SOMMELIER OF DEFORMITY

SOMMELIER OF DEFORMITY

A NOVEL

NICK YETTO

TURNER

Turner Publishing Company
Nashville, Tennessee
New York, New York

www.turnerpublishing.com

Sommelier of Deformity

Cover design: Maddie Cothren
Cover artwork: Owen Sherwood
Book design: Glen Edelstein

Library of Congress Cataloging-in-Publication Data upon request

9781684421442

Printed in the United States of America
18 19 20 21 22 9 8 7 6 5 4 3 2 1

To William B. Patrick

Writer, mentor, friend.

www.williampatrickwriter.com

SOMMELIER OF DEFORMITY

PROLOGUE

I'm not ashamed.

Should I envy him? I've never envied anybody or anything. Deny his beauty? I've got my delusions, same as anyone, but I always find myself out and feel doubly pathetic. I'm ugly. Terrance Johnson is handsome. If there is a God, he is an artist God, and he saves his careful chisel work for the rare few.

I'm like a Special Olympian. My event: lovemaking. My handicap: ugliness. My eyes are puckered inwards and darkly rimmed, so that gazing into them is like staring at a pair of twin anuses. My nose is a mashed toadstool, and my chin is a small, frightened thing, hiding in the cavern of my overbite. I'm short. Very short. Four feet nine. My spine is bent by scoliosis. Straightened out, I'd be five even, but the serpentine aspect of my skeletal structure knocks a good three inches off my height. In x-ray, you might mistake me for the missing link; in the flesh, for a human prototype that was deemed unworthy of production. My face belongs to the bullied schoolboy, to the overqualified middle manager who's banged his head against the glass ceiling of good looks. I'm the speechwriter who stuffs fertile words into handsome mouths. I'm the board operator, hidden from the audience, casting spotlights on the costumed beauties. I look like something you'd peel off the bottom of your shoe.

Yet I am not without my gifts. Or maybe *gift.* Is a "silver tongue" a gift or a skill? If it is a gift, is it a mental or physical one? I'm a strict materialist, a lapsed dualist, so I try to avoid mind–body distinctions whenever possible. Anyway, I've got a silver tongue. My other gift, and possibly, my only one, presents no metaphysical questions.

I've got a magnificent penis.

Large? Of course. Sans size, sans girth, a penis can never be "magnificent." But there's more. My penis can do a thing that other penises cannot do. Read on. All will be revealed.

"Mr. Lely, I desire you would use all your skill to paint my picture truly like me, and not flatter me at all; but remark all these roughnesses, pimples, warts and everything as you see me, otherwise, I will never pay a farthing for it."

Not my favorite historical dictator, Cromwell, but I dig the "warts and all" thing. I shall endeavor to adhere to that standard throughout.

I once made love to an ectrodactyl. A double ectrodactyl, in fact, as the deformity was present in both hands. The condition is also known as "lobster-claw hand," but that's antiquated, a slur, and if you ever find yourself chatting with an ectrodactyl—let alone *cosseting* one—I suggest steering clear of all crustacean references. Yet I cannot say she had "hands." So, "pincers." That's what she had. Calling them "hands" would do my readers no service.

Her pincers weren't sexy to me by default. I had to make them sexy. I had to choke down my revulsion and get past it so that I could get on to her beauty. Lo, there was beauty to be had! Her lips! They were full and pink, soft, forever moist, and nothing in her kiss was greedy or desperate. Her buttocks! Hers were the buttocks of an urban postal worker! *Buttocks nonpareil.* Buttocks that haunt your dreams, and all the more because they were yours for a time and are no longer. For a single shining night, every part of her was mine. She gifted herself to me, and I accepted, and the more she gave, the more I took, until the whole concept of giving and taking—what was hers, what was mine—blurred into irrelevance. It was ecstasy. All I had to do was get beyond her pincers. Rather than deny them—and let me tell you, there is no denying it when a lover has pincers for hands—I made them the star of the show. I begged her to masturbate me with those pincers. I made it sexy. Bodies were oiled. Breasts were tickled with feathers. We shifted posture. Her lordosis behavior demanded a response. "This game is *over*!" I cried, and then, after a thunderous smack on that magnificent rump, I impaled her. I thought she would implode. I thought she would implode into nothingness and take me with her, and at that moment I was glad to join her in the abyss.

Would you like to know how appreciative she was? She sent me an FTD TeddyGram bouquet. The very totem of appreciation! I still have that bear. It sits in a glass display case, alongside other treasures. Subsequent lovers have asked "Is that your childhood Teddy?" I say yes. *Yes, it is.* I'm not one for lies—even the little white ones—but there are times when the wheels of progress require the ol' lubricating squirt. We call such circumstances "diplomacy."

I'm a connoisseur of the unwanted, a sommelier of deformity, a coveter of the unloved. If I am a pervert, let it be said that my perversion is a golden Shangri-la, built upon the manly bedrock of my libido. I can be as soft as dandelion fluff or as hard as a boat anchor. I'll pull hair. I'll deliver an open-handed shot to the chops if that's what she requires. At the other extreme: a lover once requested that I wear her brassiere and panties, as well as a set of costume fairy wings, and flitter about the bedchamber like a pixie princess. After some impish frolic (pan-flute playing, jig dancing, the telling of riddles), I tossed a handful of sparkles into the air and cast a "sleeping spell" upon her. She feigned a supernatural slumber and I mounted her like a love-hungry satyr. It was her fantasy, and I never broke character. It's not that I'm an unselfish lover. I'm self*less*. It's not enough to be inside a woman. I want her to consume me like a chicken potpie: meat, potatoes, crust, and all. I want to satisfy her deepest hunger—to leave her with greasy lips and gravy on her chin. By day, I am forever chased by the shadow of my ugliness. In darkness, no shadow remains, and it's all diamonds.

My Don Juan pretensions have no truck with long commitments; my Quasimodo physique ensures that such commitments are never requested. I'm incapable of being the answer to any woman's dreams. Even for the most humble; even for those with the fewest prospects; I'm the fetid water they drink, not because they want to, but because they're dying of thirst. From the minute they meet me, they're hoping for better. They're wrong to want that. They don't deserve better, and neither do I. It's for me, through intimacy and compassion, to make them aware of this fact. There's no ideal. There's only *best we can get.*

I grip tight to my limitations. Only once have I been tempted to stray beyond them. She was attractive. Physically, I'm saying. By any measure. Her deformity? There was none. My want for her is the only shame I maintain.

As for Terrance: if you think that I am the type who likes to brag on having a black friend, you are mistaken. Blacks—especially young black males—have frightened me all my life. I have suffered grave indignities at their hands, and my psyche bears the scars. I was not seeking Terrance Johnson's friendship. On the contrary. I raged against it.

And so I begin my book. Let's call it a novel. You could also call it a pseudo-memoir, because the events within are sculpted from the soft clay of my memories. The narrative and the characters who take part in it will be cartoon renderings of the truth. Life, like war, involves hours of boredom punctuated by moments of terror. Or embarrassment. Or lust. I'll try to keep things brisk. Were it not for Homer, Odysseus would be nothing but dust and bones. I'm a repulsive little nobody, so I'll have to be my own Homer. My name is Buddy Hayes. I hope that you'll forgive me this indulgence.

March 27, 2006. A day like so many forgotten days; a day lived; a day of no consequence. So I claim it. A Monday. It is the blank canvas upon which I begin my masterwork.

- 1 -
A MORNING

Dangling. Like a side of beef in a butcher-shop window. It's how my grandfather spent his days. He had six months to live, a year at most—the same timeline they'd been giving us for the better part of a decade. He was a "fighter," they said. A "miracle." Of a type few would wish to be.

Cancer had struck. Surgery followed. They took the left eye and a chunk of the jaw. Shortly after that, a series of strokes. Atrophy in the limbs. His left arm desiccated. His legs shriveled, sores developed, gangrene threatened. The left leg was amputated first, below the knee, and months later the right, at mid-thigh.

Puppa. Pronounced *pup-uh,* lest the spelling lead you to a conclusion of *poop-uh,* which is far too cutesy a nickname for a decorated WWII veteran. Puppa's place is in the den. There is an elegant leather armchair there, and in healthier days he'd sit there for hours, reading, sipping coffee, smoking cigarettes. It was all the retirement he'd ever wanted. For a few years, he got it. Then the diagnosis. The decline was swift.

We tried to adapt. Books: easy to operate with two hands, a frustrating challenge otherwise. We got him a lap desk. His motor skills diminished further. He developed resting tremors in the functioning hand. We sat beside him and turned the pages. Then, out came the eye, the left, which had previously been his good one, the right was astigmatic, always had been, and the operation left him legally blind. From then on, Puppa took his books in audio format, with Mummy or me serving as reader.

The loss of the armchair. Of all the sad things his illness brought, this was the hardest to take. The chair had been his Florida condo; the thing he'd worked for all his life; that favorite place, that most satisfying spot, where he would spend his golden years. We couldn't make it work. We tried. God knows we did. It was the leather! The leather, damn it, with all its oily richness! It was too slick against his flannel pajamas. He lost the strength to keep himself upright. We tried strapping him in. He hated the feel of it, and we hated seeing him tied down like a mental patient. Pads and pillows didn't work. He'd be fine for a while, but sooner or later he would slip from the chair, like a frankfurter ejecting from a condiment-slathered bun. We'd hear a thud in the den and enter to find him in a heap on the floor, smarting and humiliated.

The Hoyer lift. Its inventor should win a humanitarian prize. At first, we used the device only as prescribed: to *lift* Puppa's body; to transport him from bed to armchair, from armchair to commode, from commode to bathtub. Then a surprise. Puppa came to enjoy the harness. He'd fuss whenever we unstrapped him. No telling why. Perhaps it was the womblike clutch. A swaddling effect, in other words.

A less Freudian possibility: old men possess a natural affection for rocking chairs and porch swings, and there were elements of both in the Hoyer lift. Consider also the adjustable height of the boom pole. At the top of its range, Puppa could hover at standing height, offering the illusion (from his perspective) that he was just as he had always been, with two healthy legs firmly beneath him. Whatever the case, he came to like dangling more than sitting, and dangling was certainly the safer alternative, so we left him in the lift throughout his waking hours.

Seven fifteen A.M. I stood in the center of the room facing my audience of one. Drops of spring rain struck the window, and the city brooded under a gunmetal sky. The city of Ilium. Upstate New York. Ours is a three-story brownstone. We live on a quiet, decaying street.

"It is impossible to say how first the idea entered my brain . . . but once conceived, it haunted me day and night!"

I performed the reading with great dramatic flair. Puppa wriggled in his harness, his little stumps dancing in the air, his groans mixed with laughter and phlegm. He was enjoying the show.

"Object there was none. Passion there was none. I loved the old man. He had never wronged me. He had never given me insult."

I paused. Shot a theatrical look of menace into Puppa's good eye. You may not have noticed, but you can only look a person in one eye at a time. You cannot focus on both at once, and this is for the best when you're speaking to Puppa. One grows used to empty eye sockets, but one would never say that there is a "kind of beauty" to them, or that "he looks better *without* the eyeball." Most times we keep the orifice stuffed with gauze. Out of doors, we cover it with a fine leather eye patch. Sometimes—in the privacy of our home, and only at Puppa's behest—we add a bit of whimsy and put in one of his custom ocular prostheses. He wore one then. The qualities of this false eye will take some explaining.

We used to keep a Ping-Pong table in the downstairs parlor. The table is long gone, and I'd assumed the same of the paddles and balls, but I'd been doing some spring cleaning a couple of years prior and ran across these recreational articles in the bottom of an old shoebox. Puppa was delighted by the find. Nostalgia sparked. I placed a paddle in his hand. We reenacted past duels. The old man zestfully batted at the imagined ball and I faux-volleyed back, reaching and diving, grunting like a pro, swinging at the empty air. Puppa's potent bids provoked a swaying in his harness, side-to-side, suggestive of the lateral dance performed by authentic table tennis masters. It was good exercise for him. I wondered: *might there be a way for us to play actual Ping-Pong?* Our fantasy version offered some cardio benefits, but it lacked the thrill of actual competition and did little to stimulate Puppa's motor skills. Propriety forbids the batting of Ping-Pong balls in lavishly appointed dens—that's a given—but I was excited to explore the concept, so I asked Puppa "Do you think you could catch a ball if I bounced it toward you?" He indicated yes. I bounced a ball, slowly, with lots of arc, directly toward his hand. He missed badly. I retrieved, tried again, and again he missed.

Third try. He missed again but got a hand on it. Fourth try, and he plucked the ball from the air. I cheered. Puppa raised the ball in triumph. Then, a devilish grin. He rolled the ball between his fingers. A flicker of lunacy danced across his face and then, in a flash, he mashed the ball into his open eye socket. The fit was nearly perfect. He removed his hand. The ball remained. I cried out in horror. It was ghastly! The bulbous, milky white ball transformed him into something inhuman. I begged him to remove it. He cackled demonically.

Ladies have their handbags and shoes. Gentlemen have their hats, their tiepins, their cufflinks. These small, changeable details are the brass tacks of fashion. Puppa started wedging the Ping-Pong ball into his face on a regular basis. Odd behavior, of course, I'm not claiming it wasn't . . . but is it so different than a mink stole? Than an ascot? Fashion teaches us to "accessorize around" our less attractive features. Empty eye sockets are not common in the general population. If they were, there'd be decorative eyeball sections in every department store.

We tolerated it for a while. Puppa kept the ball in his breast pocket, and he'd wedge it into his cabbage whenever the spirit moved him. That "spirit" was usually a malevolent one. It frightened Mummy every time. I found it uncouth.

"Puppa, if you insist on accessorizing in this way, can't it be done with a bit more élan? A gentleman should not be seen with sporting goods lodged in his head."

What happens when ocular science meets arts and crafts? When a loving grandson, armed with the Internet and a Hobby Lobby rewards card, commits his labors to an ailing elder's comfort and pleasure? *Progress* happens, reader. Prosthetic bijouterie happens.

The collection is up to fourteen. There's The Mobius: ashwood, painted black, with a large sapphire set as the pupil. There's The Marksman: mahogany, natural finish, with red crosshairs in the center. The Viper: tiger maple, wax polished, with an infinity symbol beveled into the face. I design and construct them. Take great care in doing so. Puppa receives a new eyeball every birthday, and another at Christmas as a stocking stuffer.

Back to the main thread. The morning. The dramatic reading. Puppa wore The Specter—a white painted number, no pupil, and sprinkled all over with silver glitter.

"For his gold I had no desire. I think it was his eye! Yes, it was this! He had the eye of a vulture—a pale blue eye, with a film over it. Whenever it fell upon me, my blood ran cold; and so by degrees—very gradually—I made up my mind to take the life of the old man, and thus rid myself of the eye forever!"

Puppa squealed. Intelligible speech was no longer an option, so he expressed his emotions in great bursts of pantomime. When saddened, he would blubber, and tears would flow from his functioning duct. If a song caught his fancy, he would bray along in indiscernible rendition. Here I had selected a tale of horror that spoke directly to his condition, as if Mr. Poe had penned it just for us. He was the old man; I, the killer. I'd even dressed the part. A tweed coat, a gentleman's bow tie, a bowler hat. This brand of playacting was a regular part of our mornings.

"Breakfast . . ." Mummy sang as she entered the den. She pushed our wooden butler's cart in front of her. A breakfast spread was arrayed upon it: slices of pineapple, bowls of blueberry and cream, toast, and homemade peach marmalade. "The Breakfast Surprise" was hidden under the lid of our silver serving platter. Steam kissed at the edges of the dome. Today's surprise smelled delicious.

My mother is not an attractive woman. Inside, in the heart of her, she is the most beautiful woman in God's creation. On the existence of a supernatural God, I am dubious, but Mummy, in all her sweetness and benevolence, could serve as proof of the divine. Maybe she's an angel. She's certainly a saint. She's performed no miracles that I'm aware of, and I doubt that anyone will deign to paint her on a chapel ceiling; but if she is ever so honored, I will demand to oversee the work. "Paint the soul, not the woman!" I would instruct. "Put some roses in her cheeks! Slim her hips! Tighten her hindquarters! And please, I beg you, take note of the sparkle in her eye and try with all your skill to capture it."

Inner beauty is of small account in this vulgar world, and Mummy does little to improve her outward appearance. She has the fashion sense of a sixty-year-old biddy, and a body to match. Her "chin" is a soft roll of flesh, and there are more than a few whiskers there. A harelip scar runs vertically from mouth to right nostril, just a bit off-center, and serves as a visual indicator of her mood. When she's tranquil, the scar blends in with the surrounding flesh. When she's agitated, the defect goes to pink; when further agitated, to red; when enraged, to blood red, and the scar looks like a live wound, open, glistening, and it's clear to all that Mummy has pulled on her war face.

She wears her hair in a style that I call "grandma puff." She calls it "fuss-free." She has the figure of a tree stump and short little arms that shoot forward from where her breasts should be. She's a chimera of sorts: a *T. rex* in miniature with an old lady's head. That morning her hair was done up in pink curlers, and she wore her blue terry robe, decorated all over with little rubber duckies. She is forty-two years old.

I'll tell you my age now. I'm twenty-eight. Do the math. As you might imagine, my entry into this world was a bit of a fiasco. It is one of the many reasons why I love Puppa so much. Without him, Mummy and I would have devolved into white trash monstrosities. We'd be living in public housing now, surviving on beans and Vienna sausages.

"What are you reading?" asked Mummy.

"Puppa's favorite," I said.

The butler's cart had folding leaves on either side. When locked into place, the cart became a small, round table.

"You're wearing the hat," she said, setting the leaves. "And Puppa is wearing The Specter. I should have known."

"They're the perfect accessories. The eyeball is Puppa's most ghoulish, and the closest match to the 'vulture eye' described in the tale. As for the hat—it instantly transforms me into dandy *boulevardier.* The rest is in the performance."

I shot Mummy a stiletto look.

"Oh my!" she cried. "If looks could kill!"

I doffed the bowler and set it gently on Puppa's bald head. The hat had been his. He'd picked it up years ago, in a thrift shop, during one of his book hunts. It was no costume piece. The hat was old, English-made, and fine. Puppa's face rent into a mangled simulation of a smile.

"Now you look like a gentleman," I said, clapping the book shut. "We'll finish later, okay? You simply *must* know what happens to the old man." I patted his shoulder. "As if you didn't know already, you old feather-duster!"

He smiled like a toothless baby. Spit bubbled at his lips.

"That certainly got your energy up," Mummy said to the elder. "Just like last Wednesday, when Terrance came over and sang. Puppa was like a Mexican jumping bean."

"Urgh!" bellowed Puppa in the affirmative.

"It was some of the loveliest music I ever heard," she continued.

"Urghhh!" A small bola of mucus spun from his mouth and landed on the cart, barely missing a wedge of grapefruit.

"I heard faint whispers of that 'music' from my chambers," I scoffed.

"Wasn't it grand?"

"As I said, it was faint, and I was otherwise engaged. 'The Wheels of Commerce' and all that. What I *did* hear, I found . . . disconcerting."

She demanded elucidation.

"The thought of that big chocolate-covered marshmallow, strumming away on his banjo and singing like Ricky Nelson," I said. "It sounded unnatural. Like someone trying to *prove* something."

"Oh please! What on Earth would he have to prove?"

"If you listened to contemporary Afro-American music, you'd know. It's all about 'sampling.' 'Mix mastering,' they call it. I call it theft! Those few strains that found their way to my ear reeked of plagiarism—as if my musical heritage were a plaything for his amusement."

"You don't have a 'musical heritage.'"

"Yes, I do. So do you."

"There is no musical talent in this family."

"Defeatist! Musically, I am an untapped fountain. The throb of primal rhythms beats in my DNA. But when I say 'heritage,' I'm speaking *culturally.* Country-inspired music. I hate that cornpone junk, but as a Caucasian-American it's mine to take or leave. I say, leave it!"

"Nonsense. If you had come out of your room . . ."

". . . my chambers."

"Your *chambers,* then you would have seen and heard something marvelous. Terrance has real gifts. Did you know that he used to perform on Broadway? As an actor, a singer, and a dancer? They call that a 'triple threat.' Isn't that wonderful!?"

"If he were so wonderful, he'd still be singing for his supper, and not peddling compassion like a TV evangelist."

"He's a nurse!"

"His family must be proud."

"A Visiting Nurse."

"And a *singing* nurse, and a *banjo* nurse. He's a good fit for a traveling circus. What's his level of certification?"

"LPN."

"LPN!?"

Trade certification is a sure marker of cognitive ability among the working classes. I'm always saying *the trades are the surest path out of poverty,* and I believe it (my darling Puppa is proof!), and accreditation in *anything* counts for *something,* no doubt about it, but to stop at the basement level—to stick there, like a clam half-buried in sand—well, it told me everything I needed to know. Terrance was a "good enough" guy. A speck. The world is covered in them. Little flakes of dandruff, riding on the shoulders of civilized society. Nothing worked for, nothing gained, and so nothing to offer. I could have bounced these bricks off of Mummy's noggin, but the indicator warned against it. Her harelip scar had lost its cool pallor. It was up to pink. Best to let the engines cool.

"I'd prefer not to discuss it over breakfast," I said.

"We need help."

"And now we have it—be it ever so humble."

"We need help more than once a week. I want to try the home health care aides."

"My stars! I agreed to the whole 'visiting nurse' business, and yes, I can see the utility of it, but I'm not going to have our home turned into some kind of—"

I cut myself off. I was going to say "nursing home," but that was #1 on our list of banned terms. We'd never consider it. We refused to acknowledge the existence of such places. Mummy and I were in total agreement on this point.

"Terrance speaks very highly of them," Mummy said.

"Of whom?"

"The aides!"

"I'm sure he does. And who speaks for him?"

"Everyone! His references were impeccable."

"Fake references are a cottage industry."

"Not when they come from the head of the VNA. We were lucky to get him at all. He's the best. A 'giving soul.' That's what the director said about him."

"'No man giveth but with intention of good to himself.' Your helper is paid for what he does. I'm sure that he spends the greater portion of his paycheck on brandy and cheap cigars. His flexible schedule allows him to drink said brandy until the wee hours and to sleep until noon the following day."

"He's here at 8:30 in the morning."

"Hung over, no doubt. Stinking of brandy."

"You say these things just to rile me," Mummy spat. "I don't like it. Get the chairs."

I moved to the den closet and retrieved the two folding chairs that are part of our daily breakfast arrangement. Mummy carefully rolled Puppa toward the cart and lowered his harness to an appropriate dining height. The hydraulic piston hissed as Puppa descended into place. I set the two folding chairs, and we took our places.

"I don't mean to upset you," I said. "I'm just not used to having strange men in our home. I may be a self-taught black belt, but he's a formidable specimen. *And* he's Afro-American. Did that fact occur to you?"

The scar pulsed.

"I've noticed, and I have no idea what difference it makes at all."

"You'll admit that Afro-Americans, as a race, possess more fast-twitch muscle than we? Well, it doesn't matter if you admit it or not because it's scientifically proven. I'm not sure that a Tiger Strike to the temple would even faze him. I would have to assume Creeping Lotus and work his legs, but you know that Creeping Lotus is not one of my better stances. He might punt me through the uprights!"

A sigh of frustration. "Why are you even talking like that?"

"Because I am the man of this house and it is my sacred duty to protect it."

"We require no protection from Terrance." Silence for a time, and then: "If you were so concerned, why didn't you come down and introduce yourself?"

"And display my plumage like a strutting cock? Ha! Maybe I would have, but I was on the telephone with a very important client."

"Well, it would have been nice. And polite. It seems like you spend eighteen hours a day in that dark office."

"Chambers!"

"There's no light in there. You live like a vampire. And you wonder why you have S.A.D." She tisk-tisk-tisked me. "A computer screen does not offer the full spectrum of light. You'll become like those poor children in Alaska."

"Occupational hazard. These tasties are not going to buy themselves. And speaking of tasties. . . ." I reached across the table and lifted the silver dome that concealed The Breakfast Surprise. The aroma of fish and smoke and butter burst from the platter like an escaped prisoner. Inside, a beautiful salmon steak dressed in hollandaise.

"Mummy! Is there some special occasion of which I am unaware? My word! Did you smoke this in the back yard?"

"You know I did," she said proudly.

"Yesterday? I thought I smelled something. Why didn't you call me?"

She performed a shooing gesture with her fingers, as if my question were a pesky fly.

"I don't need you meddling with my smoker."

"Meddling!?"

"You don't check the meat—you poke it. You pull little chunks from it and the whole thing looks as if it's been nibbled by a raccoon."

"And how do you check it? By running your tongue across it?"

"I check it with a thermometer. As you know."

"Taste is the only measure that counts."

"I didn't want any fuss."

"I do not meddle, nor do I fuss. I advise and encourage."

"You're a meddler and a fusser. But I didn't mean you. I meant *her*."

The mention of *her* was noxious, like the first whiff of a decaying mouse buried deep in the walls.

"Did she call the police on you again?" I asked.

"Don't remind me."

"The batty old crone was probably hovering above on her broomstick, snapping away with her spy camera. One of these days—and in grand fashion—I shall run a hickory stake through her heart."

"Buddy! I will not tolerate any more violent rhetoric!"

"It wouldn't work anyway. The only way to kill a witch is by drowning."

The witch under discussion was our hated neighbor. "Little Miss Sunshine," I call her. Flashback a couple of years. Mummy was in the backyard smoking sausages. Little Miss Sunshine called the police.

"There's been a report that you're burning garbage," the policemen said when they arrived. Well, anyone with a set of nostrils could tell that wasn't the case, and the investigators had four nostrils between them, two apiece, and the scents that filled those inquisitive nostrils, from the moment they exited their cruiser, suggested only the most delicious savories. After some cordial banter, we invited the lawmen to investigate our private grounds. We showed them our custom-built smokehouse. Mummy offered them sausages to take home. This was when the truth came out. A "concerned neighbor" had suggested that maybe—just *maybe*—we were cremating a human body. The policemen laughed about it. They were the only ones laughing.

"I'll never understand it," said Mummy in a huff. "As if smoking meats in your own backyard was a crime."

"At least she's on record as a bona fide kook. The police hate having their time wasted. I'm sure their report is full of coded scribbles that label her a fruitcake. It'll all prove useful when we file suit against her. Charge number one—"

". . . Buddy, please . . ."

"—Harassment!"

Mummy thrust her fingers into her ears and commenced with an obnoxious *la-la-la* rendition of Simon and Garfunkel's "Bridge Over Troubled Water."

"Charge number two," I shouted, so as to penetrate her musically induced deafness. "Slander!"

The whole "I will lay me down" bit, delivered as a series of la's. On key, but reedy. Too much breath. Mummy's tantrums might benefit from some vocal training.

"She accuses our beloved patriarch of murder!" I cried.

I will lay me down . . .

"Charge number three," louder still. "Theft of cultural relics!"

I had other charges to level against the witch, but my point was made. I interlocked my fingers and set my hands neatly on the table. Mummy ended her childish display.

"Finished?" she asked.

"I could go on," I said demurely.

"Don't. I've heard it all a million times. Can we just have a nice breakfast?"

"You know she has it."

"I don't know that."

"She stole it!"

"Even if it's in her possession—which I doubt—I don't think you can say that she 'stole it.'"

"Oh, no? Tell that to Egypt. They've been chasing their relics all over the world. A sarcophagus pops up at a museum in Dayton, Ohio, and Egypt is like *'That's ours, sucker!'* And guess what? They get it back."

She let out a tired sigh.

"It was a long time ago, Buddy."

"There's no other explanation."

"And there's no way to prove it. So enough."

I helped myself to a generous portion of salmon. I was famished. Mine was a morning-after hunger born of torrid sex play. The previous night, I had enjoyed a furious masturbation session with one of my online galpals. I know only three things about this cyberlover: her Skype username (SoggyHoochy69), her email address (I will keep that to myself), and what her vagina looks like in extreme close-up. Our relationship is purely genital. We contact each other on Skype messenger once or twice a week—just long enough to arrange a video rendezvous. At the appointed time I set my webcam on a stool between my legs and illuminate my manhood with a flashlight. SoggyHoochy69 presents her sex in a similar way—in extreme genital close-up. Our headset microphones leave our hands free, and we play our organs like a pair of dueling virtuosos. Our strokes and proddings are a pixellated blur. As for the erotic banter, let me tell you! I have no doubt that SoggyHoochy69 is the most depraved woman on Earth. She belongs in an institution. She asked me to pretend I was her cousin James! Have you ever heard of such a thing? God help her family. More than once, my online playmates have evolved into flesh-and-blood encounters. It was like that with Daphne, the ectrodactyl, and with Kelly—a Romanesque goddess whose peanut butter folds and cottage cheese crevices I still occasionally enjoy. There were no such plans for SoggyHoochy69.

I took a forkful of the smoked salmon. In my mouth, an explosion of smoke, of brine, of cream, of citrus zest.

"Mummy, this is a delicacy!"

She was pleased. "That fish smoked up very well, but it's the homemade butter that makes the real difference."

"I knew it was a good idea to build that churn," I said.

Puppa's single eye focused mournfully on my plate. He began smacking his lips.

"You can have a little fish," Mummy told him. She took a bit of fish from the platter and placed it in her mouth. She closed her eyes and moaned in chef's delight as she chewed it. Then, as delicately as a mother bird, she spit the premasticated wad onto a china saucer. This may sound vile, but it was a regular part of our breakfasts, and necessary. Puppa couldn't swallow solid food. The smallest bone could choke him. His palate was like a gaping wound; an open hole connected directly to his empty eye socket. Occasionally, a bit of gauze might slip back, and the easiest path of retrieval would be from the mouth. A prosthetic bite plate—a palatal obturator, made of translucent silicon—plugs the hole. Mummy topped the salmon-and-saliva pâté with a dollop of hollandaise and took up a tiny portion with a salt spoon. Puppa held his lips as if ready for a kiss. Mummy slid the spoonful into his mouth, and Puppa sucked at the gob like a lozenge. He emitted a low, satisfied groan. The Specter glittered. He savored the flavor. Mummy unscrewed the lid of his actual meal.

"How many calories today?" I asked.

"Thirteen hundred, I think. We've got peanut butter, heavy cream, chocolate syrup, chocolate ice cream, and an egg."

"Remarkable. The Magic Bullet people should start marketing their product as an eldercare aid."

"I agree. I've come up with a hundred different recipes. I'm working on a spicy Mexican fiesta shake that I think he'll like."

"Something savory to complement the sweet. Good thinking. You ought to pool those recipes and publish a Magic Bullet cookbook. The primary market would likely be home caregivers, but you might attract the bodybuilder market as well."

"Maybe you could help me write it?"

"A mother / son publishing project? I like it! Make a note of it in your journal. We'll revisit the concept when I finish my novel." I stuffed my face with fish.

These elaborate breakfast sessions represented our bid at normalcy. We'd always enjoyed breakfasts together. To alter the practice in light of Puppa's condition would have been a kind of surrender. Dignity, reader. It was a matter of dignity. How to assure it. How to maintain it. In this, one must realize that dignity is not a construct, but a collection of small comforts and liberties. Breakfast was a sacred family ritual. Dignity demanded that Puppa feed himself. And so again to my tinker's table. I invented a special appliance: a two-foot length of medical tubing with an inexpensive snorkel mouthpiece fitted to one end. Puppa wasn't able to operate a traditional drinking straw. He couldn't create sufficient "suck," even with his palatal obturator in place. The lips wanted a more perfect seal, and what's a snorkel but a mouth gasket affixed to a tube? A length of medical tubing, some food-grade silicone cement, and voila!

Puppa opened his mouth, and Mummy set the mouthpiece. She then inserted the rubber tubing into the Bullet-Cup. Puppa closed his good eye, and the thick brown liquid climbed the tube in a slow, incremental assent. In moments he was drinking it up, and we all set about enjoying our breakfast.

"That Terrance of yours—do you suppose he's on performance-enhancing drugs?"

Mummy rolled her eyes.

"You're not back to that nonsense, are you?"

"You must admit that he has a *dangerous* physique."

"That's a dancer's body," she said.

"It's more of a lumberjack body. A sharecropper body. I haven't seen him up close, but I've surveilled him from my chamber window. That's about as close as I intend to get. I find him extremely intimidating."

"That's good. Maybe you'll treat him with respect and not cause trouble."

"I'm imagining him now, locked in the throes of a roid rage. The bloodshot eyes. The foaming mouth. I'd have to put him down with the musket."

"Don't even make jokes like that," she scolded.

"Which reminds me—we need some fresh black powder."

"No, we don't, and I'll thank you for leaving that musket right where it is, hanging in the parlor below Mr. Moose."

"Mummy, what's the point of having a firearm if you cannot use it to defend yourself?"

"Because it's a lovely decoration, that's what. If you leave it loaded all the time, how do you know that a real intruder wouldn't find it and use it against *us*?"

"Ha! They wouldn't even know how to set the frizzen!"

"Terrance is a visitor, not an intruder."

"And I will grant him all the hospitality he is due, but don't pooh-pooh *me* just because I voice my concerns. Isn't it better to be safe than sorry? This house is full of antiques. I mean, our collection of Tobies alone! If word were to get out, we'd certainly become a target for armed robbery."

Her chin wattles danced to the rhythm of her dismissive head shakes.

"Our samovar," I continued. "The Shaker rockers. The salt-glaze stoneware. And don't get me started on the value of our library!"

More wattle dancing, more eye rolling. Mummy proceeded to pour coffee from the French press into our china cups.

"Terrance does not want our antiques, Buddy."

"Not the antiques. The *money* from selling them. This city is growing pawnshops faster than weeds! Could you imagine seeing one of our beloved Tobies in a pawnshop window? And it doesn't have to be Terrance who does the stealing. It could be one of his *stoopmates*. One of his *homeboys*."

Puppa emitted a belch from behind his snorkel mouthpiece. He begged our pardon. The pardon was granted, and he resumed sucking.

"You promised you'd work on this, Buddy."

"I have been working on it."

"Your racism, I mean."

"Indeed."

"Your 'Anti-Bias Reprogramming.'"

"That's what I call it, yes."

"And? How's it been going?"

"Wonderfully!"

"And yet your disgusting racism persists!"

I shrugged. Sighed helplessly.

"Some bells cannot be unrung."

"*No* bells can be unrung. You ring a bell, it's rung."

"Then my point is taken."

"I know you had a difficult time in grade school . . ."

". . . and in junior high, and high school, for as long as I was there . . ."

". . . but you need to freshen your outlook."

I'd attended high school until halfway through my sophomore year. The harassment I endured—the physical assaults on my person!—rendered the environment unsuitable for intellectual growth. To call my classmates "students" would be an insult to the liberal arts tradition. They were preening imbeciles. Barbarians! The strong and the beautiful sat atop the hierarchy and maintained their rule through physical and emotional violence. They hunted me in packs. They called me "Snowflake" and "Troll" and "Hunchback" and beat me without mercy. Escape was more than a desire—it was a matter of life and death! I completed my schooling at home. Puppa served as dean, Mummy as headmistress.

"Have you read the neighborhood watch emails that I've been printing?" I asked.

"I can't bear to!" Mummy exclaimed. "It's all so depressing."

"Let me tell you this: nine times out of ten, the crime is theft—often at gunpoint—and the suspect is a young black male, tall, athletically built. Is it prejudice to recognize a fact? Terrance falls into a very unsavory demographic."

"Your question was rhetorical, but I'll answer it bluntly. It *is* prejudiced and narrow-minded."

"And I will take *your* accusations and invoke my right

to counsel. My lawyer: Science. Racism is a byproduct of natural selection. Our primitive ancestors had every reason to distrust those from outside their clan. Those born with multicultural curiosities were likely to have their heads clubbed in. Man has always been man's deadliest predator. It's why 'stranger danger' remains a natural childhood impulse. Consider also the fear of rodents. That's a plague-avoidance adaptation, and another primitive relic I suffer from. My racism may be undesirable, but it's not irrational."

"Hyperbole! Cite your sources!"

"I'll provide an appendix!"

A sloppy gurgle came from Puppa's BulletCup as he sucked the dregs of his chocolate shake. Mummy carefully removed the mouthpiece. When she did, rivulets of brown goo flowed down Puppa's chin and dribbled to the floor. Mummy quickly dispatched the gunk with a linen napkin.

"Was it good, Puppa?" she asked.

"Urgh . . ." in the affirmative.

My fish was gone. I moved on to a slice of cantaloupe. Cantaloupe: nature's great oral cleanser. My blood sugar was in perfect balance. The synapses crackled like sparked kindling. I was ready to begin my day.

"When will this candy striper be holding another one of his tiny concerts?"

"Wednesday," she said, her eyes hopeful.

"Then Wednesday—and only if my schedule permits—I will come down from my chambers and watch this latter-day minstrel show. I can't promise that I'll enjoy it, but I will gently applaud at the appropriate times. If moved, I might offer more."

I rose, kissed Mummy on the cheek, and then took the bowler from Puppa's head and set it on my own at a rakish angle. "We'll finish the story later," I promised, and then retired to my lair.

- 2 -
HARD AT WORK

When I envision my fetal self—and don't we all from time to time?—I conjure a tiny creature that is one part human and one part newt, swimming in a uterine cesspool that's filled with black tar. The black-tar fluid represents the torment that my child mother endured—a gestational hellbroth that was undoubtedly passed on to me through the umbilicus. As for the image of the newt? Well, as an infant I didn't even appear human. Imagine the reaction of the doctors and nurses as I emerged from Mummy's love canal. I'm lucky I was born in a more civilized century. In the Dark Ages, they'd have thought me a demon spawn and dashed my infant brains out on the nearest rock! If you think I'm exaggerating, I welcome you to join me in our drawing room. Mummy has arranged a shrine to my birth there. Poor Mummy. Although she denies it—"You were a *beautiful* baby!"—she must have been disappointed.

The closest I've come to having a "real job" has been in a recurring nightmare. It goes like this. I'm lost in a maze of office cubicles. Each cubicle contains a stylish hipster, a stylish Macintosh computer, and one of those big rubber balls that people use for abdominal workouts. The hipsters sit atop the balls as if the balls were chairs, and they plug *XO,XO,XO,XO* into their keyboards, populating the fields of never-ending spreadsheets. The hipsters are all identical. They wear black polos. Their gelled hair is unkempt in a contrived way. Strange oily tattoos decorate their arms like runes. I know that they are slim and handsome; but try as I may, I can never see their faces. I wander the maze, looking for a cube of my own, but they are all occupied by the same infinite hipster, the same infinite Macintosh, the same infinite ab ball.

I'm terrified of the working world, yet work I must. Free of toil, a man is nothing, and hollow is the life devoted to soft leisure. There are also bills to pay.

I am a designer of web pages; a programmer of web applications; a freelance hustler who conducts himself in a very businesslike fashion. Eight A.M. to six P.M., Monday to Friday, you'll find me at the ready. These are the official office hours. Late nights and weekends are the norm. I don't take vacations. I rarely leave my station. I am an entrepreneur of necessity; a leper merchant who's found a way to peddle his wares.

Away to my chambers. As revealed in previous pages, I insist that my private lair be referred to in this manner. A bit fancy, I admit, but there's a philosophy behind it. It reminds me that life need not be compartmentalized; that walls need not define the character of a space. Sure, I could call it "my apartment." "My flat," if I wished to put on continental airs. I could also wear sweat pants in public.

Efficiency, dear reader! This, above all else, is what my lifestyle allows. Example: some of my best design concepts come to me while seated on the commode. In a traditional office setting, I would have to finish my toilet before any sketching or note-taking could occur, and by then the inspiration might be lost. This is not a problem in the flowing mindscape of my chambers. I keep a laptop in the bathroom. I move my bowels, inspiration strikes, I set the device on my naked legs, and progress marches on. It's multitasking in the purest sense. It's also my edge. I am always at work, and my work is always play.

Another example. On quiet workdays I will often plot out elaborate sexual role-play scenarios, complete with dialog beats, prop suggestions, costume design, et cetera. My chambers are a place of business; a place of inspiration; a place of gothic fornication. Art drools into commerce. Hard logic bleeds into the carnal. I've built a fortress against the world.

And so I sat at my desk, belly stuffed full of smoked salmon and hollandaise, coffee still steaming. I hit SEND/RECEIVE on Outlook. Nothing. I loathed inactivity. I did not get paid to wait. *A shot of snuff might pass the time,* I thought. A small tin of sniffing tobacco was close at hand. I popped the lid and was greeted by the peppery smell of the tobacco within. I took a pinch of the baccy and snorted it up my right nostril. It hit the sinuses like the head of a struck match. I took another pinch and sent it up the left. The nicotine was on me in an instant, followed by a sneezing fit. This is my favorite part of the snuffing experience. The endorphins released through sneezing are from the same glandular wellspring as those released through orgasm. My disposition was thus improved.

The phone rang shortly after. The caller ID displayed a 212 area code. I wiped the spiced snot from my upper lip and stood, undid my belt, and yanked my trousers and underpants to the floor.

"Good morning! Buddy Hayes." My voice was bright, like an elf on break from his Christmas toymaking.

"Hi, Buddy. This is Paula Hixon."

We exchanged pleasantries. While we did, I performed a silent striptease. I undid my bow tie and worked the buttons on my vest.

"It's nice to finally speak with you," she continued. "Megan has told me great things."

Megan was a longtime client of mine. She worked for an advertising agency in New York City. You could say that I produced "SPAM" for Megan, or "email marketing campaigns," or "HTML email blasts." I'd never met Megan face-to-face, and in this way Megan is no different from any of my clients. A few years ago, she posted an ad to the "gigs" section of a popular freelancer's website. **HTML/GRAPHIC DESIGN – MARKETING EMAIL BLASTS**. I'd never produced a marketing email blast before, so I did some research, scoured the web for samples, and created a plagiarized portfolio of my own. I then responded to the post, included my disingenuous links, and overstated my experience. I've been doing work for Megan ever since. I used the same process to secure all of my early jobs. Pretty soon I had legitimate clips of my own, and the fact that it had all started as a bait-and-switch didn't matter because I was presenting real examples of real work I had done.

What other option did I have? My ugliness is so profound that paint will not dry in my presence! As sure as a signboard slung over my shoulders, as immutable as a slave-master's brand, I am marked. The world is full of opportunities that I am too ugly to seize. Anonymity is the promise of the Internet, and it's the sweetest promise ever whispered into an ugly man's ear. To Megan, I am nothing more than a charming email, a friendly voice on the phone. I am the Zip file that contains the creative she needs, completed a day earlier than expected. I am glowing words projected on a computer screen. For $78/hr., all I know is hers, and since she will never see me and never know me, it is fully hers to claim. I sell the work and forfeit the credit. I am divorced of her skyscraper politics.

I had to convince Paula Hixon that I was "the right man for the job." In this, there's more to be learned from David Copperfield than Daniel Carnegie. Magic is in the misdirection. So as not to break the flow of my narrative—and so that you, the reader, remains in the know—I will confess my diplomacy in sidebars.

"Megan is great to work with," I gushed as if we were talking about old friends. "Please say hello when you see her."

"I will. You're located upstate?"

"Yes. I live in Ilium. Have you been?"

She hadn't.

"It's quaint," I said. "Sort of a cross between the Lower East Side and a Swiss village."

If you like sagging rust-belt cities; cities with cracked sidewalks and potholed streets and abandoned storefronts; if you relish the scent of mold and cat urine; if you are a toothless crazy, and eager to be surrounded by others of your kind, then you might consider Ilium "quaint."

"That's a description," she said, laughing. "How far is it from the city?"

"Two hours, tops."

Almost three hours, actually. That's what Google says. I've never been to New York City. I always understate the travel time, which gives the impression that my "remote office" is a little less so.

My shirt was fully undone, and I placed it, along with my vest and bowtie, over the back of my desk chair. I was now clad only in gooseflesh, save the bowler on my head and the trousers that were bunched about my loafers. I looked down at my little hobbit's belly with its weedy trail of dark hair. My eyes followed that trail down to my flaccid coil, which, in its current condition, looked like a hairless rat peeking out of a pricker bush. A fondling commenced. I was the magician now. Magic wand, at the ready. The illusion was mine to command.

"Two hours isn't so bad. It takes me an hour each way," she said.

"You live in Brooklyn?"

"I do," she said, and we discussed the merits of Brooklyn for a moment; merits that I had carefully researched.

I'm a *The New Yorker* reader, so I know about the contemporary hipness of Brooklyn. Asking if a client lives there is always a flattering assumption.

"I worked in New York for years," I said. "Lower West Side. I was a partner in a small design and development firm—only eighteen employees—but we had some great clients. A lot of fashion and beauty brands. It was a great working environment, but after a while the city began to wear me down."

"I hear you."

"Don't get me wrong—I miss the corner office and all the great people. I still see them from time to time, and even work with them on a contract basis. But my passion is for *design,* and living away from the city has allowed me to focus on what I do best, without distractions."

"It's great that you could do that," she said.

I'd stolen this origin story from someone's blog—a freelance graphic designer and former Manhattanite who had rusticated to the Berkshires. His blog was quite popular. His writing was crisp, and his designs offered much to admire, but what really struck me were the user comments. Every post, every shared image, was met with reverential praise by his followers. He'd clearly tapped into something: into a longing, held in the bosom of every New Yorker, to *get out* of New York City! I realized the power of this theme and adapted it to my purpose. My truth was in the work. I had indeed created sites for many luxury brands, but I achieved them in the diplomatic manner described heretofore.

"I enjoy it," I said. "Up here I can own a house, and a dog, and I'm still down to New York at least twice a month. The whole setup has worked out surprisingly well."

"What kind of dog?"

"A golden retriever. His name is Matisse. Matty, for short."

"Goldens are wonderful dogs. I have a French bulldog."

"That is my number one city dog. I thought about getting a Frenchie when I lived in the city, but the co-op board wouldn't allow it."

I pinched my nipple and silently kissed the receiver.

Two things here. First, the suggestion that I own a dog. New Yorkers are obsessed with dogs. Creepily so. It has to do with delayed child-rearing, suppressed maternal/paternal instincts; the requisite self-denials of the modern striver. Mix in a bit of nature worship . . .
". . . like many city-dwellers, they tend to romanticize and idealize country living and country folk, at least until the weather breaks . . ."
. . . and I think you get to the heart of the thing. Dog as child. Dog as proxy of nature. "I own a golden retriever named Matty." Including this folksy detail is always a winner.

Second thing. *"You've said that you never meet your clients face-to-face, yet here you are telling Paula Hixon that you are in the city 'twice a month.' She'll demand an in-person meet-up!"* She might. I have been asked to attend plenty of meetings, and I have avoided them all. "Next Wednesday? I'm so sorry, but I'm booked solid with production next week. How about I create some mockups for you? We can work through the details beforehand. That way, when we meet, we'll actually have something in front of us to discuss." This tactic is effective on three levels. 1) I have softly denied a request. This suggests that my services are in demand; that I'm a professional who deserves respect. 2) I've suggested that a meeting is imminent. The client is thereby reassured that I have nothing to hide. 3) By claiming to be down in New York City "twice a month," I bow to the innate snobbery

of every New Yorker. Their city is The City. Center of the universe. It's not profitable to deny them this. The important point: once a job is started and the details are worked through, there becomes no reason to meet at all.

"Well, your resume is great, and I love your work," Paula said. "Megan showed me the Flash microsite you did for Coco Chanel. It was all so shimmery and on-brand."

"I'm very proud of that one."

"Have you had a chance to look at our current website?"

"I have. Let me pull it up now." I poked the URL into my browser, and it loaded in seconds. Hixon Smyth Clothing Boutiques. A simple design. White background, crinkled parchment texture in the content frame. A horizontal nav contained the following sections: Collection, Press, About, Store Locator, and Contact. An illustrated bouquet of tulips bloomed colorfully in the lower right-hand corner. It was all neatly designed, but there was no technology to it. The pages were all flat HTML and images.

"It's a nice-looking site, Paula. Let me guess: you had a graphic designer create all of your print materials, and that same designer used those assets to create the website."

"How did you know?"

"It's not unusual for luxury brands. Have you seen the Gucci site? The design is great, but that's all you can say about it. There's no search. No e-commerce. No signup for an e-newsletter. Do you offer an e-newsletter?"

"That's on my list of things to discuss with you."

We moved through her site section-by-section and talked through the various elements. We'd redesign from scratch but retain the "spirit" of the current look and feel. We'd add two new sections—"Newsletter Signup" and "In the Studio"—the latter of which would operate as a daily blog for her buyers and designers. The "Store Locator" would offer maps and driving directions. The "Collection" section—a series of product photo galleries—would be expanded and made sortable by season, look, and product type. The site would have a new Flash-animated splash screen that would be updated each season. E-commerce would be the big-ticket item. There would be 106 products to start, with up to 40 more added each quarter. The site she wanted was substantial and expensive.

"Well, Paula, this is a big upgrade from what you're currently offering."

"We need it. Have you been to a Hixon Smyth Boutique?"

"Not yet. I certainly will, next time I'm in New York."

"Let me know when you do, and I'll give you a tour of our flagship. We've been growing big-time. Sales were up 45 percent last year. We have a new store going up in Bar Harbor, Florida, and we're in talks with The Bellagio in Las Vegas."

"That's wonderful!" I cooed, humping the air.

"We can't keep acting like we're a little Soho boutique anymore," she said.

"This will be a big improvement. Your website is the most important piece of media you have. A magazine ad, a catalog—it's very expensive to get that paper into your customers' hands. The website is there, 24/7, and the user interacts with it on their terms. As for e-commerce—well, not having it is just a missed opportunity."

The words oozed from my mouth like a sorcerer's spell.

"I couldn't agree more, Buddy. Of course, there's the big question."

"How much will it all cost?"

"Exactly."

"We've talked about a lot this morning, and I have to do some research. I'll put a spec together for you with a complete production estimate. I'll have it for you by Friday."

"Next week will be fine. We want to move on this, but I'm off to China tomorrow to meet with our manufacturers. I won't have a chance to look at it until I get back."

"China, you say? How marvelous! A visit to Chengdu is top of my bucket list. I'm such a fan of the cuisine."

She provided me with a gloss of her itinerary and then moved on to the wrap-up.

"Thank you for taking the time to speak with me, Buddy. It's been a pleasure."

Her "pleasure" sent electricity racing down my spine.

"Thank *you* for the opportunity. I'm sure we can make the numbers work."

We said our good-byes and the call was done. I nestled the receiver gently into the cradle and let out a sigh of relief.

We'd been speaking for forty-five minutes, and I was jonesing. I was also fully engorged. My rubbings had been all "genie's lamp," nothing too vigorous, and my arousal was more *physio* than *psycho*. It was a sales technique, in other words; a reassuring reminder that they don't know you, they can't see you, and that our due-diligence was being executed solely by way of vocal transmission. When the stakes are high, I always use this perverse technique, regardless of whether the opposing dupe is male or female. It's not about sex. Entrepreneurial diktat #1: no orgasms until the day's work is done. I'm monklike in this regard. Prizefighterlike. I'd push through the dull, blue ache. Come quitting time, the sweetest reward.

I took up two fresh pinches and sent them up my nose. I wasn't ready to dress. I would enjoy a moment of soothing nakedness. I waddled my way toward the window, ankles bound by bunched trousers. I must have looked like a bare-bottomed Charlie Chaplin. There, from my third-story perch, I looked out and offered my nakedness to the world. I asked nothing of that world below. Demanded no position in it. Rain slapped the windowpanes. My manhood pulsed with every heartbeat and swelled slightly, visibly, with each surge of blood. I trembled like a virgin on the cusp of penetration.

That's when I saw her. The hair on my body stood in hackles, and my penis retreated into my body like the head of a turtle into its shell. She was on the street below. She was carrying a crimson umbrella. Her dead eyes shot hither and thither, searching for something to hate. Little Miss Sunshine. The words were like acid in my mouth. Little. Miss. Sunshine! Accuser! Relic thief! Seventy years old, built like Humpty Dumpty, with a corona of golden-dyed hair framing her rotten-apple face. The face of a gremlin, forever set in an obscene pucker. She owned the neighborhood and was landlord to everyone but us. She strutted about with the squalid hauteur of a slum empress. She sucked her kingdom dry and left the people with nothing. Whereas we, the Hayeses, sought grandeur only in our private environs, Little Miss Sunshine regarded everything as hers.

I kept a spyglass on the windowsill. Its purpose: moments just like this. I took it up, cranked the tube, and focused in tight on the crone. No sign of the relic. She had it—I *knew* she had it—but only a fool would bring it outdoors on a rainy day.

I scanned the area. No sign of her toady. Her son. The ape. He was the brawn of the outfit. There wasn't a thought in his head that his mother hadn't put there. He was the super of her buildings and the enforcer of her feudal law. I dub him "Meat Foot."

"I see you, Little Miss Sunshine," I hissed through gritted teeth. "I see you!"

So much for nudist relaxation. I dressed quickly and returned to work. My keystrokes were cantankerous. My mouse clicks were bellicose. There was rage in my bosom and a niggle in my nethers.

- 3 -
THE ARRIVAL OF TERRANCE

It was to be a cloak-and-dagger affair. I awoke predawn and crept about on ballerina toes, making ready. "Be Prepared." I hadn't been permitted to join the Boy Scouts, but their earnest motto rang in my ears that morn.

Oh, how I had longed to be a Scout! To explore dark forest fantasias with my child comrades; to roast frankfurters on the blaze; to dress as Indians, to dress as cowboys, to engage in simulated war exercises. Alas, I had no child comrades. My boy adventures were limited to flights of fancy, to the fictional tribulations of the Boxcar Children, the Hardy Boys, the Great Brain, Tom, Huck, and Jim, Horatio Hornblower, Beau Geste. I was the schoolyard whipping boy. Mummy knew this, and while I begged her to let me join the Scouts, she knew it would only lead to further abuse. I see now that it was for the best. Given my diminutive stature and sultry disposition, I would have undoubtedly been sodomized by my Scoutmasters.

Thankfully, the school library offered a selection of Boy Scout manuals and guides. I could lose myself for hours in those books. Mummy took note of my interest and encouraged it. Whenever I would request some vital scouting implement—jackknife, flint and steel, canteen, et cetera—Mummy would be quick to purchase it for me. We designed our own private Boy Scouts. We spent many a summer night in our backyard—Mummy, Puppa, and I—huddled around an open fire. We'd roast mutton stew in a Dutch oven; take turns reading aloud from our copy of *Great American Folklore;* urinate in the garden to simulate the perils of authentic deep-woods camping. Mummy even assembled a Boy Scout uniform for me, complete with sash and merit badges. Most were real McCoy, Boy Scout issue, but there were a few that she embroidered herself. My favorite of the hand-stitched bunch: the *World's Greatest Son* merit badge.

Terrance had been visiting our home for over two weeks—ample time to "case the joint." Puppa took his treatments in the den. Any conflict there would be fist to fist, blade to blade. I stood no chance in that kind of duel. Should violence occur, I would need to make a strategic retreat. I would shout goading insults over my fleeting shoulder, enticing the brute to pursue. The chase would enrage him. My fearless mockery would infect him with blood lust. He would pursue me to my chambers, and there the advantage would be mine.

I paced out the route. The chase would send us hurtling from the den, down a narrow hallway, around a ninety-degree turn, into the drawing room and, through it, up a flight of stairs and through the doorway to my chambers. Sixty-two feet in total. When I bolted from the den, the element of surprise would be mine, but this was more handicap than advantage, given my pursuer's long limbs and overdeveloped thigh muscles. I needed a failsafe—a way to ensure that I would reach home base well away from my foe. And so, taking up needle and thread, I stitched a secret pouch into an old pair of trousers. I configured the pouch like a pair of large testicles, with equal portions of "scrotal sac" dangling down the sides of the inseam. I cut a three-inch slit on the bottom of each "testis," sewed velcro strips into those slits, and affixed a length of yarn to the bristly side of the closure. I ran the yarn upwards, through small holes that I punched in the pockets, and topped each with a brass button to keep it from slipping back. When pulled, the yarn would tear the velcro asunder, and an orgy of cat's-eye marbles would come flowing from the legs of my trousers. I would pull these ripcords as I rounded into the drawing room, or earlier if necessary.

Why not just load the musket, hide it in a ready place, and take it up should the need arise? That would not serve my purpose, reader. Men of Terrance's station are quite familiar with gunplay. Holding him at barrel length would do nothing but steel his resolve. He might grab Mummy or Puppa and use them as a human shield! I didn't want a hostage situation: I wanted answers.

Did I mention that I'm a self-trained aikido master? Well, now you know, and I hope it will serve as a warning to you. I'm trying to write a hip novel here. If you're reading these words, then I've probably succeeded in that goal, and maybe even achieved a small bit of literary fame. With fame comes psychopaths and perverts. If, upon completing this book, you feel compelled to seek me out—to ambush me on the street, or to knock on my door, in hopes of forcing a face-to-face encounter—please call 911 and request immediate physiological counseling. Any *excuse-me-aren't-you-Buddy-Hayes*'s will be met with an immediate throat strike, leg-sweep, or groin attack. I can't promise a crippling blow, but it will certainly be unpleasant.

Martial. Arts. Martially speaking, I'm not much. I'm small. The twist in my spine is hell for balance. I've no doubt that a green-belt aikido nymphet could best me on the mat. As for the arts? In these, I am as accomplished as any sensei. Aikido is "the way of harmonious spirit." It's about finding offense in defense. You accept the energy of an attack and reshape it, misdirect it, and turn it back against your foe. I apply aikido theory to every part of my life. I had no hope of locking Terrance in an armbar, but I might be able to lock him into a game of wits. Battlefield mine! Barbs that wound. Darts aimed at the heart. I'd agitate him. Enrage him. Cultivate his fury. I'd divorce him of his senses and send him tumbling headlong into my trap. And then? Then I would do what was necessary. *Who are you? What are your malicious intentions? How many hoodlums have you told about this home and the riches it contains? I want names, mister!*

I own a stun gun. I purchased it years ago, during the early sorties of the Hayes/Sunshine feud. It is my Excalibur. I took the weapon from its usual place (the nightstand) and moved it to a low bookshelf, not far from the entrance to my chambers. When Terrance came sprinting in, I would send him off to dreamland with a 4.5-million-volt kiss.

A sturdy chair. Zip ties. We have ways of making you talk.

In case, dear reader. Just *in case.* Remember the Boy Scout credo.

Dawn gave on to morning, and the others awoke. Breakfast was served. Mummy was aglow. I was to meet Terrance. I'd get to hear his "wonderful" music. Mummy pumped up the concert like a desperate promoter. I feigned disinterest.

"Oh, is that today?"

Puppa's excitement was evident. I played at nonchalance, but inside I burned. I was Napoleon that morn; comfortable in my palace, sumptuously provisioned, yet unable to turn my mind from the imminent fray.

Napoleon is my favorite historical dictator, in case you were wondering. Mummy is the one who likes Cromwell. She's an Anglophile. I'm not a phile-anything, I'm a zealous American patriot, but continental preferences do arise from time to time, and when they do my tastes tend toward *Franco.*

"I'm off to work," I said, dabbing the crème de chicory from my lips. "You may summon me when the nurse arrives."

Safely cloistered, I performed an aikido stretching routine, followed by one hundred squat thrusts. My chi was in balance; my body, a coiled spring. I dressed in the "escape trousers" and a smart blue blazer. A tweed cap afforded me a dual persona: part country gentleman, part Irish brawler. I sat at my computer, nibbling at the day's work, unable to focus. Then, after what felt like an eternity, Mummy requested my presence. Her voice carried up the staircase and into my chambers like a call to arms.

"Buddy, Terrance is here!"

My soul beat with the savage cadence of drums. I took a shot of snuff. I stood before the mirror and practiced my menacing glares. I was as ready as I'd ever be.

I approached the den quietly. My stealth was retarded by the payload of marbles hidden in my crotch. They rattled softly with each step. It was as if I were smuggling a pair of maracas in my underpants. The sacs brushed against my thighs. Under different circumstances, the sensation would have been titillating, but at that moment I was all business.

A babel of small talk suffused the air. Mummy was

clucking away like an enamored schoolgirl. She spoke of the weather; she related details of Puppa's condition. The other voice—Terrance's voice—was not quite baritone but deeper than I would have wished it. It was a *man's* voice. A bit of urban affect rounded the edges of his sentences, but his dialect was not the vulgar Ebonics one commonly hears on the streets. He spoke to Puppa as if they were old chums and to Mummy in a familiar way that bordered on . . . flirtation? His voice was a jazz trumpet filled with honey. The voice of a flimflam man.

I hid by the doorway and carefully peered inside. Puppa was in his swing. Mummy sat in the armchair. The tall black stranger stood in the center of the room, his back to me. His flesh was the color of dark walnut. He wore powder blue medical scrub pants, a slim-fitting black tee, and bulbous rubber slippers. The slippers were red, like something you'd see on a clown. I'd expected a thick-necked brute—and that's what my fearful eyes had seen when I spied him from my chamber window—but, in fact, Terrance was long and lean, not a trace of fat, not a bit of needless bulk. A dancer's body, true enough. He was in the process of taking Puppa's blood pressure.

In the far corner of the room was a black case. The case was shaped like a banjo, but for all I knew it was filled with rope, duct tape, and daggers.

Puppa's eye socket was stuffed with gauze, and the remaining eye was legally blind. The old fellow was faced in my direction, but his attentions were squarely on his steward, and I figured as long as I maintained my position, without any undue movements, my presence would remain unknown. Not so. Terrance shifted. Puppa's eye struck me like a laser. He muttered a string of polysyllables that asked: "Hey, what are you doing out there?" I pulled my head back and pressed my chest against the wall.

"Buddy, are you out there?"

"Yes, Mummy."

"What are you *doing* out there?"

I clung to the wall as if it were the face of a cliff.

"I dropped my lapel pin. I am looking for it." I was wearing a lapel pin—a small rose made of rubies. "Ah. There it is. I have found the lapel pin, and I am now reaffixing it to my blazer." I ruffled the jacket to make a convincing sound. "I have now affixed the lapel pin, and I shall enter." I stepped into the den with as much swagger as I could muster.

And there he was. Terrance Johnson. Had I been a cartoon, my jaw would have hit the floor like an anvil, and my tongue would have uncoiled to his feet. He was the most handsome man I had ever seen. More than this—he was the most beautiful *human* I had ever laid eyes upon. Words are insufficient here. We've all been staggered in the face of something beautiful, and so stood I, gawking, blank-faced, unable to speak. He smiled, and it was as if the sun had poked its head through the clouds and cast a single, brilliant beam upon the shadowed Earth.

Terrance stepped forward in one graceful stride and held out his hand. His fingers were long. Fashioned for precise work. His palm, a striking shade of pink.

"Hello, Buddy."

People tend to flinch when they see me for the first time. Their noses cave back into their faces, their eyes go wide, and their features go dumb as they struggle to comprehend my bizarre construction. I'm visually poisonous; their eyes want to spit me out. This didn't happen with Terrance. Not a twitch. His smile held fast. I looked into his eyes. They were almond-shaped. The irises were colored like tea leaves, and the whites shimmered, truly *shimmered,* like mother of pearl.

He towered over me. I took his hand and did my best to offer a manly grip, but my fingers barely spanned the width of his palm. What he got was something weak and clammy—as if I'd handed him a half-pound of warm bologna.

"Charles Hayes," I announced. "I am the breadwinner of this home."

It was a stupid thing to say. I was attempting to establish my authority—to make clear that I was the boss—but the word "breadwinner" was a poor choice. There was no macho thunder to it. Terrance laughed as if I had made a joke.

"Well, I guess you're the one I should thank, then."

"Yes," I hissed. "You should."

I felt silly about that one too. I was not, in the strictest sense, his employer, and I was certainly not the one who had advocated his presence. Oh, well. One idiocy deserves another, I suppose.

Pull your hand away. Pull your hand away! I looked into Terrance's beautiful eyes and tried to communicate this message to him telepathically. I'm a daily meditator. During these Zen sessions, I attempt to stimulate the brain regions that are unreachable through conscious thought. My goal: to develop my telepathic, telekinetic, and psionic powers. No luck yet, but I have felt some odd tingling sensations.

I could not be the first to break the handshake. The power behind Terrance's gaze shook me to the core, but I would not allow myself to look away. I needed to assert my dominance.

"This is a beautiful home," he said, our hands clasped. "Ruth tells me that you do a lot of the decorating."

Ruth? The nerve! To refer to Mummy in the Christian familiar!

"*Mrs. Hayes* exaggerates my contribution and downplays her own. Our shared spaces fall exclusively under her purview. My role is more 'inventory management.' I keep a ledger. If even the smallest curio is out of place, I take notice."

The torturous handshake continued. Our eyes were like lodestones, drawn magnetically together.

"I wish I was that organized," Terrance said.

"One must keep track of what one has," I said.

Terrance's dark lips curled in amusement.

"One must." He broke the handshake.

A small victory. Terrance's appearance had thrown me like a bronco, but I had quickly remounted the steed of my composure. An awkward silence followed. We spent a moment sizing each other up, like a pair of dogs sniffing rumps. He regarded my fashionable attire. He must have felt embarrassingly underdressed by comparison. Then—and I gasped when I saw it—his eyes came to rest on my crotch. His glance was indirect yet unmistakable. My heart leapt. *This man intends to rape me, here and now!* I was halfway through calculating an aikido leg-sweep when I comprehended the target of his gaze. It was the marbles. The sacks had created a substantial bulge down yonder. I clenched my butt cheeks and pushed the bulge forward, amplifying the effect. *Behold my gargantuan gonads,* the gesture demanded, *and consider the testosterone they might produce!*

"Terrance and I were just discussing *Moby Dick,*" Mummy said.

Apropos, as Terrance was considering the size of *my* Moby Dick at that very moment! I begged her pardon.

"You know . . . *Moby Dick*? The book?" She lifted our leather-bound copy from the end table beside her. I'd given a dramatic reading that morning.

"Oh? And what golden nuggets did our guest offer on the subject?"

"It's nothing," he said, attempting to kill the topic.

"No, please." I insisted. "I would love to hear your insights."

"I was in a play a while back."

"A play?"

"Moby Dick."

"*Moby Dick* is not a play."

"A stage adaptation."

It was clear that he didn't want to go into it. Terrance and Mummy had worked up a rapport—a wholly inappropriate one—and by provoking this discussion, she was hoping to project that rapport onto me.

"What manner of adaptation? A farce? Ha!"

The "ha" was not a laugh. It was a bitter, sarcastic exclamation. Mummy's face went swollen with disapproval. Her scar skipped the pinks and mauves and went right on to red.

"It was science fiction, if you can believe it," said Terrance.

"I *cannot* believe it. I suppose Moby Dick was a space monster."

"That's right."

"And Ahab was some kind of spaceship captain?"

"You got it."

"Sounds dreadful."

"I know. It sounds pretty bad."

"And what role did you play?"

"Stubb, the second mate."

"*You*? The second mate? Of a whaling ship in nineteenth-century Nantucket? Now that *is* science fiction."

The issue of race had to be broached, and this was my first attempt. Ham-fisted, I admit. Terrance said that his *Moby Dick* had been a science-fiction adaptation. Race holds no bearing on science-fiction starships, we all know that, so my quip made no sense. As for whaling ships in nineteenth-century Nantucket? My knowledge stops where *Moby Dick* ends. Vengeance, self-destruction—these are the themes that fascinate me. I'm not a big "whaling buff." For all I knew, there might have been thousands of black second mates on nineteenth-century whaling ships. I scribbled a mental note. *Afro-Americans. American whaling industry. What role?* Another point of research for my Anti-Bias Reprogramming curriculum.

I awaited Terrance's reaction. His face betrayed nothing. He displayed a regal posture, leaning neither forward (aggressive) nor back (submissive). I'd done enough. Race had been touched upon, and in so doing, a message: I was not one of those Caucasian sycophants who pretend it doesn't matter.

"So, what's in the case?" I asked, pointing with my nose.

Terrance laughed. "What do you think is in the case?"

"The configuration of the case would lead us to believe that it contains a stringed musical instrument. But I won't jump to any conclusions."

"It's a banjo," Mummy said, trying to break in.

"What's your style of playing? I'm well versed on this subject, so please be honest."

"With the banjo?"

"No, with a badminton racquet. Yes, banjo."

"A little bit of everything, I guess."

"Would you *name* the styles that you have mastered?"

That smile again. Was he patronizing me, or simply daft?

"I'm self-taught, so I sort of do my own thing, but I've picked up bits and pieces of different styles as I've gone along. Bluegrass, clawhammer, folk."

"Describe to me, in concise language, the elements of each style that are present in your playing."

Mummy rose from the armchair and set her fists on her hips.

"Charles William Hayes, let's cool it with the inquisition."

"It's a conversation, Mummy. I'm being genial."

"You're being a jerk, with a capital J. Please go make us some coffee. Would you like some coffee, Terrance?"

"Coffee sounds great," he said with a twinge of relief.

"I protest!"

"Buddy, go make us some coffee."

"There are no ground beans," I said, crossing my arms over my chest.

"Then *grind* the beans."

"The cups and saucers are soiled from breakfast."

"I have done the dishes from breakfast, Buddy. Go and prepare four cups of coffee. Terrance, how do you take it?"

"Light and sweet," he said.

My frustration was like a mouthful of bile. Here was my own Mummy, emasculating me in front of my foe. *I'm on your side, wench! Can't you see what I'm trying to accomplish? Are you blind to the intentions of this Zulu witch doctor?*

The gears in my mind shifted in a hard, greasy clunk. My face went hot. The signs had been there for weeks! Whenever Mummy spoke of Terrance, her words turned to sugar, and rainbow-colored umbrellas spun in her eyes. She was in love with him! How could I have missed it!? She was forty-two years old; at the tail end of her fertility. The pre-menopausal sex hunger was upon her! It was disgusting to consider such things—and indeed, the very thought made me nauseous—but I had to recognize that a man like Terrance could easily set Mummy's loins aflame. Through the popular media, I had learned that black men prefer women with large rumps, and Mummy certainly had that. She was an excellent cook and a stimulating conversationalist. But to take her as a lover? What a fool I'd been. I'd come prepared for a marauder but found a vile Rasputin instead! A usurper! Terrance intended to claim my Mummy as his "bro-ho." He'd come to our home under the pretense of work, beheld the majesty within, and forged a repugnant gold-digging scheme.

"Light and sweet?" My question was an accusation. "Is that the way you *like it*?"

"We're talking about coffee?" he asked.

"I hope so. For your sake." I eyed him like a gunslinger ready to draw.

"Buddy! You know full well what 'light and sweet' means. Prepare four cups of coffee. Now."

I didn't want to leave them alone. As soon as I turned my back, Mummy might toss herself into Terrance's arms. I was mind-raped by images of Terrance and Mummy fornicating roughly on the den floor, and my darling Pap, dangling above them, his single eye wide with horror.

"Puppa, would you prefer the Jamaican or the Costa Rican beans?" I asked.

He emitted a four-syllable groan. Costa Rican, then.

"Are you comfortable, Puppa?" I asked.

He flashed me his toothless smile and then gave the same smile to Terrance. The whole scene was funny to him.

"Puppa is comfortable, Buddy, but he needs to get back to his treatment." Her scar gleamed like a neon sign. She was doing all she could to tether her fury.

"I will go. I just wanted to make sure that Puppa was completely comfortable, and that there's nothing that might make him *un*comfortable."

"That's very considerate of you. Puppa will only take a half-cup, and don't forget to mix in the Thick & Easy. He would be very *un*comfortable if he choked again." The look she gave portended a vicious lambasting.

I exited the den. I trod softly and listened over my shoulder for anything that sounded like foreplay. All I heard were the test beeps from one of Terrance's devices. The kitchen was on the first floor. By the time I reached the staircase, I could no longer hear the activities in the den. I would have to place my trust in Mummy's virtue—a trust that, for the first time, was badly shaken—and hope that the two perverts could restrain themselves.

I ground the beans and set the kettle to boil. Waiting for water to boil is one of life's great boredoms, and it was doubly painful then. At last the kettle whistled, and I poured the water into the press with the ground beans. There was another agonizing wait as the beans mated with the steaming water. I used this time to ready the cups and saucers. Coffee was poured and seasoned. Black for me, sugar and lemon for Mummy, light and sweet for Terrance, Thick & Easy for Puppa. I set it all on a silver salver. The whole operation took eleven minutes—adequate time for Mummy and Terrance to slip into her bedroom, enjoy a quick tryst, and return to Puppa's care as if nothing had happened.

I reentered the den. Terrance was in the process of stretching Puppa's left arm. He took the withered limb by the wrist and elbow and moved it slowly upward, slowly downward. Puppa would let out a pained grumble as the arm rose, and Terrance would hold the arm at that uncomfortable point for a moment, then lower the limb again. Mummy looked on, inquiring after every action like some brown-nosing pupil.

"I know, I know," Terrance said, reacting to Puppa's groans. "Only three more. No-pain-no-gain, right?"

"Coffee!" I chirped.

"We'll be done in a few minutes," Mummy said over her

shoulder. "Please set up the folding chairs. Terrance is going to play a song for us."

The stupid tray made me feel like a servant. I set it down and retrieved two chairs from the closet. I sat in one and drank my coffee like a miserable drunk nursing his hooch.

Time passed. The checkup concluded. "All set, young man," Terrance said playfully. Puppa grinned at him with fatherly affection.

You old fool! Don't you know a snake-oil salesman when you see one!?

They rolled Puppa across the den, and we arranged a little seating row, with Puppa's lift in the middle. We'd face the bay window, which Terrance would use as his makeshift proscenium. He set the large black case on the armchair and undid the brass latches. I set my readiness level to "Orange Alert." He opened the case. It contained a banjo.

"Well, I'm *so* glad I made this coffee," I said. "I can see how much you are all enjoying it."

"That's okay," said Mummy, snuggling into her seat. "We'll have it after."

"After, it will be cold and disgusting."

Terrance took up the banjo and plucked a single string. It sounded like the dying cry of a small bird. He made a pained face. He twisted a tuning peg and tried again. It sounded better to him, but to me it only sounded like the dying cry of a slightly larger bird. He repeated the process with the other four strings until the banjo was—in *his* opinion—in tune.

"Okay," he asked. "What'll it be?"

"I request 'Swanee,'" I said.

That pristine smile. It was the pivot of his power, and he knew it. For a moment I almost forgot I loathed him. *No!* If I dropped my guard for even a moment, this philanderer might end up as my stepfather. I pushed my anger back to the surface. I scratched it raw, agitating the pustule of my hate.

"That's Gershwin, right?"

"Yes, it is. Please perform it in the style of Al Jolson."

"Don't think I could do it justice."

"Oh, Terrance," cried Mummy, "Why don't you play the song you played last time?" Her eyes were like hubcaps. She was comporting herself like a groupie slut! I'd get an earful later, but I had a similar portion to serve right back to her.

"Sure. Mr. Hayes, would you like to hear 'Under the Bridges of Paris' again?"

Puppa trembled. Dean Martin was his favorite musician. We had a substantial collection of Dino's records in the drawing room. I'd listened to them with Puppa countless times. "Sinatra had the chutzpah, but Martin had the talent," he used to say. I knew "Under the Bridges of Paris" word for word. When Terrance finished with his pastiche, I would be ready with an informed criticism.

Terrance took a deep breath. His back straightened and his eyes closed. Then something changed. It was as if he had slipped into a waking dream, as if some part of him was no longer present. He strummed. The sound was like nothing I'd heard before. The strings were a chorus of voices, all in perfect harmony. Terrance capered his slender fingers across the fretboard. Individual notes began to emerge—each one, a tiny promise. "Under the Bridges of Paris" worked its way to the surface and Terrance began to sing.

"How would you like to be
Down by the Seine with me
Oh what I'd give for a moment or two
Under the bridges of Paris with you . . ."

Terrance's voice was superb. His middle voice was a high baritone, but for the purpose of "Under the Bridges of Paris" he worked in the range of a *tenore di forza.* This was not one of those phony puppet voices that are so common in popular music. Terrance's musical voice was the handsome brother of his speaking one. It was the confident voice of an expert performer.

"Darling I'd hold you tight
Far from the eyes of night
Under the bridges of Paris with you
I'd make your dreams come true . . ."

Mummy was in a state of rapture. I was in shock. Puppa was "singing" along, and doing so loudly, but even this was not sufficient to break the spell. Here, in the den, was a thing sublime. The playing was delicate. Breezy. Something harplike in it. The terminus between notes was impossible to know; they blended as beautifully as the colors in a Monet. Terrance extended the chorus with an elegant instrumental solo, full of improvisations that bloomed extempore.

A hot wad formed in my chest. I felt the urge to belch and tried to do so, but the hot wad only moved to my throat. A tiny sob escaped my lips. Tears filled my eyes. I brushed them away, but it was like trying to plug the holes in a sinking submarine. What was happening to me? Our record cabinet was like a hall of masters: Pavarotti, Bartoli, Fitzgerald, Cole, Holiday, Cooke. In that moment, they all amounted to a hill of beans. I'd never beheld such virtuosity. Terrance entered into the final verse.

"Under the bridges of Paris, with you . . ."

He looked directly into my eyes. Tears soaked my cheeks. He smiled warmly and cocked his head.

I'll make your dre-e-eams . . . come . . . tru-ooo-ooo!

He changed his singing style on that final line. He adopted the tone and phrasing of Al Jolson. It was a broad, playful impression. I was moved by the effort.

Mummy burst into applause. Puppa wiggled his stumps and cried out like a child on a carnival thrill ride. I was a blubbering mess. I felt ashamed, and awed, and oh, so alive! I clapped my hands as if Tinkerbell's life hung in the balance. I cried "Encore, *encore*!" The man had earned a standing ovation, and I rose to give him one.

A strange sound came from my crotch. A tearing sound. A sound like velcro being ripped apart. A river of marbles cascaded down my legs and out of my trousers. They hit the floor and bounced off in all directions, like a mass of colored gumballs spilling from a broken vending machine. Terrance's eyes darted around the floor, finally coming to rest at my hemline. His expression was one of total bewilderment. Mummy lifted her feet and shrieked. Puppa failed to notice. He continued to celebrate Terrance's performance.

"Oh, no!" I cried. "My marbles!"

Terrance stood frozen to the spot.

"Buddy! What on *earth* is this!?" Mummy cried.

My wardrobe malfunction snapped me back to reality. The tears ceased to flow. The spell was broken.

"Marbles, as you can clearly see. I had a satchel of them, and they must have spilled through a hole in my pocket."

"Why did you have a sack of marbles in your pocket?"

"I thought we might all like to play."

"When have we *ever* played *marbles*, Buddy?"

Terrance laughed. Mummy shook her head. She looked upwards, to God, for some respite from her insufferable son. Then she began to laugh. Puppa began laughing too, simply for the sake of laughing.

I was a mockery. I felt like rolling onto my back and exposing my underbelly.

Mummy was downstairs, bidding her bed buddy adieu. I scurried about the den floor, picking up the marbles and placing them in my tweed cap. Puppa remained in his harness. He muttered a sentence. I couldn't translate it, but I knew it was some kind of accusation.

"What would you have me do?" I asked him. "Allow this stranger to violate the sanctity of our home?"

Another harsh burble.

"Terrance may seem nice, but I have come to believe he has ulterior motives. I need more evidence, but rest assured—an investigation is in progress."

Puppa mumbled four words. Each was like a wet Nerf ball—soppy, hard to catch—but I was able to understand. *What's wrong with you?* he said.

I could hear Mummy coming down the hallway. *Here it comes,* I thought. *Time to take my medicine.*

She stood in the doorway. Her eyes were fire.

"Terrance would like to speak with you," she said.

"With me?"

"That's right."

"Whatever about?"

"He didn't say. He just said that he'd like to speak with you in private."

I knew it! The whole performance had been nothing but a ruse! Well, I had news for him. My ice would not be broken!

He possessed genuine talent—there was no denying that—but I wouldn't offer my blessing just because he could win first prize in a beauty pageant. If he wanted to continue this liaison, he'd get no approval from me.

"I'm sorry, but that will not be possible. My desk is a mountain of deadlines. You grossly understated the length of this event, and I will be drowning all day because of it. If Terrance would like to speak to me, he may call my office during business hours."

I brushed past Mummy and absconded away. I needed to get back to my chambers and regroup. Terrance had won the battle that day, but I would win the war.

- 4 -
A RENDEZVOUS

I could feel Mummy's smolder. The heat of it oozed upwards through the floorboards. Thank goodness for the rule of law. The Hayes Family Contract was sacrosanct. If Mummy wished to enter my chambers, she was required to give me a full day's notice beforehand. If she needed my assistance, she could call up from the base of the stairs or use the telephone.

My mind was septic. Mummy had never shown any interest in sex before. Dating? Not that I ever saw, and an impossible thing for me *not* to see. A steady boyfriend? Unimaginable! Her only "gentleman caller" was the mailman. She was timid around men. She always had been. How jarring it was to see my sweet, naïve Mummy behaving like the neighborhood good-time girl. I could only hope that Terrance's plan was in the early stages; that I could expose him before he consummated his plot. I spent the day answering emails about jobs in progress and jobs to be. The spec for Hixon Smyth Boutiques hung over me like an anvil.

The thought of writing it made me dizzy with boredom. Procrastination reigned. I cleaned my office. Did some bookkeeping. Late afternoon, I wrote an email to a special friend. My email (re: Tonight?) contained a single sentence.

Are we on?

A response came shortly after.

Can't wait. Midnight.

My pet snake slithered in my underpants. That night, I would visit The Mute.

- - -

Eleven forty P.M. A crescent moon suspended in the haze. The sky was starless; the air, chill and damp. A climate ideal for nighttime lurking.

South Ilium is a tangle of alleys, one-way streets, vacant lots, disintegrating buildings, abandoned storefronts, crumbling churches, cars on cinderblocks, ancient refrigerators and washing machines and bicycles left out to rot. South Ilium is brick, and it is rust. Coin-op laundromats do double duty as homeless shelters. Decrepit brownstones, built in the nineteenth century, line the ghost-town boulevards. I walked south along the First Avenue alley. There are five other alleys like it. They run the length of the city, north to south, dividing each block. It's a second grid; a second city, almost, known only to locals. The back streets. Unkempt in the original cobblestone. This is where the oldest of old Ilium can be found. Gaslight buildings. Carriage houses. Some repurposed, others neglected. It's exciting to imagine a time when the alleys were stables; when the nighttime sounds would include snorts and whinnies; when manure could be counted among the acrid city smells. Silent and lifeless now, the alleys are dark, raw, lined with garbage.

My blue blazer was a holdover from the morning. A "blazer," as I blazed a path toward ecstasy; a "sport coat," for the most thrilling sport of all! I had swapped the escape trousers for a pair of flat-front khakis. I knew The Mute would appreciate my spiffy threads. She had a thing for men's casual wear.

I crossed Jefferson Street. Lubricious thoughts filled my mind, and I struggled to keep my manhood at bay. If I intended to ravish The Mute—and I *absolutely* intended to ravish The Mute—I would need to do some climbing. God is a prankster, and untimely erections are one of his choice gags; but when the urge is strong, and an emergency ladder lies between you and your lover, the joke is not funny. I would need to climb such a ladder to reach The Mute's boudoir. In the course of my ascent, I might catch my endowment on a rung, slip, fall, and smash my brains out on the stones below. I'd die in a dark alley, and that would be bad enough, but what if rigor mortis locked the erection in place? I imagined my naked corpse lying on the slab, and Mummy, standing over me, her expression a wretched mix of misery and disgust. "Is this *your* son?" the mortician would ask, raising an eyebrow toward my ghastly tumescence. Dark stuff. And useful. The thought of it reduced me to a state of semi engorgement.

The Mute's bedroom is on the third floor of a five-story walkup. The dark flank of her building loomed above and a thin, flickering light escaped her window. The light from a single candle. It was a signal: her parents were asleep, and our playdate was a go. I squatted behind a garbage can and made ready. I popped a peppermint, dusted my lapels, adjusted my tie. My traitorous wiener stirred again, but I returned to the image of the mortician's slab and regained dominion. It was time. I pulled a keyfob laser pointer from my pocket, aimed it at The Mute's window, and fired three quick laser beams into the room.

A figure appeared at the window; a shadowy silhouette, undulating with each twitch of the unseen flame. The window clattered open. The gentle rattling of chains could be heard above, and then, slowly, the emergency escape ladder descended through the darkness. My Rapunzel awaited.

Here, a brief gloss of my sexual history.

At eleven years old, I sprouted my first pubic hair. I wanted to share that pube with the world—to make the world aware of its presence—but Mummy had taught me that it's impolite to discuss "bathroom matters" with others. Not that I had anyone to tell. None of my classmates would take me as a friend. Oh, there were a few nerds and weaklings who were cordial to me, but friendship was too great a risk for them. A lion pounces. The gazelles flee. To the human observer, it appears as if the herd is running from the lion. There's a unity to their flight; a seemingly impenetrable oneness. It's an illusion. The herd is not running from the lion: it's running from the weakest gazelle.

I never questioned why it was so. My state was natural. Immutable. I was the smallest. The ugliest by far. I was the training dummy upon which they could safely indulge their adolescent cruelty.

The discovery of that silky pube filled me with hope. I was changing! What might I change into? Nothing close to handsome, I knew that, but maybe I would grow less ugly. Maybe even . . . *normal-looking*? I was full of questions, but this was before the Internet, and I had no easy way of answering them. The thought of discussing it with Mummy made me sick to my stomach. Puppa was the only option.

He sat in his armchair. His reading spectacles rested on

the tip of his nose, and a thick book was open on his lap. A cigarette burned in the ashtray beside him.

You wouldn't have called him handsome, but his looks were impressive to me. Taller, though not tall by any standard but mine. He had a broad, chinless face, which I had inherited. A large, mashed nose, but not so large as mine. Close-set eyes, but not so close as mine. His ears were his defining feature. They were too large for his head, and they're larger now, as the ears keep growing throughout our lives, and they stuck out like radar dishes, and they still do so, although his left has been reconfigured by surgery and is now folded slightly and angled downward. He dressed neatly. Slacks, dress shirt, cardigan or sweater vest. You might have confused him for a schoolteacher—maybe even a professor—but his hands would have given him away. Scarred knuckles. Thick calluses. Ragged fingernails. Stains that would never wash off. The hands of a laborer.

"I'm becoming a man," I announced.

"Agreed," he said without looking up.

"No, I mean *really.*"

"What makes you say so?"

"A hair," I said, pointing gravely at my privates.

Puppa set his book aside, removed his spectacles, and turned to face me.

"You got a little hair, huh?" There was laughter in his voice.

"Please be serious."

Puppa leaned forward, into a conversational pose, and attempted to wipe the grin from his face.

"It happens at your age. It's nothing to be worried about."

"I'm not worried. I've come to you for guidance. What should I do?"

"Do?"

"About the hair."

He nearly laughed again.

"Let it grow."

"I will terminate this conversation at once!"

"Okay, okay, okay. You've taken me by surprise. Please forgive me."

He sat back and took a moment to consider the situation.

"Have you experienced an erection?" he asked.

"Yes. Nowadays it's called a boner."

"It was called a boner in the olden days too. And?"

"And?"

"Did this erection develop when you were thinking about a girl, or did it just sort of happen on its own?"

I blushed. "Both. Usually, it happens and I don't know why it happens."

"Well . . . did you . . . I mean, *have* you . . ." His eyes searched the room as if the words he was looking for might be drifting in the cigarette smoke. "This may be something you want to discuss with your mother."

"I will *never* discuss this with Mummy, and you better not either! This topic is not appropriate for a lady."

He nodded solemnly.

"Let me ask you—have you done any reading on the subject?"

"A boy brought a dirty magazine to school, but he wouldn't let me look at it."

"Not the kind of reading I was referring to. I'm talking about literature."

I was a precocious reader. I was well ahead of my classmates in this regard, thanks largely to Puppa's influence. I'd conquered a good many "grown-up" books, but none of them spoke to my condition. I was unaware that such books existed.

"Can you suggest a reading list?" I asked.

Puppa took his cigarette from the ashtray, set it in the corner of his mouth, and rose from his chair. A large bookcase dominated one side of the den. He crossed to it and began scanning the stacks. He pulled out one book, then another, then another. He held the books out to me. The image of him at that moment is forever burned in my mind. The books in his hand, the cigarette in his mouth—he looked like a bona fide writer himself. The books were *Portnoy's Complaint, Tropic of Cancer,* and *Lolita.*

My adolescent years were a masturbatory blur. I became a regular at Rosy Palm's Whorehouse and cavorted freely with her five sisters. They were a rough bunch, those sisters. They loved me hard and left me raw. I discovered lotion. I experimented with objects. A gym sock. An oven mitt. A pair of pillows pressed together in simulation of a rump.

"Buddy, where is the cantaloupe I bought yesterday?"

"Sorry, Mummy. I ate it."

"You ate an *entire* cantaloupe?"

I was like an athlete in training. With each session, I increased the difficulty of my routines. I developed my erotic muscle memory and came to know how my body would perform under different conditions.

"Buddy, where is the feather-duster?"

"I was dusting, and I dropped it in the toilet."

How did ugly people find each other before the Internet? On my eighteenth birthday, I blew out my candles and made a wish: *This year, I wish to make love to a real woman.* I had a 486 with a dialup modem. I ate my slice of cake, licked the frosting from my lips, retreated to my room (I hadn't claimed my chambers at that time), and launched Netscape Navigator. So began my sex life.

A void of darkness pulled at my heels. I reached The Mute's window and set my elbows on the sill.

It was a small room, tastelessly appointed. The walls, a high-gloss lavender. Pink floral stenciling crawled like ivy. The furnishings—vanity, nightstand, and dresser—were of one set. A child's set. The rug was purple shag. A stuffed menagerie—teddies, elephants, pigs and whatnot—took ownership of the space. They perched on every surface. Prisoners? Sentinels? Their puerile plastic eyes had seen much.

The Mute was thirty-two—so she'd claimed, and it seemed about right—but she had the bedroom of a twelve-year-old girl. If The Mute spoke, I would ask her "Why do you keep your room this way?" She doesn't speak and she wouldn't answer. She's not The Mute for nothing.

My lover sat on the edge of the bed. Usually, she'd be nude upon my arrival, but not that night. The Mute was clad in a white brassiere, white panties, and thigh-high stockings fastened with a garter belt. A pair of sexy red pumps completed the look. Peep-toed. Patent leather. Her hair was slicked back, and her legs were crossed demurely. The signal candle burned on the vanity. In the flickering mix of light and shadow, it was possible to believe that The Mute was beautiful.

Not that I'd want to believe that. But I could have.

"I just happened to be in the neighborhood," I whispered.

She put a finger to her lips, shushing me.

I completed my ingress and pulled up the ladder behind me. This had to be done with care, as the steel chains and aluminum rungs were capable of quite a racket. I finished the task and turned to my lady.

Since I am a gentleman, let me start by stating her assets. She's lissome. She has flawless milky white skin. Her hair is a lovely shade of chestnut. She has excellent taste in perfume. Wildflower, a whisper of musk. Her lovemaking is pliant, submissive, but also quietly confident. *Take me,* her body says, *but take me on* my *terms.*

Now her defects. Her lissomness might better be described as "bony." She is one of those rare women who might benefit by gaining fifteen pounds. She's put together like an erector set—spindly limbs, heavy joints, knock-knees. Her eyes are spaced too widely and, by some freakish defect, operate *independently* of one another, with each eyeball seeking what it wants without consideration of the other. She has thirty-one perfect teeth and one horrible mutant; a central incisor at the bull's-eye of her smile that's twice as large as it should be and skewed to the side at a preposterous angle. It's like a malformed pearl set in the middle of a diamond-encrusted brooch. Its presence is unfathomable in our era of modern orthodontics.

The Mute rose from the bed and teetered over to me like a clumsy child on a pair of stilts. The Mute is not a tall woman, but the pumps added a full five inches to her height. She was not adept at operating the complicated footwear. She was making a play at "sexy strut," but the effect was more "penguin in heat."

She removed my cap and ran her fingers through my hair. Her left eye scanned my natty attire and seemed pleased by what it saw. The right eye shifted toward the bedroom door and confirmed our privacy. This googling unnerved me, but I had to recognize the utility of her skill.

"You look wonderful," I cooed. "If you would just come to my chambers, we would be free to do all we wanted, without fear of discovery." Our home features a servant stair in the back. It's a steep, twisting affair, and I'm pretty much the only one who uses it. It grants me direct access to the backyard. I call it "The Ladies' Entrance."

The Mute placed her finger on my lips and traced it slowly over my mouth. It was a dual-purpose caress, intended to tantalize and also to shut me up. I was really getting into it, but then—and this was totally unexpected—she slid the finger *into* my mouth. I nearly gagged. She pushed the finger in and out. *This is new,* I thought. I took my cue and began sucking. Her breathing quickened. She closed her eyes and began caressing her body with her free hand. She was behaving as if her index finger was her most erogenous zone! After a full minute of this odd finger fellatio, she removed her digit, took my face gently in her hands, and kissed me. In the process, she smeared my own saliva across my forehead. "*Enough of this nonsense*!" my libido cried. I took her roughly in my arms, Clark Gable style. She melted into my macho embrace. It was a moment of sweet surrender . . . and a moment is all it lasted. Her balance was shaky. Our height difference caused a teeter-tottering effect. Her knees buckled, and she fell sideways off her elaborate shoes. We engaged in a sort of spastic waltz as I struggled to hold her upright. We went tumbling sideways and fell with a thud onto the shag carpet.

"Are you okay?"

She shushed me again. I lay on my back, she lay prone, and we were completely still, like a pair of soldiers huddled in a foxhole. We surveyed the silence. I'd never been beyond The Mute's bedroom door. I had no idea of who or what might be out there. She lived with her parents. That's what she'd said in her emails. Maybe she had a brother. Maybe an uncle. Maybe her father was a drug dealer and the house was full of guns.

Another theory: that The Mute was an extraterrestrial; that her window was a portal and her bedroom was some kind of alien sex laboratory. It wasn't the first time I'd considered it. Under normal circumstances, the concept was more fantasy than hypothesis. Imagine me, Buddy Hayes, the unwitting subject in an alien sex experiment! Did her bedroom door lead to an apartment . . . or to another *world?* And just look at her! Her form might be as close to "convincing human female" as they could get. The emergency escape ladder was piled in the corner. I gazed at it from my position on the floor and considered my retreat.

Minutes passed. I drew the courage to act and was about to make for the window, when The Mute slithered across the shag and climbed atop me. She straddled me about the waist, set her hands upon my chest, and began grinding her sex into mine. A palpable heat was generated by the friction of our dry-humping; a heat that melted all thoughts of drug-dealing fathers and incestuous brothers and alien first encounters. My eyes rolled back. My toes curled in my loafers. Her gyrations grew more pronounced, and I was certain that I would go, and I was fine with that, I was always quick to rally, but then she stopped, reached down, undid my belt, and unzipped my trousers.

It's time to reveal my unique gift. The thing that makes my penis unlike other penises. Two words. Untold potentials locked within them.

Variable rigidity.

I can control the psi of my member. I do so mentally—as easily as one might flex a bicep. I am able to hold and maintain the pressure at any level I choose, and that level can be maintained throughout coitus. Or altered. On the fly. To suit my lover. To suit the moment.

A limp turnip is good for nothing but mashing. To penetrate, I must set the pressure at half-maximum. My penis is malleable at this setting, fully plumped, and approximately 66.6 percent of its potential length. It's perfect for soft, intimate lovemaking. My penis spills in like molasses. It fills every curve of the vessel. Gentle. Shudder-inducing. It's hot stuff.

"God knows what temper to put in people." That's one of Mummy's chestnuts. You rarely meet a large man who's full of piss and vinegar, and you rarely meet a small one (myself included) who doesn't suffer from a bit of the ol' Napoleonic. Furthermore: *The LORD gave, and the LORD hath taken away.* "God." "The Universe." Choose your maker. The point is about cosmic justice. If I were a handsome man, or a tall man, or a brilliant man, and you caught me bragging on the variable rigidity of my penis, you'd have every reason to doubt. But I'm nobody. I've got nothing that anyone wants, and I have never once, in my life, been an object of desire. I've only ever been an object of desperation, and so God, the Universe, granted me a consolation prize: mind control over my corpora cavernosa.

I discovered the gift in my training days. At first, it took a half minute or longer to alter the pressure. Now, after years of focused practice, it takes fractions of a second. Inherited? I cannot say. I've discussed many things with Puppa, but some topics are just too gauche. Acquired? Perhaps, but all men are vigorous masturbators in adolescence, and I've yet to hear of a penis that can do as mine does.

I set myself at three-quarter rigidity. The Mute pulled her panties aside and slowly lowered herself onto me. We made love. Heartbeats. Swallowed gasps and clipped breath. The delicious push and pull. I dropped to half-maximum. Her eyes spun like shaken dice. She settled in. Her left hand was pressed to my chest, for balance, while her right twiddled down below. I was on the precipice of orgasm. The Mute bucked and shuddered. Her thighs trembled. An ecstatic moan escaped from her chest. She tried to catch it and put it back, but it was already out, and her vow of silence was broken. I cranked the inflation to 90 percent. Spasms. A magnificent clenching. I'd never given her so much. Her eyes darted in senseless directions, and her tongue lolled about, and she pounded my chest with her fist like a malfunctioning robot blowing its fuses. I jackhammered my hips and unloaded my burden. So it ended. We lay in a heap. We stayed that way for a long time. Then she kissed me. She spilled herself into me with that kiss. I'd hold that kiss up against any kiss two lovers have ever shared.

I completed the descent. The ladder ascended away, tinging and pinging as it went, like a set of gently blown wind chimes.

I was a live wire. I wandered the streets with springs in my heels. Arms back. Chest, thrust forward. I almost wished someone would mess with me.

"Interdimensional being. Ha!"

I was strutting down 4th Avenue when I heard it. It was barely there, yet all around me. Music. Someone, somewhere, was playing music. I continued north, toward home, and the music grew louder. At the corner of 4th and Adams—a mere five blocks from our residence—I found the music's source. A saloon. "Mother's." A seedy place. A watering hole for local rabble. It made regular appearances in the police blotter. Drunken brawls. Drug deals gone bad. Needless to say, I'd never been inside. There was a picture window, brilliantly illuminated by a neon Budweiser sign. A signboard—the kind you write on with colored marker—was mounted next to the door. It read:

TONITE!!!
Terrance Johnson
Live music, karaoke
$3 well drinks, $2 Bud/Coors bottles

I gasped. The breath and sweat of the countless revelers had condensed on the inside of the window, making it difficult to see inside. I pushed my nose up against the glass and squinted through the diffusion. The saloon was choked with people. Blacks, whites, Hispanics. A few East Indians, even. Men and women in equal measure. I'd never seen such a crowd. They stood shoulder to shoulder, commingling without consideration of race. Many patrons were smoking, in clear violation of county law.

There was a small, elevated bandstand in the back. A single man was there. Terrance. He sat on a wooden stool. A microphone was poised before him. He strummed his banjo and sang out in his immaculate voice.

She's leavin' now 'cause I heard the slammin' of the door
The way I know I've heard it slam one hundred times before
And if I could move I'd get my gun and put her in the ground
Oh Ruby . . . don't take your love to town.

The crowd exploded with applause. Beers and cocktails were held high in the smoky choke. Terrance stepped down from the bandstand, and they were slapping him on the back, shaking his hand, lavishing him with praise. Someone presented him with a tiny glass of liquor, and he downed it in a single gulp. A bit more carousing, and then he remounted the stage and spoke eagerly into the microphone.

"Okay . . . so who's ready to sing?"

I recoiled backward from the window. It was as if I had just witnessed an atrocity. Terrance was more than a common philanderer. He was a kingpin! A minstrel Mussolini! That mob would have done anything he wanted. *Grab your pitchforks, light your torches—an ugly little snowflake gave me insult this morn, and I want his head on a pike!* He could have said it and they'd have done it. Terrance was master to a multiethnic militia.

Mummy, you lovesick trollop! What have you gotten us into!?

I stumbled home in a state of panic. I'd done everything I could to keep the world out, to be free of those who would do me harm. It was happening all over again. No protection, no quarter given, only one thing certain: Terrance Johnson was a very dangerous man.

- 5 -
AN UNEXPECTED INVITATION

Thursday, 9:45 A.M. I felt impure—as a drunkard might in the cruel light of dawn.

The telephone rang. The ID flashed. It was Mummy. Earlier, before she awoke, I had slipped downstairs and left a note on the counter.

> Mummy,
>
> I require a cloistered day. Do not concern yourself with my caloric requirements. I have provisioned myself with bread, sardines, and a small wheel of epoisses.
>
> Unless there is a serious emergency, please do not attempt to communicate with me for the next twenty-four hours. I intend to spend the day meditating on the importance of family and the virtues of temperance. I suggest you do the same.
>
> Your Loving Son,
>
> *Charles William Hayes*

It was not my first self-imposed exile. Mummy is a stubborn woman, I am her son, and we have been known to butt heads from time to time. She'd always honored my requests for solitude, so when the phone rang, I assumed the worst. I snatched up the receiver.

"What's happening!?"

"Hello, Buddy. This is your mother."

"I know who it is. What's the matter? Is Puppa okay?"

"Oh yes. Puppa is fine. He missed you this morning."

Her words stung. I'd been planning to perform the final chapter and epilogue of *Moby Dick*. Oh, that epilogue. The greatest two hundred and sixty-seven words in all of fiction! Terrance's loose talk of "Captain Ahab, Star Captain" had infected my imagination like a hallucinogen. No telling what idiotic anachronisms it had placed in Mummy and Puppa's minds. I had intended to purge the toxin with a traditional reading of the original source material, but then The Mute, and the tavern, and the hysterical birthing of existential triplets: Threat, Question, and Crisis. It wasn't fair. I had a sailor costume and everything. Why should Puppa have to suffer for Mummy's indiscretions?

"I missed Puppa as well," I said. "Why are you calling me?"

A long silence. The open connection crackled in my ear.

"You have a visitor."

"A visitor?"

"Terrance is here. He'd like to speak with you."

Fear. I've learned to control it—to reason my way through it—but it's always there, lurking in my guts, waiting for a chance to possess me. It did so then, and I was a little boy once more, hiding in the janitor's closet, counting the seconds until recess was over.

"No, Mummy," I pleaded. "Tell him to go away."

"I won't do that. He just wants to talk to you."

"No! Tell him to go home. Tell him to call me on the phone!"

She took a deep breath.

"I won't tell him that. Be a polite boy and come downstairs. He's waiting for you in the drawing room."

The drawing room? He was right below me! He could probably hear me through the floorboards. I'd been bushwhacked.

"Mummy, this is totally improper—"

But the line was dead. She'd hung up.

I searched for a weapon. I had a fencing foil, which I used as a prop during swashbuckling tales, and a blowgun, which I occasionally shot at a dartboard for fun, and Puppa's WWII bayonet, which was displayed in a handsome case, and a pump-action BB rifle, which I used to dispatch critters. Alas, this critter would not be so easily disposed of. The stun gun! My Excalibur! I scampered to the bookshelf, took it up, unswitched the safety, and pressed the trigger button. A tiny tempest erupted between the steel fangs. I located my courage. It bled into my fear and mixed with the hormones that were gushing from my glands. I slipped the weapon into a pocket and marched bravely toward the battlefield.

"Hello?" I stood on the landing outside of my chambers and called down to the room below.

"Hello. Buddy?"

I cleared my throat and spoke in a husky tone.

"Who else would it be?"

"Um . . . are you coming down?"

"No. I pulled a hammy in an Aikido training session. I don't want to aggravate it."

I instantly regretted saying this. I wanted to make

Terrance aware of my martial arts skills, but I also mentioned an injury. This suggestion of weakness—however false—was a serious blunder.

Terrance rose from the settee. The telltale squeak revealed his position.

"No problem. I'll come up."

He approached. Each footstep, a tiny threat. I patted my pocket. Excalibur was there, reassuring me.

He didn't step onto the landing all at once. Rather, he peeked his head into the stairwell and peered upwards, as if expecting someone to drop a piano on his head. Then he saw me. He craned his neck and gave a warm smile.

That smile! That horrible, beautiful smile!

"How're you doing?" he asked. He was dressed in stylish jeans and a tan V-neck sweater. On his feet, a pair of white tennis shoes.

It was odd. I found myself wishing for the red Crocs he'd worn the day before. The clown shoes. His tidy appearance left nothing to mock.

He moved toward the staircase.

"No further!" I shouted. The impact of my demand froze him to the spot. I had the high ground and intended to keep it.

"Can I come up?"

"I'm sure you *can.* The question is 'May you?' and the answer is 'No, you may not.' I'm not prepared for guests. My chambers are not suitably arranged."

"I don't mind."

He placed his foot on the staircase. I thrust out my hand and cast a repulsor beam from my palm.

"Not another step, Mr. Johnson! You wish to speak with me. So speak."

His hand was on the banister, his foot on the first stair.

His aspect was of one trying to solve a difficult riddle.

"Okay. It's just sort of strange, talking at an angle like this."

"It is also strange to call on someone unannounced. So much for strange."

"I wanted to talk to you yesterday."

"You did. About many things. *Moby Dick,* for instance. I've felt sick ever since."

"I meant privately."

"I was busy."

"I thought I'd stop by today."

"I am also busy today."

He maintained his smile, but I could see his bones wriggling beneath his skin.

"What I wanted to say is . . ."

Here it comes, I thought. *His disgusting confession. About Mummy. About their lustful, interracial affair. Where's a piano when you need one?*

". . . I understand what you're going through, Buddy."

"Do you?"

"I do."

"Do tell."

"Needing help. Asking for help. It can be a hard decision."

"It wasn't a hard decision for me," I said. "It wasn't a decision I made at all. This is all Mummy's doing. When I found out about it, my head exploded."

"So I heard."

"Seems like there's been a lot of talking going on behind my back. Shame on both of you."

"I could tell that you were upset, and I wanted to have a talk with you, man to man, and answer any questions you might have. It's okay if you have concerns. I'm here to help your grandfather, but I'm also here to help you and your mom."

His tone was heartfelt, but the delivery was rehearsed, as if he were trying to sell me something.

"I've read the brochure, Mr. Johnson. 'Visiting Nurses—The Perfect Balance of Healing and Home.' A bit too 'messiah complex' for me, but I can see how some sad, desperate people might find it appealing."

My sass acted on him like smelling salts. He shook his head and popped his eyes, as if recoiling from unpleasant vapors.

"Can I ask you a question?"

"You just did," I said smartly.

"Can I ask you *another* question?"

"You just did. I can do this all day."

"Is there a reason you haven't spoken to Christine?"

"Christine?"

"Our social worker."

"Oh. *That* woman. She's called on multiple occasions and has left multiple voicemails. One, two, I can countenance. Five or six? That's stalking."

"She tells me that she tried to meet with you here, twice, but on both occasions you were too busy to come downstairs. She's great, and I think you should give her a chance. You'd get a lot out of it. She can answer any questions you have about your grandfather's case, and she can also help you through any personal issues you might be having."

I searched his demeanor for signs of intoxication. I was certain he was still drunk, or at least hung over. He seemed steady enough, but alcoholics are expert at concealing their condition. I was too far away to smell him but was certain that he reeked of cigarettes and booze.

"How long have you had this job?"

"Almost three years."

"And a year of coursework before that?" I'd done my research.

"Correct."

"And you were a song-and-dance man before that?"

"Song-and-dance man. That's right."

"From flitting thespian to 'compassionate caregiver'?" I put some smug air quotes around that one. "Quite a lifestyle change. What inspired it?"

"A bunch of things."

"Elaborate."

"I wanted to help people."

"Nice try."

"It's true."

"Donate to charity. Volunteer at a soup kitchen. You can't maintain the moral high ground *and* get paid to stand there."

His face did an acrobatic pshaw.

"Are you accusing me of . . . greed?"

"I accuse the whole human race."

"No one does what I do for the money."

"And certainly, no one would do it without. What was your financial situation before you took up nursing?"

"Not good."

"As I suspected."

"It's still not great, if that makes you feel any better."

"It doesn't. What you make is beyond the point."

From professional performer to homecare nurse. At first, I couldn't jibe the two. I chalked it up to random chance; to the strange things people stumble into, and all the stranger when they stumble aimlessly. Then I pondered. Wealth. Prestige. A want of these things is the driving force behind all artistic ambition. A taboo assertion to be sure, and one that artist types will vehemently deny. They market themselves as saints of integrity, as the voice that sings for us all. They are Bolsheviks, minus the violence, minus the resolve, and in much trendier attire. Bourgeois considerations are the ultimate sin. Striving for "fame and fortune" suggests a lack of depth, yet "fame" and "fortune" are the only measuring sticks that the arts allow. A beautiful painting, exhibited on a gallery wall, and then sold to an excited buyer? That's an artistic accomplishment. A beautiful painting, set in the corner of an artist's home studio and piled among others of its like, unframed, unseen, and with no plans for it to be otherwise? That's a hobby.

Compassion. It's the whiskey incentive. One does what one wants, in service to one's own needs, and invokes "compassion" as an excuse. To suggest that nursing is a lucrative occupation, with good benefits—and a best possible option for a man whose early resume contained nothing but make-believe—is to welcome bombardment by rotten vegetable. Terrance had chased the dream and come up short. He was now a "caregiver," his life a rejection of the dream, and not a failure of it.

There can be no coming to terms when worldviews collide. Mine: that humans are motivated by self-interest alone; that "compassion" is one excuse among many, pulled in after the fact, to conceal the pursuit of one's private interests. Terrance's: that good and evil are tangible and opposing forces; that our base motivations are knowable; that perception is a fair approximation of reality. Terrance was beautiful. He could afford such naiveté.

Back to the staircase.

"Okay," I said. "Time for the brass tacks. You've got me in a category. 'Deluded grandson, in the denial stage of grief,' or something to that effect. You endure my slander because it's what you're paid to do. If I did so in any other context, you'd wring my neck."

"I'm not a violent person. And I can tell you're hurting."

"There you go again! I applaud your professionalism, but it's for naught. I deny nothing. Sometimes I'll find myself wishing for the old Puppa. The man I grew up with. When I feel this way, I remove my shirt, take up a belt, and deal myself ten lashings. If that doesn't do the trick, I taze myself with a stun gun. To wish for the man who's gone is to wish *this* Puppa away. Your presence shreds our fictions. You insinuate, and you disrupt. There's something of the buzzard in you, Mr. Johnson. You feed on the carrion of other people's lives."

He blew out his cheeks, set his hands on his hips. At last, a reaction that didn't have a wink in it. He'd plotted our scene beforehand, and I was going completely off script.

"That's nasty stuff."

"Are you insulted, or are you just *acting* like it?"

That got him. His frustration showed through and all traces of levity were gone.

"I'm not an actor, Buddy. I wish I'd never mentioned it. Can we please just forget it? I'm a nurse. End of story."

"Failed actors are like failed dictators. Always planning comebacks."

Then he did a most unexpected thing. He chuckled. He rallied his poise and smiled up at me as if my insult had been nothing more than a friendly jibe.

"That's funny. And sort of true."

Did I have to hit him with a shovel?

"Here's the deal," he continued. "When I say I understand what you're going through, it's because I do. My mom got sick about six years ago. I don't have any brothers or sisters and there was no one else to take care of her. I wanted to stay in New York. I was working. Off-Broadway stuff, off-*off*-Broadway stuff, festivals, gigging with a couple of bands."

"I believe you meant 'jigging.'"

"No. Gigging. *Playing.*"

"Oh. I thought you were referring to Irish step dance. Continue."

"It was great. The *doing* was great. No high like it. The problem is, what you're *doing* becomes what you *did,* and it does it in a blink, and I had nothing to show for what I had done, no savings, living check to check. Mom got sick. What could I do? Send her to a Medicaid Nursing Facility? So I could keep . . . playing around? Some would. Some do. Not me."

"What's her condition?" I asked.

"Diabetes. Stroke. Dementia."

"Dementia? How old is she?"

"Seventy."

"Seventy? How old was she when she had you?"

"Thirty-nine. After the stroke, things really went downhill."

"And no extended relations?"

"Just me."

"Seems odd," I said suspiciously. I had every reason to be so. An Afro-American woman from the slums, with only a single child to her litter, and that child born after she'd passed the age of twenty-one? She was a South Ilium unicorn.

Shame, Buddy. Shame! My inner progressive was outraged by my inner racist. A mental note was taken. *Only children. Age of mother at time of birth. Race and class, race vs. class, demography.* If I were to be racist here, I'd better have the data to back it up.

"So it's your intention to move back to the city once her condition improves?"

"It's not going to improve."

Silence. Soothing at first. A chance to recalibrate. But the silence grew, second by second, until it became an itchy rash. I pretended to inspect the finish on the banister. I picked at it with my thumbnail, and as the silence continued, my phony inspection dissolved into a real one. I decided that yes, the banister was in need of a good refinishing. The whole staircase needed a little TLC. A DIYer's work is never done.

"What about your father?" I asked.

"He lives in Cleveland. My parents split when I was young. I haven't spoken to him in a long time."

"I, too, have a ne'er-do-well father."

"That's what I figured. I'm sorry."

"Nothing to be sorry about. I never knew him."

My mouth spoke the words without my brain's permission. What was happening? I was sharing personal details with this chocolate interloper as if we were old chums! I was moved by his story, but for all I knew it was just another gambit. Maybe he was data-mining me in hopes of stealing my identity. Stranger things.

"Mr. Johnson—"

"Terrance, please."

"Terrance, it's my turn to ask you a question. I'm going to state it plainly, and you are going to answer it. If you try to deceive me, I'll know."

"I have nothing to hide."

Blacks possess an advantage over whites. Their dark skin is a great concealer of intent. When a white person lies, their face will go flush. It's the penultimate "tell," right behind nervous sweating. Black people don't blush—or if they do, white people are not capable of seeing it. I was limited to reading Terrance's facial expressions and body language, which were telling me very little. I looked directly into his eyes and asked my question.

"Are you attempting to seduce my mother?"

A four-year-old could have read him then. His jaw dropped. His face went slack. His expression, in any color, was one of complete shock.

"Uh . . . Wow. That's a . . . I mean . . . Are you *serious*?"

"As a funeral. Are you attempting to seduce my mother?"

"Buddy . . . I have no idea what gave you that impression."

"My instincts. They are rarely wrong."

"Well, they are *wrong* this time. No. I am *not* trying to seduce your mother."

I leaned out over the banister and focused my gaze. I was looking into his eyes and through them, to the very essence of his soul. His soul seemed clean, but if that was true then my instincts had been wrong, and I was relying on those same instincts to measure his soul. I was all mixed up.

"My mother is a wonderful woman . . ."

". . . she is!"

"But she hasn't been with a man in many years. Easy prey."

"Oh my."

"For a guy like you. Mr. Handsome. Mr. Considerate. You use your gifts to great advantage, but I warn you—I'm not some Brooklyn floozy. I am immune to your charms."

He took a moment to gather his thoughts. Angry or amused, I couldn't say. I suspect a combination of both.

"Buddy, I've got to tell you—this is one of the weirdest conversations I've ever had. No, I am absolutely not trying to start a relationship with your mother. I can't believe you'd even think that. I'm here to do a job. Things were pretty tense yesterday, and I could tell you had some reservations. I thought I'd stop by to talk. That's part of my job too."

"That's a tall glass of lemonade, and I'd like to believe you—but how can I trust a man who lives a double life?"

A mischievous smile throve on this face.

"Elaborate," he said, mimicking my earlier demand.

"I was out for a constitutional last night and happened to pass by that honky-tonk at 4th and Adams."

"You're talking about Mother's?"

"I wish I wasn't."

"I was working there last night."

"I saw your name on the marquee and peered in the window."

"Really? Why didn't you come in?"

"My tetanus shot is out of date."

"C'mon! You would have liked it. I host a music night. I play a few songs, other people sing if they want to. I have a karaoke machine in case anyone wants to do that. Sometimes I just play CDs. It's sort of a poor man's 'Midnight Ramble' kind of thing."

"Do you think it's appropriate? Whooping it up on a work night?"

"Depends on the level of whooping, but no, not generally. I don't work on Thursdays. Today is my day off."

I wanted to believe it was all a ruse—that Mummy and I were victims of an unfolding conspiracy—but my skepticism had turned to flat soda. For the first time, I considered the possibility that I might have misjudged him.

"It's all very pat, Terrance, but I maintain my skepticism. I cannot believe that a self-respecting medical professional would set foot in a place like that."

"It's really not that bad. Have you ever been inside?"

"Inside Mother's?" At least one of my suspicions was confirmed. He *was* drunk.

"I'll tell you what—why don't you come next Wednesday?"

"Terrance, please."

"I can put you on the guest list."

"Guest list?"

"You won't have to pay the cover."

"They charge an admittance fee!?"

"Only on Wednesdays."

"How much?"

"Five dollars."

"Five dollars!?"

As "cover charges" go, I wasn't sure if that was a lot or a little, but it was certainly more than anyone should have to pay to get shanked.

"You won't have to pay. Just tell the doorman that you're on the list and show him your driver's license."

"I don't have a driver's license. I'm a committed environmentalist and consider it my ethical duty to rely on public transit. It's all part of the Hayes Interactive Green Initiative. I also use recycled paper."

"You have an ID?"

"A non-driver photo ID card, yes."

"Great. Just show your ID to Tollbooth and tell him you're on the list."

My face screwed up.

"Tollbooth?"

"The doorman. That's his name."

"His parents named him Tollbooth?"

"It's a nickname, I hope. I never asked."

"Based on the 'Billy Goats Gruff' nature of his occupation, no doubt."

"I never considered that. I just figured it was because he's built like one."

"How colorful."

Did he really expect me to attend? To step onto his turf, on his terms? He could order the natives to grab me up, and before I knew it I'd be roasting on a spit with an apple stuck in my mouth.

"Thank you for the invitation, but I really don't think it would be appropriate."

"I'm not sure 'appropriate' enters into it, but it's up to you. If you want to check it out, you're more than welcome. You'll see that there's nothing to be concerned about."

The citizen and the State. The social services provider and his charge. The chain of command is always a tangled mess in such instances, but the laws of private property still applied, and we were on Puppa's property, and I was Puppa's ward, and of the two men in the staircase it was clear who was boss. Terrance's bizarre invitation was a breach of etiquette. I wanted badly to lecture him on the point, but I could see that he was ready to wrap up our conversation. I was ready too.

"I will consider it. Does that conclude our business?"

"Yes," he said with more than a little relief. "I hope you decide to come. Also, I hope you'll consider talking to Christine. You'll be glad you did."

And he left. I stood listening as his footsteps receded into the house, toward the den. He'd play the tattletale, no doubt, and relate the details of our conversation to Mummy. My day of solitude was ruined. *O Lord, why do you torment me? Please, I beg you—offer me some comfort. Show me a sign!* No sign was offered, of course, but it felt good to whine, and to pretend that someone was listening.

- 6 -
MUMMY KNOWS BEST

I've set the cadence at an up-tempo. The purpose: to horsewhip this narrative into a gallop. In so doing, I've constructed a fictional timeline that moves more quickly than life ever could. It suggests no time for the thing I spend a great deal of time doing. Writing. Writing *this book.* Also reading. These activities are essential to my life but don't lend themselves to evocative scenes.

I work on these pages every night. As sole earner (although Puppa does have a generous pension) and master of the Hayes coin, I bear a burden of responsibility, so paid work must come before my artistic pursuits. All other nighttime activities, including my liaisons, will not interrupt. My writing is a liaison in and of itself. Urges build. Juices bubble. I boot up my laptop and pray, like a heartsick lover, for my muse to visit me.

Oh, my muse! My cruel, transcendental mistress! There is no high like the high she brings, and no low like her absence. Her leave can stretch for days, for weeks, and I am left empty, wanting, with my fingernails chewed to bleeding. Then she materializes. Without call, and seemingly out of nowhere. I'm so happy to see her that I instantly forgive her. We race to the bedchamber, tearing at each other's clothes as we go, and we arrive at my writing desk, that shrine to our love, and we're gasping, groping, and I boot up my laptop and get to work.

My day job: wife. My writing: mistress. It's an apt metaphor, and it foreshadows. I've always fantasized about keeping a kept woman, you see. One of flesh and blood. I will not wed until I have the resources to maintain an extramarital affair. This fact will figure in as the narrative progresses.

For a time, I tried to hammer out my prose on an antique Corona typewriter. I bought the Corona—a 1917 model—at a flea market and reconditioned it myself. My head was full of romantic notions. I'd dress in scholarly tweed, steaming mug at the elbow, and spew forth my insipid juvenilia. I was more concerned with thinking myself as a writer than with actually writing. The "writer," as a figure, has ceased to be culturally relevant, unless he or she is a character depicted in a Hollywood film. I wanted to be that type of writer—the movie kind. I tried to take up smoking. I started carrying a notebook. I'd go to the library or the coffee house or the park, perk up my ears, and jot down overheard scraps of conversation. It was all show. My note-taking was so that others would see me taking notes. "What an interesting young man," they might think. "He's got the body of an overfed elf and a face like a boiled ham, but he's clearly intelligent. He must be a writer!"

Dreams. Always of *being;* of being something other than what we are. "Being a writer," in my case. Time passes. The veneer of youthful possibility wears away, exposing the truths that youth is blind to. Dreams are dropped. Those that remain are converted into quests. Mine: a quest for meaning. The construction of this novel is the act that guides my life. It's the foundation that my days are built on. There's a paradox in this. In my pursuit of meaning, I destroy the thing that provides it. Word by word. Sentence by sentence. At last, the final punctuation, *the end*, and a small death that portends our final estate in the void.

It's also a pleasant hobby.

I couldn't get into cigarettes. When Puppa smoked, the smell had been warm and glamorous, but I didn't have the constitution for it. Cigarettes make me queasy. This was limiting. Most of the great novelists were alcoholics or even drug addicts. At the very least, they smoked. Writers need vices, and I didn't have any, and I was dead set on developing one. I'm a nighttime scribbler and a daytime computer jockey, so I needed a stimulant—something to combat the hollow-headed exhaustion that comes with staring at a screen for seventy hours a week. It had to be legal (my anus would be forfeit in prison) and easily concealable (from Mummy). European sniffing tobacco was just the ticket. The risk/reward was wholly in my favor. I got the boost, without damage to my health or stamina. Sure, there's a warning on the tin, but who ever heard of someone getting *nose* cancer? Darwin had been a snuff-taker. So too, George Washington. Muhammad Ali. Mozart! A diverse group of bon vivants that I'm proud to be counted among.

As for illicit drugs: I'm not hip enough to have access to them nor downtrodden enough to need them. I'm curious about Benzedrine, as so many famous writers have sworn by the stuff, and I would also, under the right circumstances (and in misdemeanor doses), consider marijuana or magic mushrooms. I don't travel in any circles, let along drug circles, so the opportunity to sample these narcotics has not presented itself.

Alcohol? Never to the point of intoxication. But that was about to change.

A final note on cigarettes. I still like the smell of them, and continue to enjoy a good secondhand smoke from time to time. It sparks nostalgia. I keep a pack of Marlboros in my chambers. I'll occasionally burn one as a kind of incense.

Back to the typewriter. I was sure that once I possessed a classic writing device, fully formed prose would issue from the platen like autumn leaves falling from an oak. I was struggling to find the words. I was desperate for something—some device, something I could buy—that would unstick the valve. So I did a silly thing. I reconditioned an antique typewriter. I became something of a typewriter aficionado in the process and got lovely decoration out of it, but that's about all it's good for. I'm a creature of the digital age. I need a cursor. And guess what? Typewriters are *noisy*. Far noisier than the movies make them out to be. All that clacking—it made me feel as if I were working in a textile mill. I do use the typewriter for one thing: composing personal correspondence. The antique machine affords a classy, hand-wrought quality to a letter, in a way that my chicken scratch penmanship never could. I had used the Corona to compose my exile letter to Mummy, for example.

Terrance's visit had left me feeling at loose ends. I spent the rest of that day in irritable seclusion. I slept poorly and awoke at dawn the following morning. I was lonely, and also hungry for something other than sardines and pungent cheese. I punched out a brief letter to Mummy, informing her that I would be attending breakfast, and left it in the kitchen as before. I was dreading that breakfast. The last time we'd spoken, I had been on all fours, picking up marbles. That was Wednesday. Then Thursday, and Terrance's surprise visit, and whatever he'd told her once we parted ways. She'd had no chance to lecture me, and I was sure she'd have a hopper full of nasty quips. I was in for it.

I entered the den at 7 A.M. Mummy was away in the kitchen. Puppa was alone, in his harness, listening to AM news radio at low volume. He greeted me with a big, toothless grin. He stammered a pseudo-sentence. *Where have you been?* I gave him a hug.

"I was busy with work, Puppa. I'm sorry. I'll try to do a better job managing my time."

He patted me on the head. *That's a good boy,* he said in his special language.

I commenced with a reading from *The Poetry of Robert Frost.* When time is limited, and I don't have anything prepared, I turn to poetry, and when I turn to poetry, I turn to the American Shakespeare.

The witch that came (the withered hag)
To wash the steps with pail and rag,
Was once the beauty Abishag,

My voice soared. Puppa listened intently.

The picture pride of Hollywood.
Too many fall from great and good
For you to doubt the likelihood.

Die early and avoid the fate.
Or if predestined to die late,
Make up your mind to die in state.

Make the whole stock exchange your own!
If need be occupy a throne,
Where nobody can call you crone.

The rattling of the butler's cart announced Mummy's arrival. My heart sank. To fortify myself, I turned the dial up to ten and shredded the stanzas like a rocker on an electric guitar.

Some have relied on what they knew;
Others on simply being true.
What worked for them might work for you.

On *you,* I pointed threateningly at Puppa. He raised his arm as if to defend himself.

No memory of having starred
Atones for later disregard,
Or keeps the end from being hard.

Better to go down dignified
With boughten friendship at your side
Than none at all. Provide, provide!

I bowed deeply to a duet of cheers.

"Which one was that?" asked Mummy.

"'Provide, Provide.' My personal favorite."

"That's right. It always makes me think of *Sunset Boulevard.*"

"It makes me think of Little Miss Sunshine," I said, and then crossed to the closet to retrieve the folding chairs. "She, too, is a withered hag."

"You're awful," Mummy said with a laugh.

We proceeded with breakfast: toad in the hole with a side of beans and fried red tomatoes, Puppa with his shake. Mummy was prim. Her harelip scar was a pleasant hue. I grew concerned. With few exceptions, I was an ideal son, so Mummy had rare opportunity to play her self-righteous fiddle. A stumble on my part—the slightest whiff of malfeasance—and she'd snatch that fiddle up and start flailing furiously. The seeming calm bore the hallmarks of a trap.

"So—what did you and Terrance talk about yesterday?" she asked.

Oh boy.

"Don't pretend as if you don't know."

"I *don't* know."

"He didn't tell you?"

"Tell me what!? Oh my goodness! What did you say, Buddy!?"

Could it be? Had Terrance really kept it all to himself?

"Nothing of import. Our meeting was entirely cordial. I just assumed that he related the details of our discussion to you."

She eyed me skeptically. In my mind's ear, I could hear her fiddle being tuned.

"He said that it was a pleasant conversation. Was it a pleasant conversation?"

Misleading a client is easy. The Internet is the ultimate liar's toolkit. With a couple of keystrokes, there is nothing I don't know, nothing I can't do. Misleading Mummy is another matter. I would have to keep close to the truth and bend it only when necessary.

"He did make a suggestion that took me quite by surprise," I said. "Terrance—our home nurse—requested that I consume alcoholic beverages with him."

"What!?"

"It's true!"

"He asked you to drink with him?"

"Explicitly, no. But implicitly, oh yes!"

My confidence swelled. I was on the right path. It was true enough, and painted Terrance as a raving alcoholic.

"What exactly did he say?"

"It would seem that Terrance hosts a weekly hootenanny at a saloon down the street. He invited me to attend one of his performances."

Liars invent. The virtuoso diplomat does compose original material. I stuffed a sausage into my yap in hopes of retarding my speech. This was a diplomatic moment, and in such moments it's best to say as little as possible. Allow your opponent to fill in the unsaid portions. That way, if the whole thing blows up, you can blame it all on a misunderstanding, and on your rival's overactive imagination.

"He performs down the street? That's wonderful! You should go!"

"Go?" I muttered through sausage-lubricated lips. I took up a half slice of toast and mashed it in, thus amplifying my speech impediment.

"Why not?" she asked. "I think it sounds like a lot of fun!"

"You're crazy," I slobbered. It was a disgraceful display of table manners, but it had to be done. I added a spoonful of beans. My cheeks were puffing out like a chipmunk with a full payload of nuts.

We were interrupted by a slurping sound. Puppa had finished his shake. Mummy went to him and removed the snorkel/straw from his mouth. I chewed my way through the softball I'd created and washed it down with some freshly squeezed pomegranate juice. The antioxidants made me feel years younger. I turned the conversation to matters of state and commerce. Current-events stuff. Innocuous breakfast chatter. Mummy played along for a while, but as soon as there was a lull she returned to her topic of interest.

"Tell me more about Terrance's concerts. The ones down the street."

"Jeez, Mummy! He didn't give me a program. He said he hosts a 'music night,' whatever that means."

"It sounds like a sock hop!"

"Clean your ears. Terrance performs at a *bar.* A *drinking* establishment. You've read the neighborhood watch emails I've been printing . . ."

"No, I haven't!"

"Well, you should, because if you did you'd know that Mother's is a very disreputable place. Someone was stabbed there last year."

"Inside?"

"No. Outside. But the steel words and fisticuffs began within."

"You have to be careful wherever you go, but that doesn't mean you should just sit in your room all the time."

"Chambers," I corrected for the millionth time.

"Live a little!"

"If it sounds like such a great time, why don't *you* go? And don't forget your brass knuckles."

"C'mon, Buddy. What's the harm? You could make new friends."

"I'm a family man."

"Meet some people your own age."

The conversation was a runaway train. Up ahead: Dead Man's Gulch. Desperados had blown the bridge. I was tugging at the brake lever, but the cables had been cut.

"It's all old drunks in that place. There's no one my age."

"Terrance is your age. He's thirty-one."

Terrance's age had never occurred to me. After the age of twenty, white people are unable to discern how old black people are. So far as I could tell, adult blacks came in three ages: twenty, fifty, and eighty.

"You might even meet a girl."

End of the line. The train leapt from the tracks and fell, bomblike, into the valley below.

Mummy was unaware of my clandestine romances. If only she knew! But she didn't know, she *couldn't* know, for if she did, all of her illusions would be smashed. Genetics have been unkind to our brood. I accept it, but Mummy is a woman. We don't have the nerve to tell our ugly daughters the truth: that life, for them, will be an anthology of disappointments; that if they'd been born pretty—that, and nothing more—the cosmos would align to their desires. The beautiful choose. The ugly settle. This is law. If I were a handsome man, my wild-oat sowing would be viewed as a sign of virility. I'd be a loveable cad; a playboy; a bachelor who's "playing the field." But I'm ugly, and I'm expected to do what ugly men do. Find an ugly girl. Make her my ugly wife. Sire ugly children. Ugly people are expected to be thankful for everything that the beautiful take for granted. I raise a middle finger to that life.

"You're not going to beat that drum again," I said. "We've talked about this. The topic is off limits."

"I'm just saying. You're a young man. You should find yourself a nice girl. Go on some dates."

"Mummy. . . ."

"Everyone needs a companion."

"I've got two. Most times, I'm satisfied. Times like this, I feel as if it's one too many."

"Puppa and I aren't going to live forever."

"Neither will I."

"Have you considered Internet dating?"

"Don't be vile."

"It's what people are doing! We've got three couples at church who met online. On ChristianSingles.com. Isn't that neat? There are all kinds of sites, for people with all kinds of interests and backgrounds."

Oh, the technological insights of the middle-aged. *There's such a thing as "Internet dating"? You don't say? And please, forward me that funny chain email that Beth sent you.*

"I'm a traditionalist," I said. "I take my romance the old-fashioned way."

"In person, you mean?"

"Quite."

"Face to face?"

"As nobility demands."

"Well then, Mister Old-Fashioned—have I got a girl for you!"

"Not again."

"That sweet girl who works at the library."

"Nonsense."

"So pretty!"

"She's an attractive woman. Saying so says nothing. It's simply a fact."

"She likes you. She asks about you every time I'm in."

"And she asks about you and Puppa every time I'm in. She's smart that way. We're property owners, and there's a budget vote coming up."

"No. She likes you. A pretty girl. A *librarian!* And smart! You just said so yourself. If there's a better match, I don't know who."

"I'm sure she's taken. Please stop."

"She has a nice laugh."

"Which I'd surely hear if I asked her out."

"You'd be a great husband."

"Mummy!"

"And father."

"My heavens!" I exclaimed. "How many times must you chew *that* cabbage? I've told you—I will take a bride when my total wealth reaches an appropriate level."

"What level, Buddy?"

"A level that I deem sufficient. I will say no more."

This mother / son bickering was amusing to Puppa. He laughed, and his laughter caused him to forget himself, and he passed a mighty wind, and he laughed at himself for passing the wind, and the collision of the two humorous events—our bickering, his wind—set him into a full-on laughing fit. This scatological interruption ended Mummy's haranguing. Puppa had saved me again—this time, by way of fart.

The abbreviated timelines of looming disasters. The exhilaration of disasters averted. The solidarity of shared sin. "The forbidden": a warning label, a threat, and also a giant, floating arrow, pointing us toward our desires.

Duty. The self, as an extension beyond the individual. A hammer blow to the bestial head of solipsism. Life as a shared project.

Two sets of virtues? Of wants? Whatever you call them, be sure to add "mutually exclusive" as a preface. The wife knows the man. The mistress knows the animal. The wife is life. The mistress makes life worth living. Here, and once again, I draw my inspiration from the French.

"I will take a bride when my total wealth reaches an appropriate level." I'd run the figures. Business was good. I had the money to support a wife and family. I did not have the resources to support a wife, family, and mistress. That's what I wanted. That was the "appropriate level" I sought to achieve.

Planning, reader! It's what separates the lower classes from the cosmopolitan elite; what separates the "dirty dog" from the philandering sophisticate. My liaisons—aided and abetted by the Internet—nourished my erotic hunger, and digital trends promised an ever-growing plenty. "Unmarried partners." "Cohabitation." Such fetters are unnecessary in the information age. The Internet is, first and foremost, a self-pimping platform, and all the world is a Red Light District, and each body is free to peddle its most valuable commodities.

Companionship. Tenderness. Financial support. These are commodities too. Finite ones. There was only so much of *me,* and only so many hours in the day, and only so much companionship, tenderness, and cash to go around. Why rob from Peter to pay Paul, when I owed nothing to Paul, and Peter had nothing worth stealing? Why take from Mummy and Puppa, so that I might give to a total stranger?

Children. Expansion of clan. Continuation of the family line. "Childless marriage is dating with papers." I've heard this said, and it's not bad, but the tacit definition of "dating" is too postmodern for my taste. This "dating" has unwed monogamy as the broad stroke, with cohabiting as the finer brushwork. There's also "dating" as "scheduled recreational activity with the possibility of sex," under the pretense of "audition for monogamy." I toss these definitions aside. I'm a modern man trapped in a postmodern world.

Dating, in its pure form, is a comparison of portfolios. *I offer these resources. Column 1: material. Column 2: genetic. Column 3: social. Marry me. Offer your flesh to me, and your labor toward the expansion of my clan—toward the expansion of* my kind!—*and you'll get your cut.* It's a process, not an activity. Dating is courtship. A gentleman courts with marriage in mind.

My ugly little wife. How I love you, even though we've never met.

It's impossible to purely sexualize and purely love. Those who live ecstatically die alone, and those who live by dictate never fully live. I try, whenever possible, to leave room for my moral failings. I'm not proud of my desire, nor am I ashamed. I aspire to a set of circumstances, and I'm willing to put in the work to achieve them.

"Boxing out." It's a fundamental skill in basketball and handy as a sports metaphor. One must box out—seal off, clear out—the space in which one intends to operate. The Hoopster, if he wishes to effectively "beast" for the "board," must box out before the "rock" hits the "tin." If the successful adulterer wishes to remain so, he must box out before the tying of nuptials. Nay. He must box out before the wife has been chosen. Nay again! His bachelor life must be one great act of boxing out—of creating the space in which to pursue all future bliss.

The time for bride seeking will come. I'll scour dating websites for ugly females. I'll endure the false-starts and outright rejections. Eventually, I'll find a girl I like; one who's desperate enough, or with eyesight bad enough, to tolerate my failings. But before any of this, I'll have to make some lifestyle changes. I'll need to trade my home office for a studio apartment in a residential building. My possession of this office/studio will seem totally natural, fully legitimate, to any woman I court. "I used to work at home, but I was having trouble focusing, and besides, I get to write the whole thing off." That sort of thing. Eventually, a first date will lead to a second, and that, to an erotic third, and from there, on to commitment, and then on to marriage, and I'll have the office/studio all the while, as a place of work but also of refuge, and the need for it will never be questioned because it will have always just *been*.

Eventually, children, and The Hayes brownstone, thrumming with family life, the pitter-pattering of little feet and all that, and Mummy, our salty matriarch, a difficult mother-in-law but beloved grandma, and Puppa, our wise, ailing paterfamilias. Four generations of Hayeses, all living under one roof. Wholesomeness secured. This is when I would take a mistress. The studio would be converted into a love nest, and on to a life that most only dare to dream of.

The office/studio is just for starters. Prior to dating, I'll need to establish regular nighttime habits—racquetball league?—that can serve as cover for future trysts. I'll have to "take up golf" for "business reasons," because weekends are for lovers, and if a mistress isn't given regularly scheduled time, she'll turn to mischief. Dating is expensive. It's astronomical when you have to rent an apartment, join the YMCA, buy racquetball gear, buy golf gear, take golf lessons, join a country club, all on the off chance that a woman you ask out turns out to be the love of your life.

We finished breakfast. A wholesome affair, all things considered. It had been a trying week, but in the end family values had prevailed.

I returned to my chambers. My first task of the day: spec writing. Hixon Smyth Boutiques. They would have to pay a New York City development firm at least $50,000 to create the site as outlined. I wanted $35,000—a discount to the premium, but a serious price, arrived at by a serious operator. In a sensible world, the spec would only have to be a sentence long. *The HixonSmythBoutiques.com build will cost $35,000 because that's what I want to get paid for it*. Our world, alas, is a Rube Goldberg machine, complex for complexity's sake, a jumbled mass of cogs and springs, greased by human nonsense. I would go through the motions. Chart plans that I would not follow. Take a simple process (give me copy, give me images, I make website) and break it into fictional "project phases." Important nonsense would be marked with bullets. Technical jargon would be injected like spices into a deep-fried turkey. I would spend my Friday morning splattering five pages with fertile excrement.

She likes you. She asks about you. . . . I pushed the words away. They were silly, hopeful words, spoken by a blissfully ignorant woman. I was happy with my life.

-7-
THE ALLURING LIBRARIAN

It was nothing special. Certainly not due to anything Mummy had said. I always went to the library on Friday mornings. They opened at eight. Sometimes I'd bring a list. Other times, I'd wander the stacks without aim, plucking at any spine that tickled. If my workload was light, and no A.M. projects were due, I might grant myself two hours of languid library relaxation. Typically, it was more like forty-five minutes, and I'd be back at my station for the official start of work.

Or so it had been. For years. The boundaries were the same—Ilium Public Library, Friday mornings, before work—but my behavior within them had changed.

Because of her. The Alluring Librarian. The source of my deepest torment.

Hairstyle says so much. Hers was jet, and done in a postmodern sort of bob, with the front portion longer than the back. When she leaned forward, the hairdo closed like curtains, hiding her face and granting privacy to her thoughts. I'm not a fan of such severe coiffures . . . in most cases. On The Alluring Librarian, the look was positively bewitching. She had a beautiful neck. The hairstyle left it naked for all to see. Oh, her glorious nape!

When a Caucasian writer lays into a character description, and race is not broached, the reader is left to assume that the character under survey is of Nordic/Germanic origins. It's a racist assumption—a literary "microaggression"—but what can we do? Writers write what writers know, so they tend to write their race. *Mummy is short, ugly, and has a color-changing harelip scar. Oh, and in case you were wondering—she's white!* It gets clunky. Filmmakers don't encounter this issue. They introduce a character, the actor's race is immediately apparent, and the viewer is free to impose their biases.

The beautiful woman I'm describing is not Caucasian. She's Indian, dot not feather. What are you to take from this, reader? What's my intention? Her skin was not as dark as Terrance's, but it was as dark as, or darker than, many of the Afro-Americans who dwelled in Ilium. Afro-American darkness is both overtone and undertone. It's pigmentation and association. The Alluring Librarian's darkness was overtone alone. When I meet a black person: *This is going to be a white/black interaction. Behave accordingly.* On the rare occasions that I encounter an Indian: *Huh. This person is Indian. Proceed as normal.*

She had large dark eyes; thick, Athenian brows; a strong, slightly aquiline nose. Her mouth was my greatest challenge. One corner was pulled slightly higher than the other, and there was the small scar at the source of that pulling, almost a dimple, but one caused by defect or injury. When delivered in prose, this feature sounds undesirable. In the flesh, it was anything but. It left her with a default expression of wry amusement. When she was pleased, her resting grin would transmogrify into an authentic, gorgeous smile, and all who beheld it would have their spine sizzled to goo.

Her figure. Petite. Curvaceous. Deformity welcomes long description. Beauty can get by with a "hubba hubba."

I could go on. I shall. First, a bit of background.

I'd have been happy to go without. I mean, it's all just books, right? A diploma suggests a set of books once read; a set of core principles that the bearer has internalized. For the intelligent, this suggestion holds true. For the barbarian majority, a diploma is nothing but a participation trophy. Intellectual pursuits are absent from their adult lives, and don't even register as sub-bullets in their nostalgia. Theirs was an education in anecdotes. Parties attended. Drugs taken. Fistfights lost and won. Outfits worn. Juvenile sexcapades and piddling athletic triumphs. All that mattered was one's place in the social hierarchy. It's an ideal prep for the world my Neanderthal classmates would go on to inhabit.

Television. Three generations raised on it. A cultural mythology of 8:55 hugs, tidy A, B, and C plots, setups and punchlines, and all of this, the moral of all our stories, in service to the commercial break—to the compulsive consumerism that makes life worth living. Once you've outsourced your imagination, what other point could there be? We've purged the philosophical from our lives because philosophy inevitably leads to "what's the point of all this?," and no one escapes that rat trap with all their parts intact. Instead, entertainment. Infotainment, masquerading as truth, and the possession of that "truth" masquerading as knowledge. Teachers, who were raised on television themselves, train students for the synthetic future that television promises. Subsequent generations will be raised on the Internet.

There was a cute period, circa 1996–2003, when the WWW suggested brighter days ahead. "Encyclopedias at your fingertips!" and "an end to informational asymmetry," and other hopeful assumptions. Instantly, porn. Instantly, e-shopping, and the e-advertising for e-shopping, splashed on every page. Soon after, social media, and the self as brand, and ideas, as brand identity, and benevolence as a marketing tool, and our lives, an emojigraphic simulacrum of the popular culture we consume. The internet has been great for me—I couldn't make hay or have a sex life without it—but woe betide those who pine for a modern enlightenment.

"Experts" corner markets and form monopolies. "Expert" is an honorific, awarded to those who have successfully elbowed out.

"Eminence" is the fortress that "experts" construct. It's built of educational requirements; of proprietary language; of Ivy League nepotisms; of dildos and fleshlights, left over from the mutual masturbation society's annual prize gala.

We Hayeses are experts in nothing of value, and we've got no eminence to hide behind. Our best shot at freedom, and our only chance at dignity, is to reject eminence-based authority in all its forms. Mummy and Puppa do this subconsciously. It's implicit in their interaction with the larger world. I'm conscious and explicit. We're low-status people. Expertise is designed to exploit us; eminence demands our prostration. Educator, bureaucrat, busybody neighbor; olive branch or sword. We reject all and are grateful for nothing.

So, Mummy doesn't have a high school diploma, but she does have an unaccredited associate's in culinary arts; an unaccredited bachelor's in English, math, art history, and quilting; an unaccredited master's in domestic engineering. It's the same way with Puppa. As a boy, he had two passions: the printed word and fine woodworking. Why finish high school, when the greatest works of man are available for free at the library, or for a nickel at a used-book sale? Why endure the vocational track, when there's a world full of skilled carpenters in need of young assistants? Words hold copyrights, but knowledge is public domain. There are no jobs that cannot be mastered through on-the-job training, and there is no level of expertise that cannot be met or exceeded through focused, private study.

So says my inner populist. It's odd. I grip tight to my working-class credentials, yet I aspire to leave that class behind and join the ranks of new money. Once there, I will convert my proletarian self-hatred into an upper-class disdain, and will do so with the relish of one who has escaped the stinking swarm. My inner populist flatters the masses so that he might turn them to his whims; he insults the elites so that he might insert himself above them.

Is it all a racket, reader, or do the structures correspond to unassailable truths? Are the platitudes of possibility irreverent in absence of the caveat "so long as you're intelligent"? Does effort count for the idiot in the same way it does for the egghead? My elitist tosses his glove to the ground, draws his blade, and challenges my populist to a duel. It's a fight to the blood, not to the death, as neither side can truly kill the other, and the outcome is determined by the day, and my mood, and how the result might benefit me.

The would-be messiah, up from the multitude. The would-be novelist, who fancies himself "a voice of." The promise? To *represent.* To take them with you on the climb. This is the deceit of movements. The climbing begins on the heads of those the liberator claims to serve. The gains of the follower will always pale in comparison to those of the bringer. They welcome us in the dawn. Then the gloaming, and it's "everybody out," and we realize that we've all been unwitting invitees at a going-away party. Ever thus, and shall be evermore.

Back to my adolescence. I planned to purchase a certificate frame, leave it empty, and hang it on my wall. The absent diploma would have been a point of pride. Mummy wouldn't have it.

"What do you want to be?" she asked.

"I'm pretty good with computers," I said. "And no one over the age of forty knows how to use them. I should be able to find work as some kind of IT hobgoblin." My entrepreneurial future was but a mere twinkle in my eye.

"You're going to need a degree for that. To get a degree you'll need a diploma."

"No, I won't. I'll teach myself at home. I've got a few years to master the technologies. When it comes time to apply for jobs, I'll lie. When you claim a Harvard PhD, people check. No one checks on a state school bachelor's."

"You're getting a high school diploma."

"You didn't. Puppa didn't."

"We both regret it."

"Liar."

"It's embarrassing. We're the type of people who should have it."

"And if you're the type of person who should have it, you're the type of person who doesn't need it."

"You're getting a diploma."

I was fifteen. Not yet able to chart my course. After days of maternal censure, I submitted to Mummy's will. I would join the ranks of the homeschooled. I'd graduate regents, with honors, and would do so on an AP track. A curriculum was set. Mummy didn't just deliver it—she *consumed* it. We worked in tandem. After years of rote learning, with one size fitting all, Mummy's approach was entirely refreshing. The paradigm of "knowledge as currency"—as a treasure that they were rich with and we were begging for—flew out the window. We'd stolen the safe. It sat in our downstairs parlor, and if we weren't able to crack it today, we could try again that night, or the next day, and use whatever tools we wanted, without sanction.

Puppa was an industrial carpenter. He worked in a chemical plant for over forty years. It only recently occurred to me to ask him why a chemical plant would need a carpenter. I didn't ask. "Why would a chemical plant need a carpenter?" can't be answered with grunts and lip farts, and I saw no reason to frustrate him. A googling of "industrial carpenter" provided many returns, so I have a general idea of how he spent his days. He retired in the summer before my "senior year." The timing was perfect. Puppa had always been my mentor. That year, he became my academic administrator and distinguished professor. There were stockpiles of insight locked in his skull; decades of reading, of note-taking, of whole essays, even, written only for himself. He was a public-library intellectual and a private philosopher. We begged him to tell us everything. That which he had, he shared; that which he didn't, he pursued along with us. Puppa had no interest in telling us what to think, and every interest in teaching us how. His mantra: "There's no intelligence without curiosity. There's no curiosity without intelligence."

We'd start the academic day in the parlor. Bookwork in the required subjects—and, when that was done, on subjects that suited our fancies. Then lunch, and the "open forum" portion of the day. Then, off to the Ilium Public Library, for writing, test-taking, and the restocking of materiel.

The library. It's a grand building, but derelict, and growing more so with each passing year. American Renaissance style, built in the late nineteenth century. A mass of carved granite. The exterior is grimy, the embellishments pocked, and the massive mahogany doors chipped and peeling. The Ilium Public Library is slowly devolving into an elegant ruin. Spring comes, and with it an annual rite. Hectoring over city budget. The risk of extinction. They'd been closing the place for as long as we'd been going.

It's the type of building they no longer build. Consider the reading room. Its defining feature is a massive *authentic* Tiffany window, with a cartoon of Thomas Aquinas. Consider the stacks. Three stories, accessed by an iron spiral staircase. The floors there are glass block. The shelving is iron and wood. The aisles are little more than shoulder width, and the stock is fed by rope-pull dumbwaiters. Library insiders call this area "the maze." All of it endures. The profound loss is Puppa. He'd always been part of it. The library has a handicapped ramp, and an elevator, and we tried bringing him. It was a melancholy experience. He couldn't see anything. He couldn't flip through the card catalog or grab books from the shelves or climb the ladders. That used to be his favorite thing. "To the summit of knowledge," he'd whisper, and then up he'd go, to the top of the stacks, like a mountaineer on to new heights. He loved the library as much as I did. It had been his place of freedom. From a wheelchair, it became a symbol of all he had lost.

A gray morning, a light drizzle. I made my way. Seven forty-seven A.M. I wore my gabardine trench coat, topped off with a tweed trilby (my preferred outerwear in such climes). The hair beneath the trilby: pomaded and coiffed. The body beneath the trench: smartly dressed and amply perfumed. I am never lackluster when it comes to menswear. On Friday mornings I sought to dazzle. It's all play. I may have been dressed to the nines, but the body beneath was that of a child mannequin half-melted in a store fire. One must be realistic. On some deep, primal level, I am drawn to pretty girls, but over the years I have disciplined the desire away. To me, an attractive woman is like a fascinating bird. Beautiful, yes, but it would be unnatural to mate with it.

I shouldered through the antique doors. A blast of warm air greeted me; on the back of it, a familiar smell—the smell of words in print. I inhaled deeply. The odor gamboled with the musk of my cologne. A perfect combination. Someday I'll commission a perfumer to replicate the scent. I shall dub the fragrance "Literary Lion" and will license the brand to a major cosmetics company. I've trademarked the idea, by the way, so don't think of stealing it.

I was in the main hall. The chandelier was fully lit, but the old incandescents were grimy, and the fixtures likewise, and the atmosphere was imbued with a quality of permanent dusk. The oak tables—six of them, set in the center of the hall—were empty. There were no patrons in sight, but small echoes produced evidence of their presence. Somewhere a rustling of papers. Further off, someone clicking away in the computer lab.

A U-shaped checkout desk dominated the northern side of the hall. Behind it: The Alluring Librarian. Behind her, another stained-glass window, also Tiffany. In this one, a theatrical scene, with a group of players performing Dante's *Divine Comedy*.

Her style was alt rock business casual. A black scarf. A lace cardigan, also black. Beneath the sweater, a tuxedo-front blouse in white. She wore form-fitting ankle pants, black again, and a pair of Mary Jane flats. Nothing too-too, all quite fetching, but black and white, with purpose; and while of modest cut, the fit accentuated all, and, when taken with the hairstyle, one registered a disposition as much as a fashion sense.

She had a book open on the counter. She was lost in it. Instinct compelled me to ogle. I'm not an ogler by nature. Any conscious ogling I perform is as an accessory to foreplay. My blemished lovers are unaccustomed to a gentleman's gaze. Most shy from it at first, but if my desire is genuine—which it will be, if I've done my mental prep—and if I take my time and escalate my ogling along with their comfort level, I've found that most of my lovers come to bask in my sleazy gaze. *That's right. I'm looking at you. I'm objectifying* you. *And I like what I see.* My ogling of The Alluring Librarian was a different thing. It was nonconsensual and covetous. The very things I sought to purge. She was just so pretty.

I approached the desk. The Alluring Librarian looked up, the hair fell away, and her beautiful features emerged. She smiled. It took all of my muscle power to remain upright. And why the gulp reflex? Why has evolution allowed this tendency to pass unchecked? What's the utility? Anyway, I did it. I gulped.

"You're a creeper," she said. Her voice had a Terry Gross–like quality—erudite, but with a simmering sensuality playing at the edges.

"Most would agree," I said.

"You *creep. Around.* Do you put felt pads on your shoes?"

"Just practice. I prefer to move through the world unnoticed. What are you reading?"

She told me. A poetic novel about America's atomic age. It was the subject of much buzz. "I'm not one for verse novels," I said.

"It isn't in verse. It's just stylized. You'd like it."

"I doubt it."

"It's free to try."

"Well, if my dealer says so—and given the state of my

addiction—I'm in no position to argue. One, please."

"They're all checked out."

"Then what's that?" I asked, pointing at the copy in her hand.

"The one *I* checked out," she said.

"Talk about corruption! You insiders hoard all the hot stuff for yourselves. What should I read? *Beowulf?*"

"We've got copies available. But you don't like verse novels." She said it jokingly and tilted her head while doing so, and even threw in a tiny hair toss. It tested me, reader. I won't deny it.

"*Beowulf* is an epic poem," I chastised. "Shame on you."

"You're not a fan of those either."

"Fandom doesn't figure in. They drain me. Epic poetry is a powerful sedative. One requires no sleep aid so long as *Beowulf* is on the nightstand."

"The world is noisy," she said.

"Not in here," I said.

"That's how I like it," she said. "Out there, it's getting noisier all the time."

"That's fair to say."

"And when everything gets noisy, you have to scream to be heard," she said.

"A provocative notion, but apropos of nothing."

"I like art that puts you to sleep. I think it's daring. How's that?"

"I'm not sure the epic poets had such courage of intention."

"'Intention of the author is neither available nor desirable as a standard for judging the success of a work of literary art.' Don't get trapped by the Intentional Fallacy."

"So says the Master of Library Science, University of Buffalo, class of 2004."

"You remembered."

"I asked. Doctors maintain the statuary of our bodies. Librarians tend the gardens of our mind. You ought to know something about the people who fiddle with your organs."

"Nicely said."

"Which part?"

"Doctors, statuary, librarians, gardens."

"Glad you liked it. Now, if I may offend: you cling too tightly to new critical orthodoxy. Art cannot be made a science of. You must shake the fetters of your education. It's left you with an affective head cold."

"How's your book going?"

"Lousy, thanks for asking. It is the lousy efflux of my lousy soul. But it is mine. Take that!"

Okay. Sure. This was not your typical librarian-to-patron banter. There was an odd sort of intimacy to it, a bit of something, hidden between the lines. I attribute it to my resistance. The Alluring Librarian was the most attractive woman I'd ever had to resist. I'm not referring to "her advances." Oh no! The only thing she advanced to me was reading material. I had to resist my *want.* Want is the bane of men like me. In my attempt to resist her charms, I ended up treating The Alluring Librarian like a human being.

I know what you're thinking, reader. *We've seen this movie before.* The Alluring Librarian has "love interest" written all over her. All the pieces are there. The moral takeaways of a romantic outcome would be tangible and uplifting. I need not outline them. They are the flatus of popular entertainment.

Seventeen months prior. The first time I saw her. I was gobsmacked. I was familiar with the "sexy librarian" archetype, of course. The title of this chapter, and the identity-concealing handle I've assigned the character, are plays on it. The concept didn't even cross my mind at the time. "Sexy librarian" is not a woman who exists in the world—she is a character in pornographic films. She's a sexualized representation of female intelligence. Off with the glasses! Down with the hair! The fantasizer strips "sexy librarian" of her trappings, of her intelligence, and fornicates freely with the whore beneath. I don't find that appealing. Authentic eroticism is a balancing act between desire and rationality; between instinct and intelligence. The wham-bam-thank-you leaves me cold.

The sexy librarian porno character is always Caucasian. Why would this be? I've attempted to research the subject as part of my Anti-Bias Reprogramming. *Racially-based porno genres. Archetypes. Cultural aspects. Shifting trends in masculine desire.* Seems like a rich thesis topic, but I haven't found much. I did run across some interesting articles on India's obsession with lighter skin. Further digging revealed the global nature of this phenomenon. It seems that brown people, the world over, discriminate *amongst themselves* on the basis of skin tone, with lightness as the ideal, and darkness as an unwanted mark of lower-class standing. The Alluring Librarian was quite dark. I assumed that her relatives shared similar pigmentation. Perhaps it's why her grandparents moved to the states. Anyway, The Alluring Librarian is not Caucasian, nor is she particularly leggy, or unnaturally busty, and she doesn't wear glasses, and her hairstyle wouldn't work in a bun, and I had never seen her in a pencil skirt or low-cut blouse. She was young and pretty. She was of exotic parentage. She was, by her handling of staff-only equipment, a clear practitioner of the information sciences. I've known plenty of librarians, but none that had looked like her.

The Alluring Librarian has a way of disappearing into what she's doing. On that day, when I first saw her, she'd been loading new arrivals onto a roller cart. She didn't notice my approach.

"Who are you?" I hissed.

She shrieked. It was the placement of the shriek that tells. She didn't cry out when I said the words. Had she done so, the shriek could have been attributed to surprise. She shrieked when she saw me. When she *laid eyes on me.* The eyes tell all. I was a monster to her; a troll who'd been living in the library cellars for hundreds of years, only then to emerge, drawn by the scent of delicate young flesh.

"You scared me," she said. It took her a moment to screw her face back on.

"I have a way of doing that," I said. Over time, she's grown accustomed to my appearance. She'd never grow used to it.

Speaking of "the scent of delicate young flesh": lilac! It's the empress of fragrant flowers and the backbone of The Alluring Librarian's singular aroma. A powder? A lotion? Eau de toilette? No telling, but titillating to wonder. The lilac mixed with the pervasive fragrance of printed words, and with the slightest hint of cigarette smoke. I dub her odor "Literary Lioness." My future cosmetics concern will offer a "his and hers" set for the holidays.

Back to the main thread. I chitchatted with The Alluring Librarian for a while longer. We spoke about the weather. It was dreary. Her favorite kind of weather, and mine. We explicated on the tangible and ontological aspects of the gloom. She asked after my family. I asked after hers, even though I didn't know them. Parents, grandparents, a younger sister, all living in Chicago. I said that it must be hard, being so far from her "indigenous culture." I got a smile for that one. I asked if she ever got lonely. She said that she did, but that all in all, one place was much the same as another, and that she spoke to her family more "now" than she had when they cohabitated in Cook County.

I pulled a crumpled list from my trench coat pocket.

"Do you need me to look anything up," she asked, "or are you researching today?"

"Well, Mummy wants me to pick up *Cooking the Russian Way*. She means to expand her aspic repertoire. Other than that, today's shopping will be topic-based."

"Care to share?"

"Oh, let me see. Whaling. The whaling industry. Specifically, in nineteenth-century Nantucket."

"Interesting. Why?"

"We just reread *Moby Dick*. I want to know more about the men who undertook such soggy work. I'm also seeking data on single motherhood and postwar manufacturing."

"All these disparate things. I'd love to know what you're trying to get at."

"A satisfaction of curiosity. Not everything has to lead to something."

Her eyes scanned for eavesdroppers. The coast was clear. She set her hands on the counter and leaned toward me. The curtains of hairstyle drew in slightly, framing her face, and that wry, off-kilter grin, and those beautiful, sparkling eyes.

"Have you stolen it yet?" she whispered.

I did my own scan, leaned in closer, and whispered back. "It's not stealing. It's cultural repatriation."

"So you haven't."

"A plan is in the works."

"I've been thinking about it," she said. "Ever since you told me. It's crazy stuff."

"My neighbor toes the line between reason and insanity. There's also the matter of her son. He'd kill me if he had the chance."

"You're sure she has it?"

"It's the only thing that makes sense."

"And 'cultural repatriation' is the only way?"

"What choice do I have? It's a sacred family relic."

"Maybe she's sold it."

"I'm sure she would have found a way to let me know about it. To gloat."

"But what if she didn't know it was yours?"

"That thought has crossed my mind."

"You can't ask her about it."

"I know."

"Because then she'll definitely know."

"I know."

"Because if she has it, she'll keep it just to spite you."

"I know."

"Or sell it."

"I know!"

Our speculations were interrupted by a brief, electronic ditty—a text message notification, emanating from a cellular flip phone on the checkout desk. The Alluring Librarian gave a mild curse, grabbed the phone, silenced it, and tucked it away. The phone had been acting as a sort of paperweight. Her actions drew my eye to the stack of documents where the phone had rested. Atop the stack, a photocopied flyer. It looked like this.

WEDNESDAY NIGHTS!
9PM-CLOSE

TERRANCE JOHNSON

LIVE MUSIC, KARAOKE

$5 COVER
DRINK SPECIALS

MOTHER'S TAVERN
201 4TH AVENUE
ILIUM, NY

I snatched the flyer from the desk.

"What. Is. This!?" I spoke at full throat.

"You haven't heard? There's a music thing happening Wednesday nights . . ."

"I know all about it. The musician is our nurse."

"*Terrance Johnson* is your nurse?"

The syllables danced off her tongue. She spoke his name in the same way Mummy did.

"Not mine, Puppa's, and not for long if I have anything to say about it."

"You know him?"

"I just told you. He's Puppa's nurse. I'm appalled by this flyer."

"I was too. I think that's the point."

"Did he make it?"

"He must have. There was a stack of them by the door."

I gasped. My hand trembled as it came to my lips.

"What *door*?"

"*The* door. At *the bar*."

A shot of vomit ejaculated from throat to mouth. I choked the bile back with a pained gulp.

"You can't mean!?" I exclaimed.

"I go every week."

"To Mother's Saloon!?"

"Terrance is a friend of mine."

"Good God!"

"You should see the place. It's a great group of people. And diverse! Terrance does that. He's an incredible roots artist . . . if that even describes him."

"I'm familiar with his repertoire. He performed for us just the other day."

"Really?"

"In our house."

"That must have been amazing."

"'Amazing' is a chorus of dogs barking 'Jingle Bells.' It's not some two-bit LPN who can carry a tune. To me, the man is an insinuator and a con. Mummy is in love with him."

"I think all the girls are in love with him. You should see the reaction."

"Never!" I cried.

She shushed me. I shushed her shush with a louder shush; a shush loud enough to warrant a return shush, which she provided.

"I'm taking this flyer," I said sternly. "My inner liberal is outraged by this 'jigaboo minstrel' iconography. He can't have made it himself. If he did, I will demand an apology, because it's *too much, too far,* and I will send a copy of the thing to his employer, and another to the local chapter of the NAACP. Good day!"

As tantrums go, dramatic exits are pretty satisfying. Here's the thing: when you leave a place, you have to go to another, and your problems will always beat you to where you're going.

- 8 -
INDULGE THE DEMON

Sunday mornings are man time. Mummy leaves for church at 7:30. There's a "coffee social" after services. After that, she runs errands. She ventures this weekly pilgrimage by bus. She looks forward to it, and I look forward to the quality time I get to spend with Puppa. For seven hours every Sunday, Puppa and I play the part of bachelor roommates. We don our robes and slippers, watch the morning news programs, and discuss the day's stories. It's more an interview than a discussion, really. During commercial breaks, I'll mute the television and ask Puppa questions relating to the previously viewed segment. "Puppa, do you agree with the Senator's assessment of XYZ?" He'll indicate yes or no, and I'll follow with another polar question that digs deeper into the topic.

The news programs end at eleven, and I break out the checkerboard. Puppa was a checkers champion in his Navy days, and I rarely beat him now. The game board is set on a stool, close to his harness, and he points out the moves that he would like me to execute on his behalf. He's always black. The game usually ends with two or three black kings straddling the board and a pile of bloody red chips littering the floor. We play for about an hour, and then settle in for a reading of the Sunday paper. World news, local news, arts and leisure, and, at last, sports. This leads us into the afternoon, to the sporting portion of our day. Puppa was born in Buffalo. In the chambers of his heart, the penthouse is reserved for his daughter and grandson, but choice accommodations are given to the Buffalo Bills. In autumn, we listen to every Bills game on the radio. In the off-season, I fire up the laptop, and we scour the web for every scrap of news relating to the team.

Puppa and I were well into our first checkers game, and it wasn't looking good for me. I was down 6–9. Puppa had a clear lane up the right wing. In three moves he'd have a king. Once Puppa had a king at his command, he was almost impossible to beat. Murder beamed from his eye. He'd chosen The Marksman as his sporting prosthetic. That's the mahogany with the red crosshair pupil.

"Puppa—there has been a startling development over the past week."

"Urgh?"

"I've been invited to attend an event."

"Mmm hmmm. . . ."

"Terrance's music night."

"Ahhh!"

"Well—and you're going to say I'm crazy—I'm thinking about going."

"Boo booooo!" That's as close as I can get to the way his words came out. He said: *You should!*

"I'm curious. Sociologically, I mean. We Hayeses are of academic temperament, and our private library contains the greatest thoughts of history's greatest minds—but one can distance himself too much from the common man."

The crosshair pupil aimed right between my eyes and Puppa fired a sour look along the trajectory. He didn't like it when I put on airs.

"There's also a psychosexual component."

"Huh?"

"The Alluring Librarian. She's a regular attendee of this depraved soirée. She said so yesterday."

"Oooooo!"

"Nothing like that. It would just be interesting to see her. Outside of a municipal context, I'm saying. The line between patron and provider would blur. The civic veil would lift. It might cure me of my unhealthy fascination."

He nodded enthusiastically.

"But it's a *public house*, Puppa. I wouldn't know what to do."

His face ground into a smile, and he pantomimed a drinking motion with his good hand.

"That's not a good idea, given our family history." It was a diplomatic way of putting it. Puppa waved his hand, shooing my concern away.

"I've never partaken of spirits—except in church, and then only a thimbleful. I see no reason to take up the habit now. What if I'm a dormant alcoholic?"

"Baaaaa."

"It does lurk in the genes, wouldn't you say? That first drink could awaken the disease and send me into the downward spiral."

"Blah ba ba."

"I have zero experience with mind-altering substances."

"Kaktus," Puppa said.

"Cactus?"

"KAK-TUS!" he bellowed.

"Practice?"

"Mmm Hmmm."

"Practice *drinking!?* Absurd!"

Puppa pointed toward the closet door. His face was gay with amusement. I asked him what he wanted, but he just kept pointing, so I did as he bade. The closet was filled with old coats and hats, the folding chairs, a spillover of books; miscellaneous debris for which we no longer had a place. There was a set of shelves built into the back wall, behind the hanging coats.

"What am I looking for?"

"Up," he said, clearly enough, and indicated, with an upward pointing gesture, that what he wanted was up high. There were some old sweaters peeking out from the top shelf, but that was all I could see. I removed the folding chairs and pushed the coats aside. The closet smelled of leather, warm wool, and the stale memory of cigarettes.

"You're about to make a monkey of me. You know that, right?"

"Up! Up! Up!"

And so, for the second time that week, I was climbing. The shelving was custom-built and nailed into place, so the climb was easy enough. I passed the various compartments as I ascended—each filled with the forgotten detritus of our lives. Old photographs; half-burned candles; tools, hardware of lost provenance; Othello, Parcheesi, Backgammon, a 1989 edition of Trivial Pursuit; a broken desk lamp; a silver cigarette case, a collection of Zippo lighters, an ancient bottle of lighter fluid; a globe, on which I had received my first geography lessons. I remembered every one of these artifacts, although I hadn't seen many of them in years.

"This is quite a climbing wall, Puppa. It's filled with memories."

I reached the top shelf and pulled the old sweaters away. An array of bottles was revealed. Liquor bottles. A few were half-full (or half-empty, depending on your disposition), but most were sealed.

"You old rake! Were you running a speakeasy out of here?"

It was as if I'd uncovered a hoard of magic potions. The bottles were green and emerald and charcoal, some squat decanters, others tall and lean, still others earthenware jugs. Some had large wooden stoppers, or else fat corks, or screw tops. They stood like armored soldiers with silver breastplates or gold chainmail or bronze placards, and their labels were like banners of war, complete with regal crests. There were a dozen such bottles, maybe more, and to the right side was a stack of four wooden liquor boxes. I took one of the boxes and carefully made my descent.

I'd never, in all my life, seen Puppa take a drop. Such drop-taking was done down in our basement woodshop, away from prying eyes. Puppa would arrive home from work, retreat down to his private sanctuary, and proceed to glaze himself with therapeutic libations. It wasn't until years later—until the death of Little Miss Sunshine's husband, and the dark accountings that followed—that I pieced it all together. There was a padlocked steamer chest under the workbench. It was the only place in our home that was off-limits to me. Mummy had said that she'd gotten rid of it all, but apparently Puppa had held on to "the good stuff."

"Does Mummy let you drink this?" I asked.

He shook his head sadly.

"I should think not, given the state of your liver."

Hindsight clarifies. Puppa, passed out in the backyard. Puppa, slipping and falling down the back stairs; a broken wrist, and lucky to have avoided a broken neck. I've mentioned his amputations, but there is a smaller, nonmedical one that predates them all. His left pinkie. That digit, and neighboring ring finger, were gobbled by the table saw. The doctors successfully reattached the ring, but the pinkie was mangled and doused beyond repair. The unfortunate digit was tossed by the blade, splattered against the wall, and then it rebounded off, into an open can of lacquer. I didn't witness this gruesome spectacle. "I thought he had a handle on this," Mummy had said, and I'd had no idea what she meant.

He was a kind, happy man. There wasn't a trace of violence in him. Either he had a constitution of iron, or else he'd been drinking so much, for so long, that intoxication had become inseparable from his personality. He always seemed so lucid; so sober. They say a drunken mind speaks with a sober tongue.

Puppa eyed the wooden box in my hand. He beckoned me to open it. The box was made of dark wood and covered in a twenty-year layer of dust. Inside the box was a nest of velvet, and in that nest nestled a clear bottle. The liquid within was the color of black coffee, and there was a label, also black, trimmed with silver flake. The label read:

BLACK BOWMORE
1964

FINEST
ISLAY SINGLE MALT
SCOTCH WHISKY

"Wow . . . this is old," I said.

"Mmmm Hmmmm. . . ."

"It's probably gone bad."

He got a good laugh out of that. I knew what scotch was, of course. I knew it was sophisticated liquor, enjoyed by gentlemen, but regarding connoisseurship I was completely naïve. He pointed at the bottle, then at me, and again pantomimed drinking.

"You think I should drink this?"

He pointed at me, then at himself.

"You think *we* should drink this?"

He slapped his nubbin knee and gave an enthusiastic thumbs-up.

"Are you insane!? Mummy would crucify me!"

The old rascal raised an eyebrow and put his finger to his lips. His expression communicated the old axiom: *What Mummy don't know can't hurt her.*

A few sips? What harm? And what an experience to share! I went to the kitchen, where, for the first time in my life, I tried my hand at bartending. This would be my first real drink, and I was glad that it would be a manly one, shared with my beloved Pap. I wasn't a total rube—from literature and film, I knew that real men drank their scotch "on the rocks" or "neat," and that volume was measured in "fingers," as in *Hey, barkeep, give me two fingers of your best hooch.* I broke out a pair of good crystal glasses, gripped one across the bottom, and drew a mental mark at the two-finger line. I then peeled away the black foil that sealed the bottle and wrenched the cork free. I placed a nostril at the mouth of the bottle and whiffed. The smell was warm and musky, like a spent campfire, with quieter notions in the background; a mix of earthy notes that suggested a pine forest after a soaking rain. Complex, certainly, but not something I'd think to put in my mouth.

I dispensed two fingers' worth into each glass, and then carefully spooned some Thick & Easy into Puppa's glass and whisked it thoroughly with a fork. It was a sad necessity, and I hoped that it wouldn't diminish the quality of the scotch too much. I placed the glasses, the bottle, the tin of Thick & Easy, and a tablespoon on our silver salver, and returned to the den.

"Here we go. Before our first sip I want you to realize—if this ends up being my first step down the road to ruin, you only have yourself to blame."

"Sheesh."

"It's why I've never tried alcohol. I don't think I'll hold my liquor as manfully as you did. My temperament is too volatile. I also don't want to slice off any fingers."

Puppa wiggled his pinkie stump and winked his working eye. The Mobius remained, its crosshair aimed directly at the scotch bottle.

I held my glass in my left hand and the tablespoon in my right. Puppa lacked the dexterity to drink from his glass directly, and the snorkel/straw was ill-suited for sipping, so Puppa would have to take his scotch from the tablespoon, like medicine. It was a sacred moment. Dignity demanded that he be able to hold his own glass and that we behave just like two regular guys, sharing a good drink and good conversation. Puppa held out his glass, and I took up a full tablespoon of the thickened scotch. We gently clinked our glasses together.

"Cheers." He opened wide, in went the spoon, and in the same moment, I administered a dose of elixir to myself. The flavor was revolting. It slithered down my esophagus, into my stomach, burning a trail as it went. I felt as if I had swallowed a centipede—a live one, biting and clawing at my delicate inner tissues.

"Plech! People actually like this stuff?"

Puppa inhaled deeply, relishing the fumes. He said, *"Ooove."*

"Smooth? The narcotic effect must be more powerful than I thought."

"Kaktus."

"I don't think I can practice anymore."

"KAKTUS!" he thundered. His harness shook with the force of his command. He thrust his glass toward me. I ladled up another dose, then raised my glass and examined the contents. My bottom lip trembled at the thought of consuming more.

"Now I know what Socrates must have felt like."

Puppa smacked his lips. I delivered him his shot of sauce, in time with my own swig. The taste remained awful, but not so awful as the first time. My taste buds were braised senseless. An unpleasant warmth was kindling in my guts.

We proceeded in this manner for some time. We'd sip, I'd recover, we'd sip again, and with each snort, the scotch became more agreeable. We finished our first glass, and at Puppa's insistence, I prepared another round.

"When will I start feeling drunk?"

I was keeping close track of my senses. My speech patterns remained fluid. The hardwood felt sturdy beneath me, and my mind was free of absurdity. I reassessed my mental status with each sip. I didn't want to make a clown of myself in front of Puppa, but he'd forgive me that. My true fear was of the beast. The beast within. Aroused, who knew what it was capable of? I made a reassuring promise to myself: if I detected even a spark of malice in my heart, I would set down my drink, go to the bathroom, and induce vomiting. So far, I felt nothing that could be classified as "intoxication." Quite the contrary. The novelty of our activity imbued me with a lightness of spirit. I was jocular. My joints felt loose in their sockets.

"They call them 'spirits.' Is it because they make your spirits so high?"

"Mmmmmm."

"I feel like music. Do you feel like music?"

"Oooooo!"

I rolled Puppa into the drawing room and fired up the hi-fi. We needed a record that was equal to the occasion, and the choice was easy: Dean Martin's fabulous LP, *Hey, Brother, Pour the Wine*. I'd had Dino on the brain ever since Terrance's performance. I pulled the record from the shelf and presented it to Puppa. He raised his glass to my good taste. I set the record on the turntable and delicately placed the needle in the vinyl foothills of track two. The speakers fizzled like a glass of fresh seltzer as the needle made its circumnavigation of the well-worn groove.

A blast of horns; a swaggering beat; a grungy, high/low swing. Then it was Dino's turn.

Standin' on a corner watching all the girls go by,
Standin' on a corner watching all the girls go by,
Brother, you don't know a nicer occupation
Matter of fact, neither do I,
Than standin' on a corner watching all the girls
Watching all the girls, watching all the girls go by.

We knew every word, every note. We sang along. I was overwhelmed by the urge to dance. The rhythm was perfect for an ol' soft-shoe—a dance that Puppa had taught me as a boy. I tapped my toes. I circled and sashayed. Puppa bebopped in his harness. Pupil and crosshair were locked on my feet. My movements transported him. It was as if my feet were his, and he was executing the steps, and at that moment he had two good legs and my soft-shoe was his soft-shoe, and he was dancing like he had in the old days. The glass of scotch was a perfect prop. I sang. I danced. I sipped. I was Dino at the Sands. I was in the present tense of a cherished memory, and I knew it, and I took care to savor every moment.

What if Mummy smells the alcohol on our breath?

I was back in the kitchen. The afterglow of the experience had faded. In its place, an anxious dread. I could suck a lozenge or gargle mouthwash, but what about Puppa? Should I pulverize a mint and serve it to him as a paste? Puree a pickle? I searched the refrigerator, then the freezer, and found the solution: a tub of mint chocolate chip ice cream. It would be the perfect topper to a perfect morning.

"The Mute sat on the bed. She teased me with her eyes. She tossed her hair and pursed her lips. Her flirtation was like gasoline, tossed upon the flames of my desire! At last, she rose from the bed, crossed to me, and submitted to my embrace."

A spoonful for Puppa, a spoonful for me. We ate the ice cream while I recounted my adventures. I always gave the G-rated version, of course. I stuck to the romantic details, or the humorous ones, and left the rest to Puppa's imagination.

"I held her. Our hearts beat as one. And then, the unthinkable!"

His eye was a saucer. His lips and chin were covered in minty goo. We were like a pair of teenagers reveling in a tale of sexual conquest.

"She fell. She was wearing these massive high heels—like something a chanteuse would wear—and she fell over!"

Puppa gasped. This autonomical wrenching of features pushed The Marksman beyond its operational tolerance. It fell from Puppa's face down to the floor, and rolled under the armchair. This malfunction sent Puppa into hysterics. A neon green spritz exploded from his mouth. Little droplets of mint ice cream hit my shirt. My laughter matched his.

"I couldn't hold her!" I said, forcing words through the gasps.

Puppa cackled. If you didn't know him, it would have been hard to tell whether he was laughing or crying.

"So we . . ."

I choked on a chuckle.

". . . fell . . ."

I choked again. Tears broke from the corners of my eyes and made hot trails down my cheeks.

". . . to the floor. Together! I was afraid to move! I was afraid her father would burst into the room in nothing but his boxer shorts!"

We laughed for a full minute, and then the laughing subsided, and then it came again in a series of small, snickering aftershocks.

"Murr murr unny," he said, out of breath.

"It was funny." I fed him another spoonful of ice cream. He smiled gladly, and then reached out with his good hand and tousled my hair.

Monday:

Spec writing complete. Beneath the technobabble and pseudo-legalese was a classically structured short story. Introduction. Body. Conclusion. A real page-turner, too, filled with twists and turns, intrigues and feints, all ending in a satisfying climax: $35,125. Round numbers sound made up, so I always fray the edges of my figures. Read, edit, read, edit, send. There was nothing to do but wait.

Monday night:

I emptied my closet onto the bed and considered various

getups. My cheval mirror would serve as my private fashion runway. I sipped scotch. I was going to return the Black Bowmore to the closet but Puppa said no, that I should take it and continue with my *kaktus*.

As any haberdasher will tell you, the trousers are the foundation of an outfit—choose them first and build from there. I settled on a pair of flat-front charcoal slacks. They were form-fitting and gave clear definition to my buttocks. I was bare-chested and bare-footed. I twirled in front of the mirror. My trousers said, "I'm casual and contemporary. Pair me with a turtleneck!" I had a beautiful cashmere turtleneck in black. Yes! I looked like a poet—a *wealthy* poet—in search of his living muse.

The turtleneck spoke next. "Oh, don't you think I'd look *fabulous* under that leather blazer of yours? The black one, which you never have the nerve to wear?" I pulled the blazer from the pile. The leather felt cool and sexy. I slipped it on and regarded myself in the mirror. I was dumbstruck by the reflection that stared back at me.

"I'm trendy!" the slacks cried.

"I'm artistic!" the turtleneck proclaimed.

"I'm dangerous," the leather blazer warned.

The blazer knew which hat it wanted. "Give me the bowler," it growled. I took up the hat and set it on my head. The man in the mirror looked better than he ever had. He was ugly, and small, with a crook in his back and a toadstool nose, and there was the overbite, and a chin that was defined by its absence, and the close-spaced, deep-set, anuslike eyes. But the man in the mirror had nerve. The man in the mirror was used to getting what he wanted, in spite of his obvious limitations. Cock of the walk? In no one's eyes. But in the right light, and from certain angles, and with a bit of distance, he might be mistaken for king of the cockroaches.

Tuesday morning. Breakfast was served.

"When Terrance gets here, why don't you come downstairs and say hello?"

"I cannot."

"What about his music night? You're *going,* aren't you?"

"There's only a ten-percent chance that I'll be able to attend."

"I don't understand you! Why wouldn't you go?"

"A major pharmaceutical company. A microsite that promotes a new eczema cream. It launches on Thursday."

"You should tell him yourself and not be rude."

"Not a moment to spare. Please extend my apologies."

I hid behind the curtains and peered out from my chamber window. Terrance approached. He was dressed for business, in scrub pants and the red Crocs. If I were appointed emperor for a day, my first edict would be to outlaw those stupid shoes. The sole purpose of their design, it seems to me, is to make a joke of the human foot.

The birds were singing. A gentle breeze slow-danced in the treetops. Terrance walked at a leisurely pace, hands in his pockets. He was whistling a song—possibly *Yankee Doodle.* The thin strains of it carried on the wind. The gentle day seemed to be an extension of his mood; as if his emotions determined the state of nature. If he stopped for a moment and held out a finger, I was sure that a bird would swoop down to perch upon it. He was handsome to the point of unreality.

It's up to you, Terrance had said. *If you want to check it out, you're more than welcome. You'll see that there's nothing to be concerned about.*

He didn't expect me to go. I'd had him wriggling on the grill, and he'd been desperate to escape the sizzle. I should have gone downstairs, made nice with him, and formally RSVP'd. It would have been the polite thing to do. But I couldn't. I'd be taking him up on an invitation that he hadn't wanted to make. He'd be surprised, then regretful. He'd backpedal. *Oh, tonight isn't a good night. You can come if you want, but my banjo is broken so I won't be playing.* Or maybe: *My voice is off so I won't be singing. I should be better in a couple of weeks.* His way was the nicest way possible, and in his way he'd tell me that he didn't really want me there. I'd worked up my nerve, and I didn't want to lose it.

I had my wits. My aikido training. I had Excalibur, and an inner jacket pocket to conceal him in. I was ready to try something new.

- 9 -
I AM THE MYSTERIOUS STRANGER

It was a cool, clear night. Perfect turtleneck weather.

My heart beat like a timpani. A mustache of nervous sweat had formed on my upper lip. The streets were desolate. My footsteps echoed off the brick. Ilium is a city of echoes, whispers, ghost sounds. By day this ambiance is barely noticeable, but then day gives on to night, and it's only you and street after street of nothing and no one, and your reverberated footfalls sound like a pursuer, stalking you step for step. You move, he moves. You stop, he stops. It does a job on the nerves.

At last, my echoed paces were subverted by the dull throb of music; by the whoops and cries of a wassail in full swing. Up ahead: Mother's Saloon. The face of the building was illuminated by a single street lamp. I receded into shadow, took a double shot of snuff, and then advanced.

A man guarded the entrance. He was of average height, but with a chest like a barrel and arms like fence posts. He wore camouflage short pants and a black hooded sweatshirt and also a baseball cap, the bill of which was pulled low over his eyes. He was the physical embodiment of blunt-force trauma.

Tollbooth.

"Greetings," I said, bowing slightly at the hips. I wanted to show deference to this powerful warrior and not cause him offense. "I am here to attend Terrance Johnson's music night."

"Five dollars," he announced blandly, and I saw that his face—his *face!*—was covered in tattoos! His visage was like a cave wall, decorated with iconography! His nude calves bore similar markings, and the ink spilled out from his sleeves, onto his hands, like consuming leprosy. I swallowed hard before I spoke.

"Good sir, I have been invited to attend by Mr. Johnson himself, as his special guest. Here is my New York State Non-Driver ID card."

"I don't need that. What's your name?"

I told him my name, and he pulled a folded sheet of paper from his pocket. His expression grew less taut, and the faint traces of a grin emerged from under his facial artwork.

"You're friends with Terrance?" he asked.

"I think 'associates' would be apter."

"Terrance is awesome," he said. "It sucks that I have to be out here."

"That does *suck,*" I said, trying the vernacular on for size. "You should be stationed inside."

"No room," he said with a shrug.

I peeked through the window. The scene within was the dictionary definition of "fire hazard." The interior was packed to overflowing. The building seemed to breathe, collapsing inward and expanding outward like a giant lung.

"You're all set, Charles. Have a good time."

"Please," I said. "Call me Buddy." I popped my leather lapels and entered the fray.

I had imagined that all eyes would be upon me. I'd push through the door, and the instant I crossed the threshold the music would stop and the crowd would turn to inspect the ugly little stranger. The men would snicker. The women would gasp. I'd be seared by the heat of their gazes, but I would stand firm, puff out my chest, doff my bowler, and announce: "Buddy Hayes. Entrepreneur. Might I join you for a drink?"

I was greeted, instead, by a wall of rumps. It was like entering a showroom of rumps. Fifty rumps, maybe more, all crammed together. From my unfortunate perspective, Mother's Saloon was a tight maze of rumps and crotches. I couldn't see the stage or the bar.

The ceiling was pressed tin. No telling what color it had been a hundred years ago. Shined up, it would have been beautiful, but age and neglect had given it a sickly brown patina. The walls were wooden plank. Illumination was provided by three dangling bar lamps and five neon beer signs. The temperature leaped twenty degrees the instant I was through the door. My eyes burned. Glowing cigarette embers darted about like fireflies. I would have to run the gauntlet, despite the risk of being burned, trampled, or farted upon.

I've described the challenges I face as an ugly man, but I haven't talked too much about the difficulties presented by my stature. So here goes. A crowded room renders me near-blind. It's like navigating in a fog—a fog of unclean human bodies. It's an awful, claustrophobic experience and the primary reason why I avoid crowds. The mob absorbs me, and I am beholden to its will. Not to mention the smells! The lower half of the human body is a vile perfumery. The sweaty groin. The unclean anus. The odoriferous feet. It's a trinity of filth from the waist down, and at four feet nine it's a filth I'm forced to wallow in.

I wasn't ready to reveal myself to Terrance. I'd take a barstool first, lay low, and observe him in his natural habitat. He was the most powerful presence in the bar in spite of the fact that I couldn't see him. He was working his way through an upbeat country number. I kept my eyes on the floor and worked my way toward the bar. The assembled revelers were tall as trees. Beers and cocktails dangled from their limbs like fruit. It was a colorful canopy—ambers and oranges and reds and greens—and the glasses shimmered in the neon light. The floor was hardwood. Black with grime. There was a scattering of cigarette butts, and also a strange, flaky dust. The dust was everywhere, covering the floor like sawdust in our basement woodshop.

I reached an impassible point—an escarpment formed by two large men. Their massive bellies were like co-orbiting planets. I was at eye level with these corpulent planetoids. If the men had chosen to embrace at that moment, they would have crushed my head like a grape.

"Excuse me," I said. My voice absorbed into the soft matter of their guts. "Excuse me!"

One of the giants decided that it was time to play litterbug. He opened his hand, and dust fell from it—the same kind of dust that littered the floor. I realized, then, what the dust was. Ground peanut shell. Apparently, the proprietor served them as an appetizer, and this slob had dropped his spent shells right onto my hat. They cascaded down, covering me in peanut dandruff.

"Hey!" I cried. They realized my presence with great surprise.

"Oh, man, I'm sorry," said the litterbug, shouting above the music. "I didn't see you down there, buddy."

They were pachyderms. Lumbering and skittish. I was a feral opossum. It must have been quite a sight—a face like mine, popping up between their legs. Alarm registered on their faces. Each man took a step backward, but there was little space to step into. The crowd forced them into an uncomfortable proximity.

I removed my hat and inspected it. The brim was lousy with flotsam. I slapped it against the side of my leg and put it back on.

"I am not a trash receptacle, sir!"

The litterbug was built like a snowman. His bald head was blistered with sweat, and he wore a stained white T-shirt that advertised an equatorial vacation spot, and knee-length cargo shorts, and leather footwear that was neither fully shoe nor fully sandal. The sandal/shoes left portions of his foot flesh exposed to the air. His fellow was of near-identical appearance and dress, except for a goatee beard, flip-flops, and a novelty tee that read "Who needs hair with a body like this?"

"Sorry," said the litterbug.

"Yeah, we're sorry," said his doppelgänger companion.

"I didn't see you down there," said the litterbug.

"We didn't see you down there," said the other.

The litterbug reached down with his paw and proceeded to brush the peanut dust away from my chest.

"That's better," he said.

"My word! Please! Stop it!" I pushed his hand away.

"You want a peanut?" said the other.

"You should have a peanut, buddy," the litterbug said.

Were they mocking me? Angling for a fight? I'd been in the bar for forty seconds and was already on the verge of a brawl.

"I've had enough peanut for one night," I said coldly. "Are you brothers?"

"We are brothers," said the first.

"Twin brothers, yes," agreed the other.

"The *Tweetle* brothers?" I asked, baring my teeth. I knew how this worked. They were "trying" me. I had to bite back, or before I knew it they'd be shaking me down for money.

"Tweetle? I don't know any Tweetles. I'm Viktor."

"I'm Oleg," the bearded one said.

My face: glazed in ennui. I picked the crumbs from my cashmere sweater. Oleg asked my name. I told him.

"Your name is *Buddy*?" Viktor's eyes were wide with amazement.

"That's right."

"I only heard of a *dog* named Buddy."

"Well, that's just charming."

"But I called you buddy already, you know? I called you buddy before I knew *your name* was Buddy. That's funny!"

The brothers exploded into a riot of laughter. Their bellies jiggled from the force of their convulsions.

"Oleg, Viktor, if you please . . . I have an appointment at the bar."

"An appointment?" asked Viktor.

"Like, with a doctor?" asked Oleg.

Here were two of the stupidest clowns I'd ever met. I'd lost five IQ points through the course of our conversation. I was desperate to escape.

"Yes—an appointment with Dr. Scotch. Will you please excuse me?"

"DR. SCOTCH!?" cried Viktor. "That's funny!"

The idiot brothers vomited laughter once more, and Viktor gave me a playful shove, which sent me stumbling toward Oleg, and then Oleg delivered me a lively slap on the back, which sent me back toward Viktor, and Viktor put his arm around me and squeezed as if we were old friends reunited. I felt like a dinghy tossed by stormy seas. It was the very definition of a manhandling.

"Coming through!" announced Viktor. He used his considerable bulk like a plow and pushed his way toward the bar, pulling me along in his wake.

The counter came nearly to my chin. Most of the patrons were standing, so there were a couple of unoccupied stools pressed in between the bodies. I climbed onto one, like a child mounting a jungle gym, and took my place.

Viktor summoned the bartendress. "Connie!"

Connie was of late middle age, with bottle blond hair and an exhausted, ruddy face. She was nearly six feet tall. Her affect was arthritic. The effort required for movement seemed to pain her. I could tell that she had endured much nonsense in her life and had little taste for it now.

"Another Michelob?" she asked Viktor.

"Not for me. For my new buddy, Buddy!"

Connie found no humor in Viktor's lousy wordplay. I instantly drew a liking to her. Her face was all wood and nails, and a smile from her would have to be earned. As for Viktor, I assumed that he would buy me a drink, given his crime, but he just patted me on the shoulder and vanished into the swarm.

"Hello, Connie. May I call you Connie?"

I had to shout to be heard. Connie regarded me in the same way that a primatologist might regard a lemur species that, before that moment, she'd only read about.

"That's my name," she said. "What'll you have?"

"Black Bowmore, 1964."

"Is that a scotch?"

I nodded.

"We don't have it."

A buffet of liquor bottles was arrayed against the mirrored backbar. Connie had a staggering array of potables in her arsenal, and I had no idea what to order.

"May I be frank with you, Connie?"

She responded with a bored shrug.

"I am here in support of my associate, Mr. Terrance Johnson. I don't usually indulge in spirits, but tonight I'm feeling intemperate. Will you suggest a drink for me?" I got the feeling that no one had ever asked her that before.

"You like scotch?"

"The *idea* of it, yes."

"Good scotch?"

"Only the best will do."

When a gentleman is chatting up a lady, and he's trying to establish some level of distinction, and he says a silly thing like "only the best will do," a flirtatious wink is pretty much required. The wink signals conviction. A *cheesy* conviction, sure, but a little cheese is better than blown smoke. I gave Connie a flirtatious wink. Her expression didn't change, but there was a barely perceptible flush to her cheeks. The "sex flush." Connie was an unfeeling oak on the outside, but inside—beneath her barmaid's cynicism—were traces of velvet.

"I got Chivas."

"Is that a Mexican drink?"

"Chivas Regal. It's scotch."

"It sounds like a Mexican name. *Chivas.*"

"It's Scotch."

"Is it a flavorful scotch? One that will add hairs to an already hairy chest?"

Her crow's feet shifted like fault lines and the resulting tremor forced a smile up to the surface.

"I guess."

"Would you say that the intoxicating effects of Chivas Regal are *more* or *less* potent than those of Black Bowmore, 1964?"

"Probably the same," she said.

"I will have two fingers of Chivas Regal, then."

"Rocks?"

I dipped my answer into a pot of innuendo. "Neat," I said, and used another wink as punctuation. It wasn't the best word to season with flirtation, *neat,* but there it was. I was rewarded with another tectonic smile.

Was I titillating the wench? Not likely. What she had was a raunchy little imp, cooing at her from his booster seat. But she was amused, and that was something. She didn't exactly "saunter off" to fix my drink—her sauntering days were well behind her—but it was clear that I had charmed her.

I'd found a refuge of comfort, away from the press of the crowd. From my barstool, I had a decent view of the goings-on. I caught occasional glimpses of Terrance through the gaps. *You are a recording device,* I said to myself. *Observe, and maintain your academic sense of remove.* I was an undercover agent. A cop on a stakeout. I pivoted on the stool, set my elbows on the bar behind me, and proceeded with my surveillance.

An attractive young lady was sitting beside me. Attractive in form, I should say, for in terms of function she appeared to be a prostitute. Her pink mini-dress left very little to the imagination, and what remained could easily be gleaned through sidelong glances at choice moments. Her perfume was a pimp's idea of what a rose garden should smell like. She was Caucasian, and a young man—a young *black* man—stood behind her, his hands resting on her shoulders.

Four Hispanic men stood by the pinball machine. They wore grimy white tees and black pants—the stock uniform of food-service professionals. There was a boldness about them—that touch of devil-may-care that laborers project after a long day's work. They had been joined by four women. Four white women. Regarding type, these ladies could best be described as "soccer moms." They were plump; they wore elaborate sweaters; their hairstyles were primped to leonine proportions; their jeans were of an unfashionable cut. One of the men told a joke, and it appeared to be a good one, and one of the moms playfully kissed the comedian on the cheek.

Viktor and Oleg were close by, in conversation with another man—a black man, dressed in bib overalls, with a railroad cap on his head and a red kerchief tied loosely around his neck.

Over by the pool table—which was not being used, as the crowd was pressed too tightly around it—was a diverse grouping of souls. A Persian couple hobnobbed with a trio of heavyset black women, and there was a gray-haired man—a Caucasian senior citizen—mingling among them. There was a weirdo in a purple wig, and three Army reservemen in digicamo fatigues, and a pair of biker dudes and a pair of biker mommas, and young coeds in sweatshirts and pajama pants, and no one race could claim a majority, and the generation gap seemed to hold no relevance here. It was colorblind bonhomie all around, and I was thrilled by the strangeness of it and more than a little frightened by it.

I scanned for The Alluring Librarian. No sign. Given the crowd, and my fixed vantage point, she could have been feet away yet totally concealed. I waited and hoped.

Connie set a drink in front of me.

"Eight dollars," she said.

I dug out my wallet and gestured toward Terrance with my eyebrows.

"Quite a performer," I said.

"He's the best," she said. "He makes my week."

"Financially or emotionally?"

I got another smile.

"Financially. Which helps with the emotions."

- - -

I finished my Chivas, ordered another. I felt comfortably invisible.

"Hey, everybody," Terrance announced. "How you all doin'?"

Warm applause. From the heart of the mob, a woman shouted: "I love you, Terrance."

"I love you too," he said with a laugh. "I'm Terrance Johnson—"

He was interrupted by a flirtatious wolf whistle. He accepted it with an *aw-shucks* grin.

"Okay, okay, okay. Welcome to Mother's Saloon. We all know the drill by now, right? If you'd like to sing, if you have a request, just write it on one of the little slips of paper that are around the bar and bring it up to me. Okay. Put your hands together for the lovely and talented . . . Dolly!"

That's not her real name. One must protect the innocent. The rationale for the moniker will soon be plain.

The crowd cheered heartily. I searched the room for the subject of this affection, but no one was making way. I sat up straight and craned my neck to get a better view. There was a small folding table up-left on the bandstand. An assemblage of audio equipment was arranged upon it. Terrance crossed to the table, fiddled with some knobs, studied the blinking of various indicators, and then he grabbed a second microphone, along with a device that looked like a television remote control. He had two microphones now—both of the wireless handheld variety—and the remote, and he crossed to the lip of the bandstand and sat there, on the edge, his legs dangling over. That's when I saw Dolly. She was already in position. She had been in position all night, seated in a wheelchair at the foot of the stage.

Her shriveled legs rested in polished silver stirrups. She was so small, and sunk so deeply into her chair, that she didn't look real. Her body was like a balloon with half the air let out. Without the benefit of her name, it would have been impossible to tell whether she was male or female. Her hair was done in a clumsy bowl cut.

The microphone looked gigantic in her hand—like some kind of slapstick joke. A hush fell over the room. Terrance took the remote and aimed it back at the equipment table. A press of a button and the speakers came alive, and I instantly recognized the easy listening classic that dribbled forth: "Islands in the Stream" by Kenny Rogers and Dolly Parton. It was a lousy Muzak instrumental, with synthesized horns and an overmodulated drumbeat, but there was no mistaking it. Whenever Mummy worked in the kitchen or the garden, her portable radio was with her, the dial locked to 95.5 Lite FM. I could have glued the dial there, and she would never have noticed. I'm not saying that Mummy has bad taste in music—she has no taste in music at all! Soft rock is like birdsong; it can be annoying at times, but it doesn't really affect your life, and eventually it just blends into the background. I knew "Islands in the Stream" as well as I knew "You're So Vain" or "Tonight, I Celebrate My Love," which is to say I knew it better than I should have, since I never actively tried to know it. Such is the nature of soft rock. It seeps into your brain through a slow process of osmosis.

There was a karaoke monitor set up at the foot of the stage, but they didn't seem to need it. Terrance picked up with the first verse.

"Baby when I met you there was peace unknown.
I set off to get you with a fine tooth comb.
I was soft inside,
There was something goin' on. . . ."

His voice was pitch-perfect, as always, and he added a bit of gravel in the lower register. His vocalizations were loose and breezy, definitely country, but with some interesting herbs and spices mixed in. Little R&B runs. Hints of black gospel. His partner took the second verse.

"You do something to me that I can't explain . . ."

Dolly hit the first line like a sledgehammer, and the misfit crowd hit the ceiling. My senses spun. It was impossible to believe that such a powerful voice could come from such a broken figure. She sounded almost exactly like Dolly Parton.

". . . Hold me closer and I feel no pain
Every beat of my heart
We've got something going on . . ."

Then Terrance.

"Tender love is blind.
It requires a dedication . . ."

Then Terrance and Dolly, in unison.

"All this love we feel,
It needs no conversation
We ride it together, uh-huh.
Makin' love to each other, uh-huh. . . ."

The lead vocal was a hot potato that they tossed between them. Each performer took focus without reservation, and then gave it back, and they didn't cling to it too tightly, yet neither was anxious to be rid of it.

"Islands in the stream,
That is what we are.
No one in-between.
How can we be wrong. . . ."

I was singing along—*screaming* along—and so was everyone else. I felt as if I were a part of the performance—as if the song was *ours,* all of ours, and we all had an equal stake in it. They were the ones making music, but without us—without the crowd—they'd be singing into a void, their glorious voices unheard.

"Sail away with me
To another world,
And we'll rely on each other, uh-huh,
From one lover to another, uh-huh. . . ."

She was in love with him. That was clear. You could tell by the way she looked at him when he didn't know she was looking. I watched. She loved him the most when his eyes were not upon her.

Terrance: tall, trim, black, and handsome. Dolly: the very opposite of all those things, but at that moment their pairing seemed totally natural. Obvious, even. The music would end and the enchantment would be gone, but it was beautiful to believe in everything the lyrics claimed. Cheers rained down. Dolly soaked them in. She was totally alive.

You get it, right? "Dolly," like Dolly Parton, but also because dolly*ing* was her primary method of locomotion, and also because—and I take no pleasure in saying this, reader—she looked a bit like one of those old-fashioned, bisque-headed dolls, but of a type that no child would wish to play with.

Has this broken songbird ever experienced an orgasm? A seed of compassion sprouted in my bosom. I experienced the early stirrings of an odd, pitiful lust. It was all wrong. To attempt a seduction would have been monstrous. It would have been charity, of a type I'd never accept, and would never force on another. It would have been an insult to her, and a repudiation of everything I believed.

The seed. In my bosom, I'm saying. It required nourishment. I'd fertilize it with base intentions. Water it with taboo. Erotic meditations. Manual stimulations. At last, a tree of desire, sprouting from my chest. A smallish tree, mind you. A healthy houseplant at the very least. I wouldn't present myself until the seed had taken root. Dolly would have a suitor. A genuine one. If she rejected me, she would be rejecting a cad, and not some perverted Samaritan who felt sorry for her. The pursuit would be vacuous if she weren't capable of hurting my feelings. If she accepted, she'd be accepting a man with only one thing on his mind. I'd make an object of her. Just enough to let her know she's worthy of it.

I eyed Dolly and considered the course ahead. It would be an aesthetic pursuit of worldly longing. I'd grow to want her. It could be done.

- - -

I was beginning to wonder if I was immune to alcohol intoxication. I've read that many Native Americans lack the enzyme to break down alcohol, and can be drunk for days on only a drop of liquor. Perhaps I was the opposite. Perhaps I had overactive glands that produced the alcohol-consuming enzyme in freakish abundance. Puppa had been a functional alcoholic; so functional, in fact, that I hadn't known about his condition until illness forced an end to his covert drinking. His lush life was "a contributing factor," the doctors said. With the exception of the pinkie affair, and a handful of slips and blackouts, Puppa had exhibited a deft inebriation. I had attributed this to strength of character, but maybe it was enzymes! Enzymes that I inherited! The Chivas calmed me. I felt a certain *joie de vivre,* no doubt about it, but I attributed this to the titillating strangeness of the environment. I was like a space explorer crash-landed on an unknown world.

So the alcohol didn't seem to work for me, but it appeared to be having a profound effect on everyone else. Its reputation as a "social lubricant" was proving out. There was a drink in every hand. They clanked them together; raised them in celebration of small triumphs. In idle moments—moments that would otherwise be filled with awkward silence—the patrons used their drinks as crutches and hobbled their way toward the next satisfying encounter. I found it hard to believe that anyone would drink the stuff for flavor's sake. Maybe everyone hated it. Communal suffering has been known to draw people together. I treated myself to another libation. My *joie de vivre* swelled. I was growing more comfortable in my surroundings.

I observed the women. It was my first time in a saloon; but even knowing as little as I did, it was clear that Mother's was not a place where beautiful women congregated. This was to my benefit. For me, a perfect ten is a perfect zero. I won't even masturbate to the thought of a beautiful woman. The ones are my tens. I'm a smooth operator with the twos. Three and above is risky business. *What's* wrong *with her? Is she mentally ill? Planning to use me in some kind of satanic ritual? Whoring herself, in hopes that I'll fund her drug habit?* An ugly man's dignity comes only through force of will.

Terrance played on. I drank. I helped myself to some peanuts. Communal snacks are always rank with fecal matter, but I had to give Connie credit—she'd made a good choice in serving peanuts as a complimentary hors d'oeuvre. The shells protected the nuts from unwashed hands. I didn't care for the unsanitary way in which the shells littered the floor, but this behavior seemed to be encouraged, and there was a primitive satisfaction in cracking the nuts and tossing the husks over your shoulder.

Sitting on the bar, next to a basket of nuts, were some slips of paper. They looked like this:

Your Name: ____________________

Your Request: ____________________

Check one of the following:

☐ I want to sing!

☐ Sing it for me, Terrance!

☐ Play me the original record!

There was a scattering of golf pencils too, and I took one up and wrote my name, checked the "Sing it for me, Terrance!" box, and then took a moment to consider the implications of "Your Request." The concept was disturbing. Why Terrance would take such an egalitarian approach was beyond me. Did he really expect these nitwits to make informed musical decisions? Was Terrance's internal songbook so vast that he could play *any* random tune from memory? He was pushing the democratic process too far; placing too much faith in the wisdom of the common man. The masses should not be given the ballot in matters of art. I, as a man of refinement, understood the great responsibility of "Your Request." It wasn't enough to choose a song I liked—it had to be something that the group would recognize and enjoy. It also had to be a good fit for Terrance. I wanted to pick a song that he could really kick the stuffing out of. It was an opportunity to show off my good taste, and I didn't want to blow it. I settled on my choice and summoned Connie.

"I would like to submit a request to Terrance, but I'm afraid I won't be able to press through the crowd and get it to him. I would also hate to lose my seat, and in turn, the pleasure of your company. Might it be possible for you to pass this slip along to him?"

I held the paper out to her. She looked at it as if it were a dead mouse. I smiled up at her, wiggled my eyebrows, and waved the slip back and forth in a teasing way. Her expression asked: *Are you serious?* I just kept wiggling my eyebrows.

"Okay," she said, relenting. "But only this first time. After that, you have to bring it up to him just like everyone else."

"You've made me feel very welcome, Connie. Thank you."

There was another worker behind the bar; a young

man who served as dishwasher and busboy. Every so often he'd leave the bar and disappear into the crowd, to return with a tray full of empty glasses and spent beer bottles. Connie went to him, and they held a private conference. She pointed out some things that needed doing, and he nodded along with her instructions. Then she handed him my slip of paper, and he disappeared into the crush once more.

⸻ ⸻ ⸻

Time passed, the crowd executed its slow, circular churn, and I was able to draw a complete model of the saloon's occupants. The front door opened and closed every few minutes, granting entrance to cool bursts of air and an array of cretinous characters. The Alluring Librarian was not cretinous, nor was she among them.

Her absence was like a dull ache—or maybe I was just a little queasy from all the smoke, and from the ethyl and peanut slurry sloshing in my stomach. I put a philosophical spin on it. My longing was not for her, but to be rid of any longing I might possess. Beautiful women never want for attractive escorts. She'd likely arrive with some hipster hunk on her arm. Such a sight would serve as a visual illustration of facts I already knew. If she came alone, she wouldn't be so for long. I'd have to machete my way through brambles of jackanapes just to get near her. There I'd be, in my "Munchkin Bad Boy" costume, smiling at her with my little gremlin face. We'd be outside the structures that permitted our affable acquaintance. She'd recoil. Her eyes would tell the truth, as they had the first time we met. It might be enough to cure me.

The music was heavy in the atmosphere but had faded from my attention. Terrance finished another song. I was lost in thought, so I scarcely noticed the transition to quiet. Then Terrance announced my name over the PA system.

"Buddy! Where are you, Buddy?"

I didn't know that he'd announce my name. At most, I thought he might give a dedication. "This one goes out to my man Buddy," or something along those lines. I certainly didn't expect to be made the center of attention. I pulled my hat down over my eyes and burrowed into the bar.

"He's over here!" cried Oleg. Had I been near him, I would have stomped his foot.

Silence. I could feel their monstrous eyes burning into my back. I wanted badly to take a shot of snuff but feared that my actions would be mistaken for illegal drug use. I would have to rely on the fortifying aspects of my new prescription. I downed the scotch and pivoted on my barstool. They were all staring at me, every one of them, and their eyes reaching out, clawing at me like the talons of some prehistoric bird. I set my jaw. My legs were shaking, but I commanded them to cease their cowardly vibrations and *obey!* and I took a deep breath and set my feet on the footrest of the barstool and stood erect. I rose to a height above them, and they were looking upward, gawking, awestruck, like a pack of natives undecided on whether I was God or lunch.

Terrance spotted me and offered a warm smile. He was bathed in stage light and floating in a haze of cigarette smoke. His banjo was slung casually over his shoulder.

"Everybody, this is my friend Buddy. This is his first time at Mother's, so let's give him a warm welcome!"

Suddenly I was being applauded. It was a polite kind of applause, nothing too enthusiastic, and quite frankly chilling. Who applauds a stranger for nothing? I gave the crowd a quick tip of my hat and sat back down, into the safety of the shadows.

"So, Buddy—you picked a great one. One of my favorites." He made some quick tuning adjustments and settled into his stance. "If I get this wrong, my friend will beat me with a sack of marbles. Inside joke. It's called 'Mr. Pitiful.' It goes like this."

Music, like an explosion. Terrance operated the banjo like a dual-purpose weapon. In a blur of syncopated handiwork, he pounded out an up-tempo beat on the head while simultaneously plucking out a funky rhythm. The groove went right to everyone's hips. Terrance sang like a man possessed by demons.

"They call me Mr. Pitiful.
Baby, that's my name.
They call me Mr. Pitiful:
That's how I got my fame. . . ."

The floor bowed toward the earth and then rose upward, toward the heavens, and everyone, *everyone,* was dancing. There is no name for this type of dancing. It was a simulated orgy; dry-humping set to a beat. The dance was just a pretense. The laws of personal space were repealed, replaced by an edict to grope and fondle. I was witness to a mating ritual. I'd intended to observe the animals at a safe distance, and like a fool I'd climbed right into the cage.

"But people just don't understand
What makes a man so blue.
They call me Mr. Pitiful
Because I lost someone just like you. . . ."

A pair of ladies ejected themselves from the orgiastic mass and came to stand before me. They were handsome women. Far too handsome to be a target of my affections. One of them was a mousy blonde, the other a brunette, and the blonde shouted, "Are you Terrance's friend?" right into my ear. I recoiled and proceeded to massage my aching eardrum with my pinkie. She seemed oblivious to the permanent hearing damage she had caused and just stood there, palpitating with the music.

"I suppose," I said.

She leaned in again, and this time I created a barrier with my hand, restricting her access to my ear canal.

"You want to dance with us?"

Except for Mummy, no woman had ever asked me to dance before, and now I was being asked to dance with two handsome women at once! Sexual butterflies invaded my lower abdomen. My imagination flashed and we were transported to my chambers, the three of us, and we were nude, slithering about on satin sheets, our bodies twisted in an erotic ménage. Shameful, I know. I was the ugliest man in the bar. Mother's was stocked full of ugly, but it was all the same brand; the familiar kind that is the hallmark of bad breeding. I'm not just ugly—I'm *irregular.* I'm *strange looking.* Mating with me is an unpredictable genetic risk that no handsome woman would ever take. They wanted Terrance. He was the prize stud, and I was the donkey. Terrance had introduced me as "his friend," without qualification, and for all they knew we were bosom chums. They didn't want to dance with me—they just wanted to ingratiate themselves to the chocolate balladeer.

"Not interested," I said coldly.

The brunette leaned in and grabbed me firmly by the arm.

"Oh, c'mon!" she shouted. "Don't be lame."

The blonde grabbed my other arm. I was being molested by a pair of lusty broads! Their lust was for Terrance, and I knew this, and I resented it. Dignity compelled me to resist.

"Unhand me! I am not in the mood for dancing!"

They had the strength of milkmaids. I struggled helplessly. They yanked me from my stool and dragged me through the sweaty sieve of bodies to a place in the center of the room, not ten feet from the stage. A tangle of humanity loomed above me, but this time the mass was shaking and twisting, like a humid jungle tossed by a storm. A gyrating buttock hit me in the face. A swinging arm whacked me on the shoulder, and someone stepped on my foot. I was about to scurry away when one of the girls stood behind me, set her hands firmly on my hips, and guided my rump into the cradle of her *mons pubis.* The other faced me directly and spread her body over me like a smear of mayonnaise. I was made the meat of a very tasty sandwich.

I was being used. They were making a show of it, and it was all for Terrance, but at that moment I didn't care. To the backside, it was bump; to the front side, grind; I followed their lead and did my best to simulate the movements of the other dancers on the floor.

Terrance was dancing too. He kept his knees locked and swung his legs out to the side as if propelled by springs. My partners cried out for Terrance's attention. They waved their arms above their heads and pummeled me with their bodies and they caught Terrance's eye, and he smiled at them, and then at me, and gave a coy wink.

I located the beat and began snapping my fingers. The rhythm worked its way down my arms, into my chest. My head bobbed, and the beat oozed down my hips, to my knees, to the very tips of my toes, and before I knew it I was dancing of my own volition. I closed my eyes and allowed the music to soak into my bones. The women caressed me, and I took this as an invitation and caressed back. I grasped the blonde about the hips and operated her pelvis in concert with my desires, and then I reached back and stroked the twizzling flanks of the other. The blonde slid her hands inside my blazer. The brunette spanked my bottom—and I deserved it, for I was a very naughty boy.

And then the song was over. We offered our gratitude at the top of our lungs. Terrance was exhausted. His T-shirt was soaked with sweat. I was a mess of soggy cashmere and leather. It took me a moment to readjust to the static world.

He set his banjo on a stand. The remote was in his back pocket, and he took it up and aimed it at his AV table. A hard rock ballad materialized in the speakers, and he hopped down from the stage and pressed through the throng.

"You made it!" he said, his teeth shining.

He reached down to shake my hand, but the blonde intercepted the gesture. She embraced him, planted a kiss on his cheek, and said something into his ear. Terrance laughed, feigned an expression of shock, and leaned in to respond. The look on her face suggested that he'd said something fresh, but it could have been anything. *Have you tried the peanuts?* It was his nearness that got her. The brunette swept in. She slithered her hand around his waist, pulled him close. When Terrance turned to me, he did so with a milkmaid under each arm.

"Whatdaya think?" he asked.

My expectations had been correct. The bar was filthy. Dangerous possibilities were as thick as the smoke that hung in the air, and it was cheap and sordid, and common, and I had been right about *all of that*, and none of it mattered so long as Terrance was on that stage. "Master of Ceremonies." Never had a title been apter.

"It's . . . fun," I said.

A kiss for the blonde, a kiss for the brunette, and he freed himself. He patted me on the shoulder.

"The fun's just started."

He raised the remote, twiddled it, and the rock ballad cut off. Some quick button presses, and in moments a beat emerged from the speakers at full volume. The sound was like something out of a cheap Casio keyboard. Electronic beeps and tones. A deep male voice came in after a few measures and commanded everyone to "get funky."

"Cha Cha Slide!" cried the blonde. The crowd swelled once more. *Everybody clap your hands,* the voice ordered, and the dancers clapped as one. *To the left . . . to the back now y'all,* and my feet did as they were told. The room shook. *One hop this time, right foot let's stomp,* and Terrance stomped and Oleg stomped and Viktor and the railroad engineer and the two milkmaids stomped and Dolly slapped the armrests of her wheelchair. We were dancing. *Left foot let's stomp, cha-cha real smooth.* We were a multicelled organism. One flesh. Ancient instincts stirred within. We were dancing together.

- 10 -
BREAKFAST SURPRISES

Get in, get out—that's my motto. Once you've got what you came for, there's nothing to gain by hanging around. Leave. Hang up the phone. Those who linger are sure to have their good works undone.

We danced the Cha Cha Slide. Terrance returned to the stage, and I watched him perform a few more songs, I finished my drink, and then, like a draft through a doorjamb, I effervesced into the night.

- - -

I awoke the following morning. I was lying on my bed, nude, face down and crossways, atop the ruffled flounce of my satin bedspread. My nudity was unusual. Longshoremen sleep in the buff, not gentlemen, and I had an array of fine pajamas that I always donned before bedtime. There was a crust on my eyes. My mouth was vile with residue. It was a disgraceful state to find oneself in.

Thank goodness for my bedchamber. The motif of this space serves three functions: artistic (my writing), recuperative (my sleeping), and erotic (you get it). The walls are pink. "Schauss pink," the shade is called. The bed is an Elizabethan four-poster. It's a prized possession. Curtains open, the bed is elegant, romantic, like a stage in a grand old theater, upon which all manner of fantasies—comedic, dramatic—have been expertly performed. With the curtains closed, the bed is like a bunker. Total darkness. It's the way I prefer to sleep.

I could recall leaving the bar; but the walk home, and whatever followed, was coming up blank. I sat up and scanned my surroundings. Where were my clothes? I was not a willy-nilly clothing-tosser. I had a system. Worn articles get hung on the oak valet. Each article is inspected and assigned a status—soiled, wrinkled, all-clear—and attended to as necessary. I eyed the valet. It was unburdened by garments.

Had someone slipped me a mickey? I stood and probed my anus for signs of unauthorized coitus. All seemed good. I crossed to the cheval mirror. My eyes looked like two urine holes in the snow, and my color wasn't good, and I was overdue for a manscaping, but there were no mysterious marks or injuries.

I toddled out to my chambers and searched for the shorn garments. They weren't on the floor, or hanging on the coat stand, or tossed on the Chavanon loveseat. I gazed toward my office space.

"Egad!" I exclaimed aloud.

The previous night's ensemble was seated at my workstation. It was perfectly arranged—as if I'd been working at my desk, and suddenly melted away inside the clothing. The bowler was perched atop the office chair. The leather blazer was laid on the chair back, with the left sleeve resting on the armrest, and the right sleeve extended out, onto the desk, as if operating the computer's mouse. I moved to explore. The cashmere sweater was inside the blazer, and laid in as neatly as a jacket lining. The charcoal trousers were laid on the seat itself, and my shoes were on the floor, directly below their appropriate trouser cuffs.

Why would I do such a thing? I've been known to lay out sartorial tableaus—what clotheshorse doesn't?—but I always used my bed as the moodboard, and I never went to the trouble *after* a wearing. My workstation was on. My snuff tin was open on the desk. I punched the spacebar to wake my machine. Outlook was open, and within Outlook, an open message.

> Buddy, sorry for the wait. Trip to China was extended. Taking Thur-Fri off. Talked numbers with team. Can you do $30,000?
>
> Paula Hixon
> -Sent from my Blackberry

I blinked at the screen. That $30,000 would push me past a threshold I'd been closing on for some time. When the HixonSmythBoutiques.com site was complete, and when the check was cashed, I'd be a self-made millionaire.

My total wealth was about to reach an appropriate level.

"At Hayes Interactive, we can always find a way to work within your budget," I said to the empty room.

It's tacky to talk turkey. I'd avoid the figures if I could, but they play a pivotal role in my tale. Please forgive me.

Cash, which one could pull together at a week's notice, and shove in a bag, and carry down the street. That's the kind of millionaire I'd be. "Liquid." It's not much in the grand scheme, but quite something for a twenty-eight-year-old nobody; for a grubby little hustler who works solo, in his private chambers, by way of phone and email, and has never met a client face to face; for a hunchbacked masturbator who lives with his mother and grandfather, in the provincial cesspool of South Ilium.

It didn't start as a grand scheme. I was simply looking for something I could do. The first year brought $17,000. I was delighted by the figure because it allowed me to pay my share. The next year, $28,000. I couldn't imagine doing better. Year three: $78,000. I was getting passed around. I had become a secret asset—that "guy upstate" who could do the work, who was always available, and who had no ambition beyond payment. Year four: $145,000. I got wise. I began inspecting the innards. I realized that I wasn't selling web pages, or web applications, or digital marketing materials. I was selling *hours.* The client would ask, "How much?" and I'd say "Eight hours," which wasn't a price, but a multiplier of the $78/hr. they already knew.

It was a special time. Perhaps the only time in human history when such shenanigans were possible. My clients were "project-managing" technologies that they didn't comprehend. Those who could comprehend—the members of their IT departments (if they even had such staff)—were salaried employees. The hustler, if granted access, will always outperform the nine-to-fiver. There's a popular understanding of how companies exploit workers—see *Das Kapital*—but there's a self-serving ignorance, among the working classes, of how the worker exploits back. Productivity, reader. This is what the worker steals. Languid lunch breaks; shirking of unwanted tasks; in a bit late, out a bit early; flirtations with coworkers; sports betting pools; Secret Santa; chatter around the water cooler; prevaricative bathroom behavior. The list goes on.

My clients are all in marketing. Television, radio, print: these were their areas of interest. They understood these platforms. They were schooled in them. Growing up, they dreamed of working in these media, on the creative side, for what is the marketer but a thwarted actor, a thwarted writer, a thwarted artist? The Internet was a dirty, unwanted interloper. Dot-com was not a thing they could name-drop to friends.

"We'd prefer to keep this one in-house, but our web team can't get to it for two weeks, and then it will take them another two weeks to complete. Can you give me an estimate?"

"Eight hours. I can have it done on Wednesday."

"Great!"

Eight Buddy Hayes hours. That's the product. How long the work actually took—how an eight-hour gig might only require four hours of labor on my part—was irrelevant. In the world of exploited productivity, my eight-hour product was bargain basement. On my best day ever, I worked an eight-hour gig that took me four, another eight that ended up taking five, a six that took three, a five that took two, a three that took one, and a couple of twos that took half an hour apiece. It all made for a savage day—sixteen hours of bleary machine work—but I was able to bill thirty-four, and my actual hourly for the day, $165.75, and a total takeaway of $2,652.

Year five: $165,000. Year six: $200,000. I've been holding around there ever since.

I'm not a hard worker by nature. Ask Mummy. I was a lazy child, and I have the soul of a lazy adult. If I had my choice, I'd do nothing but write. Oh, the soft world of letters. That's the world I'd prefer to inhabit, and I might have gotten there more quickly had I not tripped headlong into the pig trough of earning potential. Hard work is not a special thing when the annum is celebrated with six figures. I'm an authentic picaro, ruined by opportunity.

I performed a long turn in the hot 'n' sudsy. The loofah scoured every nook and cranny. I emerged from the steam and dressed for breakfast. Silken pajamas, eggshell blue. Satin smoking jacket, forest green with black lapels. I regarded myself in the cheval. Buddy Hayes, self-made millionaire. They say the first *m* is the hardest. I intended to push harder still—not for position, or for recognition, but for total control of my existence.

Eight A.M. The smell of breakfast and, shortly after that, the ring of Mummy's tea bell. The chiming had a Pavlovian effect on me. I bounded down the stairs, hungry for sustenance and human contact.

I stepped into the den. The butler's cart was set in typical fashion. Puppa was in position. Mummy stood beside him, tying his bib into place—and there was Terrance, seated in a spot next to mine. He smiled up at me over the rim of his coffee cup.

"Oh, Buddy," Mummy said. "You look awful!"

"It's a work-related deficiency. I've been nothing but a brain for the past four days. My body is a spent husk. Hello, Terrance."

He greeted me warmly. I took my place and fixed a coffee. We watched in silence as Mummy seated Puppa's snorkel/straw into his mouth. Terrance eyed the contraption with great interest.

"So," I asked after a time, "to what do we owe the pleasure of your visit?"

Mummy gave me the hairy eyeball.

"I invited him," she said. "And he was very generous to accept the invitation."

I harrumphed loudly.

"It's his day off, Mummy. You're imposing on his private time."

"Terrance is a grown man, Buddy."

"It's no imposition!" Terrance interjected.

I avoided eye contact with our guest. An inevitable topic loomed, and it was not a thing I wanted to discuss. The music night. He'd want to know what I thought; and I would have been happy to tell him, but not over breakfast, and certainly not in front of Mummy. I searched for a way to silently communicate this to Terrance. Telepathy was off the table. I'd already tried it on him, with zero success. My troubled mind considered various gesticular options, but my gray matter was like chowder, and by the time I settled on one—head shake, finger pressed to lips, conspiratorial wink—I'd forgotten that Mummy was in the room.

"What was that?" she asked.

"What was what?"

"That 'shush' you just did?"

"Oh. Quite right. I was trying to inform Terrance—nonverbally, you see—that your curiosity is insidious, and he need not bend to it. Terrance has earned his downtime. What he does with it? How he spends it? That's his business and none of ours."

The harelip scar increased in temperature.

"Why don't you let Terrance speak for himself? We were just talking about his music night."

"Oh?" I asked dumbly.

"Yes. He hosts it on Wednesdays. Remember?"

"That's right. You'll have to forgive me. I thought *today* was Wednesday."

Not true, of course. I was trying to confuse matters.

"You see what I told you?" Mummy said to our guest.

"He works nonstop for days on end, just sitting at his desk, poking at the computer like some kind of . . . robot! And he comes downstairs, and he acts like a robot. I've got a robot for a son. Tell him it's not healthy."

He turned to me and smiled—"It's not healthy," he said—but his tone suggested that he was placating Mummy on my behalf.

"So it's Thursday," I said, throwing up my hands. "My circadian rhythms have turned to experimental jazz." I turned to Terrance. "I can still read a clock, though. You must have been up quite late, what with your 'music night' and all. Why are you here so early?"

This was a softball version of the question I really wanted to ask: *Why are you interrupting a sacred family ritual?*

"It's the time I gave," said Mummy through gritted teeth. "And we're *very* glad he could make it."

The snorkel tube dangled from Puppa's mouth like a giant, overboiled macaroni. His patience exhausted, he emitted a series of muffled cries that said: "Hey, I'm ready to eat here!" Mummy apologized and inserted the tube into the BulletCup.

Puppa proceeded to siphon his strawberry-vanilla breakfast shake. Terrance was rapt. He seemed totally shocked by what he was seeing. His curiosity transformed the moment into a novel experience for us all. Puppa enjoyed being the center of attention. He bobbed his head and amplified the sucking sounds in an attempt to illustrate the usage of his unique appliance.

"What if he chokes?" Terrance asked, addressing Mummy.

"I worried about that," she replied. "But you know what? He never chokes with the straw. We have more problems with spoon feeding, if you can believe it."

"And he can breathe?"

"Thank you, Mummy," I said, inserting myself. "I'll pick it up from here. To answer your question, Terrance: Yes. Puppa breathes through his nose and can do so freely and easily. When he stops sucking, the excess liquid returns to the vessel below."

Puppa winked his good eye and nodded enthusiastically.

"The only danger is sneezing," I continued. "His meal has been known to shoot out his nose in such instances. If a sneeze is particularly violent—and this has happened only once—the meal can shoot out his eye hole!"

Terrance recoiled at the thought. In regards to human frailty, he was prepared for anything, but the possibility of such a thing took him totally by surprise.

"Are you serious?"

"Tomato soup! Surging from the socket like a spew of gore!"

"Don't dramatize!" Mummy snipped. "It was a little trickle."

"It was a *spew,* and not a thing I'd ever like to see again. I had nightmares for a month. Small price to pay, though. The occasional mess is no bother, so long as Puppa can eat on his own. The snorkel/straw is all about dignity."

Terrance showed a genuine interest in my invention. I'd never discussed the snorkel/straw with a palliative-care professional. It felt good to talk shop. He suggested that I was a good engineer. "Just an able tinkerer," I insisted. Mummy took her seat.

"Ruth tells me that you built a lot of the furniture here."

"Then *Miss Hayes* has been caught in another exaggeration. Puppa built the furniture. I'm just the custodian."

"You're the one who's caught—being falsely modest!" Mummy exclaimed. "Buddy helped with everything, and he's done a lot on his own."

"As I said . . . custodial work."

"What about the kitchen pantry? You did a wonderful job with that."

"A simple DIY job."

"And the breakfast nook?"

"It took me a month. Puppa could have done it in two days."

"And the floors?"

"You did the floors?" Terrance said. "They're beautiful."

"Terrance is always saying how beautiful the floors are," Mummy said as if his motion required seconding.

"I didn't *install* them. I just refinished them. Grunt work. Anyone could do it."

Mummy wanted to brag on me, and I wasn't having it. Puppa was the master craftsman, and I'd accept no false credit at his expense. I puttered in the woodshop from time to time, but not in the way he had. The shop hadn't seen serious work in years.

"Well, I couldn't have done any of it," Terrance said. "It's a skill, and you should be proud. It's one of my regrets. I wish I had taken shop and spent a little less time in the music room."

"What an idiotic thing to say," I scolded.

"Seriously. Our house is a wreck. I want to do something about it, but we're talking some serious work and I don't have the knowledge to do it myself."

It was bold of Terrance to admit such a thing. The condition of a home speaks to the class of its occupants, so his pronouncement could only serve to diminish him in our eyes. I respected his honesty. He lived somewhere south of Franklin, in the single-story neighborhoods that had once been home to Italian and German immigrants. The area had gone black long ago, and Franklin Street had become an unofficial line of demarcation. "Old Town." That's what his neighborhood used to be called. Forgotten now. Little Italy, Little Germany, Pottery Row, the Southside docks—all a rubble of memory. Terrance lived "South of Franklin." That's all it was now.

Horrible. Offensive. I scribbled some mental notes. *White flight. Assimilation of US immigrants, first and second wave. Urban sprawl. Gentrification.*

Breakfast commenced. The spread featured poached eggs, potato latkes with sour cream, a small loaf of black bread, a selection of fresh fruit, and yogurt with blueberries. The Breakfast Surprise remained hidden. Terrance kept sneaking peeks at the silver platter, but he didn't inquire as to its contents.

"Mummy, our guest is curious about The Breakfast Surprise."

"Is it time for the big reveal?" She stood and lifted the silver lid with a flourish, like a waiter presenting a flambé.

"Smoked beef tongue!" I cried.

It was a gorgeous tongue, nearly a foot long. The cartilaginous root was the size of my fist. The flesh was pink, almost electrically so, with just enough caramelization on the fatty underside. I'm a stickler for even grill marks and the char on Mummy's tongue was a bit helter-skelter, but overall she had done an excellent job.

Terrance eyed the meat dubiously. It was clear that he'd never seen its like before.

"I made it just for you," Mummy said to Terrance, batting her eyelashes. "A little taste of New York City!"

"Oh . . . my . . . it's . . ." He acted as if she'd just presented him with a severed human foot.

"Smoked tongue," I said, matter-of-factly. "Like at Katz's Deli."

He took a deep breath and tried to rally himself.

"That's something. I've just . . ." His eyes returned to the tongue. His lips drew taut. "I've never actually *had* tongue before."

Mummy's color, which had been all rosy excitement, went to ash.

"I'm so sorry," she moaned. "I thought everyone in New York ate tongue. I thought it was a New York *thing*."

Too often, Mummy's naiveté is a source of embarrassment, but this time she was right on the money. Real New Yorkers *love* delicatessen. Beef tongue is one-third of the sacred deli trinity. Father: Roast Beef. Son: Tongue. Holy Ghost: Pastrami. The problem here—Terrance was not a real New Yorker. He'd been a temporary transplant. Mummy had given his taste more credit than it deserved, and there she was, wringing her hands like a little girl who had done wrong.

"How long did you cook this?" I asked, wafting the delicious aroma toward my nose.

"Six hours."

"Six hours! And last night—it must have taken a couple of hours to parboil and peel it."

"You have to peel it?" Terrance asked, sounding both interested and repulsed.

"It's a beef tongue, not a jar of peanut butter. It takes a little work to get it right. Eight hours of work, in Mummy's case." I was trying to guilt him. Mummy had gone to great effort. He'd try the tongue, or I'd toss him out on his ear.

There were a carving knife and fork on the tray, as well as a small bowl of vinegar-infused *jus*. I stood and proceeded to cut the tongue into thin slices. My disappointment with Terrance was tempered somewhat by my anticipation. I hadn't had tongue in months.

I took a piece of black bread and folded a fatty slice of tongue onto it, and gave the arrangement a quick dip in the brine.

"*Nostorovia,*" I said and slid the whole thing into my mouth. The tongue was juicy, and smoky, and salty, and perfectly tender. The flavor reminded me how long it had been since I'd had it last. I chirped with delight.

Terrance reached across the table, grabbed a substantial slice of tongue, and shoved it into his mouth. He did so in a flash—like a man who'd psyched himself up for a dare. His need to please had left him with an overstuffed mouthful of something unfamiliar. *Take that, philistine!* My eyes darted to the lid of the silver tray. If necessary, I would take it up, turn it over, and use it to catch Terrance's spray of barf.

He chewed carefully, as if the tongue were full of bones and he was scared of breaking a tooth. His eyes grew wide. He nodded his head. His chewing grew more rapid, he pumped his fists, and then, at last, he swallowed.

"That's *good,*" he said. "Really good."

"You like it?" Mummy begged.

Instead of answering, he took up a second slice, and a piece of bread, and dipped it as I had. Down the hatch it went.

"Oh!" he exclaimed. "It's like corned beef, only twice as tender!"

I'm proud of my prejudices. They're like marble blocks, cut from the rough quarries of my experience. I'd spent a lifetime stacking them up. By my teen years I had a wall; by my early twenties a battlement; and still it grew, year by year and block by block, until I had a fortress of prejudice. Why stray beyond the walls? My castle was appointed as I wanted it; filled with paintings and tapestries that depicted the world in terms I preferred.

Afro-Americans are not adventurous eaters. I'd cut that block in childhood, upon witnessing the awful slop that my classmates ate for lunch. The fried, the factory-processed; these were the limits of their enjoyment. I probably wouldn't have given it much thought had it not been for the way they mocked my provisions.

"What sick thing you got today, Snowflake?"

"Sardine-and-cucumber sandwich, seaweed salad, and cold gazpacho."

They'd laugh, gag, feign vomiting, and toss all kinds of vulgar insults at me. I ended up wearing my soup course on more than one occasion. My cuisine was just another excuse for their torture and ridicule, and I took it as every weakling must, but all the while I'd be thinking *there's a whole world of exciting flavors that you'll never know.*

Once, I claimed that my lunches represented a "speed-skating diet," and thereby added "Nancy Kerrigan" to the list of offensive handles used against me. *Liars invent. The virtuoso diplomat does compose original material.* I learned a valuable lesson.

Terrance had stepped into my culinary wheelhouse, and I expected him to fall flat on his face. Instead, he helped himself to a third slice of tongue.

We dined. Idle chitchat commenced. Terrance sampled each dainty and complimented every bite. Mummy tittered stupidly. I thought Terrance was spreading it on a little thick. He was acting like an alien from a planet where breakfast did not exist. Mummy removed Puppa's snorkel straw and spoon-fed him tiny samples of the various treats. She shredded and mashed them before doing so. Premastication was too intimate for mixed company.

"So what's the rest of your day look like?" Mummy asked Terrance.

"Boundaries," I admonished.

"It's called 'conversation,'" Mummy said.

"It's called 'prying,'" I admonished further.

"Our church offers a respite program on Tuesdays and Thursdays," Terrance said. "For seniors. Mom enjoys it, and it gives me a chance to do some visits and run some errands."

"Who do you visit?" Mummy asked.

"My patients. Like what we're doing now, only without the world-class cuisine."

Mummy luxuriated in the compliment. I was astounded.

"Let me get this straight. You visit *patients* on your day off?"

"If they ask, sure."

Mummy glowed. The "sex flush." I wanted to claw my eyes out.

"There's a place for you in heaven, Mr. Johnson."

"I enjoy it," he said nonchalantly, and then turned to me, and looked directly into my eyes. "No one does what I do for the money."

"So who's on your goodwill itinerary today?" I asked coldly. "After us, I mean."

"A young woman named Dolly."

His utterance sent shivers.

"Which Dolly?"

"Dolly. My patient."

"*The same* Dolly?"

"Are you sure you want to do this?"

"*Wheelchair* Dolly?"

"She's in a wheelchair, yes."

"*Singing* Dolly?"

"That's the one. I visit her every Thursday. I bring my banjo. If you were impressed by her singing, you should hear her play the piano. She's excellent."

"Who knew that Ilium was such a wellspring of hidden musical talent?"

"It's true."

"Last night was a real eye-opener," I said.

Mummy had been feeding Puppa with the salt spoon. The spoon slipped from her fingers and fell to the floor. The obnoxious *ting* of silver clanging on hardwood served as an exclamation to my outing.

"You *went*!?" Mummy cried. "Why didn't you tell us?"

Puppa smiled broadly and started grunting like a baboon. He knew of my intentions and was excited to observe the subject in open air. I crossed my arms over my chest, buzzed my lips, rolled my eyes. When hale, I'm as slick as an eel, but when sleep-deprived I've been known to slip on my own secretions. I wanted Dolly. Or, more aptly, I wanted to want her. I'd thought she was just another face in the crowd. Now I knew that she was one of Terrance's pet projects. If I played it right, he might wingman me to the ultimate triumph.

Exciting possibilities, but irrevelant to the matter at hand. Mummy was a bloodhound for gossip, and by God, she was going to sniff it out.

Fart, you geezer! Fart! I badly needed an assist and hoped that Puppa would provide one, but his lower intestinal issues would not prove a boon that day. I had to improvise, and so I took up my butter knife and speared a tangerine from the fruit-bowl centerpiece.

"Hi-yah!"

My strike was as fast as a cobra's. I lifted the impaled fruit and held it before me as if it were a still-beating heart cut from the chest of a slain opponent. I turned the blade and inspected my kill. Juice oozed through the pierced skin. I placed my lips and the point of penetration and slurped at the nectar. It was, admittedly, an odd thing to do, but I was desperate to break the rhythm of the conversation.

"Wow—I think someone needs a nap," said Mummy.

I slurped harder.

"That's disgusting," she scolded. "Stop sucking that orange at once!"

"It's a tangerine, you boob! Learn your fruits!"

I resumed my vigorous sucking.

"Buddy—could you please stop doing that?" Terrance asked politely. "It's sort of turning my stomach."

"How rude of me!" I said sarcastically. "The next time you violate someone's privacy, I hope this feeling of nausea will return to you."

"Not to make an argument, but I think you violated your own privacy."

"Revisionist history," I said, pointing at him with my tangerine-tipped cudgel. "You must have seen, and wanted to manipulate me into admitting it."

"Seen what?"

"My nascent desire!"

"For Dolly?" He was dumbstruck.

"What's this?" Mummy asked. "Did you meet a *girl,* Buddy?"

"I spotted a girl, not that it's any of your business."

"You can't be serious," Terrance said.

"What a monstrous thing to say," I replied.

"Tell me about her," Mummy said.

"Enough! I am terminating this thread at once. It is in clear violation of the Hayes Family Contract. Press further, and you can expect a lawsuit."

"Buddy has a policy—" Mummy said to Terrance.

"*We* have a policy," I interjected.

"—that we're not supposed to discuss anything he does after nine P.M."

"Anything *we* do. It's for your benefit too."

"I don't do anything after nine P.M.," Mummy said.

"That's private."

"I just watch television with Puppa."

"How nice. For *you*. Please keep it to yourself."

"Sometimes I read."

"Mummy! Enough! Our guest is going to think you're an old spinster."

Terrance clapped his hands together and said, "Okay, guys. I'm sure that Mr. Hayes doesn't like to see his family fighting."

We all turned toward Puppa. The old man's eye glittered with mirth.

A long silence followed. We took up our coffee cups, sipped, hid behind them. I could have endured that silence forever, as it was better than the alternative, but Mummy couldn't help herself.

"Well, maybe Buddy doesn't want to talk about it, but I do. How's your music night been going, Terrance?"

Terrance granted me a quick, apologetic look and then turned to Mummy. He told her that everything was going great, that attendance was growing, and that the owner was very happy with the response.

"What type of music do you play?" she asked. "Any of the same songs you played for us?"

"Yeah, Mummy," I said. "He plays 'Under the Bridges of Paris' to a roomful of drunks. After that, he moves into Broadway show tunes."

"Oh! It sounds wonderful. Like a cabaret."

I shook my head snidely.

"I love the standards," Terrance said. "I get an occasional

request for Frank Sinatra. That's always a lot of fun. But it's a bar, so they mostly ask for rock, R&B, and country. Songs you'd hear on the radio. It's funny. There are a lot of corny pop songs that people ask for, and I look at the request slip, and I'm like 'oh, no, this is going to be awful.' Then I start playing the song, trying to make it work, and once you strip it down to its basic elements, you find that the song is pretty good."

"Can you give an example?" I asked.

He thought for a moment. "Do you remember that song from the nineties titled 'If You Love Me,' by an all-girl R&B group called Brownstone? I played it yesterday."

"I do recall you singing a song with those words in the chorus. I was not previously familiar with it."

"They were a one-hit wonder, and that was their hit. Anyway, you can tell that 'If You Love Me' was written by a talented songwriter. And the record is good, but it all comes off a little . . . sugary. Like a cake covered in too much frosting."

"Oh—I like that analogy."

"Thanks."

"And you take these sugary cakes and scrape away the frosting."

"I don't have a choice, right? I'm just one guy with a banjo."

This conversation was, in some ways, a violation of my privacy policy. We weren't directly discussing my experience at Mother's, but we were talking about Terrance's musical philosophy, which I had witnessed in practice at that very location. Mummy would paint a picture of the event in her mind, and I'd be in it, dancing and drinking and making a fool of myself. It was untoward. A mother should not fantasize about her son in this manner. I should have ended the discussion then and there, but I was too interested to draw back. It was the first time I had ever spoken to a real artist about his craft.

"About that banjo," I said.

"What about it?"

"Well . . . it's just that . . ."

I looked to Mummy for approval. Her face was blank. She had no inkling of the course I was trying to chart.

". . . It's not an instrument that one associates with Afro-American musicians."

"Buddy!"

"*Buddy* me all you want! It's the truth."

"Please excuse my son," she said to Terrance. "As he said, he hasn't been sleeping. In fact—I think it might be a good idea if he excused himself and took a nap *right now*."

"No. Buddy's right. You don't hear banjo in modern black music, which is weird. The banjo is an African instrument."

And he proceeded into a lengthy dissertation on the banjo's history. They were originally made from hollowed-out gourds, slaves introduced them to America, so on and so forth. I had already researched the topic as part of my Anti-Bias Reprogramming, so his insights bored me. Mummy was all in, right up until Terrance mentioned the S-word. The mere mention of slaves—even though it was a black man doing the mentioning—caused her to shrivel. Slavery, for her, was a historical concern, best pondered in the context of PBS documentaries. Her white guilt was painted on her face.

"So your mastery of the instrument is something of a reclamation project? A sort of 'getting back to roots?'"

He shrugged.

"That's part of it. Surprise is the bigger part. It's the thing in any performance. There're a lot of preconceptions about the instrument. About what it's capable of. And there are a lot of preconceptions about black musicians and the type of music they're expected to perform. I like to play with both. Put the banjo into places people don't expect. Put myself into places people wouldn't figure. If you're at a bar and you see a white man on stage tuning a banjo, you have a pretty clear idea of what's going to happen, and you're either up for that or you're not. When it's a black guy? You almost *have* to stay. 'What's *this guy* about?' That's what I've been chasing after for the past few months."

Terrance possessed a wide-angle view of performance. He presented ideas that I'd never considered.

"Now, about your flyer."

"The racist one?"

"Exactly! I was deeply offended by it. If I understand you, 'offense' was the very thing you meant to achieve."

"Call it 'cognitive dissonance.'"

"It's too much."

"Just a little too much, I think."

"A *lot* too much, in my opinion."

"I can live with it."

I pressed him further.

"Where did you get the image?"

"From the internet. Just search 'racist banjo player.' There's a ton of them."

Later—and in the interest of furthering my anti-bias education—I did just that. I found Terrance's image on the first page of returns and clicked through to the source. The Library of Congress. It was part of their "minstrel poster collection." Calvert Company, Detroit, Michigan, circa 1892. It was one of a set, and that set, part of a larger canon of racist nineteenth-century lithography. Interesting stuff. Not a thing I'd wish to collect.

"Let's go further back," I said. "What was your playing like in the past? Before you started chopping away at these race-based genre restrictions?"

"I've only had the banjo for a few years. It was never my main instrument."

I was astonished.

"You're able to play *other* instruments?"

"Sure. I've been playing piano all my life. Also guitar. Drums. I can even do some trumpet and trombone."

"Jesus Christ!"

"Charles William Hayes!"

"Sorry, Mummy." Back to Terrance. "How long have you been playing the banjo?"

"Seriously playing, about three years."

"Three years!? But you're a virtuoso."

"It's not a huge leap from the guitar."

"So why not just play the guitar?"

"For all the reasons I told you."

His musical talents seemed depthless. The banjo was just a lark for him! The man belonged at Carnegie Hall, not wearing scrub pants and crocs!

"How is it possible that you know so many songs?" I asked. "Are you just a good memorizer?"

"Only with music. I hear a song once, and I've just . . . got it. Every once in a while someone will give me a stumper, and I'll see if I have the karaoke CD for it, and I'll play along to that. That doesn't happen much. I just know a lot of music."

"You're like a genius!" said Mummy.

"*Like* a genius is a good way to put it," Terrance joked. "I can remember a thousand silly songs, but I can't remember my own cell phone number."

"These people at the saloon—and you should see them, Mummy—represent the dregs of society. Terrance accepts their requests, which are almost always tasteless, and reworks them. Infuses them. Truly, Terrance, you're not taking requests like some tacky wedding DJ. You're taking inspirations."

There was a shifting of color in Terrance's cheeks, from dark walnut to a tawny port. A question was thereby answered. Blacks are capable of blushing.

"I don't agree with the whole 'dregs of society' bit, but thank you for the compliment."

Another silence followed. Mummy offered Terrance more coffee, which he took. She turned her attention to Puppa.

"How are you doing, Dad?"

"Goooo!"

"Isn't it nice to have Terrance over for breakfast?"

"[Gurgle]!"

She stood, removed Puppa's bib, and cleaned his face with a napkin.

"Well, it sounds like you're having a good time." She continued wiping the chin and kept her eyes on her work, so it was unclear to whom she was speaking.

"If you're not having fun, it's not worth doing," said Terrance.

Even with her back turned I could detect a look of mischief. I set the lasers in my eyeballs to "annihilate" and fired them into the back of her head.

"Oh, I know *you* do, Terrance. How could you not? It must be the most wonderful feeling in the world—doing something you're good at, having a room full of people there to appreciate it." She finished the cleanup, playfully pinched Puppa on the cheek, and turned back to face us. "I was talking to Buddy."

"I should have had the Contract notarized by an attorney," I sneered.

"I'm just glad you had a good time."

"I'm glad you're glad."

"I knew you would."

"No, you didn't."

"I was the one who said you should go."

"What would I do without you?"

She turned to Terrance.

"I don't think he's ever been to a nightclub before."

"Untrue!" I lied.

"I can only imagine how nervous he must have been."

"This is an outrage!"

"I said to him: 'It'll be fun. You'll make new friends. Maybe you'll meet a girl.' And look what happened!"

I'd had enough. I threw my napkin down on the table and stood up, clattering my place setting as I went.

"Good job, Mummy. I feel completely violated. You have spoilt the morning. Now, if you will excuse me, Terrance, I must go and earn a living."

How I wished I was wearing a cloak at that moment. Had I been, I would have stomped my foot, swept my cape around me, and made a dignified exit. I was still in my moccasin slippers, so when I did stomp it sounded more like a package of cotton balls hitting the floor, and I had no cape, so I popped the lapel of my smoking jacket and scuffed my way to the door.

"I hope you come next week," Terrance called out behind me. "I enjoy having you there."

I pushed forward, down the hallway and into the drawing room, up the stairs and into my lair. I had a million things to do. Once more unto the breach.

- 11 -
THE NEW REGULAR

I look forward to my Friday morning excursion, but I am forced to skip it on occasion. Work comes first, and sometimes my workload doesn't allow for a trip to the public archive. Such was the case that week. I had mountains to climb. It was a convenient excuse, but not fully honest. I had hoped to see her at Mother's. She hadn't shown. My mind was heavy with thoughts of what might have been. Flirtation? Outright rejection? I was awash in hallucinated scenarios. My unhealthy fascination was giving way to illness. I hoped that an application of truancy would serve as a soothing balm.

I'd be looking at a fifty-cent library fine. It chafed me. I was eager to begin my life as a self-made millionaire, and I felt that any debit, however small, was sending me in the wrong direction. I'm a bit of an aesthete, and my taste is for the finer things, but I'm no spendthrift. Consider my sailor costume. Some would call it an extravagance. I considered it an essential prop, as an inspiration for home theatricals and erotic play, to be used and reused down the years. Going chintzy may be cheaper, but chintz defeats the purpose. I'm inspired by Edith Head. She didn't dress the performer to look like a pirate, or a cavalier, or an Edwardian debutante; she dressed them to *be* those things. A costume is nothing if it doesn't inspire the wearer to inhabit a different life. Aesthetically, the choice is clear. As for the additional cost: if one invests in a sailor costume, and one properly cares for said sailor costume, then one need only buy a single sailor costume in one's life. Mine is theatrical quality, purchased online and on clearance. A coupon code conferred free shipping. Some live cheaply. I prefer to live well, with thrift in mind.

My library visits were part of this theme. A library card is more than a "passport to knowledge"; it's a savings card to frugal living! A trip to the library is not unlike a shopping excursion, except that the products are free, and good for you, and incapable of provoking buyer's remorse. You "shop," you leave with heavy armloads, and the amygdala receives its shot of consumer-grade heroin. Library membership is an on-demand shopping spree. Upward to prosperity!

Just not that week. I needed to recalibrate my chi.

* * *

The weekend came and went. With the exception of Sunday "man time," I worked straight through. Monday, Tuesday, and Wednesday, all a blur. Megan needed ten email blasts: cut, programmed, and ready to be delivered *yesterday*. My pharma client wanted an animated Flash banner—a 300x600—that advertised their newly released cold-sore gel. FamousFashionMagazine.com was having a problem uploading images via their CMS and they hired me to troubleshoot. New to the slate: Hixon Smyth Boutiques. I was running on a jet-fuel mixture of coffee and snuff. It was the busiest I'd ever been.

Not the ideal time to develop a new late-night habit, but I had to go back. To say that Terrance's music night had "exceeded my expectations" would be thin soup. It had stimulated my every organ! My synapses fizzed; my heart swelled with emotion; my liver was given a rigorous working out; when I was harassed (by way of peanut), my spleen went hot; my ears feasted on all they heard; my gonads surged with manly readiness. Before the event, I would have considered "escaping alive" as a triumph. I didn't expect to leave with a bundle of bonus prizes clutched under my arm. Wednesday night, 9:45 P.M. "That's enough for today."

Sex, reader. It was a palpable essence; one stink among the many; a prime note in the irreligious bouquet of Mother's. We were all there for it. I glued my back to the bar and watched. I wanted to see how it was done. How to deliver that first glance. How to roll it over into a second. The smile. That wordless statement of intent that the good ones master, and where *on earth* did they learn it? It seemed to be the key. The man sends out a smile, or the woman does; and if accepted, the smile would be returned, and then the two would break it off, as quickly as it started, and they'd look at their shoes or into their drinks, pretending, for a time, that the trade had never happened. Then, over the course of minutes or hours or an entire evening, they'd circle one another. Wide. Concentric. Aware of each other but unaware of this circling. More glances. An adult game of peek-a-boo. More smiles. He gets up the nerve, or she does, and the circles converge. This is the start of things.

I was a shotgun of glances and smiles that second night. Occasionally my buckshot would graze a target, but I never hit one true. I wasn't getting back what I was sending. I wasn't doing it right. I continued to watch.

Here and there, a parting of the crowd, and I'd get a full-on view of Dolly. I'd transmit my signal through the gap. Nothing but static in return.

"Eight dollars," Connie said, sliding my Chivas across the bar. I turned to face her.

"Here's twenty. Eight for the drink, two for the gratuity, and an additional ten, which will cover my entrance fee for the past two weeks."

Connie looked at the money as if it were a handwritten insult.

"Aren't you on the guest list?"

"I am, and I don't wish to be. It makes me uncomfortable. I'm no charity case."

She pinned the ten to the bar with her index finger and slid it back into her hand. The pair of fives remained where they were.

"You're not takin' anything from me. Terrance gets the gate. You wanna pay, talk to him."

I wasn't aware that Terrance and Connie had such an equitable arrangement. I did the math. The fire department had deemed Mother's suitable for sixty-two occupants, but Wednesday night attendance was closer to ninety. $5 x 90 = $450. A paltry sum considering Terrance's talent, but not bad for four hours of work.

I had a new question: Why was Terrance paying me to attend his music night? Each free pass was like five dollars taken directly from his pocket. And for what? What was he getting out of it? It certainly wasn't the pleasure of my company. Our interactions had softened, but an air of suspicion continued to hang over all our dealings. The obvious explanation—that he actually wanted to be my friend—was too saccharine to believe.

I was Terrance's pet troll. That's how they saw me. Word

had gotten around. I was forced to endure an interview process with each new acquaintance. *How are you doing? Been rainy, eh?* General barroom malarkey, until finally, and without fail, they'd trail on to the only thing that made me worthy of their interest. *So, how do you know Terrance?* His attention counted as currency. He bantered with me in spare moments. A minute here, five minutes there. It counted as a monopoly. My association was the envy of all.

Oleg occupied the stool to my left; Viktor, to my right. They had their request slips and each man agonized over his choice.

"This is hard!" exclaimed Oleg.

"It's like a test," said Viktor.

"Just think of a good song that everyone likes," I said. I'd already made my selection: "Send Me Some Lovin'" by Little Richard. Terrance would be impressed.

"I already *know* one that everyone likes, but you told us it's no good," said Viktor.

"'Chicken Dance'!" cried the other.

"No 'Chicken Dance,'" I demanded firmly.

Oleg sang, "With a little bit of this and a little bit of that now shake your butt" and flapped his arms furiously. His interpretation perfectly captured the spirit of the fat, flightless bird for which the song was named.

"In small doses it's okay," I said. "But you can't force it on us two weeks in a row. It's too much."

"Then why do they all dance when Terrance plays it?"

"They dance whenever Terrance plays anything. You can request the Chicken Dance once a month. That's all the Chicken Dance anyone can stand."

The idiot brothers returned to their impossible task, and I took the opportunity to observe the scene. Eleven P.M. The railroad engineer was there. His name was Leroy. He wasn't a real railroad engineer. Rather, model railroad hobbyist. *The* model railroad hobbyist. He was the president of a local society dedicated to the pastime. He was featured in magazines, so they said. Those who had seen his scale arrangements spoke of them with awe.

The Milkmaids were in attendance. Kerri and Kiera. They were elementary school teachers! I was appalled when I learned this. *I believe the children are our future* . . . and what chance did a juvenile mind have under the stewardship of these bawdy tarts? I considered the subject further. My opinion shifted. Terrance was nurse by day, bard by night. I was a new-media entrepreneur during business hours, aspiring novelist/gigolo after closing. Kerri and Kiera were pretty loose and sloppy, but so was everyone else. Better elementary than secondary, I decided. Boys should have to work for their masturbation fodder. Sixth grade is far too early to set up ePay on the spank bank.

Rodolpho, Luis, and the two Jorges—The Mariachi Quartet, I called them—were packed around a corner pocket of the pool table. The four of them ran a food truck: "The Cantina Wagon," which operated in semi-permanence near the paper mill in North Ilium. They invited me to "stop by anytime," and I intended to, first chance I got.

Dolly was at the foot of the stage, ogling Terrance with a religious intensity. She lived five blocks from Mother's, so I was told, in the rotten guts of South Ilium. The sidewalks there are like paths through ancient ruins, smashed to bits by the hammer of time. It's difficult to walk on them, let alone roll. It's a municipal disgrace. Dolly needed help with the trip, and this was provided by her mother—a careworn woman of middle age. They arrived minutes after I did. The entrance to Mother's features a concrete step, a high threshold, and nothing in the way of a ramp. Handicapped accessibility was provided by Tollbooth's muscles. Dolly rolled up to the front step, locked her wheels, and Tollbooth grabbed her chair by the armrests—while Dolly was *in it,* mind you—and then, without so much as a grunt, he levitated the apparatus upward and through the door. The man was as powerful as a forklift.

Dolly's entrance was a choreographed event. The mob welcomed her, and then parted, without having to be told to do so. Dolly rolled to her place. Her mother shared some words with Terrance, then with Connie, and then disappeared into the night.

There were other faces in the crowd—some familiar, some soon-to-be. I'd enjoy a few more servings of courage juice before making the rounds.

"We want to ask you something," said Viktor.

"It's been on our minds," said Oleg.

Viktor leaned in. For a moment I thought he might kiss me.

"What do you *do*?" Viktor whispered, as if he were asking a deeply personal question. I turned to Oleg. The sight of him was vertigo-inspiring. He was leaned in as well, and he wore the same grave look that his brother did.

"That's it?" I asked. "You want to know what I *do*."

"We've heard rumors," said Oleg.

What were people saying? I didn't advertise my vocation. There would be assumptions, of course. I had assumptions about everyone. Oleg and Viktor, for instance. I imagined them working behind a deli counter at the local supermarket.

"I do what I want," I said haughtily.

"Do you ever *do it* for people like us?"

What on earth did they think I was? A dope peddler? A male stripper? Sure, I was dressed a little flashy: seersucker jacket, straw fedora, herringbone trousers. All Jay Gatsby, nothing male prostitute about it!

"Okay, you perverts. What have you been told?"

"Perverts?"

"We're not perverts, Buddy."

"We're married. Married people aren't perverts."

"Married, huh?" My hand had found its way to my inside pocket, to the smooth plastic of Excalibur's housing. "To each other?"

I'd been trying to make friendly acquaintances. Instead, I had made myself the potential victim of a murder-rape. My reptilian cortex formed a combat strategy. I'd set my feet against the bar and eject away, backward, off of my stool. I was elbow to elbow with the brothers, and if they seized me I'd be caught in a vicious cross-pummeling. My aikido tumbling skills were not all that they should be, owing to the fact that a tripod does not move on its own, and Mummy is always "too busy to play cameraman while you flop around in the backyard." It'd be a hard landing. Better than being drawn and quartered by a pair of giant infants.

"Who told you!?" bellowed one.

"That's the joke," said the other.

My feet were pressed against the bar, but goateed Oleg slapped my back, and the impact bent me forward, and my feet fell to the footrests of my stool. I was ready to take my stun gun and electrocute myself.

Connie effervesced out of nowhere.

"This one's on me," she said. Her timing was impeccable. She set a fresh scotch before me, offered a thin, empathetic smile, and returned to her work.

"Okay, I'm lost. If you wish to explain, feel free. I would not be disappointed if you chose to drop the subject altogether."

"Our wives are sisters," said Viktor.

"Twin sisters," said Oleg. "Like us."

"Not like us," corrected the brother. "They're *sisters*."

"They're twins."

"But we're not twin sisters. That's what you said."

"I didn't say we were sisters!"

"You said that our wives were twin sisters, like us.'"

"He knew what I meant."

"He's confused."

I half expected them to start bonking each other on the head.

"I get it," I said, waving my hands. "You're twin brothers, married to twin sisters. Unique. Continue."

"Our friends are always joking: 'It's like the four of you are married.'"

"Like Mormons," said Oleg. "That's part of the joke. We're not really Mormons."

"We're Methodist."

I asked if their wives were identical or fraternal. Identical. I asked if they all lived in the same house.

"We used to, but now we have our own places."

"We work together every day. Me and Oleg. We're partners."

"Brothers get sick of each other too."

"I live at 43 Fourth Avenue. Oleg lives right next door."

"45."

"But we share a backyard. You should come by!"

"We'll grill hamburgs!"

I was getting a headache from whipping my head back and forth. The polite thing would have been to ask about their children, but I was afraid that their response would spin my melon loose.

"What business are you in?" I asked.

"We asked you first," said Viktor.

"I asked you second."

"I'm asking third," said Oleg. "Two beats one."

I suggested that we split the difference. I was never in the mood to discuss my work, especially with the technologically ignorant, but I was curious as to what they had heard.

"We've heard you make web pages," Oleg said.

It was strangely disappointing. The male prostitute angle had somewhat grown on me.

"I can't see how that constitutes a rumor," I said. "It's true. I'm a designer-slash-developer of web pages. So why all the intrigue?"

They huddled closer.

"It wasn't a rumor," confessed Viktor.

"Terrance told us," said Oleg.

"And he said you might not like it if we let anyone else know."

Terrance! I shot a glare at him, but he was under his AV table, fiddling with wires. My glare rebounded harmlessly off of his peerless buttocks.

"We were talking to him, and he asked us 'how's business?' and we told him business was good, and we talked about that, and other stuff, and he said we should get a website, and Oleg said 'we don't know anybody who makes websites,' and Terrance said 'yes, you do, Buddy makes websites!' Will you make a website for us, Buddy?"

Wonderful. Another local with $100 burning a hole in their pocket. "Hey, I got your number online, I need a webpage, I run a flower shop, do you have affordable rates?" I tell them $78/hr. and they choke on their tongues.

"All of my clients are from New York City," I said, pointing my nose in the air. "I don't deal in the local market."

"It wouldn't be a big website," said Viktor.

"Just some pictures and words and how to contact us," said the brother.

"You could do it when you have time," said Viktor.

"What's your business?" I asked tiredly.

"Novokhatsky Brothers Plumbing, Heating, and Cooling."

"That's you guys?" I was shocked. I had walked past their business a thousand times. It was down on Canal Street, in a repurposed warehouse. It was more than a two-man operation. There was the main building and a big concrete yard, and there were always quite a few cars parked there, and they had some red work vans with their logo painted on the side. You'd see the vans all over town. I did my own plumbing, so I had never used their service, but I knew that they had a good reputation.

I told them I was too busy. I'd be another month on the Hixon Smyth job, at least. When that site was done, I intended to take two weeks of staycation. Putter around the house. Spend more time with the family.

"I'm fully booked until the end of the spring," I told them, hoping they'd get the drift.

"Perfect! We can do it in the summer. Do you have a card?"

I didn't. Business cards are antiquated and bad for the environment. Oleg presented a couple of Novokhatsky Brothers business cards, told me to keep one, and had me write my information on the back of the other. What was the harm? I had no intention of taking the job—I dealt in New York City dollars, not South Ilium pesos—but there was no need to deny them too harshly. It was all bar talk. They'd forget about it. Or summer would come, they'd give me a call, and I'd give them the same excuse. Too busy. It would likely be true.

Minutes passed. I eyed Dolly and considered an approach. Just a hello. Maybe a compliment on her singing, maybe a mention of our shared association with Terrance. Light chatter. A gentle tilling of the soil.

"Evenin', everybody," a voice boomed, shaking my reverie. "Looks like the gang's all here. How are you?"

It was Terrance, of course. Everyone sprung to attention.

"My friend and I are going to do a song for you," he said. He held a request slip in his hand. My request slip. "Buddy, can you come up here? I don't know where you come up with these great songs."

He gave me a sly smile. My lips formed a giant *oh, no!*

"Thanks anyway," I called out. "I prefer to watch."

"Just get up here," he said, laughing.

"I checked the 'sing it for me' box!"

"Just get up here."

"You need to follow your own rules!"

"Everyone give a warm round of applause to my man Buddy!"

Bastard! He was encouraging the mob to peer-pressure me! They goaded me with claps and wolf-whistles. It was all part of the ritual. I'd never sung before. I was to be a "virgin" sacrifice, disemboweled by my own shame.

Oleg hollered "Don't be a chicken, Buddy!" so that everyone could hear, and his brother said "Yeah . . . or we'll make you dance the Chicken Dance!" Viktor placed his hand on my back and pushed, causing me to slide from my barstool. The cheers grew louder. Terrance had put me in a very uncomfortable position, and by the look on his face, it was exactly where he wanted me.

I skulked my way to the stage. I reached the foot of it, and there was Terrance, towering above. I trembled. My knees turned to door knockers. Terrance crouched down and offered me his hand. I took it, and he pulled me up and over the apron of the bandstand.

Faces. A roomful of faces, all staring at me. Their gazes were like crawling insects. The stage was only two and a half feet high, but it seemed much higher than that. I felt huge. Totally exposed. A small bank of stage lights illuminated our position, and I squinted at them, like a guilty perp in an interrogation room.

Terrance put his arm around me and leaned in close.

"It's easy," he said, away from the microphone. "I'll take the first verse, you take the second, I'll do the third, and we'll do the fourth together. It's a short song. You only have to sing four lines by yourself."

"But I can't *sing*," I said desperately.

"Everyone can sing. Just give it a try. There's almost no one here."

"*Everyone* is here. I don't even know the lyrics."

"We'll karaoke it. The words will be on the monitor."

"I've never done this before." My voice quavered. I was afraid.

"First time for everything. Follow me."

He placed a wireless microphone in my hand. It felt warm and greasy; certainly not the kind of thing I'd want to put near my mouth. And then, with a wave of his remote control, the music started. A 4/4 blues beat flowed from the speakers and filled the room. Terrance took up his banjo and quickly worked his way into the song. After a few notes, he was in full control. It was as if the recorded version followed him.

"Okay, here we go," he announced over the opening instrumental. "This is a Little Richard tune. It's Buddy's first time on the stage, so let's give him some support!"

Hooray! Do it, Buddy! Connie smiled. Oleg gave me

a double thumbs-up. One of the Jorges toasted me in the air. Dolly bobbed her head and snapped her fingers in time with the sexy groove, and Leroy the scale modeler gave me a solemn, reassuring nod.

Terrance crashed into the first verse.

"Send me some lovin',
Send it I pray;
How can I love you
When you're far away?"

My turn approached. I formed a simple plan. I would never be the best singer in the place, but I would try, with all my power, not to be the worst. He turned to me on that last line, and counted me in with four nods of his head. The moment of truth. Just don't be the worst. I sang.

"Why don't you send me your picture . . ."

I'm on key. That's the first thought that occurred to me. Compared to Terrance, my voice was feeble, but at least I wasn't off. Thc supportive cheers that followed were like food to a starving man. My emotions surged, and my confidence with them. I put a little mustard on the lyric.

". . . Send it, my dear
So I can hold it
And pretend . . . you are here."

Terrance tore at his banjo as if it were the source of all torment. He closed his eyes. Threw his head back. He played as if it was his honor to accompany me. I started shuffling my feet, then pumping my fist, and by the time Terrance entered into the next verse I was fully involved in the music.

"Can you send me your kisses?"

he sang.

"I still feel their touch . . ."

It wasn't my turn to sing yet, but for some reason, it felt natural for me to take the next two lines. Terrance sensed the impulse, and he encouraged me, with the slightest nod of his head, to follow my musical instincts.

". . . I need you so badly,"

I sang.

"I miss you . . . sooo-oh-oh much."

The spirit moved me. I aimed the lyrics directly at Dolly. I placed a hand over my heart, looked into her eyes, and finished the line with a coquettish air kiss. Her jaw dropped. There was a slight lolling of tongue. My flirtation went over like a dirty joke in church. No time to dwell. The final verse had arrived. Four lines, sung in unison. This would call for harmony. I had no idea how to do that. I decided to keep on singing as I was and allow Terrance to make the proper adjustments.

"My days are so lonely,"

we sang as one.

"My nights are so blue.
I'm here and I'm lonely.
I'm waitin' for you."

We were given a standing ovation. Terrance threw his arm around my shoulders. My smile was ear to ear.

"Ladies and gentlemen, give it up for Buddy!"

Their praise vibrated every molecule in my body. I wanted to adopt a triumphant pose; to throw my arms wide, thrust out my chest, to soak in their adulation; but modesty demanded otherwise. I waved, gave a small bow, and returned the microphone to Terrance.

For ten to sixteen hours a day, I sit at a desk, staring at a computer screen. After a while, I start feeling like a peripheral—like an accessory to the machine. Without music, I'd go mad. I have a collection of over ten thousand illegally downloaded MP3 files, and I keep them in constant rotation. Sometimes I listen to Pandora or streaming radio stations from overseas. I thought I was an expert. I thought I knew what music was. Then Terrance called me to the stage and put a microphone in my hand.

Until that day, music had been like a letter from a distant pen pal; the transcription of a moment I could not attend. Suddenly, it was alive! I'd taken part in its creation. I understood, for the first time in my life, what music actually was.

I dismounted the stage. There, standing by the lip, was a set of newcomers. I'd never seen them before. Four young black women, aligned in a row. They were sipping sugary cocktails through tiny red stirrers. On the left: a knockout. Slim, busty, with a push ponytail, highlighted ombre style from base to end. On the right: the unfortunate one. Short, stocky. Puglike features. She was nearly as ugly as I was. The two in the middle bridged the divide between the others. They had subconsciously arranged themselves in order of attractiveness. Taken together, they looked like an inverted *March of Progress* illustration.

"Good job!" said the beautiful one.

"Thank you," I replied. "It was my first time."

Her mouth was painted blood red, and it glistened, as if covered with the residue of her last man-eating.

"You're friends with Terrance?" she asked sweetly.

I inhaled deeply and considered the question.

"Yes," I said at last. "I suppose I am."

"I'm Angel. Nice to meet you."

She smiled, and placed her hand on my forearm. It was an outrageous gesture. I knew the score.

"Angel, eh? Did it hurt when you fell out of heaven?"

"Wow—never heard that one before."

"I know I don't have a chance with you. I just wanted to hear an *angel* speak."

She made a *yick* noise and rolled her eyes. I continued to play the creep.

"I didn't know that angels flew so low. But I'm glad you did, because from this distance I can see heaven in your eyes."

"You're Terrance's friend?" she asked again, this time in disbelief.

Her ulterior motives shone like coins in a wishing well. *How lucky,* she must have thought. *The ebony stud has a gremlin familiar. I'll flatter, then manipulate.* I abruptly broke off our conversation and turned my attention to the ugly one.

For a Caucasian man to rank as an authentic Casanova, he must have at least one Nubian notch on his headboard (the flip side is true for lascivious Othellos). My Anti-Bias

Reprogramming has a degree requirement: *Graduate Seminar, Interracial Lovemaking.* I haven't taken that course yet. I've tried, using my typical online courtship methods. The ISO issue looms large. Black women show a strong proclivity toward SBM, and it's as true for the attractive ones as it is for the uggos. The beautiful can afford to be choosy, but it's an insane posture for an ugly black woman to take. Happiness is a numbers game for all ugly, regardless of race, culture, or creed. *Please. Reply to my query. We're too ugly to let race come between us. I may be paler than what you're used to, but I do have an adjustable penis, and aren't we all black once the lights go out?*

Her outfit was a disaster. A spinach-colored dress, and shimmery, like something a dimwitted bride would choose for her bridesmaids. Her chocolate bosoms rose from the plunging neckline. I'd venture to say that 49 percent of her breast flesh was visible. She was putting too much faith in her brassiere; a single unfortunate jiggle would reveal all mysteries. The chain of her necklace had fallen into the cavern of her cleavage. Pendant or no, I couldn't say, as it was buried deep in the crevice. On her feet: an awful pair of lime green high heels. Pointed toes. She looked like a sad leprechaun who'd just had her pot of gold stolen.

I was enthralled by her breasts. Not in the way a man is expected to be. It was the inept presentation that fascinated me. *Really?* I thought. *This is the best you can do?* I understood her intentions. We ugly are told to *accentuate our assets,* and this is generally good advice. It can also be dangerous. Clothing should tell a story. It should not serve as a confession of everything you hate about yourself.

"I like your shoes," I said, my lips pursed. I didn't like her shoes, of course. No tasteful person could, but it was all I could think of at the time. She acted as if I was speaking in a foreign language. She turned to her girlfriends as if hoping one of them might translate.

"I like *your* shoes," she said after a moment. I was wearing a pair of Church & Company wingtips. They had belonged to Puppa, and he'd taken great care of them, as men of his generation did with their fine footwear. My Churches bore the distress of miles walked and the marks of skillful cobbling. She was right to like them.

So, her outfit was a nightmare, but she had put some thought into it; and when she had, it was not with a guy like me in mind.

On the one hand, Dolly. On the other, Spinach Dress. Was I torn? Not a whit! I'm not the kind of man that a woman can want at first sight. If Dolly were to want me at all, she'd need to see that another woman was capable of taking the leap. And who knew? If I toed the tightrope just so, I might end up with two lovers in the offing. Forbidden lovers. Exotic lovers. The possibilities were delicious.

I bought Spinach Dress a drink. She sucked it down, and I bought her another. We talked nonsense. Her friends left us alone, but their ears were like police scanners, covertly tuned to our frequency. I asked my companion to dance. She resisted, but after another drink—also on me—she obliged. Her dancing was a self-conscious shuffle; a repeated series of timid shoulder bobs. She kept a buffer of air between us. I'd step into the buffer and she'd step away. Her attention remained tethered to her "friends." She kept looking over her shoulder, not so much for approval as for fear that they were mocking us. And they were. She'd look over to them, they'd be all smiles, but then she'd turn her back, and they'd huddle up and make light at our expense. She didn't know what we were. She didn't understand the role we were playing for them.

"Yee-HAW!" I cried out, cowboy style. I stomped my feet, clapped my hands, attracted the attention of all. I drew my finger pistols and shot the room full of lead. Chest shimmy, butt wiggle. Belly dancing? A bit of pigeon fandango. The dance floor was a hotplate, and I was cranking the dial. I was an ugly little white man, dancing with an ugly black woman. No inhibitions. All in the spirit of fun. I earned bona fides with every plié, relevé, and tendu. The other dancers closed in like moths to a flame.

Things got frisky. Before I knew it, my dance partner was wearing my hat and pulling me about by the tie, and I was spinning her and tracing my fingers across her body as she twirled. The other revelers formed a circle around us. Their cries pushed us to new levels of improvisation, their claps, like a thunderous metronome, providing the cadence of our movements.

I worked into a boogie-woogie kickball change, and worked that into a jazzy half-turn. The goal: to end up facing Connie, and then to cast an imaginary fishing lure toward her. I'd yank the imaginary pole, set the imaginary hook, and reel her in. She wouldn't do it, of course—she'd roll her eyes and shoo me away—but I figured she'd get a kick out of it.

I executed my turn. I stopped where intended and adopted a razzamatazz pose. I was about to pick up my rod and tackle when a vision froze me to the spot.

There, standing between self and bar, was The Alluring Librarian.

- 12 -
BOOTY CALL

I stood agog. She was the most beautiful thing I'd ever seen.

Her hair was an expression of artistic asymmetry. The left side was pulled back and bobby-pinned; the right, free-swinging and luxuriant. Her cat's-eye makeup was evocative of a young Barbra Streisand. Her flesh was molten milk chocolate. Her black, off-the-shoulder tee advertised a recurrently trendy punk band. A bra strap. Its presence a contrivance of the outfit. Red. Silky. Faded pencil jeans clung magnetically to her curves, and one knee was ripped, exposing the fertile protuberance of her kneecap.

Fertile protuberance?

I know, reader. I know. I'm only describing the image that came to me: of her kneecap mating with another kneecap, a male kneecap, and becoming impregnated, and swelling, flush with child, until it birthed a litter of little kneecaps.

I would have expected flats. I'd never seen her in anything but. Her Mary Janes would have gone nicely. Her checkered Chucks would have agreed with the "rocker spirit" of her getup. She had elected for more provocative footwear. Peep-toe pumps, red patent leather, five-inch heel.

They couldn't be! No chance! Yet there they were: the same pair of heels that The Mute had worn during our last rendezvous. On The Mute, the heels had been a fetish object. They'd been sexy for their own sake, and too hot for The Mute to handle. On The Alluring Librarian, the heels reached their maximum promise. There was nothing wishful about them. They afforded everything a sexy heel can.

I could have abandoned my dance partner. I could have thrown myself at The Alluring Librarian's feet and planted kisses on her sizzling stilettos, and my actions would have felt entirely natural, entirely appropriate, as they were fully in concert with my yearnings. My glands were mutinying. If I'd obeyed their riotous cries, I would have lost everything. I gave The Alluring Librarian a wink, spun on my heel, and returned to my ugly dance partner.

- - -

Is alcohol a gateway drug? Until that night, I would have said *no,* or *not necessarily.* Now—and given what I've learned—I'd give an emphatic *yes*! Drunkenness, as a high, has a lot going for it. It's easily had, cheaply bought, socially acceptable. At a place like Mother's, it's socially *expected.* There's only one detriment.

Hangover?

Nay! That's another benefit. The discomfort of a hangover reminds us that we overdid it; that we exceeded the recommended dosage. It's a built-in slap on the wrist. Bully to hangovers! They've saved the human race from extinction by cirrhosis.

It's the urination, reader. The incessant urination! I lost Spinach Dress because of it. The thought made me furious. How many people switch from alcohol to the hard stuff, so that they don't have to tinkle all the time? I considered the alternates. Ganja? Opium? I wouldn't have to urinate, but these are smoking drugs, and as a martial arts athlete I couldn't abide the loss in stamina. Heroin? It would certainly help my writing career, but needles are one of my phobias.

I wanted to score Spinach Dress's digits. Urological necessities interfered. We finished our dance, I gave her a gallant tip of the hat, and then made for the powder room. I had never asked a girl for her number before. I stood at the urinal and considered the possibilities. Casually: *Can I call you?* Politely: *May I have your telephone number?* Contemporary: *Do you prefer phone or email?* Devil-may-care: *Call me if you'd like to party.*

I emerged from the bathroom. Spinach Dress was gone.

Her friends had been entertained at first. *He's buying her drinks! He asked her to dance!* Our urges were a mockery: unearned, grotesque, unsuitable for public display. Something changed while we were on the dance floor. Spinach Dress stopped asking permission. She forsook their authority. How long can you make fun of a person who's having more fun than you are? They grew bored. I went to the loo, and Angel took the opportunity to yank the leash.

There was another possibility: that Spinach Dress had given me the slip. The thought burned, but I had to admit it was possible. Women slip me all the time. They stop answering my calls, stop responding to my emails, and I realize that my services are no longer required. Sometimes it hurts. Usually, it just irks. Guilty pleasure is the best I can be, and you don't sit a guilty pleasure down to discuss why things aren't working out.

It had been a fine evening, shared with an enchanting, ugly female. Spinach Dress owed me nothing. I should have just let her go, but disappointment compelled me to play the ass. An Angel had impeded our love. Beautiful forces had altered the course of our romance. I convinced myself that it had to be true. I'd been in the bathroom for little over a minute. They couldn't have gotten far. I wormed my way through the throng and exited the establishment.

"You leavin'?" asked Tollbooth.

"I'm not sure. Did four females just exit the premises?"

"Yeah. They went that way."

He pointed to the south, down the long and broken expanse of 4th Avenue. The city was dark and grew darker still in the direction indicated. I was ill prepared for such a sortie. My hand found its way to my inside jacket pocket. I gripped Excalibur for courage. If I moved quickly, I might be able to apprehend the ladies before they reached the all-black neighborhoods.

"You don't want to go that way this time of night," Tollbooth said, perceiving my intent.

"Did you say the same thing to them?" I asked.

"That's different," he said.

I ran. The cool night air whistled in my ears, caressed my face, and Mother's receded behind me. It felt good to run. It felt romantic.

Here's the thing. Melee outcomes are usually decided in the first ten seconds. If a fight goes longer than that, I'm doomed. I train for the quick strike, not for the slobber-knocker. There's also the twist in my back. My dressage gait is quite majestic, but my thoroughbred sprint is decidedly less so, and it grows more awkward as I tire. There's also an issue with my nasal passages. They don't care for endurance activities, and when I conscript them into such service they rebel and fill themselves with snot. My stomach contents also figured. Chivas Regal is a fine scotch, but it's a lousy sports drink. By the time I reached the ladies—if I ever did—I'd be dragging one leg behind me, and they'd find themselves overtaken, on the meanest of South Ilium's mean streets, by a shambling, gasping, boogerfaced Caucasian troll. I ran two blocks, pushed myself to run another, and then pulled up lame. I was at the corner of 4th and Jefferson. Franklin Street—the unofficial DMZ between white Ilium and black—was only three blocks off. I was tracking them on race-based assumptions. Shame on me. They could have turned off anywhere.

Just go home and satisfy your urges manually, I thought. Safe in my chambers, apart from the world and all its dangers, I could lie in my bed, take up a silken hanky, and wander from one fantasy to another. I'd try each fantasy out, settle on one that stuck, and then on to private ecstasy, and all while the vulva-soft hanky served as proxy of things divined.

All of this fantasizing about fantasizing caused me actually to fantasize. To my right—a half block down Jefferson—was the opening to the 3rd Street alley. The Mute's window was only a short walk away. I recalled our previous rendezvous. Her lingerie. The swell of her bosom, the knock of her knees, the google of her eyes. The smell of her flowery perfume flowed from my memory to my olfactory receptors. No. Masturbation wouldn't do.

Twelve-oh-nine A.M. I'd made no prior arrangement with her, and it was too late, too presumptuous, to be trying such a thing, but my acid blood had dissolved my reason. It had been a strange and wonderful night. Strange sex would be the perfect topper.

I sidled down the 3rd Street alley, gathering pebbles as I went. A rat darted across the cobblestone. I reeled back, went up on one foot, and nearly shrieked. The rat disappeared into a pile of rubbish. I could hear it there, gnawing and scratching in the garbage.

"I'll break your neck, you filthy creature!" Simple as the sentence was, it was difficult to articulate and came out in a whispered mush.

"I'll break your neck and take you by the tail and fling you at my lover's window. Ha!"

The threat was spoken quietly, but I shouted the "Ha!" as if it were the punch line of a joke that I wanted everyone to hear. Shocked at what I had done, I clasped my hand over my mouth, slunk toward the dark side of the alley, and hid behind a row of trash cans.

Could I be drunk? I'd only had . . . four drinks? Maybe five? I'd done at least that many during my *kaktus*, but that had been in a controlled environment. A sobriety test was required. I stood in the middle of the alley and performed a series of shadow-fighting exercises. Standard front kick. Side-kick. Two-three-two combo, sweep kick, tiger-claw neck strike. I attacked the air in front of me with deadly force, but silently, like an oriental assassin. The maneuvers spilled effortlessly from my muscle memory; each delivered with snap and precision. I was too lethal to be drunk.

The Mute's window was above. A Shakespearean pebble-throwing commenced. Turns out, it's hard to throw a pebble at a window that's three stories up. The lights were off, the window black, and I couldn't trace the projectiles once they left my hand. I'd fire, wait for the sound of the impact, recalibrate, and fire again. My first attempts collided uselessly against the brick wall, or in unfortunate cases, against a window on a lower level. I could achieve no measure of accuracy with the tiny stones, so I rooted through the garbage in search of munitions with greater heft.

"Spring on me, and you'll be sorry," I warned the rat. "I'll squish your brains between my fingers!"

I tore into the nearest bag and found:

- ❑ An apple core
- ❑ A chicken bone
- ❑ A half-eaten pork chop, slathered in sauce
- ❑ A broken calculator

I took these up, set my feet, and fired them into the darkness one by one. *Splat! Clack! Whap! Ping!* I hit the window dead center, three out of four. I waited. My groin throbbed.

Here's what I had in my mind.

The Mute awakens. At first, she's frightened. Who could that be, knocking gently on my bedroom window? She turns to her Hello Kitty alarm clock: 12:17. Could it be . . . my gentleman lover!? Her ingredients start to marinate. She rises, crosses to her vanity, and lights the special candle.

I was surprised when the light bulb flicked on. The candle was discreet. It could be seen from below, but just barely so. The electric blub lit up The Mute's window like a display case, and the light from it ricocheted off of the opposing building and down into the alley, greatly diminishing my concealment.

No matter. My visit was unannounced. She probably couldn't find a match.

The surge of light retarded my night vision. I squinted against it, my eyes adjusted, and I could see great splatters of gunk on the window glass. There were three distinct gobs: one of fruit, one of poultry, one of hickory molasses.

Bad form, Buddy. But no damage done.

A figure stood at the window. I gasped. It wasn't The Mute. It was a child; a young girl, not more than six or seven years old. She wore a white flannel nightgown. Sleep pulled at her eyelids. She gazed out through a smear of barbecue sauce.

She spotted me. From her vantage, I must have looked like a goblin; like some monster out of a fairy tale. Our eyes met. My stomach clenched like a fist.

It *was* The Mute's window. No doubt about it. I pulled my hat down over my eyes and walked on as if it all had been a casual mistake.

Oh, the vicissitudes of the male sex organ. Mine had experienced multiple states throughout the evening. These unrequited ups and downs had turned my seed into poison, and I needed to get the poison out; but my lust had gone to ice, and masturbation would have been a difficult medical procedure. The scene in The Mute's window had filled me with questions, and they were anything but erotic. I needed to reboot the hard drive. I decided to return to Mother's, have another drink, and try to convince myself that the ill-begotten booty call had never happened.

I re-entered the saloon. Terrance played on. Dolly was in her spot, watching. The Alluring Librarian sat at the bar. She was unaccompanied. In her right hand, a smoldering cigarette. Her red stilettos twinkled in the neon light. She sipped a cocktail and watched the goings-on.

Dolly: my yin. The Alluring Librarian: my yang. At that moment, I chose yang. I had some sorrows that needed drowning and was in no mood to pick my way through a mosh pit.

"Where'd you go?" she asked.

"On a fool's errand," I said. "Mind if I join you?"

"I was wondering when you would," she said. "What are you doing here?"

I climbed the barstool beside hers and settled in.

"Terrance invited me," I said.

"I thought you were disgusted by all this," she said.

"I was. Terrance and I talked through it. I was here last week too."

"I couldn't make it," she said.

"I noticed. When did you arrive tonight?"

"Right before you started singing."

"I wish you hadn't seen that."

"I'm glad I did. And who knew you were such a dancer?"

I was calm. Her appearance was affecting, her carriage beguiling, but I wasn't as nervous as the circumstances should have made me.

"It's all research," I said.

"You've moved from the theoretical to the practical. That's good."

"Quite. I figured it was time to get my beak wet."

She laughed. She seemed genuinely happy to see me.

"Speaking of wet beaks," she said, "can I buy you a drink?"

"A gentleman would never accept such an offer. I will gladly replenish yours when you're finished."

That crooked little grin of hers. The large, dark eyes. She appraised my threads.

"You look handsome," she said.

No one, besides Mummy, had ever said those words to me.

"That's a lie," I said, "and patronizing, coming from someone as pretty as you."

I couldn't remain in that moment. It was too heavy. My eyes darted away, I searched for a place to set them, and they came to rest on the librarian's oddly familiar footwear.

You're going to think I'm a foot fetishist, reader. I'm not. A particularly nice foot can be something of a turn-on, I admit, and I've sucked my share of toes, don't get me wrong, but it's not my "big thing." I'm simply a ganderer.

A lady's choice in footwear doesn't tell you everything you need to know, but it tells you much. The Alluring Librarian's heels were pure sex and unadulterated confidence. They also posed some daunting metaphysical questions.

"Your shoes," I said. "They're quite something."

"They're murder," she said. "But it's fun to wear something slutty every once in a while."

I didn't like it. *Slutty.* The heels were provocative. Suggestive. *Slutty* was too cheap for her.

"I'm sure I've seen them before," I said.

"Not unless you're spying on me. I'd never wear these to work."

"Where are they from?" I asked.

She sipped her cocktail, took a final drag on her cigarette, snuffed it.

"From a different life," she said.

I considered asking her to dance. It would have been the chivalrous thing to do—but what would it have done to *me* if she said yes? My perspective on modern party dance was from the outside looking in. I wasn't raised on it, so I was able to see it for what it was. Party dancing is sexual selection behavior. This has always been true, but the styles of yore—lindy, bebop, tango, et cetera—offered greater testament to a partner's reproductive soundness. Footwork requires agility; dips and turns require strength; the forms themselves require timing and precision. Modern party dance—that improv orgy of rump-shaking—suggests nothing more than a willingness to mate. The classical forms are foreplay. The current forms are pornography. A skilled tango dancer *is* a skilled lover. The sophisticated undulations leave no doubt. The skilled lindy hopper will likely beget healthy, nimble children. It's there, in the genes, for all to see. The bumper-and-grinder tells us nothing. If I asked The Alluring Librarian to dance, I'd be doing so on modern terms. Her beauty shouted her reproductive soundness from the rooftops. Further shouts were unnecessary, and the styles available could not have made them any louder. Any dancing we did would have been an innuendo of *willingness,* and that would be more than I could bear.

Terrance was working an old-school rock 'n' roll medley. The medley concluded. Cheers tore at the smoky air.

"Ladies and gentlemen, it's been my pleasure to share the evening with you," Terrance announced. "My girl Dolly gets the final request. It's a great one." He shifted his gaze to her. "You sure you don't want to sing it with me?"

"You do it," she said over the din. Dolly's speaking voice was somewhere between husky and singsong, and her tone was full of wishes.

"All right. Grab a partner, everybody, and sing along. This one is called 'Always and Forever.'"

Another easy-listening classic ripped from the playlist of 95.5 Lite FM. I knew it well. Mummy and I had danced to it on more than one occasion. The spirit moved me. Supernatural forces pushed me from my barstool.

"Always and forever,
Each moment with you
Is just like a dream to me
That somehow came true."

I was off, through the crowd, weaving between the intermingled bodies, until I came to a spot directly beside Dolly. She didn't register my approach. Her attention remained fixated on Terrance. I tapped her shoulder. She turned to me with a start.

"And I know tomorrow
Will still be the same,
'Cause we've got a life of love
That won't ever change."

I knelt before her. She shriveled away, into her wheelchair, like a time-lapse video of a rotting mushroom. I extended a hand to her and backed it with my patented eyebrow wiggle. She softened. She took my hand. My scoliotic spine was made for the moment. It arched me toward her, over the seat of her wheelchair, allowing for an intimate proximity that a straighter back would not have permitted. She slid her left hand onto my shoulder; I slid my right down to her waist. Her body was like an empty husk. There was an energy to her, but little in the way of matter.

"And every day,
Love me your own special way.
Melt all my heart away
With a smile. . . ."

I held her. We couldn't turn, so we swayed. Her breath was hot on my neck. She smelled of antibacterial soap, latex rubber, and just a hint of urine. The smell of the ailing and infirm. She smelled like Puppa.

What do you want, reader? She was what she was. I was what I was.

I perceived a shifting in the room. I looked up and saw that the crowd had formed into a semicircle around us. They were singing along with Terrance, but they were watching Dolly and me, and a few seemed close to tears. I was outraged. *This is a seduction, not a freak show!* My masculinity stirred violently. I was struck by the urge to grope Dolly's breasts, to open my mouth, project my tongue, and deliver her the frenching of a lifetime. They had usurped our dance, and turned it into their life-affirming moment. I wanted to take that moment and snap it over my knee.

I didn't. Nothing about it would have been right. I leaned in, set my head on Dolly's shoulder, and remained there until the song concluded.

The final applause of the evening was for Dolly and me. It was sickening. I couldn't stand to look anyone in the eye, yet I couldn't remain where I was, fixed to Dolly's shoulder. I stood and looked over to the barstool I had vacated, and to the half-empty scotch that held my place.

The Alluring Librarian remained where she had been. We locked eyes. I detected something. A desire? I think so. For me? Not quite. She was looking *at* me, but not *for* me. She was looking for a different man; a thoughtful man; a man with a dark sense of humor, and a love of literature, and a predilection for life's inevitable decay. I shared a lot in common with the man she was looking for. If only my face. If only my body. The look in her eyes wasn't for me. It was for the man she wished I was.

I sat on the apron of the stage, in front of Dolly. I didn't want to mingle. I feared what would happen if someone complimented me or, worse yet, *thanked* me. Someone had taken photos of our dance. I'd seen the flashes.

"You made a kissy face at me," Dolly said. "During your song."

"I did. I apologize for being fresh. It was my first time up there. I was looking for a friendly face to grip on to."

"I do that too," she said.

"Well, considering the makeup of this crowd, I didn't want to start picturing people in their underpants."

She gave little wheezing laugh, and then looked toward the bar. The Alluring Librarian had been joined by the man himself—Terrance Johnson! There was an obvious warmth between them. They conversed easily. Connie brought them drinks. Terrance insisted on paying. Connie insisted that his drinks were on the house.

Dolly cast a sad eye toward the handsome pair.

"How do you know her?" she asked me.

"She's my librarian."

"She's pretty."

"She's also smart."

Dolly sighed.

"That must be why Terrance likes her."

Her words jarred.

"Terrance likes everyone," I said. "He's a good host."

"That's his girlfriend," Dolly said.

I was aghast. She had to be mistaken.

"Don't go reading in, my dear."

Terrance placed his hand on the small of the librarian's back.

"A simple rapport-building technique," I said dubiously. "Platonic physical contact. He's just making her feel welcome."

The Alluring Librarian leaned over and planted a kiss on Terrance's lips. It was a quick one, but decidedly more than a peck.

"See?" Dolly said.

"Yikes!" I cried. "How long has this been going on?"

"A while, I guess."

I was racked. I had no claim on The Alluring Librarian, nor any right to jealousy. I'd been trying to rid myself of the illogical cravings I held for her! It was *my* struggle, *my* philosophical exercise, and not a thing I wanted Terrance's help with, yet there he was, accepting smooches from the inappropriate object of my desire. I held title on my internal struggles. Nurse Johnson had lovingly insinuated himself into every corner of my life.

How did they meet? I brushed the question away as quickly as it occurred. There is no tale as boring as that of attractive people falling in love. The details are irrelevant. It probably happened at the saloon. It could have happened at the library. At some point, they saw one another. He liked. She liked. The end.

I turned to Dolly. She looked miserable.

"Can I tell you a secret?" I said. "That girl? I'm thinking of making her my mistress. Crazy, I know. But I can't shake it."

Dolly turned to me with a start.

"Terrance's girlfriend?"

"That's no girlfriend. That's a passing fancy, at best."

"You're married?"

"No. I've still got to find a wife. Details, you know."

"I like Terrance," Dolly said.

I hopped down from the apron, got down to one knee, and leaned in close.

"People like him—people like *her*—are made for people like you and me to want."

Telepathy. It was the only way I could give Dolly what I knew. My hands balled into white-knuckled fists. My eyes rolled back. I mentally massaged the nether regions of my brain. *You want Terrance in the way men want cars they cannot afford; in the way women want homes that are beyond the reach of their status. Don't measure yourself by petty trinkets. It's not love you feel—it's consumer instinct. Rage against it!*

A tug on my pant leg roused me from my lucubratory state.

"Are you sleeping?" Dolly asked.

"No. I'm trying to communicate with you telepathically."

"Like, with your brain?"

"That's the preferred organ, yes. Unfortunately, my parapsychological skills aren't what they should be. How would you like to blow this place?"

"Blow it up?"

"Leave. Go for a walk. I'll push."

My suggestion expunged her melancholy. She looked back, over each shoulder, as if scanning for secret listeners lurking in the shadows.

"My mom will be here any minute," she said.

"We'd better hurry, then."

"She'd be worried sick. I'd get in trouble."

"I, too, have an overbearing mother. It's good to tweak her from time to time. Makes her realize where things stand."

"She'll call the police."

"My chambers are only minutes away. We could slip inside and lie low until the heat blew over."

The possibility excited her. I'd like to think that some of the excitement was on account of me, but I knew that it was owed primarily to the novelty of my offer. For a moment, I thought she might go for it. She looked like she had right after her song with Terrance, when the cheers had been raining down. She thought it over. The look vanished.

"I can't," she said.

"But you'd like to?"

"Maybe. It sounds interesting."

I looked over at Terrance and The Alluring Librarian. They had vanished into a world of two. Everything else—myself, my companion, the saloon and all its occupants—had ceased to exist for them.

"Wait here, Dolly. I'll be right back."

- 13 -
AFTER-PARTY

The red-hot heels proved too much. The Alluring Librarian had shed them when we passed through the backyard gate and had left them in one of our garden boxes, alongside a decorative gnome. The gnome was one of my early attempts at hand-carving. Not my best work.

"You can bring your shoes upstairs," I told her.

"I think I'm done with them," she said.

What would it have been to be alone with her? To mount the back stair; to behold the sway of her as she ascended my private flights, and to know that that sway was for me? I couldn't picture further than that. Anticipation was as far as my fantasies dared to go.

The guest list: Dolly, Terrance, The Alluring Librarian. The party crashers: Viktor and Oleg. The brothers had overheard my proposal and begged to be included. I'd tried to refuse, but their pleas were unrelenting, and I was afraid they would draw in other ne'er-do-wells. My acquiescence was in service to shutting them up.

We arrived at my sitting room. This space represents one-half of the main chamber proper, with my office occupying the second half, and the two spaces separated, in both function and spirit, by a magnificent Tudor archway. Did I mention the vaulted dome chandeliers? One in the sitting room, one in the office space? I'm sure I didn't. Now you know.

"This is some place," Viktor said.

"Some place," agreed Oleg.

"But those stairs are pretty steep," said Viktor.

"Not easy for big guys like us," said Oleg.

"Especially when you're carrying a wheelchair," said Viktor.

I assented to their complaint. The Ladies' Entrance was arduous. My firm gluteus is a testament to this fact. Viktor had lugged the wheelchair. Terrance had carried Dolly up the flights. She'd held tight to him. His embrace was the fulfillment of all she wanted.

Back at the bar.

"There's zero chance that her mother will let her come," Terrance said. "Besides, I'm not sure I like what you're trying to do."

"What's nobler?" I demanded. "My ignoble intentions, or the unrequited love you inspire? Dolly worships you, she dreams of you, but she can never have you. Is it friendship you offer, or sadism?"

"She's got a little crush," he conceded.

"Easy to call it 'little' when you're not the one feeling it."

"This is not a girl you can just screw around with," he warned.

"Screwing around is the third thing on my mind," I said. "The first: seduction! The second: intellectual control of baser instincts! These would be grotesque objectives if motivated by compassion. Mine is a cold, considered depravity. The obstacles to this courtship are obvious. It's not likely to go very far, but I'm excited to give it a whirl."

The Alluring Librarian was listening along. She chimed in.

"This is interesting," she said. "Ethically speaking. In a feminist context. I mean, she is a grown woman, right? If she wants to go, and if you and I go too—"

"You don't know what he's up to," Terrance interrupted.

"I think I do. He's interested in pursuing a relationship. His word choice is a little . . . *icky* . . . but I can't say the same about his intentions. He's articulating motivations that most of us keep to ourselves. He's 'speaking from the id.'"

"He's speaking from his pants."

"Trousers!" I corrected. "And they speak for themselves. Tonight, they tell a tale of old-world elegance. Use that irresistible Johnson charm. Tell the mother that you've breakfasted with us, that Puppa is one of your charges, and that the Hayes home is a safe home, a stately home, and that you will be there the whole time. One hour. An hour and a half tops. It's something that Dolly will never forget."

Dolly's mother entered the saloon. She exchanged some pleasant words with Tollbooth and then worked her way toward her daughter. Terrance harrumphed and hopped from his barstool. The mother received him with an embrace and a kiss on the cheek. A dialog commenced. Dolly grew excited and started pulling on her mother's jacket, entreating her to agree. The mother registered protests. Terrance offered assurances. It was a tense two minutes, but two minutes was all it took.

Flashback over. Back to my chambers.

My hands rested on the handles of Dolly's wheelchair. I helped her along and keyed her into the various decorative delights. Viktor plopped onto my Chavanon love seat.

Oleg delivered similar punishment to the matching accent chair. Terrance and The Alluring Librarian eyed my bric-a-brac, fingered my tchotchkes, and expressed various appreciations for my cluttered feng shui.

There was a palpable heat between them. They did not kiss, nor did they pet, but there were caresses in their shared looks and portents of lovemaking in their continuous proximity.

"Is this a phrenology object?" asked The Alluring Librarian.

"Indeed. A miniature phrenology bust. Porcelain. Circa 1870. It was once the head of a cane."

"What's this?" asked Terrance.

"A surveyor's compass. Made in Boston. George Washington had one just like it."

The librarian demonstrated an antiquarian delicacy that is the hallmark of her trade. She innately knew what was for looking, what was for touching; and when she wished to touch, she'd confirm my approval with a wordless glance and nod. Terrance lacked such refinement. His hands were tactful and precise, but they were all over everything, and without consideration of risk/reward mathematics. What did my collection say to him? Many of the objects were pre-Civil War, and there wasn't a piece that postdated Jim Crow.

Antiquing—Caucasian v. Afro-American. Another topic for the pile.

"Oh, Buddy!" exclaimed the Librarian. "Look at these!"

She stood before my bookcase. It contained over six hundred volumes—a mere fraction of the total collection, but the rarest of it, and the most valuable. The librarian made a random selection and pulled it from the shelf: *Following the Equator: A Journey Around the World,* by Mark Twain.

"This is a first edition, isn't it?"

"They're almost all first editions. We're always on the lookout."

"They're *almost all* first editions?" she asked, awestruck.

"And some with inscriptions. Take that blue volume up top. *Herzog*, by Saul Bellow. A first edition, and signed on the title page. Black ballpoint. Very strong. Puppa bought it for ten cents at a garage sale."

"That's impossible!"

"It's how we got most of them. The common man sees no value in literature and treats old books as trash."

The Alluring Librarian clutched Mark Twain to her breast. Her affect turned puckish.

"Buddy, you have to tell these guys about your neighbor."

I recoiled as if she'd farted aloud.

"Please! I revealed that to you in confidence!"

Terrance had moved on to my Uncle Sam mechanical bank. Circa 1885. Original paint. He had it in his left hand, while his right fished around in his pocket, looking for a coin to shove.

"What's up with your neighbor?" Terrance asked. I was surprised by his tone and expression. Both seemed authentic. When young lovers trade secretions, secrets tend to flow with them. I was surprised that The Alluring Librarian hadn't played my saga as afterglow gossip.

"It's nothing," I said. "Just a bit of Hatfield and McCoy business. We've been at war with her for years. By 'we,' I should say 'me,' because Mummy is a conscientious objector and Puppa is well past his soldiering days, and by 'years,' I should say 'for eternity,' because our battle is cosmic in nature."

"What started it?" asked Dolly.

"Oh, you know how these blood feuds go. My neighbor believes that Puppa killed her husband. I think she's a demented despot. Her unquenchable thirst for rental property won't be sated until she's absorbed all of South Ilium. There's also the question of a stolen artifact. Typical neighborhood drama."

"Your neighbor is a woman?" asked Dolly.

"Yes. And ancient. Like a demon."

"And she thinks your grandfather killed her husband?" asked Terrance.

"I told you. She's insane."

"How old is she?" asked Dolly.

"Around seventy-five. Maybe eighty."

"Maybe eighty!?" exclaimed Terrance.

"I get what you're driving at. 'Why not just puff up your feathers and physically intimidate the old broad?'"

"That's *not* what I was driving at."

"She's got a son," I said gravely. "A brute of a man. He's her leg-breaker. If given a chance, he'd murder me in an instant."

Viktor and Oleg were amused by my exposé. They chuckled along from their comfortable reclines; but as the revelations mounted, they grew more erect, and by the time Oleg spoke there was a dawning awareness painted on their matching faces.

"What's her name?" asked Oleg.

I told them.

"*That* bitch!?" cried Viktor.

"Please!" I admonished. "There are ladies present."

"She owes us twelve hundred bucks!" Oleg bellowed.

"She had a furnace go in one of her buildings," said Viktor. "You should have seen the place."

"Falling apart!"

"Oleg almost fell through the basement stairs."

"And we told her 'all this pipe is lead, it's gotta go.'"

"And she says 'just fix the furnace.' So we did. And guess what!?"

"She never paid us!"

"And she poisoned our cousin's cat!"

The others recoiled. My jaw dropped. It was confirmation of a long-held suspicion. Mummy thought I was crazy, but I knew better.

"She poisoned a cat?" asked Dolly.

"Oh, that old bag has poisoned lots of cats," Viktor said. "Dogs, too. They get into her garden . . ."

". . . Her blasted garden . . ." I sneered.

". . . and she lays out poison for them."

The Alluring Librarian brought her hand to her mouth. Dolly was white as a sheet.

"It's true," I said. "I've seen the corpses. Maybe five, over a span of as many years. If you live in a city long enough, you'll run across the occasional dead stray, but this was something different. They were all in this neighborhood, and all within a one-block radius of her compound. Four cats. One sad little mutt. I thought of tossing the dead dog over her fence, as a kind of primitive biological warfare, but I'm a devoted naturalist and could never be so disrespectful to one of God's creatures."

"She's messed in the head," said Oleg.

"And she's a thief," said The Alluring Librarian. She was attempting to expand the narrative. I was pleased that my guests were enjoying the party chatter, but I wished for a different subject.

"What did she steal?" asked Dolly.

"Something of ours," I said. "Something irreplaceable. Let's leave it at that. Who's thirsty?"

"We are!" said the brothers in unison.

"Well, then, make yourselves comfortable. I'll slip

belowdecks and retrieve a bottle of vintage Scotch. Be right back."

I wanted to keep my guests lubricated and, if possible, to prime Dolly's pump. My methodology would not be that of a horny undergraduate, mind you. Dolly was a drinker. There was a cup holder affixed to the right armrest of her chair; and when she was at Mother's, Connie's boy helper kept the holster stocked with cold cans of Coors Light. A lowbrow drink, and no telling if she'd go for the sophisticated aperitif I offered, but I had nothing else on hand. I had no illusions that our night would end in the boudoir. My mind didn't even want this, although my swollen testes, heavy from their night of unanswered exertions, begged for unwholesome satisfaction. *Down, traitorous wiener!* The whiskey I served would be in service to memory, not persuasion. Later, when Dolly looked back on the evening, I hoped her reminiscences would be tinted by a pleasant buzz. I hoped they might be brighter than lucid sobriety would permit.

I scampered down into the darkened house. My mind felt crisp, but my agility was hampered by the dimness, and perhaps a wee bit by the intoxicating chemicals that pumped through my veins. The drawing room proved a crucible. I nearly knocked a vase from the hutch. I banged my knee on the divan. I collided with Mummy's antique sewing table. The impact knocked some sense into me. My freakish enzymes rendered me nearly impervious to intoxication, and if I was feeling the effects, my guests must have been on the verge of blackout. This called for hors d'oeuvres! I'd go to the kitchen, prepare an enticing assortment of nibbles, and stop by for the scotch on my way back.

Speed. *Cuisine d'inspiration.* It would have been an unforgivable faux pas to leave my party waiting. I raided the larder. A tin of black caviar, a can of chickpeas, a jar of tahini, a jar of cumin, a decanter of olive oil, a box of *petits toasts*. I threw open the refrigerator. Grapes? Quite right. Pont L'Eveque, Fourme d'Ambert, Buche de Chevre? Mummy was clearly planning a cheese plate; hospitality demanded that I commandeer her provisions. A clove of garlic. A lemon. And what was this? A peeled beef knuckle, hiding in the crisper tray? Mummy intended it for smoking, no doubt, but the cut was perfect for a quick tartare. I set all of these ingredients on the butcher block. A gastronomic marathon commenced: grinding, squeezing, julienning, cubing. The Magic Bullet made quick work of the hummus. The tartare was topped with a raw egg. The caviar was accompanied by a small bowl of sour cream. Total prep time: nine minutes, forty-eight seconds. It had to be a record. I arranged the munchies on our trusty salver, along with four crystal rocks glasses, and trekked toward the scotch supply.

The den door was ajar. The light was on. I offered a silent, bitter curse to Mummy's environmental consciousness. I had warned her: "If you continue leaving the lights on, I shall install a timer on the appropriate circuits."

I entered. Puppa was in his harness. Mummy sat in the chenille wingback. I swooned like a lady in a Victorian novel. This near-fainting spell almost proved fatal to the hors d'oeuvres. Some *petits toasts* fell to the floor, but I righted myself in time to save the works.

"Buddy! What are you doing up?"

"What am *I* doing up?"

Puppa smiled warmly. Mummy smiled as well, but hers was a bit suspicious.

"Puppa was having trouble sleeping. This can be a tough time of night for him. It's not unusual for us to be up at this hour."

"I didn't know," I said, setting the tray on one of the Shaker candle stands.

"It's past ten P.M.," Mummy said. "Hayes Family Contract, right?"

I was pleased by her nod toward constitutional legitimacy. That's how I viewed the Hayes Family Contract—as a founding text, secular yet sacred, that sets our union on a footing of long-term sustainability. Mummy understood the terms, she'd signed on the dotted line; but as with all legal documents, there was some wiggle in the interpretation. I'm an originalist. Mummy's a loose constructionist. In cases regarding Puppa's health, I was fine with her dancing outside the framework.

"If you had told me, I could have researched possible remedies. Melatonin. Milk of magnesia."

"Milk of magnesia is a laxative."

"Exactly. Some research would have sorted that out."

"Why are you dressed like that? Did you join a barbershop quartet?"

"Hardy har har. I'm as shiny as a new penny. Spring is the perfect time for seersucker." My head wobbled. I spit a little on the Ps.

"Goo shick ite!" exclaimed Puppa. Translation: Music Night.

"Did you go to Terrance's music night!?"

"Maybe."

Her eyes narrowed to slits.

"Are you . . . intoxicated!?"

"How dare you."

"You are! I can smell it from here." She cast an eye toward my salver of savories. "And clearly, you've worked up an appetite."

"I have company," I said.

"Company?"

"A couple of friends."

"Friends!?"

"I prepared a nosh."

"Caviar, I see."

"American bowfin. I'll replace it with sturgeon."

"And you got into my cheeses."

"*Our* cheeses, I should think. Unless you intended to hog them all to yourself."

"Your hors d'oeuvres looks very tasty, Buddy. I'm shocked you were able to prepare them in your current condition. What brings you to the den?"

I blinked dumbly for a moment. Mummy blinked back.

"I thought to retrieve a bottle of scotch from Puppa's private reserve. For my guests. Puppa has indicated that I may help myself."

Mummy's harelip scar went a ghostly white.

"How do you know about Puppa's scotch?" she asked.

"That is between grandfather and grandson."

"And you've been *drinking* it?"

"'Sampling' would be apter. Not that it's any of your business."

She shot Puppa an accusatory look. He responded with an innocent shrug.

"This is alarming news," she said.

"All things in moderation."

"Moderation does not run in your genes." She shot Puppa another nasty one.

"It is you, Mummy, who placed the forbidden fruit in my hands. Without your badgering, I would never have gone to Terrance's shindig. What would you have me do? 'Oh, just water for now'? The 'water' would peg me as a cheapskate; the 'for now' would peg me as a liar. One does not go to an opium den and order a fish sandwich. I had zero experience with drinking, social or otherwise, and Puppa graciously offered a few pointers."

She took a calming breath.

"Just be careful, is all. I'm delighted that you have friends over. There is a Lord, and he is good. Just one more question."

"Fire away."

"Is that girl up there?"

I hadn't expected that one. My darting eyes searched for pretexts.

"Which girl?" I asked obtusely.

"Dolly. The one in the wheelchair. You mentioned her when Terrance was over."

"That is leaked information. True, I was the leaker, but I was sleep-deprived and unable to bear up under your scorching emotional abuse."

"So she's here?"

"Perhaps."

"And there are other people up there, right?"

I was like a rat backed into a corner. Thank goodness for my diplomatic training. Without it, I might have thrown my hands in the air and run off screaming through the unlit house.

"Grip tight to your knitting, Mummy. *Terrance* is up there."

"He is!?"

"And that librarian you like so much."

"The pretty one? My goodness!"

"And a pair of buffoons. Local businessmen. I may do some work for them."

"Buddy! You're blossoming before my eyes."

"I have been at full blossom for some time."

"And you're not going to do anything shameful, are you?"

"Like what?"

"Like take advantage of a girl in a wheelchair."

Her words enraged me. A slap was called for. Mummy was across the room, so the logistics didn't allow for it, and I wouldn't have done it besides, but her comment was worthy of a good crank to the kisser.

"What makes you think that *she* isn't taking advantage of *me*?" I sneered.

"Be a good boy."

"You overstep your bounds."

"Be noble."

"Dolly is Terrance's friend and patient. You may take his attendance as a ringing endorsement. Your favorite librarian is also here. Do you think she'd participate in anything untoward?"

She considered my petition.

"Well, if Terrance thinks it okay, who am I to argue?"

I rolled the eyes and buzzed the lips.

"The fact that you would trust in the virtue of a friendly acquaintance, and not in that of your own blood, gives one pause," I said. "You have questioned my integrity as a gentleman; I question *yours* as a mother. Enough of this. I have friends to entertain. Puppa, by your leave, I shall retrieve a bottle of the good stuff and then bid you goodnight."

He gave one of his broad, toothless smiles. He was excited for me. I looked forward to the coming Sunday, and to the recounting of gory details.

I carefully ascended the flights. I had to rearrange my plating to allow for the bottle of Anderson's Fine Old Scotch Whiskey, and the whole assembly was a bit precarious, but I managed it well. I reached the landing outside my chambers.

From within, I heard a cacophony of merriment that could only be described as a "ruckus." Laughter in bales. Shrieks of delight.

I was struck by a humiliating vision. My adult playthings! My ticklers, teasers, probes, and spankers; my cooling and warming ointments. These erotic items were in my bedchamber and padlocked in my footlocker, but my guests were all denizens of South Ilium, and there very well could be a lock picker among them. *A silly notion, Buddy . . . but what if you left something out?* A stray butt plug, tossed away in the heat of passion; a forgotten bullet vibrator, lost between the couch cushions. *Be steady, man! You would never be so careless.*

I proceeded into my chambers with great uncertainty. My companions had left the sitting room and were now away back in the back passage. I couldn't see them, but I could hear their whoops and hollers. Who knew what scene awaited? After ten timid steps, all was revealed.

They had found my blowgun. They were shooting it at my dartboard. They were also fully bedecked.

The Alluring Librarian was wearing my fairy wings, and my costume fairy skirt, and my curly-toed elfin shoes. She had one of the latex ears in place and was working the other onto her bare lobe.

My centurion helmet sat askew on Viktor's enormous cabbage, and he had somehow squeezed himself into my bronze breastplate. The armor remained unbuckled in the back, and his corpulence bulged out beneath it, leaving his lower vitals exposed to killer blows.

Oleg had on my Ghanaian spirit mask and had paired it—in a fit of sartorial miscegenation—with my authentic tartan kilt. The kilt didn't fit around him, so he had tucked it into the waistband of his cargo shorts, causing it to hang like a waist apron. He was shirtless. A more terrifying native I could not imagine.

Dolly was wearing my royal headpiece. The crown was gold plated, lined with red felt, and topped with an iron cross. She had also helped herself to a selection of my costume jewelry. It suited her. What had been a wheelchair was now a mighty throne.

Terrance had the blowgun to his lips. He aimed it at the dartboard down the hall, at the tight grouping of barbs that were already buried in the bull's-eye. He inhaled deeply through the corners of his mouth. He was dressed as a pirate. Leather tricorne: more than a little snug. Leather eye patch: all boon, no bane, as it clarified his right-eyed aim down the barrel. My taxidermied parrot was affixed to his left shoulder. My satin cape—which was more Dracula than Blackbeard—billowed down his back.

His breath exploded into the tube. The barb flew. It split the grouping dead center and scored a perfect hit. The crowd went wild.

If you've never fired a blowgun before, you're missing out. It's a thrilling diversion. Aiming is as easy as pointing your nose, and even a novice can achieve great accuracy with only a couple of tries. I'm shocked that there aren't more blowgun enthusiasts. I believe that a few were made that night.

"Wow!" exclaimed Viktor.

"You're really good!" exclaimed his brother.

I cleared my throat. The costumed merrymakers turned to face me.

"Buddy!" cried the elfin princess.

"Where were you?" demanded the Roman centurion.

"You brought us snacks!" exclaimed the Ashanti/Celtic warrior, his voice muffled by his ceremonial mask.

"I hit seven out of ten, right in the bull's-eye," the Queen proudly boasted.

"Why do you have this?" asked the pirate.

"For assassination purposes, me hearty. Poison is the thing with blowguns, and I've experimented with a few concoctions, but only in preparation for the coming apocalypse. I've never shot anyone with it . . . but I have been shot *by* it."

The costumed jesters gasped.

"Have no fear. It was with rubber training darts, and Mummy was doing the shooting. I was practicing my missile defense."

Apparently, my guests had never considered the possibility that they might be attacked by an archer, or an arbalist, or a slingshotist, or a spearist. Anything can happen on the streets. They laughed uproariously at my comment. It was a mocking laughter, delivered by a group of costumed fools. The serving tray, chock full of dainties I had painstakingly prepared, only served to double my disgrace. For the second time since I'd known him, Terrance had relegated me to the position of "dimwitted butler."

"Let's drink!" bellowed Viktor.

"Let's eat!" cried Oleg.

"We've decided to help you," said Dolly.

"To get your relic back," said The Alluring Librarian.

My eyes fell to Terrance. He had only one eye to return to me, as the other was obscured by a leather eye patch. The available eye beamed with amusement, and a little trepidation, and a little incredulity, but also, I think, with genuine excitement.

"Why don't you tell us what happened? With your neighbor. Maybe we can help."

And I told them a tale.

- 14 -
TARZAN OF THE APES

Spring 2001. Five years before this telling. I was not yet aware that the relic was missing.

Mummy and I were in the kitchen. She was huddled over the butcher block, slicing beets. That night, we'd enjoy her famous cold borscht.

"The South Ilium Garden Tour is fast upon us," I said.

"It's June already? How time flies."

"I've been thinking. We should participate this year."

"In the Garden Tour? Oh, Buddy—you know that she always wins that. The fix is in."

"It's true. The South Ilium Historical Society is an oligarchy, masquerading as a democracy."

"And they run the Garden Tour."

"Indeed."

"And *she's* on the board."

"Quite right."

"And you think we should participate in their annual snobfest?"

"You've always wanted to."

"You distort the facts!" she exclaimed, waving her beet-stained knife in the air. "I would like to be *invited.* We have a very nice garden ourselves . . ."

"A beautiful garden."

". . . And just because it doesn't look like a wannabe Keukenhof . . ."

"Ours is more rustic. Victory-style, with English and Japanese design influences."

". . . And that ridiculous, dress-up croquet party she throws every year . . ."

"It's obscene."

"'Oh, look at us, all dressed up like the British aristocracy.' No one is fooled by your trash pageant!"

"Hit 'em, Mummy!"

"Our garden doesn't have to pretend."

"It's got soul."

"Exactly."

Her scar was like a murder scene. I tended to view Mummy's mood indicator as a personal foghorn, warning me away from dangerous waters, but in this instancc it served as a beacon. I was charting the proper course.

"I've fashioned a plan," I said. "If we chose to engage, I believe we could be victorious."

She set down her knife and wiped her hands on her apron.

"I'm listening."

"That beet you're slicing. Where did you get it?"

"You know where I got it."

"You know *I know* where you got it. Play along."

"It's from the Ilium Farmer's Market."

"Ah ha!" I cried, thrusting my finger into the air. "Over

the past few years, would you say that the Farmer's Market has become more or less popular?"

"It's a zoo."

"Ah ha ha ha!" I cried, thrusting again. "Excellent use of double-entendre! It is a zoo, in the 'overflowing with people' sense, and also because it's filled with freaks."

"Zoos are filled with animals."

"Right. I was thinking 'carnival.' But you have noticed, right? I've never seen so many hipsters in all my life!"

"What's a hipster?"

"Those unwashed young people. The ones covered in 'tramp stamps.'"

"What's a tramp stamp?"

"Jeez! A tramp stamp is a tattoo. Really, Mummy, you need to get out more."

"If that isn't the pot calling the kettle black. You haven't left the house in a week! Since we went to the Farmer's Market, as a matter of fact."

"I was outside just this morning. I did an hour of training in the backyard. Go out there if you don't believe me. You'll find my dummy, twisted up like a pretzel."

My melee calisthenics had been especially vigorous that day. I always superimpose a hated figure from the real world onto the training dummy. Such violent fantasizing imbues the simulation with vim, and allows me to "blow off steam" that might otherwise explode in the face of those who irk me. My fists are stones. My feet are . . . maybe daggers? My head is capable of devastating butts. I don't claim my bod as the deadliest thing going. My size, my physical defects, and my love of buttery cuisine all conspire to dull the edge. But believe me, if you're a training dummy, you wouldn't want to run across me in a dark alley.

So who did the dummy represent that morn? Not Meat Foot, not Little Miss Sunshine. It was the Organic Cheese Boy! He operates a stand at the Farmer's Market. This would-be monger is slim, bearded, ponytailed, and tattooed. He calls his nitwit operation "The Cheese Traveler." The Farmer's Market operates on Bay Street—a cobblestoned ribbon of hipster gentrification, and the area most cited as evidence of Ilium's "coming up." What was once a German butcher shop is now an "artists' co-op"; what was once a bait 'n' tackle is now an artisanal coffee shop. The River Street Pharmacy is now Rx Vintage Clothing, and the old porno theater—closed when I was a boy, so I never got to take in a picture there—has been converted into a see-and-be-seen nightspot. In between what was and what is, a long era of shutting down, boarding up, and moving out.

"All of our cheeses are sourced from local farmers, from the Hudson Valley up to Vermont," said the Organic Cheese Boy as he offered me a sample of one of his coagulated "re-imaginings."

"Wow. That's some cheese traveling you've been doing. I don't know if you heard, but they make some pretty good cheeses in Europe."

They've planted their flag on Ilium's scorched earth and erected their own private Gomorrah. Their creep has been contained to the south by a Section 8 housing complex. This low-income stockade has kept the hipster carpetbaggers from spilling into South Ilium, but how long can the poverty hold? There's been talk of moving the public housing up the east hill, into the outskirts. This velvet roping will "allow the development district to expand more quickly," and "raise the standard of living for all residents." I prefer the ruin, so long as I know my place in it. Little Miss Sunshine is the last of my industrial-age enemies. My future opponents—those of the information age—lie to the north.

Back to the beets. Mummy was perplexed.

"The Farmer's Market. Hipsters. Tramp stamps," she said. "I don't see what any of that has to do with the Garden Tour."

"Sustainable living, Mummy. The Green Movement. We're on the vanguard! We grow our own vegetables. We smoke our own proteins. We also recycle and rely on public transportation."

"So what? We've always done those things."

"Exactly! What we've been doing all along has suddenly become *a la mode!*"

"I guess I'm a hipster," she quipped, and proceeded into a little shimmy-shake. Apparently, she thought the etymology of "hipster" had something to do with the hips. "Can you help me pick out a tattoo?"

"Don't be disgusting. As you know, I'm very good at spotting trends, and this whole 'sustainable living' business has traction. In 1999, everyone was faux-rich. By 2010, everyone will be faux-hippie. The backyard garden will be the new Mercedes-Benz."

"Okay?"

"We can't beat Little Miss Sunshine in a traditional gardening duel. She's too well capitalized. She employs a squad of Latino mercenaries. We must deal with the situation as it is."

She eyed me skeptically. "So how can we win?"

"We must alter the Garden Tour discourse. As it stands, tourees are asked to vote for the 'best garden.' We must redefine the meaning of 'best.'"

"They bribed the people with food!" the hag cried at the garden tour awards ceremony. She was bent on our disqualification.

"What you call bribing, we call hospitality," I said

coolly, standing before the assembled. "And there's nothing against it in the rules."

"They printed phony ballots!" she bellowed.

"This 'phony ballot' business is too much," I rejoined. "Present evidence or I shall sue you for slander."

Deny, deny, deny. This is the first-best tactic that every diplomat must master. Had I printed extra ballots? I had, reader. Did I supply said ballots to all tourees who didn't have one in hand? Indeed. Does a facsimile of a facsimile count as "phony?" Not a whit, I say, so long as the votes cast upon them are genuine. Ballot control was the autocracy's primary protection. They kept the supply tight. This planned scarcity—if that's what it was, and not just an attempt to save money on photocopies—ensured that "the right people" were given the vote, and that the wandering suburbanites (who held no stake) and late-arriving hipsters (still blinking through their hangovers from the previous evening) would be denied suffrage.

"They don't even have a garden!" Little Miss Sunshine shrieked. "It's more like a working farm back there."

"It's a victory-style garden, with English and Japanese design influences."

"They were handing out pamphlets!"

"Some simple tri-fold brochures on sustainable gardening practices. I designed them myself, and I suspect they will encourage an urban gardening revolution. Now, may I have my blue ribbon?"

I won the crowd that day. The committee members—all women—fell into two camps: those who would usurp the Empress, given a chance, and those who coveted her patronage. It was easy to tell which was which. She lorded over all but didn't have a friend in the bunch.

Mummy refused to attend. "We know who won,"

she said. "Let her have her silly ribbon." I wouldn't stand for that. I returned home with our gaudy blue prize and presented it to Mummy like a bouquet of roses. She nearly wept. It was the first award she'd ever won.

"Mummy, I don't think we should enter the competition again. Too much trouble. Too polarizing. Let's retire as champions." And it *had* been a lot of trouble, but that wasn't the true motivating factor. Not for me. I wanted to add insult to injury. I wanted to spike the ball, perform a mocking touchdown dance, get flagged for taunting. There'd be no rematch. She could win the contest every year from then on, but she'd never get the chance to prove that she could beat us. I'd hold our victory over her forever.

I hadn't considered the connection. I hadn't considered the significance that the month might hold for her; that her garden had been *their* garden, and that the Tour day, for her, was a memorial as much as it was a competition. Little Miss Sunshine did not view our Garden Tour victory as an example of harmless neighborhood rivalry. To her demented eyes, we were dancing on her husband's grave.

The rancid stew of our mutual hostilities had been at a simmer. The blue ribbon sent them boiling over. We fell victim to regular acts of vandalism. On four occasions, our garbage bags were removed from their cans, torn open, and thrown into our backyard. This was obviously an attack on our prize-winning garden, and it was clear who did it. As retaliation, I snuck into Little Miss Sunshine's yard and sprinkled her flower beds with rock salt. "Someone" smeared turds—human turds!—on our front steps. I defecated in "someone's" birdbath. Our Christmas wreath was stolen. I stole their snow shovel. Our mail slot was coated in maple syrup. I stuffed a dead fish into their dryer vent.

We were locked in a dangerous game of brinkmanship. Mummy begged me to cease all provocations. I threw up my hands, denied any wrongdoing. She invoked Gandhi, Martin Luther King, and scripture. *Turn the other cheek.* I could not abide. Bullies had stolen my childhood, and there I was, a grown man, being bullied again. If I could build a time machine and visit my schoolboy self, I would encourage the boy me to *go for the eyes, go for the throat, fight until they break your arm and then fight with the other, never stop fighting, for if you do, you'll regret it evermore.* I determined that this conflict would end in one of two ways: with me dead, or with Little Miss Sunshine and Meat Foot taken away in irons.

Our residence contains many beautiful articles, but nothing impresses so much as our collection of fine wood furniture. If it's Early American or Shaker, you can be sure that it bears Puppa's hallmark. I was his boy apprentice. On weeknights, once I was done with my homework, I'd be permitted to join him in the wood shop and serve at his elbow. Hindsight would indicate that he was smashed for every one of these wholesome episodes, but I had no concept of such things at the time.

Those basement hours were my most formative. Ostensibly, it was hobby work, but Puppa approached it with zeal. No shortcuts. An eye for detail. There are many grades of error in fine woodworking. The most minor: an imperfection that is known to the builder but would be undetectable to all but the trained eye. Puppa vetoed such works. He'd never permit them a place in the house.

"It's beautiful otherwise," I'd tell him. "And besides, no one will notice."

"We're the ones who will be looking at it every day. And when we look at it, all we'll see is the mistake."

- - -

They were one of those mismatched couples. Little Miss Sunshine was into everyone's business. Her husband minded his own. He was friendly and well liked. She was that prototypical urban antagonist that one finds, and takes pains to avoid. The affluent busybody. The neighborhood snoop. She trotted her position as if she'd earned it, but owed everything to her husband's successful bootstrapping. She was a provoker of eye rolls throughout South Ilium. Our dealings with her were cordial if a little itchy.

Puppa called him a "time bandit," but he seemed to enjoy having him around. I'd arrive home from school, throw a cold steak on my black eye, have a quick snack, run through my homework and chores, and then make for the basement. My first greeting: the smell of cut wood, stain, poly. My second greeting, like as not, would come from The Husband, dressed in shirt and tie, not yet changed from his day of work. He was handsome in a heavy, tired sort of way. Silver hair. Metallic, almost. His complexion was a bit mottled, his jawline a bit jowly, but that hair was fit for a presidential run.

The Husband would sit on a bench, off to the side and out of the way, and he and Puppa would shoot the breeze. When a task required Puppa's concentration, The Husband would break off what he was saying—often, mid-word—and pick up where he left off once the operation was complete. He never offered assistance and his assistance was never requested. He just wanted to watch the work, and seemed to admire the man who did it.

He never stayed long. An hour at most. At some point, Mummy would call from upstairs.

"Your wife is on the phone."

The Husband would shut his eyes. One, two seconds. A deep, meditative breath. Then his eyes would open, he'd offer a grim smile, he'd clap his palms against his knees and rise stiffly from the stool.

I trust my memories of him. They move at a very low frame rate—almost like those historical documentaries that are nothing but still photos and voice-over narration, with the flow of time suggested by slow zooms, tilts, and pans. Children make for lousy cameramen. As an adult, I try to take a more active role in the production process. *This is important,* I tell myself. *Record for posterity.* I was witness to over a thousand conversations between The Husband and Puppa. I recall about ten. They discussed a lot of things, but what I remember most were their discussions about books.

▰ ▰ ▰

"Reading should be like anything you do," Puppa advised me. "If you're going to spend time, spend it wisely."

Who ever heard of a part-time orphan? I hadn't, until Mummy keyed me in. Hollyridge Children's Home. It still operates in Northeast Ilium. Puppa's father—my great grandfather—would leave him there for months at a time. Mummy says that it was a common practice during the Depression—for a widower to leave his children in an orphanage while he sought work.

There had been a Brother at the orphanage—Brother Anthony—who loaned books to Puppa. They were the great books of boy-adventure: *The Three Musketeers, Treasure Island, The Swiss Family Robinson, Tarzan of the Apes.*

Tarzan of the Apes. A red-cloth hardcover with gilt lettering. Puppa must have read that book to me fifty times when I was a child, and I must have read it myself fifty more. It was only in the context of our shared appreciation that I learned about Brother Anthony. "I kept asking to borrow it," Puppa told me. "Eventually, he told me to keep it."

Tarzan of the Apes thereby became the first book in

Puppa's private library. As far as I'm aware there's only one other artifact that remains from his childhood—a jackknife that his father gave him, and that Puppa has since passed on to me.

Puppa didn't set out to be a book collector. That's an effect. The causes: a lifelong love of reading and a nose for a deal. The discarded. The just out of fashion. Always used. Local book purveyors knew him by name. Every March, the Ilium Library would hold an annual book sale, and Puppa would be there an hour early, the first in a line that never actually formed. Garage sales. Estate sales. A nickel here, a quarter there, *dollar for the box.* He got the great works of the twentieth century before they slipped into the canon. People were leaving nineteenth-century masterpieces on the curb. For instance: Puppa found a ten-volume set of *The Diary of Samuel Pepys,* published 1893, leather-bound and in good condition, just sitting in a shoebox beside a dumpster. "They were *throwing them away,*" he said, presenting the box as if it were full of gold ingots.

He built bookshelves into every room. Our downstairs study is wall-to-wall, floor-to-ceiling. There's a large bookcase in the den. "Any more books," Mummy likes to joke, "and this house is going to cave in!" Not that she minds. Mummy is a reader herself. Her feminine tastes tend toward the romantic and mysterious. Of course Agatha Christie, of course Jane Austen, but also Graham Greene, Somerset Maugham. My sweet, anglophile Mummy. When Princess Diana died, she cried for a week, and I busted her stones every day about it. Her favorite contemporary author is American (thank God, as we did not fight a revolution for nothing!), and he also happens to be her dream hunk. It's sad—a middle-aged woman, pining after a celebrity—but at least his talent is worthy of it.

"Russell Banks!" she gushed, clutching his latest opus to her breast. "So talented . . . and *so* handsome!"

"And doesn't he know it," I sneered. "His back flap photo is so 'come hither' that it might as well be a centerfold."

"I like knowing what the author looks like." She opened the back cover, ogled the photograph of her literary lion, and planted a kiss on it.

"Oh, *yuck*!" I gargled. "Someone else might like to read that book some day."

"He lives in the Adirondacks. Could you imagine if we ever ran into him?"

"On our next bear hunt?" We never left Ilium, and ours was not a city that famous writers deigned to visit. "If you ever 'ran into' Russell Banks, he'd probably hiss at you and make the sign of the cross."

Back to *Tarzan*. It's a book for children. I enjoyed it as a child, and then moved on to more age-appropriate material. Years passed without thought or mention of it. Then Puppa got sick. He became reading-disabled, and we developed coping mechanisms. We read aloud to him every day, sometimes for hours at a time, but I wanted to offer something extra, something a little punchier, a little more theatrical.

I presented the concept to Mummy during one of our brainstorming sessions. She immediately agreed—a dramatic reading, performed before breakfast and composed of flash-and-bang material, would certainly get Puppa's appetite up. It would also afford me the chance to season the ol' acting chops.

"What story are you going to do first?" she asked excitedly.

"Good question. It's got to be something that will hook him."

I put finger to chin and pondered the options.

Tarzan of the Apes!

It was too perfect. I'd lift the first performance from the pages of Puppa's first book. *Our* book. A book we hadn't revisited in years. A costume! I'd leap into the den, clad in nothing but a loincloth, and let forth a powerful jungle yodel. I'd pound my chest like a gorilla. Puppa would be amazed!

"I could hang a rope from one of the beams!"

"Maybe just the costume. He'll get a kick out of that."

"Fair enough. We'll keep the special effects to a minimum—*this* time. Have you seen our copy of *Tarzan*?"

Mummy's face scrunched up, and she drew squiggles in the air with her index finger.

"It was . . . down in the study? Maybe the drawing room. I think that's where I saw it last. I feel like it wasn't on a shelf. It could be locked in the secretary. I'd hate to think it was in the basement. There are some boxes down there in dry storage."

I commenced a lazy search. I rediscovered books I'd forgotten and figured *Tarzan* couldn't be far behind. My looking turned to digging; my digging to a frantic tearing-apart. Days of this. No corner left unturned. The book was nowhere to be found.

Maybe it was in a secret place that only Puppa knew. I couldn't ask him about it, of course. *Tarzan* was not in his active memory. I'd never have that luxury again, but it seemed best that Puppa remain blissfully ignorant. I endured the loss on his behalf. How could we have misplaced something so precious?

For my first reading, I played the part of Viktor Frankenstein. I wore one of Mummy's aprons and splattered myself with artificial gore. I menaced Puppa with a plastic cleaver. It was a huge hit, he was delighted, and for a time I allowed myself to forget about *Tarzan*.

We don't watch a lot of television, but on Monday nights, 8 P.M., our family gathers in the den and watches *Antiques Roadshow.* We make a game of it. We watch every week, but we're only able to play the game with episodes we haven't seen before. WGBH Boston produces fourteen new *Roadshow* episodes per season, so our games are special events, endeavored upon with great intensity. Each segment constitutes a "bout," and each bout has two rounds.

Round one. At the start of a segment, Mummy and I will venture guesses as to the object's provenance. Our agreed-upon syntax: classification, date of manufacture, point of origin. "Art glass vase, early twentieth century, Bavaria," for instance. Specifics top generalizations. "Honesdale vase" would beat "art glass vase"; but if the object in question turned out not to be Honesdale, the less-specific "art glass" would trump. The segment progresses, the appraiser reveals all, and Puppa declares a winner for round one. It's usually me. Mummy always goes for the knockout—"Sweet Sue Doll, 1947, Cleveland, Ohio!"—whereas I play the percentages. Puppa used to be house champ, but given his impediments, he now plays the part of referee.

Round two. After the appraiser asks, "Do you have any idea how much this is worth?" and before the owner says, "I have *no* idea," we blurt out our estimated values. For reasons I cannot explain, Mummy always wins this. She has an innate ability to determine an object's value. She watches *The Price Is Right* every day (against my wishes), and she's just as good at that.

September 2004. We were watching *Roadshow,* enjoying our game. A bout commenced. A handsome older gentleman had a book. "What have you brought for us today?" the lady appraiser asked.

"Oh, boy," said Mummy. "*The Time Machine* by H. G. Wells, 1880, London."

Puppa gave the up sign. She had submitted her answer before the close-up of the book/periodical.

I leaned forward in the armchair and squinted at the screen. It was a medium-sized volume, quite worn. A green leather cover, abundant gilt stenciling. I didn't speak. The title of the book was revealed.

"This is a book," said the handsome old man. "*Twenty Thousand Leagues Under the Sea,* that my great-uncle used to own."

"Disqualified!" Mummy cried. She started in with the trash-talk. I was a "snoozer," and so a "loser." I silenced her with an upraised finger.

"Quiet, Mummy! I think we might own this book."

We kept individual scorecards of our *Roadshow* bouts. I turned mine over and took notes.

First American Edition.

Imprint—Boston: James Osgood and Company, 1873.

Copies burned in the Boston fire. "One of the true rarities in fiction."

Cover: Under the Sea. Title page: Under the Seas.

Jellyfish vignette. Later editions, Captain Nemo.

"Have you ever had this appraised?" the expert asked.

"Fifteen hundred dollars!" I shouted.

"No," said Mummy. Her eyes flashed. "It's more than that. Five thousand. Maybe ten."

Then, the denouement.

"The issues that predate this one are worth less," said the appraiser. "That first British edition you can get for about $1,000 today. This copy is probably a $10,000 book—$10,000 to $15,000 at auction."

I sprung from the armchair and searched the nearby

bookcases. Nothing. Without pause, I surged from the den, smoke trailing at my heels, my scorecard fluttering in my hand. Into the drawing room. Two bookshelves, a hutch, and a mantel, all lined with books. The spines were like rows of piano keys. I ran my finger across them as if performing a long arpeggio. No *Twenty Thousand Leagues.* Downstairs, to the study. More searching. My respiration quickened. My silken pajamas grew damp with perspiration. Still nothing. I fled the study and tore up the stairs, back to the second story, my open robe flapping behind me like a cape.

"Have you found it?" Mummy shouted from the den.

"Not yet!" Thank God I was wearing my ballet-style slippers—if I had gone with the moccasins, I might have slipped and broken my neck.

I exploded into my chambers and spotted it at first glance. The binding seemed to glow with an inner light. I pulled it from the shelf with a hooked finger. I couldn't tell what was vibrating—my entire being, or the book itself!

Green leather cover. Gilt lettering. A circular graphic, depicting a smack of jellyfish. The book I was holding was a point-for-point match with the notes on my scorecard. Some flaking on the title inscription, some minor toning on the pages, but not a single tear or crack. Ours was in better condition than the example I'd just seen on television.

Of course, I knew that some of the books were valuable. Or, more aptly, I figured they had to be worth *something.* Puppa had assembled an heirloom-quality library, but value, for him, had always been determined by author and title. So too for me. The words were all that Puppa and I ever discussed and the only judge of value I'd ever seriously considered.

You're going to think me false. "You're a *Roadshow* watcher, yet it never occurred to you to look into the value of your own collection?" In self-defense: most of the *Roadshow* books I had seen were atlases, collections of prints, old bibles, autograph books, civil war diaries. We don't have any of that on our shelves, and besides—*Antiques Roadshow* is on *television.* The cathode ray lends an unreal quality to all its projections. Our books had always been there. They were as permanent as the walls. I never thought of them as a thing for selling.

So there I was, in my chambers, our copy of *Twenty Thousand Leagues* hot in my hand. The phone rang. Exhausted, exhilarated, I padded over to my workstation. It was Mummy on the line.

"Well?"

"I think it is. I'm going to do a web search to confirm. I'll be down shortly."

"Really! That's wonder—"

I hung up the phone, set the treasure on my desk, sat in my chair. A wiggle of the mouse woke my machine. I launched a browser. I was about to enter my search terms—"1st Edition Twenty Thousand Leagues"—when I was interrupted by memory.

I was six, seven years old. We were in the downstairs study, seated on the Queen Anne sofa. Cigarette smoke built bridges in the light. I nuzzled close to Puppa. He held a book and I turned the pages. An old book. A book with a red cloth cover. Our mutual favorite.

Jules Verne could wait. The Google search box gaped like a hungry mouth, and I fed it. "1st Edition Tarzan of the Apes." The top return was from a rare-book emporium in New York City. I clicked. The page loaded. It was like seeing a ghost. A photo of the book I remembered. Thumbnails below, a gallery view, scans of illustrations that I hadn't seen in years. I read the listing. There were variations. A Toronto printing. A New York. Same cover. The title page colophon held the key. *Chicago: A. C. McClurg, 1914.* That was the mark of purity. The website offered one in "very good" condition for $40,000.

I returned to the den. Mummy and Puppa were as gleeful as lottery winners, and were eager to celebrate our find. They beheld our copy of *Twenty Thousand Leagues* as if they'd never seen it before. Mummy turned the pages for Puppa. Each turning was like a new discovery; like treading on virgin ground. Her hands worked delicately. She wondered aloud if she should be wearing rubber gloves.

"Just don't lick your fingers to turn the pages."

"Should we get a safe?"

"And lock it away? It's a work of art, not a pile of cash."

Mummy eyed the surrounding shelves. Her harelip scar took on a treacherous shade.

"Do you think there are any other valuable ones?"

"Nothing in this house is for sale, Skipper. You can sail that yacht back to the docks right now."

"I'd never! It's just . . . exciting! To know what they're worth."

I slumped into the chenille wingback.

"They're worth a lot. To us."

I turned to Puppa. What I had to say was going to bring the whole night crashing down. I sighed. Puppa focused his eye. He could tell that something heavy was coming.

"Puppa—there's a book I've been looking for. One of yours. I've searched everywhere. Everywhere! And no sign."

"Bar-bar gar argh epps!" he blurted. My jaw dropped.

"That's right! *Tarzan of the Apes!* Do you know where it is?"

His lips parted, and he released a long, hissing breath.

He turned toward the window, raised his knotted hand, and pointed toward the street.

"It's outside?"

He angled his finger to the north and stabbed at the darkness.

The Husband was a reader too. He tended toward the genre stuff: mysteries, spy thrillers, anything with a submarine. Puppa called them "gumdrops." The Husband would bring one of his paperback recommendations, Puppa would present *his* suggested reading material, and the two men would swap. The Husband called it "The First Street Book Club."

Sometimes, after our guest left, Puppa would perform a little sight gag for me. He'd hold the dime store novel aloft and read the title—"*The Icarus Agenda*!"—in a cheesy announcer voice, and would pretend to throw the book in the garbage. He always read them, though. He'd blow through them in a day, a smile on his face the whole time, often chuckling aloud, as if we were reading a great work of literary humor. It took The Husband months to finish the books that Puppa gave him, and they wouldn't discuss until both men had finished their homework. When they did, *The Icarus Agenda* would be given the same intellectual consideration as *White Noise*.

I disliked the practice. Our books were far better than The Husband's, so the collateral terms didn't line up. Not that I voiced my displeasure. They were Puppa's books.

I was fitting a dovetail on a dresser drawer, if memory serves. The work required concentration, and the words flew loose behind me. A few scraps fell into my ear, and the scraps were book-related, so I tuned in to what was being said.

"You talkin' about the comic books?" asked The Husband.

"No," said Puppa. "The adventure books. The novels."

"Nope. I saw the movies."

"Oh, the books are better. Much darker. In the movies, he's just some handsome actor. In the books, he's a real savage!"

"Sounds goofy."

"It's classic! I think you'll love it. I've got the first one. I'll see if I can find it."

Blood pooled in my organs. Hands, feet, face—all numb. I turned to Puppa.

"You let him borrow it, didn't you?"

He closed his eye and hung his head.

"And then he got killed. And you never got it back."

No response. The eye remained closed, and his head down, as if he were in an uncomfortable state of sleep.

"And now . . . *she* has it."

Puppa's face was a Rorschach interpretation of regret. Clearly, the loss of the book had haunted him all these years. It had haunted us both, separately, and neither had wanted to reveal the loss to the other.

Puppa didn't remember any "Chicago: A. C. McClurg, 1914." I occasionally consulted the copyright line in a given work but never paid any attention to the contents of the colophon. Again: we collected literature, not books. No telling what edition we'd had. What edition *she* had.

"What's this all about?" Mummy demanded. "Who is *she*?"

Testosterone gushed down my brain stem and through the plumbing in my spine. I turned to Mummy. She recoiled from the violence in my eyes.

"You know who," I sneered through gritted teeth. "LITTLE MISS SUNSHINE!"

- 15 -
SHERMAN'S MARCH

The previous evening was still warm in my heart. There'd been singing! Costumed dancing! In between exuberances, we ate and drank, and we plied the lost art of conversation. Once *Tarzan* was out of the bag, there was no getting him back in. My guests were fascinated. The party morphed into a gumdrop thriller pitch session. The scenarios varied, but they all had me as the hero and my guests as an ensemble of colorful accomplices. Our mission: to rescue the fabled feral man. The Alluring Librarian, Viktor, and Oleg swore fealty to my cause. Dolly was noncommittal but did show some interest when the role of "lookout" was presented. Terrance was dubious throughout. He stood, arms crossed across his chest, shaking his head at our clandestine hypotheticals.

Dolly's ringtone was the only unpleasantness. It interrupted our fun every thirty minutes. Dolly would lift the device with annoyance and *urgh* at the caller ID, as if surprised by the identity of her fervent late-night harasser.

She'd apologize to the group, request our silence, and take the call. "Everything's fine" and "we're just hanging out" and "go to sleep, Mom." It was an amusing conspiracy. The brothers fought to hold their giggles at bay. A bit more back-and-forth on the wireless, and then Dolly would cover the receiver and confirm that Terrance was good to remain. "Just thirty more minutes. Yes, Mom. *Yes*, Mom. Terrance will bring me home." With that, she'd clap her phone shut, and our merriments would proceed in another half-hour burst until the phone rang again and the process was repeated. Five times in total. Four A.M. arrived. Dolly's mother would be put off no longer. It was time to draw our evening to a close.

There was a matter of footwear to consider. Terrance had to roll Dolly home. The Alluring Librarian wished to accompany them, but she perished at the thought of enduring the sojourn in stilettoes. The laws of chivalry offered me guidance. When a gentleman escorts a lady and the temperature falls below her comfort level, he must offer her his jacket. I would not be escorting, and The Alluring Librarian had a jacket of her own, but she was in need of trekking shoes, of which I had plenty. I presented the concept. We performed a stocking foot comparison. My feet, and those of the beguiling Hindu, were of near-identical size.

As every sophisticate knows, it's bad taste to leave a bedchamber door open when guests are about, and one must never include the boudoir on any "grand tour" of a private residence. The current situation challenged this etiquette. My bedchamber door was closed, and the bedchamber was where I kept my shoes.

"Wow," said The Alluring Librarian upon entering my sanctum. "This is a *pink* room."

"The shade has been scientifically proven to lower

anxiety and promote a tranquil, compliant disposition," I informed. "They use it in prisons and drunk tanks."

The brothers piled in after, and Dolly rolled in after them, and Terrance brought up the rear.

"Look at this bed!" exclaimed Viktor.

"It's a Scrooge bed," said Oleg.

"Like in *A Christmas Carol*," agreed Viktor.

I was shocked. The twin gorillas were exactly right. Puppa and Mummy had given me the bed for my sweet sixteen. "Ebenezer Scrooge bed" had been the top item on my Christmas list for years, but I'd never thought I'd get one. Puppa constructed it at work, during his breaks, and threw a tarp over it so the bosses wouldn't get wise. Mummy sewed the sumptuous drapery. Erotic confession: Sometimes, to punctuate an orgasm, I'll cry, "There's more of gravy than the grave about you!" It just leaps out. Best not to analyze pillow talk.

The ghosts of Christmas Past, Present, and Future were joined by a new specter—that of a mind-bending, misfit orgy. I suspect that I was the only one so haunted, but who can say? I'd never hosted guests before or attended a private house party, but I couldn't imagine doing either and not, at some point, considering group sex as a possible recreation. This immoral instinct could be the impetus for the "closed bedchamber door" rule. Door closed: *This party is a wholesome, Christian affair.* Door open: *This party is a bacchanal, and your host is DTF.*

My cooler head prevailed. *Too soon,* I thought. If anything were to happen between Dolly and self, it would have to proceed slowly and naturally. A young couple should not experiment with the swinger lifestyle before sharing their first kiss. I opened the closet and revealed my array of footwear.

"I recommend these," I said, pulling forth a pair of blue suede penny loafers. "They're practical, but the color imbues them with a little rock 'n' roll flair."

The Alluring Librarian tried them on.

"I love them," she said.

A thought flashed. A forbidden one. Were it not for the hour, and for my slight crapulence, I don't think I would have dared give voice to it.

"I'll trade you," I said.

She didn't gather my meaning.

"Don't worry," she said. "I'll get them back to you."

"No. I'll *trade* you. My shoes for yours."

You could have heard a pin drop. Eyes were agog, mouths were agape. You'd have thought I'd gone for the orgy suggestion.

"Are you serious?" she asked.

"I am, but please, don't think it's some all-or-nothing proposition. If you prefer to borrow the loafers, and carry your heels with you, then by all means. I was just thinking of what you said. 'I'm done with them.' If that's so—if you were going to throw them away, or stuff them in the back of your closet—I'd like to have them."

"He's a fruit!" cried Viktor.

"A tutti-frutti!" seconded Oleg.

"Don't say that," The Alluring Librarian chastised.

"What are you going to do with a pair of high heels?" Terrance asked. He was amused, but also a little creeped-out.

"I'm disappointed in your reactions," I said. "What do you think I'm going to do? Wear them to the grocery store?"

"Maybe," said Viktor.

"To buy . . . *fruit*," said Oleg. The brothers laughed as one.

"Not appropriate," the Librarian chastised again. She was a good chastiser. Part of her training, I assume.

"Let me put your minds at ease," I said. "You've seen my costume closet. You've partaken of its wonders. Do you think I maintain this theatrical assortment for my own pleasure? Nay! My costumes are eldercare aids. I've told you about my daily performances. Some days, it's drama; other days, it's comedy; it's the latter that draws me to the stiletto heels."

"You're going to perform for your *grandfather* in drag?" asked Terrance.

"As Lemmon and Curtis! As Hanks and Scolari! Puppa will lose his mind. I've wanted to do it forever. Mummy has plenty of dresses I could use, but primitive gender stigmas have prevented me from securing the appropriate footwear. Only an idiot would purchase shoes online, and the thought of going to an actual store, and having a salesperson assist me in the process . . . could you imagine? I'm an open-minded person, but I'm also a local businessman, and one does have a reputation to uphold."

The miasma of perversion was lifted. My guests were now laughing with me, not *at* me. The Alluring Librarian examined her penny-loafered profile in my cheval mirror.

"I'll wear these all the time," she said.

"And I'll wear yours only as Blanche DuBois." I shifted into "fading southern belle." "'I . . . I . . . I took the blows in my face and my body! All of those deaths! The long parade to the graveyard!'"

The deal was made. Our revels had ended. My guests exited via The Ladies' Entrance. Terrance carried Dolly. Oleg hauled the wheelchair, which he claimed as tit for tat but Viktor disputed, as the latter had done the more difficult upward climb.

"The shoes are over there," said The Alluring Librarian. "Next to your little gnome."

We stood at the back gate and exchanged farewells. The brothers embraced me. I got pecks on the cheek from Dolly and the Librarian. Terrance patted me on the shoulder. My guests dispersed into the darkness.

The ruby slippers. What magic did they hold? At last, I understood why the Wicked Witch had gone through all the trouble. I moved to the garden box. I almost expected them to be gone—to have vanished back into the shadow realm from which they had sprung—but there they were, resting on the soil. I lifted them. My body shuddered. I brought the shoes to my nose and whiffed. There was a hint of foot odor—just enough to ground them in the real world—and other smells. Lilac. Cigarette smoke. Wildflower. A whisper of musk. They were The Mute and The Alluring Librarian in equal measure.

I stood nude before the cheval. On my feet: the glittering red stilettos. I felt indescribably sexy. The five-inch heels tightened my calves, lifted my buttocks. I turned my back to the mirror and consulted my reflection over the shoulder. In the dim light, and when viewed from this perspective, my backside was stripped of its gender. It was a backside that any man, myself included, would be happy to find himself behind. I turned again. The feminine illusion fell away, replaced by one of a sensuous pansexuality. My penis was as rigid as a maypole. For the first time in my life, I felt beautiful. I proceeded to stroke. All I had done, all I had seen, every fantasy, every possibly; I seized them all. I licked my lips. I moaned like a harlot. The psi of my member dropped to half-maximum, and then shot up to three-quarters, and then dropped again, and then pinned the needle, and such a thing had never happened before, and I had no control of it, and my corpora cavernosa expanded and contracted like a blowfish in the death throes. I grew weak in the knees. My magma sought its destiny as lava. At last, the release, and the great silver ribbons flew, splattering against the mirror. There was no shame; no wishing I hadn't done, or pious apologies to all the souls I had violated. I felt clean. The cure was better than the disease. I collapsed on my Ebenezer Scrooge bed and immediately lost consciousness.

I've never been one to impose my company. I'm genteel in this regard. I resist kindnesses imposed by outsiders for fear of the recompense that will be expected. I'm a stoic. A rugged individualist. You could call me many things, but never needy.

These virtues are inseparable from my character. Unfortunately, I've had little chance to exercise them. Rugged individualism is no big accomplishment when you don't have any friends. Until Terrance, I'd never had anyone to impose upon. It was Thursday. Terrance's day off. An imperfect opportunity for a pop-in visit.

I went down to the wood shop and gathered accouterments. Items included:

- ❏ A tape measure
- ❏ A flashlight
- ❏ A voltage tester
- ❏ A small pry bar
- ❏ A changeable screwdriver, a variety of bits

All of this, in service to the "generous offer" I planned to present. I holstered the items on a tool belt.

Puppa had had a special tool—an aluminum skewer, about three feet long. He had used it to probe for rot. Attics, basement ceilings, around chimneys; decks, exterior door frames, anything near a gutter; these are the most common areas of infection. *"En garde!"* Puppa would cry as he thrust the spike into an area of questionable soundness. I performed a thorough search but was unable to find the old tool.

"My fencing foil!" I cried aloud. It was in my chambers, in a wooden barrel with my other prop weaponry. It was the perfect implement for the task. The foil was well balanced and designed for stabbing. The pommel guard would protect my fingers from splinters and creepy-crawlies. It was also a sword. My crusade would take me into Ilium's lower intestinal tract. Who knew what dangers I might encounter? White people didn't go to South of Franklin. It was a rule known to all. A lifetime of folktales had ingrained it. Local news reinforced it. There are those who subscribe to the Neighborhood Watch Newsletter and those who generate the content.

I returned to my chambers, retrieved the foil, and then moved to the bedchamber. I stood before the mirror and practiced my feints, parries, ripostes, and passata sotos. I curled my lip and threatened my reflection. I had no scabbard, but the hammer loop on my tool belt held the weapon quite nicely. The rapier hung dashingly at my hip—a warning to any who might accost me. It would certainly deter any would-be knifeman—assuming, of course, that the knifeman was in his right mind. South of Franklin is a narcotics hotbed and, as we all know, junkies will do anything to get their next "fix."

Victimization always comes at the point of something. South of Franklin, one of three things: knifepoint, gunpoint, or the point of a rapist's penis. So went the narrative. I had knifepoint covered. Penispoint? Any man intent on raping me had better be a necromaniac too, as he'd have to kill me first! Gunpoint was the toughie. The Neighborhood Watch emails weren't filled with tales of urban swashbucklers.

Guns were the thing. I needed a firearm. I slipped down into the parlor and pulled the musket from the wall. I'd be in hot water if Mummy noticed it missing, but she was in the den, liquefying her mind with her daily viewing of *The Price Is Right*. With luck, I'd have it back before she noticed it missing.

So I had the tool belt, the rapier, the musket, and a problem. What if I was stopped by the police? There's a precinct South of Franklin, and the officers there were always on the lookout for misplaced Caucasian wanderers. It's common knowledge: any white person South of Franklin is there to buy drugs or solicit prostitution. The color of my flesh was enough to make me conspicuous; the fencing foil and the muzzle-loading long rifle would stick me out like a sore thumb. I needed a cover story.

Was I . . . a Civil War reenactor?

It solved everything! I was on my way to visit Terrance Johnson, famous local musician, in an attempt to recruit him into our "regiment." We needed . . . a drummer boy! *"Did you know, officer, that freemen were often employed as drummers, owing to their innate sense of rhythm?"* The statement would be false, so far as I knew . . .

Music and the Civil War. Field musicians. Drum corps. Brass bands. Race?

But what chance that an apprehending patrolman would be a history buff?

My weapons weren't period. Our musket is an original 1795 Springfield Flintlock, .69 caliber, nearly four feet long. Any action it saw likely came in the War of 1812. Puppa had received it in trade for some cabinetry work. As for the rapier—it was a sport foil. I purchased it online, and it arrived with a metal button on the end that rendered the tip inert. I ground that off and continued grinding until the blade featured a needle-sharp point. I was inspired by Orson Welles. I've read that he preferred to use actual, sharpened blades in his stage plays. Occasionally an actor would be sliced or impaled, thereby affording a level of violent realism previously unseen in the American theater. I aspired to a similar effect in my morning performances. I'd read from *The Three Musketeers* and cleave the air with my blade, dueling with imagined foes. "Watch where you're swinging that thing!" Mummy would cry, and I'd point the blade, suggesting that the next cut might be for her.

In any case—Civil War soldiers carried sabers, not fencing foils. Again, I would have to rely on the ignorance of any who might intercept me. "It's a practice blade," I would say. "My saber is an antique, it's quite valuable, I only draw it during simulations, and then only to direct maneuvers."

Diplomacy, dear reader. The skilled diplomat must deliver his evasions with total conviction. Look your mark squarely in the eye. Darting pupils, never, and especially not up and to the left, which clearly indicates deception. Speak in a level tone. Too meek: obfuscating. Too zealous: baiting and switching. *Uhs* and *Ums* are as telltale as bloody fingerprints. If you require a pause, fill it with silence. And there you have it. Adopt these techniques, and you'll be able to convince the masses of just about anything.

I was embarking on a dangerous mission, and my sole wish was to complete it unmolested. I certainly didn't want to shoot anyone. I had only fired the musket once in my life, years ago, shortly after Puppa acquired it. He showed me the various steps: half-cock, tear the charge, ball, powder, wadding, ramrod, prime the pan. We reflected on the difficulties that such a process must have posed to our revolutionary ancestors. We didn't shoot anything. Our backyard is far too small for that, and no telling where the unpredictable projectile would have ended up. We skipped the lead ball and fired the weapon blank. No boom. A jet of flame, a puff of smoke. Anticlimactic, really.

Our black powder was kept in the kitchen, in a rusted tin under the sink, behind the cleaning supplies. Not an ideal environment in which to store a combustible. I retrieved the tin and gave it a shake. There was very little powder in it—one or two charges, tops—and what was there was decades old. It would have to do.

I searched for the balls. We had five of them. They'd been in the parlor for years, in a pewter gravy boat that sat on the hutch. No sign. Their absence had the stink of Mummy's doing. I had mentioned my desire to load the musket on more than one occasion, and she came with the same objections every time. "It's a decoration! You'll shoot yourself!" The stock patter of the urban liberal. I had no doubt that she'd hidden the "bullets" from me. Her chicanery was a clear violation of my Second Amendment rights.

Fortunately, Mummy knew nothing about the design or function of the weapon. I had the charge—I just needed a round projectile of the appropriate circumference. My marbles! Mummy's bleeding heart had not deigned to seize *them*. The glass cat's-eyes—which had so recently served as an object of humiliation—were back to their usual place, on my office windowsill, in a Mason jar. They played beautifully with the light. I picked through them and found that the shooters were a near-perfect fit to the musket's bore.

I had my ball and power. I cut some strips of wadding from an old T-shirt. Munitions, present and accounted for. The same could not be said for my confidence in the weapon's reliability. A misfire was probable; catastrophic failure, highly possible. The barrel hadn't seen a projectile in God knew how long. Firing a marble from a Springfield

Infantry Musket seemed like something you *could* do, but I wasn't sanguine as to the *should.* There were also legal concerns. Marching through South Ilium with an unloaded antique? I couldn't see there being anything illegal about that. Doing the same with a loaded long rifle? I would carry the munitions in a fanny pack. If sprung upon, I would have to load the weapon *in medias res.* Nothing ideal about it, but our forefathers had fought a revolution in similar fashion, and we had a nation to show for it. The musket was an antiquated weapon, but time had not served to diminish its destructive promise. No one—not even a smackhouse junkie—would want to be shot by a .69-caliber ball. I would put my faith in the intimidation factor.

My attention turned to dress. I'd planned to wear my workman's overalls over a crisp white oxford. Any inspection of Terrance's home would undoubtedly lead me into some dirty nooks and crooks, but I was also meeting Ms. Johnson for the first time, and it was important that I make a good impression. The overalls were worn but clean. They suggested quality work tidily done. I have an old Greek fisherman's cap that I don for manual tasks. It's a bit ragged, but in a casually manful sort of way. The hat promised "old-world craftsmanship with a dash of flair." A red bow tie completed the getup. I was buttoned up and put together. Had I been handsome, I'd have looked exactly like the type of man you'd want working on your house.

The rapier and musket were unforeseen accessories. A Civil War uniform—a *Union* uniform—would have been just the ticket. Parading boldly through South Ilium, clad in Union blue, musket at my shoulder and rapier at my hip, my brass buttons gleaming in the sun . . . the story would have sold itself. "Oh," a passing patrolman would say, "there goes a young Civil War reenactor. Such a fine display of patriotism in so low a place." The uniform might also afford me safe passage. The local thuggery might fall upon a random Caucasian stranger, but a Union soldier? I'd be clad in the uniform of their liberation! It had to count for something.

Alas, I didn't have a Civil War uniform. I had the pirate costume, and the musket and rapier would have paired finely with that, but what excuse could I use? "Officer, I am the treasurer of the Northeast Buccaneer Appreciation Society, on my way to recruit a new swabby." Ridiculous. It had to be Civil War. My Greek fisherman's cap might pass for a Union forage cap from a distance. As for the jacket, the closest thing I had to Civil War issue was a tuxedo tailcoat. I owned a tux, as every man must, and I wore it once a year, for our family's black tie New Year's celebration. It was not a military garment, but it was, essentially, a frock coat, tails and all, and frock coats were standard issue for Union officers. If only it had been in blue. Then again, that would mean that I owned a blue tuxedo, which is only appropriate for professional clowns.

"What's with the tux?" the officer would ask.

"It's a Union funereal jacket," I would tell him. I dressed it up with a red sash and some of Puppa's Navy insignia pins.

Eleven ten A.M. The cool bluster of previous days had given way to an unseasonable balminess. The conditions didn't call for a jacket, and I perspired as a result of wearing one. I was a soldier. My discomfort heightened the reality. I marched south. A Google map printout informed my course.

Funny how walking unmasks the details. My neighborhood. Terrain so familiar that it has long since passed beyond reflection. Scenes. Details. As unexamined as the air we breathe. Now I was looking.

The sidewalks. Slabs of blue slate. A hundred years of shifting. One slab, slanted to the east; the next, sunken, a four-inch drop, and encroaching on the previous like an ingrown toenail, and the next tile straight, the next smashed, with a sharp edge jutting skyward.

Frankencars. At least one example per block. American beaters. Example: a 1990 Chevrolet Caprice. I'm not a car buff—the registration sticker said so. Blue hood. Front fenders, white. The rest, champagne-tan and rust. Cars like patchwork quilts.

Brick. The flesh of Ilium. From high above (my chamber window), from behind glass (while riding the bus), it all seems as one brick, with the city as bas-relief carved into it. The brick decays. Pillows of moss pop the mortar. Ivy clings to walls. Consumes the walls. Pulls Ilium slowly to the grave.

Graffiti. Another symptom of the social disease that's spreading out of Brooklyn. Not the graffiti itself, but the attitude toward it. I've read credentialed journalists who take the word *graffiti,* set it before *artist,* and use that grotesque nomenclature to suggest a new class of savant. Oh, the Caucasian culturati and their endless glom for "authenticity" and their obsequious endorsement of lower-class folkways. Everything is permissible, all wrongs forgivable, so long as they're "real" and done in someone else's neighborhood.

I passed a piece of "street art."

MaG/neTo

It was a block script composition, spray-painted on the side of an abandoned pizzeria. What's the message? What was I to take from this? Is it a name? A concept? Artistically, it had the value of a burning bag of dog feces left on a doorstep.

Smashed bottles. The shards ground smooth under foot and tire, and sharper bits nestled in beds of sparkling dust.

I was perspiring heavily. I removed my cap and wiped the sweat from my brow. The air smelled strangely of cut hay. In the distance, the clattering sound of a freight train.

Across the street, two adolescents. One black, one white. *Why aren't they in school?* They straddled BMX bicycles. Their union implied nothing good. They followed me with their eyes but said nothing.

My journey took me past the Quix Mart bodega. Pakistani-owned. I knew the proprietor. He kept me "in the snuff," through special arrangement with his tobacco supplier. A vinyl banner advertised "Cold Beer—Soda—Cold Cuts—Sub—Coffee—Grocery." A string of pennants celebrated the New York State Lottery. A black woman, enormously fat, sat on a milk crate outside the store entrance and stabbed her finger into a cellular phone. She glanced up at my passing and took note. Musket. Rapier. Caucasian troll in tails. She'd seen stranger.

Corner of 3rd and Division. A ratty old pickup rolled up and impeded my progress. The engine hacked, and oily smoke belched from the tailpipe. On the rear window, a decal of a mischievous boy urinating on a Ford logo. The truck's bed was filled with scrap. A Caucasian barbarian piloted the jalopy. His arm rested on the open window. His hands were black with grime and his lower lip was stuffed full of chaw. He was filthy, and the filth seemed to have shaken off of him, caking the cabin. He spotted me and did a double take.

"Hey!" he shouted.

"*Hey* yourself," I replied.

"There a parade or somethin'?"

"Not today. July 4th. We've got practice."

He smiled. His oral tobacco was like a rotten lip. His teeth were stained with juice.

"Good luck," he said and rattled away.

Third and Van Buren. Brownstones gave on to row houses; brick gave on to chipped paint and aluminum siding. The city flattened and widened. Strange businesses. A shop that sells used vacuums and sewing machines. A china shop that's always been there but I've never seen open. I was rarely down that far. Two, three times in my life.

My greatest fear: to encounter a pack of young black men. A racist fear, sure, but not one born of ignorance. I was right to fear it. A lifetime of experiences had borne it out. The timing of my expedition had been informed by the old stereotype—urban blacks never arise before noon. The streets were empty. I could count on two hands the people I had seen. I consulted my pocket watch: 11:35 A.M. On schedule.

Native guides are the best way to secure safe passage. Every paleface adventurer knows this. At the risk of mixing historical metaphors: I was in serious need of a Sacagawea. Franklin Street lay ahead. It was all "south of" from there. I thought of Spinach Dress. Running across her would have been balm for the weary. Women love a man in uniform. My musket and rapier might give her pause, but they might also work some phallic symbolism on her subconscious. I scanned in all directions. No sign of her, nor of anyone else. Last call for tobacco. A meaty shot up the left nostril, another up the right. I marched on.

I feared street-corner barbecues. I feared Japanese and German automobiles with blacked-out windows, resplendent in gold or silver trims, throbbing with R&B heartbeats. I feared double-dutching black girls. I feared arguments, shouted cross-street from one open window to another. I feared elderly black men in concrete parks playing chess. I feared the occasional white woman, a fat one, always a fat one, towing a row of mulatto children behind her, cussing them out in that implacable urban dialect that lies somewhere between black inner city and rural white trash. I feared young black men. Gangs of them, lounging on front stoops. I'd seen all of these things. An example here, an example there, over the course of years. Whenever South of Franklin came up in conversation—whenever I pictured the place—I would gather these disparate observations together and dump them in that hallucinated place. A place I had passed through, but never set foot in. A place that wasn't for me. South of Franklin was Caucasoid Ilium's fever dream.

Desolation. That's all there was. South of Franklin was a bit grimier than my neighborhood, but not much, and it would all shine up nicely, and my neighborhood would too, if more people had the will and money for it. Those who had the will, and had the money, had left long ago. South of Franklin was South Ilium; South Ilium was Chernobyl after the meltdown. There were no people. Signs of them, everywhere, but nothing in the way of life. Row homes in clusters—three, four of them adjoining—and then a small house, a cinderblock cottage or a one-story bungalow, and then something condemned, windows boarded up, and on and on this way, along the pockmarked pavements. Tiny backyards and side lots, rusted chain link fences. A crippled swing set. A plastic kiddie pool filled with muck.

It was early. A quarter to twelve. If my prejudices held, they'd all be waking soon, and the streets would become the monster I had learned to fear. Or maybe not. Maybe the noontide wake-up rule was just a myth. The greatest danger lay in darkness. So the fables said. So I believed. I'd be nowhere near that spot when darkness fell. My racism was a huge part of who I was. It gave me reasons. If it helped me to stay alive, it was worth having.

I knew the address because Terrance had mentioned it in passing: 38 Liberty Street. Single story, eggshell blue. You'd call it craftsman, although it was age and neglect, not architectural style, which defined the structure. The roof was in rough shape. The gutters hung like a broken collarbone. The windows were barred on the outside and shaded within by heavy drapes.

I mounted the front porch. The boards did not so much creak as mush underfoot. I drew my rapier and stabbed. It would all have to go.

There was a brass door knocker. I tapped out *shave and a haircut* in tight, percussive raps. The cadence and amplitude of a knock speaks to the intentions of the knocker, and I wanted mine to sound playful, friendly, like a pleasant surprise. I stepped off the porch, down to the walkway, and sculpted my features into a mask of benevolent joy. Puppa taught me: when paying a visit, you must always step away from the door after knocking. If possible, down to street level, so that your host can view you in full from above. This will increase their comfort and provide adequate space for the trading of salutations. So that's what I did. There was a peephole in the door. I couldn't see through it, yet I had the sudden impression that I was being watched. I smiled gaily at the glass eyeball. A bit of waiting. Maybe a sigh, maybe a *"What the . . . ?"* from the other side, or maybe I was hearing things. A racket of lock tumblers. The rattle of a door chain. The door swung inward and there stood Terrance.

"Buddy?" he asked, dumbfounded.

"Terrance! So good to see you!"

He was dressed in a white V-neck tee and nylon athletic shorts. Always with the V-necks. Tight collars itched him, he said, but I suspected a different motivation. He had marvelous pecs. If I had such pecs I'd go shirtless to the library.

Terrance leaned out the door and scanned the street.

"What are you doing here?"

"I was out for a stroll. Lovely day for it. I happened to find myself in your neighborhood."

"Who is it?" cried a shrill voice from inside the house.

"Don't worry, Ma," Terrance shouted back over his shoulder. "It's a friend of mine." Then to me: "This is not a neighborhood where people 'find themselves,' Buddy."

"You mean physically, or spiritually? Because I meant—"

"What the *hell* are you wearing?"

"Overalls, tuxedo jacket, fisherman's cap—"

"Gun, sword!" he interrupted.

"Those are just accessories."

"Why do you have them?"

I unbuttoned my jacket and opened it, revealing the arrangement of utilities about my waist.

"I came equipped with many tools, Terrance. The rapier is a weapon, that's true, but its purpose today is purely utilitarian. If you look down to where you're standing, you'll see a deep gouge where I stabbed your porch. As for the musket . . ."

"Is it loaded?" he asked sharply. His eyes continued to scout our surroundings. I took a step closer and spoke softly.

"Not at this moment, but I am prepared with the proper armaments."

"Terrance!?" came the voice again. "Who's out there?"

"It's okay, Mom. One second." I had pushed him into a quagmire. There appeared to be no one else around, but his apprehensive ogling suggested that the street had eyes and they might be upon us now, absorbing the spectacle of my arrival. I had created a "scene," and scenes were exactly the type of thing you wanted to avoid South of Franklin. Politeness demanded that he invite me in. Anything short would throw me to the wolves.

"My mother is sensitive about things like this. Structure is big for her."

"I'm Mr. Structure!"

"She's going to be upset, and not very pleasant."

That was unfortunate. I felt sorry about it, but was no other way. I removed my cap and placed it over my chest.

"I know it's inappropriate, but I felt compelled—in the name of friendship—to pay you a visit. Not so long ago, you imposed upon me. I was furious. And if you hadn't done it—if you'd been unwilling to endure the awkwardness—we never would have gotten to know each other. Today I'm violating you. It's for your own good. Now invite me inside."

He hung his head. His mother warbled again from inside the house.

"Give me the gun," he said.

"Of course," I said, and mounted the front steps.

"The sword too."

"Are you sure? It might be a nice conversation starter."

"I'm sure."

"I could use it to 'cut the ice.'" I transformed my index finger into a tiny rapier and pantomimed a possible ice-cutting technique.

"No."

"Get it, though? *Cut the ice*?"

"I get it."

"I promise—the sword will stay on my hip."

"No."

"It's really just a piece of jewelry at this point."

"No."

Phase One: Complete. I'd made it. My body chemistry adjusted to suit the challenge at hand. We were in a small entryway. Terrance seized my weapons and stowed them in a closet.

I'd never been inside a black person's house before. I had some expectations. Black people, it seems to me, possess a design sensibility that's unique to their race. I was prepared for tribal art. African masks and whatnot. I'd seen this manner of bric-a-brac in the discount sections of discount department stores and wondered *who buys this stuff?* and then I realized *oh, black people must!* I expected animal prints. Cheetah in particular. Zebra also. To my Caucasian eyes, these patterns are tacky to the extreme, but I could understand the cultural significance they might hold for Afro-Americans. I expected it to be hot. Black people prefer temperatures above eighty-five degrees. I know this because I heard Little Miss Sunshine's husband complain about it all those years ago. "I keep a lock box over the thermostats—and they put a bag of ice over them!" He was a great font of racial insight. Anecdotes. Bons mots. I've yet to meet an urban rental property owner who doesn't sling them.

Terrance's home did not match my expectations. It was dim and cool. The kitchen was worn but clean. Formica table, a mismatched set of dining chairs. Dated fixtures and appliances, nothing newer than the middle 1980s. In the dish rack, a carnival of silverware, plates, and mugs, no two alike. Yellow wallpaper, blistered, seams peeling, a section repaired with packing tape.

An archway connected the kitchen and living room, and Terrance pointed in that direction and shushed me. I perked my ears. A television could be heard. Chimes, whistles, a game-show host chirping like a piccolo. *The Price Is Right.* The audioscape of this show typically repulses me, but it was soothing in that movement. Mummy and Puppa were watching the same program, at that very instant, in a safer part of town. The showcase totals were about to be revealed.

Terrance indicated, through hand gestures, that he was going to enter the living room and that I should remain where I was. I took the opportunity to visually inspect the kitchen ceiling for water damage.

"Mom . . . we have a guest," Terrance said as he entered the other room.

"Who's out there?" The voice was old and tremulous, like someone speaking through a tin-can phone.

"It's my friend Buddy. He's just paying me a visit."

"I'm not dressed for company," the voice complained.

"You look great, Ma."

Discoloration. In the far corner, above the cabinets. A bad sign.

"My program isn't over," the old woman said.

But it was. The bell chimed. The loser had overbid. The winner had bid a dollar.

"Hey, Buddy," Terrance called. "Come on in."

I straightened my appearance by feel. Bowtie, collar, cap. I gave my tuxedo tails a ruffle. Nothing more to do. I slid my hand under my lapel, upon my breast, *à la* Napoleon, and entered.

The living room. White stucco walls. A picture window, drapes drawn. An upright piano. The piano seemed to glow with the heat of recent use, like the tubes in an old radio. A recliner. An old console television. A sofa with a gold lamé slipcover, threadbare, stained at the armrests. The air was stale.

Terrance's mother sat in a wheeled chair. Not a *wheelchair,* with the large wheels that can be operated by the sitter, but that other kind, higher-backed, more like an accent chair with a set of casters on the bottom. She wore a turquoise muumuu. She was a large woman. There was a sag to every part of her. The effect was amplified by a bad case of dropsy. Her legs were bare from knee to ankle, from muumuu hem to house slipper, and these lower extremities were grotesquely swollen. The mother's complexion was darker than her son's—a fact that I wouldn't have thought possible, as Terrance was one of the darkest men I'd ever seen. She wore a wig. A hint of stocking cap could be seen peeking out below it. Terrance stood beside her.

Her eyes were on me from the moment I entered. Those eyes! I nearly gasped at the sight of them. They were Terrance's eyes! Yellowed, yes, and the lids rimmed with pink and the whites shot with capillaries, yet they were still beautiful. I studied her features. The edema swell was also present in her face, and her features were buried underneath, but you could see the traces, the hints of what had been, like gazing upon an ancient ruin and estimating its former greatness. It would not be clear to many, but I am a student of appearance, so it was immediately clear to me. Terrance's mother had spent her better years as a total knockout.

I removed my cap with a flourish, swept it in the air before me, and bowed deeply at the waist.

"Ms. Johnson . . . it is *my pleasure* to make your acquaintance."

She cocked her head at my regal display.

"Who are you?"

"This is Buddy," said Terrance. "He's a friend of mine."

The volume of his voice was turned up a click. I took this to mean that I should do the same. I rose from my bow and held my cap over my heart like a schoolboy reciting the pledge of allegiance.

"My given name is Charles," I told her. "You may call me that if you prefer."

"Terrance didn't tell me you were coming. I'm not dressed."

"If you will permit my objection," I said, "I think you look very nice. I'm quite taken by the color of your dress. Turquoise becomes you."

She didn't know what to make of my compliment. It seemed to please some part of her, but it was coming from me, an ugly Caucasian stranger, who was standing in her living room. My presence had her totally off-kilter.

"Why are you dressed like that?" she demanded.

"Oh . . . these old rags?"

"You look like a butler."

"My other jacket is at the cleaners."

"Are you in the army?"

She squinted at my jacket. I followed her gaze. The sash. The WWII insignia pins. Their presence had slipped my mind.

"I wear them in appreciation of our veterans, and to honor the boys currently in action. You know, I considered joining the Navy, but the whole 'communal bathroom' thing just wouldn't have worked."

She was annoyed. Her beautiful eyes disapproved of me. She looked at me as if I were an aggressive panhandler.

"Are you sick?" she asked.

"I don't think so. Why?"

"You don't look right."

"Oh, I see. I'm quite well. Just strange-looking."

"You ain't kiddin'."

"Ma," Terrance scolded. "Be nice."

"You're an ugly little thing," she said.

"Ma. . . ."

"I don't mind, Terrance. Your mother is right. I'm an *ugly little thing.* I've been so all my life."

"What do you want!?"

"He's just paying a quick visit," Terrance said.

"Well, I never heard of him," she said and flicked her wrist as if to rid the air of me.

I sighed. Stepped closer. Terrance's hackles went up. I could smell the change in him, his heightened readiness, his uncertainty about my intentions, but he stayed where he was and permitted my approach. I got down on one knee, directly beside his mother. Ms. Johnson cocked her head and leaned away.

"Ms. Johnson, I've come for a simple reason—to express my gratitude. To express my family's gratitude. To you. For raising such a wonderful son. My Puppa is not well. He's been ill for a long time. Terrance is his nurse."

I related some basic details about Puppa's condition and about Terrance's role in caring for him.

"Terrance would say it's nothing special. That he was just doing his job. That's not so. I've never met anyone who cares more. I didn't like your son at first, Ms. Johnson. I didn't like what he *represented.* Help. The assumption that we needed it. That we were lacking. It was an insult to me. Oh, I wanted to hate your son. I tried. I just couldn't keep it up.

"He invited me to his music night. It might seem like a small thing—and again, I'm sure he'd say that it was no big deal, that he'd invite anyone, all are welcome—but it was the first time anyone ever invited me to anything. I was scared to go. Came up with every reason not to . . . but curiosity finally compelled me. An *invitation*! I had to see. I'm so glad I did, Ms. Johnson. Your son is the rarest thing in the world: an authentic talent. In South Ilium, Terrance Johnson is not a name you say in vain.

"I'm sorry to spoil your morning, but I knew there was no other way. I just had to meet you. Your son means a lot to a lot of people. He means a lot to me. Please forgive my intrusion."

She'd grown emotional about halfway through. Nothing moves a mummy like hearing kind words about her son. There was also her age. Senior citizens are always on the verge. The gentlest strumming of heartstrings can set them over the edge.

I rose and turned to Terrance. He had a dumb look on his face—as if he hadn't understood a word of what I'd said. Then he smiled.

"Would your friend like to stay for lunch?" Ms. Johnson asked.

I did stay. Terrance wheeled his mother out to the kitchen. I sat across from her at the table while Terrance made lunch.

"Tuna melts and tomato soup," he said. "Sound good?"

"Oh . . . well. . . ." I was stammering. Ms. Johnson gave me a muddy look. "Yes! Sounds fantastic."

Terrance retrieved fours cans from a cabinet—two of tuna, two of soup—and a jug of generic mayonnaise from the fridge. My stomach clenched. Mummy and I are avid picklers and smokers, so I can appreciate the utility of preserved foods . . . but this? Canned tuna? Canned . . . *soup*!? Who knew what chemicals they contained!? I'd expected many dangers South of Franklin, but dysentery had not been among them. It was a wonder Ms. Johnson wasn't dead already. What could I do? Mummy and Puppa had raised me right. Please, thank you, and never refuse a meal offered in kindness. When the visit was over, on my walk home, I would find a dumpster and shove my fingers down my throat.

Terrance and I chitchatted while he prepared the noxious meal. We remained in shallow conversational waters. Ms. Johnson said next to nothing.

"So, Terrance—I was wondering if I could ask you a favor. I have a small home-improvement project that I'm getting into. The closet in our downstairs foyer is not insulated properly. The air from the basement seeps through and creates a nasty draft. I'd like to rip it all out, spray-foam it, and replace the old paneling with sheetrock. I could use an extra pair of hands. Just for a couple of hours." I turned to Ms. Johnson. "These old houses. It's always something."

"I know it," she said.

I returned to Terrance.

"And of course, if you need any help with projects of your own, I'd be happy to lend a hand." Back to the mother. "I'm a do-it-yourselfer, Ms. Johnson. Home improvement is my passion! You've noticed my tool belt, no doubt. I wear it at all times—just in case there's a thing that needs fixing. 'Mr. Fix-It.' That's what they call me. Feel free to do so yourself!"

"Okay, Mr. Fix-It," said Terrance. "Do you like your tuna melt with pickles or without?"

"Excuse me?" I'd heard him just fine. What kind of hot mess was he making over there? The whole fish and cheese thing was bad enough. Fish is *never* to be paired with cheese. That's a given. And now pickles? Was he going to serve this lunch in dog bowls?

"Do you want sliced pickles on your sandwich?" He articulated each word in a most annoying manner.

"Of course! That's just how I like it!" *Never refuse a meal offered in kindness.* "May I ask—what are our cheese options? I'll take gruyere if you have it."

Terrance opened the refrigerator and retrieved a yellow, brick-shaped box.

"We've got Velveeta, Velveeta, or Velveeta."

"Velveeta?"

"You've never heard of Velveeta?"

"Is it Czech?"

He held up the box and read from the face of it.

"'Processed Cheese Food.' I'm guessing it's American."

Gouda I could handle. A mild emmental, even. I would have settled for a pedestrian cheddar! As for this block of Yellow #5 and hydrogenated oil, masquerading as dairy? I'd have preferred waterboarding.

"I'm unfamiliar but *so* excited to try it."

Butter sizzled in the frying pan. The bread: "Wonder." This I knew. Mummy had a joke about it. "I *wonder* how they call it bread?" The only natural component of this meal would be the tuna, the *canned* tuna, full of mercury and bits of dolphin. I averted my eyes and steered the conversation back on course.

"Anyway, Terrance—about that project."

"You want me to help you out? No problem, but I don't think I'll be much help. I told you before, I don't know anything about that stuff."

"I remember. You lamented the costs of home improvement and your own lack of DIY experience. Well, Terrance—well, Ms. Johnson—I've come to make an offer."

"An offer of what?" Terrance asked.

"I'm about to come into some money. Thirty thousand dollars. Not an earth-shattering amount, but if we apply it wisely, and do the labor ourselves, it could go far."

People perk up when there's talk of money in the air. Ms. Johnson went all ears. Terrance was nonplussed.

"You've got thirty thousand dollars laying around?"

"Not yet. I'm just wrapping up a job for a boutique fashion retailer based in New York City. When it's done, that's what I'll get."

"That's a lot of money."

"My vocation is quite lucrative."

"I guess so."

"I'd like to loan it to you. I say *loan,* and not *give,* because you are clearly a proud people, and it is not for me to offer charity. Thirty thousand dollars, at 1 percent non-compounding annual interest, with a ten-year term. The loan balance will be $33,000, to be paid back at a rate of $275 a month."

"You want to loan us $30,000?"

"And my expertise. And Puppa's. And I'll grant you full access to our workshop. We'll rope in the Novokhatsky Brothers. Their reputation for HVAC and plumbing is quite good, and I'm sure they can swing a hammer with the best of them. They admire you. This job will call for some grunt. Who better than a pair of trained apes?"

Ms. Johnson was turned toward Terrance. She seemed interested in what I was saying but far more interested in how her son reacted to it.

"Buddy, it's very generous. And sure, the house could use some work. But $30,000 is a lot of money, and I know you could find plenty of ways to use it."

"The cash does represent some—aesthetic virtues—that I've been chasing after for some time. A benchmark, if you will. An accomplishment. How fleeting they can be if we don't stop to ask ourselves: am I ready for this? Is *now* the time? I've decided it's not. I'm enjoying the current state of affairs. I'd like to live in this time for a while."

I owed the man. I truly wanted to help him. I also sought dominion over him, so that I might keep him, and also bend him toward my objectives. Terrance opened doors. He had things that I wanted. Prestige. Access. I disdained the bona fides that our interracial friendship granted me, but I was coming to know their power. The deepest bonds are based on mutual exploitation. If I was to use him, I had to offer him a way to use me back.

"What do you think, Ma?"

Ms. Johnson turned to me. Her expression remained incredulous, but there was some softening to it, and the first hints of a smile.

"What kind of work do you have in mind?" she asked.

Without the benefit of a mirror, can one say that one's own eye "twinkled"? One can't, but I'm sure mine did. I could feel it.

"An inspection is called for," I said. "Terrance—bring my rapier!"

- 16 -
A TRAGIC TRUANCY

Storywise, and from a marketing perspective, it would probably be better to say that the events described in this novel all happened "over the course of a madcap week." I tried for that level of compression, but it was too much. The best I could do was to stick it all in a season. Spring 2006. Even that feels a bit too tight. I hope it doesn't push your credulity too far. "Yes, and. . . ." This is the foundation of comedic storytelling. This tale operates in picaresque time. I've spooned enough. On to the conclusion.

- - -

Sunday. I told Puppa about Spinach Dress and the after-party, and of my fearless expedition through South Ilium's meanest streets. I told him about my visit with Terrance and Ms. Johnson, and of my munificent home reno proposition. "The interest rate is generously low," I told him, "but it's there, in deference to the fact that time is—and always shall be—money." He applauded my approach. If the offer had been pure charity, his working-class ethos would have choked on it. I had taken the lessons he'd taught me. When Mummy returned from her Sunday errands, she found Puppa and me in the drawing room, running through some rough concepts and estimates. I keyed her in.

"I think it's a wonderful idea," she said.

"Puppa will serve as Project Manager, I as foreman. Can we recruit you as an interior-design consultant?"

"I'd be thankful for the opportunity!" she gushed.

"This could be an exciting new venture for you. Terrance is our community's top celeb. Do a good job for him and you'll be beating off new clients with a stick."

"I'm just excited to help," she said. Then she pondered. A chin stroking commenced. The chin was whiskerless. She had just received a fresh plucking at the beauty parlor. "It would be nice to start my own business, though."

"Then again," I said, "you'd really be working for *me,* since I'm forking over the dough."

"You're not the client in this scenario," she said. "In this scenario, you're the bank."

"I'm the benefactor. He who pays the piper calls the tune."

"I refuse to be employed under such terms. If you want my help, you must give me carte blanche."

My eye for interior design was advanced, but Mummy had a real panache with the feminine touches, and it was a panache I lacked. Her palate was "refined hominess"; mine, "muddled sophistication." If you're a gentleman and looking to appoint your stateroom or hunting lodge, you'll find no better designer than me. As for the tasteful beautification of family spaces? Nobody beats Mummy.

"Very well," I said. "You may consult with Terrance and Ms. Johnson directly. I'll push back where necessary, but only when architectural or budgeting considerations demand it. Puppa and I were talking. We're thinking bungalow. Crank up the Arts & Crafts elements."

"Love it!"

"Expose the rafters."

"Yes!"

"A dormer up front."

"How could you not?"

"The front porch. Theirs is fit to be condemned. It needs to be fully redone, and turned into an outdoor oasis where mother and son can while away the hours."

"I couldn't agree more."

"I pray your agreeability will continue. I will defer to you on interior matters, but I remind you—this will be your first contract job. A design job, no less. Like son, like mother. In business matters, I insist our relationship be that of mentor and protégé, with no confusion as to who's who."

"I'd be honored," she said without a hint of sarcasm.

"Moving along: I know it's important that we keep Puppa to a regular schedule, but do you think we could push our Wednesday breakfast up to eight o'clock and invite Terrance to join us?"

"I'd love to have Terrance over for breakfast again."

"I'd like to make a regular thing of it."

"You mean . . . every week?"

"If he's up to it. Wouldn't it be nice for Puppa to have a regular visitor? We'd make a rule—at breakfast, no one is allowed to talk about Puppa's condition. Terrance would be like a family friend, just stopping by."

Mummy and I did our best to provide Puppa with stimulating diversions, but it was *Mummy and I,* all day, every day. Puppa liked Terrance, and having him as a regular breakfast guest would be a welcome break from the norm.

"So, we'd all have breakfast, and then Puppa would have his therapy session?"

"Like the morning tongue feast we enjoyed a fortnight ago."

"I don't know," Mummy said. "I'm sure Terrance has better things to do."

"If he's not free, no one will be offended. We'll tell him that. But I think he will accept. Did you know that he doesn't currently eat breakfast?"

"What!?" Mummy gasped.

"That's what he told me. We're his first stop of the day, so he's fine when we see him, but can you imagine what he's like at four thirty in the afternoon? Skipping breakfast, for him, is a one-way ticket to a lawsuit. We'd be doing him a favor."

"That's for sure."

"It's settled. Please contact Terrance and invite him for breakfast this coming Wednesday. This will be a 'working breakfast.' We'll put pen to paper over the next few days, and be ready to present our client with various concepts and considerations."

"A Hayes Family venture," Mummy sang.

"Gitz gow gowt ime!" burped Puppa.

"Let's put out an impressive spread," said I.

Wednesday arrived. Terrance was late. We sat around the butler's cart, twiddling thumbs, eyeing the treats. The concept of a "working breakfast" was previously unknown to Mummy, so she'd done some research and settled on a more brunchlike approach. Cornish hens, topped with a curried remoulade. A pistachio pesto quiche.

Quiche. They say real men don't eat it. Who are these "real men" who don't like eggs and cheese, baked in a savory, flaky crust?

"Do you think something's wrong?" Mummy asked. Terrance had never been late before.

"I'm sure it's nothing. Car trouble, perhaps. Let's dig in."

We did so, tentatively. A taste of this, a morsel of that, hoping, all the while, that the doorbell would ring and activities could proceed as intended. Puppa and I had put a production schedule together, along with some rough architectural mock-ups. Mummy had clipped inspirations from her archive of home décor magazines.

We ate glumly. The time for Puppa's appointment came and went. Mummy cleared the things.

"Is there someone we can call?" she asked.

"Like who?"

"Visiting Nurses?"

I snarled.

"Well, maybe they know where he is!" she said.

"And maybe they'd fire him for his truancy. We Hayeses are many things, but never rats. If I know Terrance, he'll ask to do a makeup day tomorrow."

A plausible excuse would get him a reprimand. A lousy one would earn him a lecture. I had no tolerance for slippery work ethics.

The Wednesday workday came and went. No call from Terrance. Evening came. Time for the music night. I mooched along the dark streets and rehearsed my righteous indignation.

I reached Mother's. The first thing I noticed: no Tollbooth. The threshold was left unguarded. The marquee advertised *$3 well drinks, $2 Bud/Coors bottles,* but there was no mention of the evening's entertainment. I pushed through the door. The regulars were all there: Viktor and Oleg, Dolly, the soccer moms, The Mariachi Quartet, Leroy the scale-model engineer, The Milkmaids, and others who I knew by face but not by name. There was no music, and none of the usual bar chatter that might fill its wake.

"Where's Terrance?" I demanded.

"He called in," said Connie.

"Well, he didn't call me. We had an appointment this morning, and he was a total no-show."

"It's his mother," said Connie.

I felt a swell of relief.

"Oh, thank goodness. I was worried that it was something serious. Is she all right?"

"She died last night."

It was nonsense. I'd seen her six days ago; enjoyed a disgusting lunch with her. How? It didn't work that way. It wasn't possible that six days could spell the end of her existence.

▬ ▬ ▬

"You've reached the cellphone of Terrance Johnson. Leave a message, and I'll get back to you as soon as I can."

"Hey, Terrance. This is Buddy. I heard the news. If there's anything. . . . Just give me a call whenever you feel up to it."

▬ ▬ ▬

"You've reached the cellphone of Terrance Johnson. Leave a message, and I'll get back to you as soon as I can."

"Just following up. I haven't heard from you. Not that you're required. . . . Anyway. I've been thinking about you. And your mom. Hope you're okay."

▬ ▬ ▬

As you know, Mummy's access to my chambers is strictly limited. There was some Yaltaesque wrangling over the third-story landing, and over the flight of stairs that runs from the second story to the third. I would not have Mummy eavesdropping on my affairs. She deferred to my claim on the landing but demurred on the staircase. "I need to clean," she said. "*I'll* clean," I said. "There should be no borders in a family home," she said. "Our terms must satisfy the collective and the individual," I said. Back and forth this way. After days of tense negotiation, I secured the entire flight. Mummy may not tread beyond the second-story landing without prearranged clearance from me. The price for this hegemony was dear. I am required, in perpetuity, to join Mummy for Christmas and Easter mass. I am a confirmed volunteer—also, in perpetuity—for the church's Lenten fish fry, and a conscripted usher for the annual Passion Play. These activities are brutal on their face and were made more torturous by fellow congregants. *Where have you been, Buddy? When are you coming back? We'd be happy to help with Puppa.* I'd grown up in the church. Puppa's need for Sunday supervision had been right in time with my crisis of faith. Church had always been a thing that Puppa could take or leave, and we were both happy to use his illness as cause to lapse.

There's a brass mailbox mounted on the wall of our second-story landing. Mummy uses it to transfer correspondence to my attention. Occasionally she'll slip in a personal item: a recipe she's found and wants my opinion on, a newspaper article that interests her and is of no interest to me. Friday. I opened the box. Inside, there was a single scissor-cut clipping. An obituary. It featured a photograph. As previously stated, I'm incapable of pegging an Afro-American's age by appearance, but I placed the woman in the photo at somewhere in her early twenties. The photo was black-and-white newsprint, but little was lost in that, as it was clear that the scanned original had been black and white as well. In the background, a restaurant kitchen. A rack full of dishes.

The subject of the photo was trim and shapely. She was wearing a white dress and a fitted apron. Her arms were tucked behind her back. Hair in ringlets. Small hoop earrings. That bright Johnson smile. She was gorgeous.

I moved on to the text. The checklist items were there: date of birth, where she'd been born, who she'd been born to. She'd had a sister. She was survived by a son: Terrance J. Johnson, thirty-seven, of South Ilium, New York. She had died in her sleep.

The next paragraph offered a recounting of brighter days. Lindsay's Sky Bar. A famous jazz establishment in Cleveland. She had worked there in the late 1950s. All the greats had passed through. She'd seen them all. Served them personally.

Further details followed. Usual things. The text was a life, sliced down to a hundred and fifty words.

Services would be held on Friday at the Echoes of Mercy Baptist Church. Terrance served as "Director of Music" there. The fact that a church could have a musical director came as news to me. At Bethany Presbyterian, we had tone-deaf Esther, knuckling away at her wheezy pipe organ. If anyone required "echoes of mercy," it was the poor congregants at our house of worship. As a rule, I do not thank God; but if I did so for anything, it was for the fact that I only had to tolerate that noise on Christmas and Easter.

"I've made arrangements with the car service," Mummy told me that evening. "Would you have time to sew up Puppa's funeral trousers? Last time he wore them, he still had a right leg."

"I'll do that for you," I said, "but I won't be going."

Her jaw dropped.

"Buddy!?"

"You know my policy about funerals."

"I do. It's selfish and disrespectful. In this case, I think it's despicable."

Once I let go of the idea that God was watching—that the deceased was up there, in the clouds, looking down, and would be offended by my absence, and possibly even *haunt me* as a kind of revenge—what was the point? There's also the matter of the corpse. Right there. Lying in an open box. You line up and sign a book to prove you were there, and then wait your turn to "pay respects" to the next of kin. And how do you pay them? With clichés! "My condolences" and "I'm sorry for your loss" and "He's in a better place." You blush at the futilitiy of your words—at your Hallmark-style attempt to put a positive spin on the thing—and all the while, you're ashamed at your actual thoughts. *This event is an unpleasant reminder of my own mortality. I'm not glad to see him go, but thank* God *it's not me!* Then you move past, to the corpse itself, to inspect the thing, to say good-bye to it or to make your peace with it or just to be sure that the thing in the box isn't pretending, but how could it pretend, it's not a person, it's just a grotesque dummy in pancake makeup, and sure, it looks like someone you know, someone you saw yesterday, or the day before, or last week, or a couple of years ago, but that person—the one you're reminded of—isn't really dead to you. They won't be for years. Then, one day, and for no reason at all, you think, *I wonder how ol' John is doing?* And you realize. *John is dead.*

A whole lineup, waiting its turn to inspect a corpse. Some kneel before it. Some kiss it! It's all too ghoulish to be endured.

"I can't do it," I said.

"You knew her."

"It's a black church, Mummy. You have no rhythm, and we don't have any drums or rattles."

"Your disgusting, racist humor is completely inappropriate."

"They probably won't even let you in."

"They will let us in, fool. We have an open invite to Terrance's church. He's offered on numerous occasions. I would have gone myself, if it wasn't for the cakes."

She was referring to her role as "Queen of Cakes" at Bethany Presbyterian. They didn't call her that. "Queen of Cakes" was a tease on my part. "Oh, Ruth, you make such a wonderful lemon bundt, your toffee crumble is to die for, won't you take care of the cakes for the coffee social?" It's an old hustler trick; a middling responsibility, presented to a mark, and made grand by the illusion of inside access.

"I know you're disappointed in me," I said to Mummy. "I'm sorry."

"No son of mine would even consider not going."

"I'm sorry."

"It's an insult!"

"I'm sorry."

"But Buddy . . . Terrance is your friend."

"I know. And I'm sorry."

She was right. My behavior was everything she said it was.

Friday came. I stood at my window, peeked through the curtains, and watched Mummy and Puppa go. The house was mine alone. I passed through walls. Levitated between stories. The wood shop. A place so rich with fragrance, and each note, so heavy with memory. The parlor. My finishing school. Unused now. The study. Puppa would read to me there. I'd done my grade school homework there. The den. Puppa's penultimate resting place. The silence was surreal. Dust floated in the sunbeams.

I ended up in the drawing room. I switched on the hi-fi, searched the archive, and pulled a 45. The B-Side: "Under the Bridges of Paris." I set it on the turntable, positioned the stylus, and moved slowly to the center of the room.

I cried. I cried because I would be the last one. I would be alone. Then my time would come, and this home, our home, would go on to someone else, some "investor," and the whole thing would be converted into apartments. That was the way of it. Our things would be sold off, our bones picked clean by the vultures, and not a trace would remain and no one left to remember.

I wish I could have cried for Ms. Johnson. If not for her, then for Terrance. I couldn't muster either, so I tried making my tears for Mummy and Puppa. Nothing doing. I'm a selfish little troll. I could only cry for myself.

"You've reached the cellphone of Terrance Johnson. Leave a message and I'll get back to you as soon as I can."

"Hey. I'm sorry I missed your mother's wake. Mummy told me it was a beautiful service. She said the music was incredible, and that you sang 'Amazing Grace,' and that she didn't think you'd get through it, but you did, and that it was the most heartbreaking version she'd ever heard. I believe it.

"I sent some flowers. . . .

"Mummy says there were a lot of white people there. She met Dolly. She said she was quiet, but very sweet. She also met Viktor and Oleg. And their wives! What a scene! I hope it wasn't too embarrassing.

"How's your lover holding up? Mummy says that she was pretty upset. I thought to bring some flowers to the library, but I don't want to do anything untoward. I respect the boundaries of the patron-librarian relationship.

"I dropped by your house the other day. You weren't home. I left a fruit basket by the back door. I hope no one stole it.

"Before Puppa got sick, I could have done five wakes in a day. Not that I ever did. I'm just saying I *could* have. Now, with Puppa the way he is . . . I didn't want to be a mess. And I would have been a mess.

"So here I am. You know where to find me. I'm sorry about everything."

We got a call from Visiting Nurses. Terrance was taking an extended leave. The news shook us.

"Did he say anything at the wake?" I asked.

"He didn't, but we only spoke for a moment," Mummy said.

"We're not replacing him," I said.

"Not right away."

"Not *ever.*"

"We'll give it some time."

"We were doing just fine before he came."

"No, we weren't."

"And now we're doing worse."

"No, we aren't. We're doing better. And we're going to keep doing better."

I cloistered for the next two weeks. No library visits, and certainly no music night. There'd be no music there. If there was—if Connie had pulled in a local band, or a karaoke DJ—the music would have no value. Terrance transformed Mother's into something other than what it was. Without him, the place would be back to what it always had been: a watering hole for the local rabble; a place of drunken brawls and drug deals gone bad. It was no place for a self-made millionaire. HixonSmythBoutiques.com was a wrap. The check had arrived. The scales of my life had tipped. They would remain so. The Johnson Reno was off the table. I had no friend to help.

I called Terrance's cellphone one more time. It was my fourth call, which planted me in stalker territory. No answer. No message left. I determined to call no more.

It should have ended there, but heartsickness got the better of me. I took up the musket, donned my "Civil War uniform," and made a final march through South Ilium. 38 Liberty Street. There was a FOR SALE sign on the front lawn. One of those realtor's locks on the door. I went around back. My fruit basket lay moldering in the sun.

- 17 -
A DEADLY BALLET

April gave on to May. Mummy called a summit.

"It's been four weeks, Buddy."

"I'm still in mourning."

"In mourning? You didn't even go to the wake."

"You've misplaced the source of my bereavement. I mourn my lost innocence. I mourn the fact that I thought I had a friend."

We were in my chambers. If Mummy insisted on pushing the issue, fine, but I got to choose the venue. I sat at my desk. My chair was cranked as high as it would go. Mummy was seated on the opposing side, in an antique spindle chair. The chair was sound, but a little rickety. An uncertain foundation. These are the tactics that every self-made millionaire must know.

"You could have friends if you wanted them. What about Viktor and Oleg? They said nice things about you."

"I can admire the noble savage, but I wouldn't invite one to tea."

"And what about Dolly? You were developing feelings for her."

"I've called off all development."

"And the pretty librarian. She must be as hurt as you are."

"Maybe. Maybe they're still together. I haven't gone to the library."

"I'm sure Terrance is just sorting things out."

"The whole thing has sparked an existential crisis. In my soul, if you take my meaning."

"I take it."

"Endings. Loss. These are the concepts I've been grappling with."

"I'm sorry to hear it. Truly."

"I only ask for a reply. 'You threw a pork chop at my window. I never want to see you again.' That I could accept."

Her concerned matriarch bit faded in a flash.

"You threw a pork chop at his window?"

"No," I said glumly. "I threw a pork chop at someone else's window. Similar situation, though, with the same result."

"I don't think I care to hear about that one."

"You're right about that. Now, about this new nurse."

"She's available to start on Monday."

"I'll need to review her CV."

"No."

"And run a background check."

"Absolutely not."

"Well then, it's closed-circuit cameras in every room of the house."

"I said no."

"It's not negotiable."

"And this is not a negotiation. I'm telling you how it's going to be. Up here, in your 'chambers,' you make the rules. Down below, I'm in charge. It's going to be the nurse on Mondays and home healthcare aides on Wednesday and Friday."

"And who are these 'aides'?"

"I don't know. Whoever they send."

"Strangers!?"

"At first. But you'll come to know them."

A pause. We were like a pair of circling pugilists, measuring up, looking for soft spots in the other's defense.

"Didn't you notice?" I asked sweetly. "I did not inquire as to the race of the strangers."

"How big of you."

"I've made progress. My Anti-Bias Reprogramming Curriculum. That's what it was all about, I've decided; about me, and my journey towards more enlightened personhood. I now reserve my disdain for all members of the lower classes, regardless of race, creed, or sexual orientation. Terrance was a fine mentor. I think he learned a lot from me as well."

I expected her scar to boil, and for a torrent of hostility to spew from her gob. The opposite occurred. The scar went pale. Mummy hung her head and sighed.

"I told him he should quit. Early on, and a few times after. You know that, right?"

"Quit what?"

"Quit us. Quit working with us."

"Why?" I was incredulous.

"Your behavior, you swine! The things you say! You hurt me sometimes; you offend me…" She trailed off. Gave a cold laugh. "Why should anyone else have to take it?"

"Mummy? Are you experiencing some kind of

pre-menopausal hot flash?"

"You think you're too small—too insignificant—to hurt anyone."

"Not so. Insult is my explosive shell. Unfortunately, the mortar will only fire sideways or downward. I'm incapable of injuring Terrance Johnson. That much I know."

"Proving once again that you don't know anything. You hurt him plenty. You offended him plenty. I told him that he should go—that we didn't deserve him—but he wouldn't. 'Buddy is acting out of pain,' he said. 'Because of his…'"

A world of possibilities in that ellipse, reader. A nod toward intention. A wink and a nudge that explains it all away. Can't do it. I'd had enough. I cut her off.

"It's closed-circuit cameras in every room. That's that!"

"No."

"Front of house, entryway, kitchen, backyard, parlor, den, drawing room."

"Not acceptable."

"Please note that I did not include the bathrooms on my list. You see? I'm being flexible—which is more than can be said for you."

"The answer is no."

"Okay. This will be my final offer. Reject it, and I will act unilaterally as commander-in-chief. A camera in the den, of course. This is essential for Puppa's protection. It will also allow us to monitor him when we have chores to do. One camera on the exterior front, so we can record all arrivals and departures, and another in the entryway, so that we have a clear confirmation of all parties who enter our home. The backyard. We should have had that years ago."

She puckered her lips and considered.

"That's all?"

"You'll let me do more?"

"No. Approved."

Mummy rose. Her affect was victorious. She scanned my chambers. This was a rare visit to the friendly confines, and she took the opportunity to rubberneck. "Oh, that's new," and some other small comments on my forever-evolving milieu.

"I need to get back to work, Mummy. Is there anything more?"

"There is. Terrance called."

My jaw fell to the desk.

"Terrance called *you*?"

"He's coming by tomorrow."

"Coming here?"

"That's right."

My head spun. It took me a moment to regain equilibrium.

"It's a shame," I said. "My pharmaceutical client is launching a new IBS drug and I've got a suite of mockups due on Thursday. I simply can't make the time. Please extend my apologies."

- - -

The phone rang later that day. Terrance's cell number. I let it go to voicemail.

I took up a pinch, vacuumed it up a nostril, and repeated the process on the other side. A fitful sneezing commenced. Not pleasant. I'd taken too much.

The phone rang again. Terrance's cell number. Straight to voicemail.

I hit SEND/RECEIVE on Outlook. Nothing. I loathed inactivity. I did not get paid to wait.

The phone rang once more. Once more, Terrance. Stalker territory. I grabbed up the receiver.

"Hayes Interactive! Buddy Hayes speaking!"

"Hi, Buddy. It's Terrance."

"Terrance!" I gushed. "How are you?"

"I'm well. Doing well."

"That's great. Oh, by the way—my condolences on the loss of your mother."

I unzipped, reached in, and uncoiled my kielbasa. *Get sizzlin', you magnificent sausage!* I gave it few tugs. Tickled around the circumference. It wouldn't do. My penis was outraged at my intentions. *Not like this,* my penis said. I left it alone. My manhood hung impotently from my open fly.

"I saw your mom and grandpa at the wake," Terrance said. "It was a nice surprise."

"I'm sorry I couldn't make it. You know me. Business, business, business."

"I got your messages."

"Did you?"

"I'm sorry I didn't get back to you."

"Water under the bridge, Terrance. It's all water under the bridge. Is there some way I can be of help to you today?"

"I was wondering if I could stop up tomorrow."

"I'm booked solid with production."

"I'm moving back to New York."

"I see."

"I wanted to come over and say good-bye."

"You're saying it now."

"And thank you."

"Nothing to thank me for. We didn't do anything."

"I spoke with Ruth. I'll be over tomorrow."

"Mummy and Puppa will be so happy to see you. Does that conclude our business?"

"It does," he said.

I hung up.

A Wednesday, of all days. The April showers had brought

May flowers, but the showers had returned, and, with them, a whipping wind. It was one of those days that makes you happy to be a desk worker, as there is no better place to be on such days, in contrast to the opposite, the sunny ones, when nature cruelly reminds you of how much life you're missing. I did some work. The doorbell rang and, minutes later, the phone.

"Terrance is here."

"I'm aware."

"He's waiting for you. In the drawing room."

I sighed.

"Send him up."

V-neck tee. Over it, a stylish denim jacket. Motorcycle cut. Machine-distressed. A hipster bid at rough-and-tumble. His dark jeans were cuffed at the bottom. Where the Crocs had been, a pair of chunky hi-tops. The ensemble was topped off with a fitted New York Yankees baseball cap. I searched for the nurse but couldn't find him. The man of practicality; that man who had settled on the best of what circumstances had to offer; that man was gone.

"It wasn't my plan," Terrance said.

"Ah. Plans. Always subject to change."

"I called an old friend after my mom died. My old roommate, in fact. He's a mime."

"You said a *mime*?"

"I did. He trained in Paris. But he gets more work as an actor and dancer."

"And waiter, I'm sure."

"Bartender, but you're right. Anyway, he's the director of a theater company. Off, *off* Broadway."

"Sounds glamorous. Let me guess—it's at an 'experimental performance space' in Brooklyn."

"No. It's at an experimental performance space in Queens."

"Goodness. Does he pay his troupe in anchovies and crackers?"

"Pretty much. I needed someone to talk to . . ."

I felt the urge to smash something. I was standing within arm's reach of my mantel, and there was a bisque figurine there. Three monkeys. See no evil, hear no evil, speak no evil. I almost grabbed it. I almost flung it across the room and smashed it to bits. Doing so would have exposed the depth of my hurt. He'd know that he was capable of hurting me.

"You could have talked to me," I said calmly.

"I should have. At the time, I just needed a little distance from everything, so I called my friend in New York and I told him 'I don't know what I'm going to do, I don't know what I'm *doing*,' and he said 'We just lost a member of the company and I need somebody, and if you don't have a place to stay I've got a pullout with your name on it.' "

"And how did you feel about it?"

"Good. And scared."

"And relieved," I said, certain I was right.

He had perfect posture. The kind of posture that a person cannot force. I'd have thought it impossible for him to stand straighter, yet he was straighter still, taller than he'd ever been, and in his eyes a resolve, a purpose, and I thought I'd seen those things in his eyes before, but no, not like this. He was free. Utterly free. Nothing bound him.

"Come down and visit me," he said.

"I can't."

"Of course you can. And I'll come up here to visit. You. Oleg and Viktor. Dolly."

"What about The Alluring Librarian? Does she fit into

your new life?"

He took on a sheepish, regretful look.

"We were just hanging out, you know? We'd only started . . ."

". . . *hanging* out."

"Right."

"*Hooking* up."

"I hate that term, but okay. We'd only been seeing each other for two months before Mom died."

I hadn't known that. I brightened at hearing it. Theirs was a brief and thwarted romance. It bode well for the possible futures I liked to consider.

"So you two weren't serious?"

"I wasn't in a place to have anything serious. But we like each other. We're friends."

"And with a face like yours, you'll make friends wherever you go. How's she taking it?"

"Fine. I mean, she's not happy—"

"Are you still fornicating with her?"

"C'mon, Buddy."

"She wouldn't lie with you if she could help it. It's her instinct. She's using her body to try to persuade you to stay. Be a good boy and don't take advantage."

"It's not like that. We talk on the phone. I'm staying at her place right now. As soon as I have a place of my own, she'll come down to visit."

"I'll bet Lord Byron made similar assurances to Caroline Lamb."

"I don't get the allusion, but I know what you're driving at. I'm going to be back and forth. Connie says I can do a show at Mother's any time I want. I figured maybe once a month."

Terrance towered over me. He towered over all of us. I

told him so.

"You're my friend, Buddy. Let's keep being friends."

I crossed to my barrel of weaponry, extracted the blowgun, gathered the darts. Terrance's expression grew concerned. He wondered at my intentions.

"It only works here, Terrance. In South Ilium. Out there? Out in *the world?* People like you aren't seen with people like me."

He protested. He was "sick of hearing me talk like that." I was sick of his kind—the beautiful kind—acting as if the same rules applied.

"I can't spend the rest of my life pining after my handsome black friend. Waiting for your calls, fantasizing about the glamorous life you're living, picturing myself in it—maybe even popping into it from time to time to chew the scenery. There's more to me than comic relief, Terrance. I've got to be my own leading man."

On the inside, I was a mass of trembling. On the outside, I was stock-still. We shook hands. A solid, manly one. He looked into my ugly, sunken eyes. I looked into his beautiful ones.

"Take this," I said, and presented the blowgun to him. He laughed sadly.

"That's okay," he said.

"You're a crack shot with it. Where you're going, it might come in handy."

"I don't have any use for it."

"Apparently, you've never considered the possibility that you might be attacked by an archer, or an arbalist, or a slingshotist, or a spearist. Anything can happen on the streets."

He took the blowgun and the darts. We traded good-byes. Then he was gone.

I wasn't satisfied with my performance. My injuries had shown. What I said had all been true, but with an edge that didn't suit my dignity. No helping it. I needed that edge. That sharpened blade. Without it, I would have felt no protection. I might have fallen to his feet and begged him to stay.

It had all passed without tears. Now I felt the tears coming. Entrepreneurial diktat #2: No outbursts of temper. Business is business. No use crying when the deal doesn't go your way.

I crossed to my chamber window. A repose was necessary. I'd take a moment, reminisce, and then proceed with the rest of my life.

Alert level: Orange. The alarm bells sounded. Meat Foot was on the street below. He was wearing a filthy workman's unitard. He stood next to his mother's silver Cadillac. The hood was open and the rain was soaking him. *Strange day to be doing auto repairs,* I thought, and took up the spyglass. The brute cast his eyes about like an anxious drug dealer. When he saw that the coast was clear, he took a single wrench from his pocket and climbed under the vehicle. He emerged moments later with an oily bolt in his hand. The hand was covered in sludge.

"Oh my GOD!" I shouted. "He's emptying the oil into the storm drain!" My eyeball nearly popped out the other side of the tube.

My enemy had chosen a rainy day, as it would wash away all evidence of the deed. Who knew where that spent petroleum would end up? In our soil? In our asparagus? Our drinking water? Most of it would be swept out to the Hudson, where it would mate with the rest of the industrial pollution, killing fish and fowl. I burned. I dedicated a silent prayer to Mother Earth and vowed to avenge her.

"Criminal! I am placing you under citizen's arrest!"

I stood in the center of the street. The rain soaked me in a most heroic manner. My fists were balled at my sides.

Meat Foot turned to me from under the hood. His dead eyes glared out from behind the mask of his fat, soulless face.

"Get the fuck out of here," he said.

"Haven't you heard the news, Meat Foot?"

"You call me Meat Foot again and I'll snap your fuckin' neck."

"The news, you slob! Answer my question!"

He came out from under the hood. There was an empty quart bottle of oil in his hand and he tossed it to the sidewalk, where it came to rest alongside four others. A slight grin played at the edges of his lips. My impudence amused him, but not so much that he wouldn't deal me a beating.

"Go inside. Before I hurt you."

"The news is—we live in a post-9/11 world. If you see something, tell someone. What I see is a terrorist dumping oil into the storm drain."

"I got a pan down there, cocksucker."

"Please stop cursing. This is not a locker room." I slowly lowered myself to one knee. It was a compromising combat position, but if he attacked, I could quickly shift into Dragon and work his gonads. I took a quick glance under the vehicle.

"No pan that I can see."

The Sunshine residence was only a stone's throw away. The front door burst open and popped loudly against its stop.

She emerged.

Little Miss Sunshine waddled toward us. Her orthopedic shoes scuffed along the sidewalk. In one gouty hand, an umbrella; in the other, a croquet mallet. Such a mallet would typically be viewed as harmless conduit to backyard fun. Her malevolence transformed it into a war hammer. It was an unbelievable spectacle. I didn't know whether to laugh or scream.

"You get out of here!" she cried. Her voice was like an air-raid siren. She stopped short of us, about ten paces, and waved the mallet in the air. "You son of a bitch! Go home and mind your business!"

"So you know about this!" I cried. "Ordered him to do it, no doubt. If you come at me with that cudgel, I'll seize it from you and beat your head in!"

"Stay where you are, Mom!"

Meat Foot scanned the street again—this time, with apprehension. He turned away from me and moved to the sidewalk and gathered up the oil containers he had thrown there.

What followed happened in a flash. I sprang to my feet and scampered up to the luxury sedan. There was an open toolbox on the back seat, and next to it a case of Valvoline—all the evidence the police would need. The keys were in the ignition. I opened the door and leaned into the cabin. Meat Foot cried out from the curb . . .

"What the fuck are you doing!?"

. . . and I hit the switch for the electric door locks. They engaged with a heavy *ka-chunk* and I retreated, closing the door behind me and sealing the evidence inside. Meat Foot rounded the front of the car, his paw extended, intent on grabbing me. By the time I slammed the door, he was only a stride away. His eyes were embers; his face, bloated with rage. I turned and ran, made a few steps, but his momentum was his advantage, and he caught me by the collar of my sports coat. I could feel his filthy knuckles on the back of my neck. There would be no escaping his nutcracker grip, so I moved my arms backward and wriggled my shoulders and allowed the sports coat to slip from my body. I left him holding my jacket like some kind of post-apocalyptic maître d'. I darted around the back of the Cadillac. He gave chase, but I was quicker. We circled the car. He'd try to head me off and I would cut back in the other direction, keeping the vehicle between us.

I had spent years planning the assault. A basement window. That had always been the way. But how to do it? Little Miss Sunshine rarely left home. When she did, it was only for brief periods, and there was no discernible pattern to her comings and goings. This was the moment, reader. She hadn't shut the door behind her. The Sunshine compound was wide open! This fact represented only 5 percent of what you might call a "perfect opportunity," but it might be the best I'd ever get. I was by the trunk. Meat Foot was by the hood. My only obstacle: a seventy-five-year-old woman armed with a croquet mallet. I broke off and sprinted at her like a linebacker cutting through the A-gap. Meat Foot cried out. I entered Little Miss Sunshine's melee sphere, and she swung the mallet. It was a sidearm delivery. Her aged muscles couldn't muster much pop, but the aim was true. If I had kept going as I was, she would have drilled me right between the eyes. I performed an *onegai shimasu*—a forward aikido roll, front shoulder tuck. The maneuver brought me crashing through a mud puddle, and left me soaked, but cleared my brains of her semi-vicious swing. I rolled though, barely breaking stride, and came up on the balls of my feet. The path was clear. I bounded up their front stoop. In I went. At last, I had penetrated the portcullis of my enemy's fiendish lair.

Their home was the doppelgänger of ours—the same floor plan, built by the same hands, designed by the same architect, one hundred and forty-six years ago. A comparison of exteriors suggests this similarity; my research at the library confirmed it. I knew where the rooms would be, and the stairs, and had some sense of how the home was purposed within. I'd been surveilling her for the better part of a decade. It was one thing to know these facts, and quite another to experience them. The interior was alien yet familiar. It inspired vertigo. In The Mute's bedroom, I had considered alternate universes; in the Sunshine home, I had irrefutably stepped into one.

It would be satisfying to denigrate her décor, but it wouldn't be honest. Her home was finely appointed. The bric-a-brac was tasteful and expensive; the furnishings, rugs, and textiles hit the appropriate Victorian beats. She was a higher-up in the South Ilium Historical Society, after all. Little Miss Sunshine might be evil incarnate, but she did have sophisticated taste.

In our home, it was the parlor. In theirs, a living room, if by *living,* I mean, "Where the large television is." There was a bookcase there. Looking in from the outside, through the spyglass, I could only ever see one-half of it. Now I saw all. Cookbooks. Gardening books. How-to's. No *Tarzan.*

A rumble of footsteps. Meat Foot was hot on my trail. I retreated, out of the living room and into the kitchen, which, in terms of floor plan, was in the same spot as ours, and as I passed through I took note of the brass pot rack that hung over their kitchen island, and of their vintage farmhouse sink, and I thought *Huh, nice touches.* I soared through the kitchen and into the back stair, the servant's stair, and up I went, to the second story, and into their "drawing room." There was a fainting couch, a pair of exquisite Chippendale-style armchairs, and, of all things, an antique sewing table, quite similar to the one that sat in our space. No bookshelves, however.

I heard Meat Foot coming up their ladies' entrance. Here's what I should have done. I should have made for the main stair and headed upwards, to "my chambers." There would have been plenty of real estate to search, and I would have had two options for my retreat. If he followed me up the main stair, I could slip to the back, and vice versa. Instead, I cut hard to the "den." In their home, it was not a den. It was Little Miss Sunshine's bedroom. I knew this. It faced the street, as our den did. It featured a beautiful bay window, as our den did. I'd seen her at the window. At night. In a nightgown. It was a sight sufficient to cool a young man's libido, let me tell you.

Her bedroom was our den. Our den was Puppa's special place. I was searching for Puppa's book. That was my manic calculus. It's what happens when you allow your animal mind to take hold of you.

I burst into Satan's boudoir. There was a brass bed, neatly made with a patchwork duvet, and a Pennsylvania Dutch blanket chest off in the corner, and a Steiff teddy bear resting on top of that. Below the bay window, a built-in seat. Little Miss Sunshine's looking post.

Wall shelves. Up high and out of my reach. Books, nestled in among more teddies. Mostly paperbacks. Mysteries. Spy-Thrillers. *Gumdrops.*

And there it was.

Three books from the right. An old book. A book with a red cloth cover. On the spine, printed in gold flake: *Tarzan of the Apes.*

Footsteps thundered in the hall behind me. This was when I realized my folly. I was trapped. I backed myself into the room, toward the bed, and drew Excalibur. Safety off. I pressed the trigger button. A ball of lightning exploded in my fist. Meat Foot flew headlong into the room, stopped short, and reeled back at the sight of me.

He was holding a pistol. A modern one. 9mm? That's the caliber of the popular imagination, and I imagine it was the case here. It was a real gun—one of those chrome-nickel slabs you see in movies. He aimed it at the center of my face.

"You fuckin' faggot! What the fuck you doin' runnin' into this house!?"

"I was *fuckin' runnin'* from you!"

Self-defense. This is the tail that gun owners like to wag. Not the sportsman. That's a different thing. I'm talking about the pistol and assault-rifle guys; the ones who never go traipsing through forest and glade; the ones with personal armories; the ones who practice on human-shaped targets. For these men, guns are totems to bloodlust. They dream of murder. They pine for the opportunity, and they chafe at the restrictions that civilization has placed on their homicidal wants. I suffer from this. You can take my musket when you pry it from my cold, dead hands. I would love to murder an intruder because it would not be murder, but *self-defense*. I would be in the right. I would get to know the ancient satisfaction of killing another man, and the killing would be righteous.

When it came to Meat Foot and his gun, I was close to satisfying all terms. I'd threatened his mother. I'd invaded their home. I was now standing in the old woman's bedroom, holding a weapon of my own, and while it wasn't a match to his he could say that I'd drawn it quickly—that while it was actually all *stun,* he'd mistaken it for all *gun*—and had fired for fear of his life. This was his chance to kill, the only chance he might ever get, and me of all people, a blood enemy, a man he hated and who hated him right back.

"You gonna shock me with that toy?" he said, his voice quavering.

"You piece of garbage," I said, rough as I could but scared out of my mind. "Put that pistol down this instant!"

Act now, I thought, *or you may never act again.* A plan coalesced. I would explode forward and downward, onto my knees, and slide toward my foe. I was still soaked from my *onegai shimasu,* and I hoped that the leftover precipitation would provide some lubrication against the hardwood. Successful execution would place me in range. With my weapon, it didn't matter where I struck, so long as I made a solid connection. I'd stab for the belly and hope for the best.

A risky plan. Likely performed through a hail of gunfire. I coiled—

Terrance materialized in the doorway. The blowgun was at his mouth. He aimed the weapon at the back of Meat Foot's head. Terrance maintained that aim and pulled his lips back from the mouthpiece. He spoke calmly.

"I'm behind you. Take your finger off the trigger and lower the gun."

Meat Foot spun on Terrance. Terrance took a gulp of air and pressed the mouthpiece to his lips. Meat Foot saw the lean black stranger, saw the blowgun, and aimed his pistol at the new threat. I sparked Excalibur. My weapon popped and crackled like a 4.5 million-volt bug zapper. Meat Foot whipped back and pointed the pistol at me. He continued shifting his aim this way, whipping the pistol back and forth, undecided on which man posed the greater risk, and then he started a slow sidestep, deeper into the room, keeping his back toward the wall. This move took him out of the crossfire. He stopped in a spot below the bracketed shelves. *Tarzan* was directly above his head.

"Where's my mother!?" the slob shouted at Terrance.

"Working her way up the staircase. She's fine. Why don't you lower that gun?"

He swung the pistol to and fro.

"Or how about I kill this little faggot, and then I kill you?"

"And splatter my brains all over your mother's duvet?" I mocked. "She'd never forgive you."

"Is that a *blowgun?"* he asked incredulously.

"It is, unfortunately," said Terrance.

"Shoot me with that thing and you're dead."

"Wrong!" I cried. "He shoots, and *you're* dead! The darts in that blowgun are poison-tipped. My own concoction. Rat poison, cyanide, and just a drop of sodium pentothal, so that you'll bleed out all of your disgusting secrets right before you die."

"Bullshit."

He was right, of course. Terrance may have hurt my feelings, but what kind of monster would give poison-tipped darts to an inexperienced blowgun operator?

"You must not know Buddy that well," said Terrance.

Meat foot was confounded. He lowered his weapon. We lowered ours. Everyone took a breath.

Terrance turned to me. Telepathy! I tried with all my power. *It's right there! Right above his head! If we can get rid of this thug for ten seconds, you could come over and pluck it with those nimble fingers of yours.* My face must have performed some vigorous calisthenics in the effort. Terrance didn't take my meaning. He looked at me as if I were a loon.

"Just let us go," Terrance said to Meat Foot. "Everybody fucked up today. You let us out of this shit and we'll all act like none of it ever happened."

Such language. Such dialect! I didn't know that Terrance possessed it. He'd shifted into the gutter vernacular, so as to build rapport with the violent Meat Foot before us.

Our aggressions were interrupted by a scraping sound. It was Little Miss Sunshine's talons, ambling across the planks. Terrance stood at the threshold. He stepped back, into the hallway, and turned to face the new arrival.

"You get out of this house, nigger!" the witch cried.

Little Miss Sunshine proceeded to beat Terrance with the croquet mallet. I couldn't see her, but I could see that mallet, dancing in the open doorway, and I could see Terrance, raising his left arm in defense, and taking a series of not insubstantial whacks to the forearm and shoulder. He gave an *"Ow!"* and a *"Quit it!"* and then he seized the croquet mallet by the handle and wrenched it from Little Miss Sunshine's grasp. He was now equipped for both missile and melee combat—blowgun in his right hand, mallet in his left—or for a backyard game that had not yet been invented.

Meat Foot responded unkindly to his mother's disarmament. He raised the pistol once more.

"Drop it!" he screamed.

"You drop it!" I screamed, sparking my weapon.

"Get *out of here,* nigger!" screamed Little Miss Sunshine.

"Beat her head in, Terrance!" I seethed.

"Drop it *now!"* Meat Foot demanded.

My insults. Our trespass. The years of bad blood. The ape in him could not forgive these transgressions. He couldn't jibe his manhood with the idea of letting us go, and yet the logical side of him—that tiny speck of gold, cradled in the flab—saw it was the only way.

"You're not gonna call the cops about what I did outside?"

Terrance looked him squarely in the eye.

"Bygones." He turned to me. "Isn't that right, Buddy?"

"We Hayeses are many things," I said. "But never rats."

We lowered our weapons. Meat Foot took the pistol, popped the clip, and placed it in his pocket. He then took the gun by the slide, pulled it back sharply, and ejected a round from the chamber. It was my first time in the presence of an actual handgun, so the process was interesting to watch. He picked up the loose round, placed it in his other pocket, and then took the gun itself and shoved it into his waistband, below his abundant gut, and straightened his shirt above it. The gun absorbed into him. He put his hands up in a show of submission.

"I want them out of my house!" Little Miss Sunshine bellowed from the hallway.

"They're goin', Mom."

She squealed like a mortally wounded swine. It was a terrifying sound. The crone was apoplectic. Terrance's gritty expression gave on to one of genuine concern.

"Take deep breaths, ma'am," he said. It was the nurse speaking. Terrance turned to Meat Foot. "She's having a fit out here. She's going to give herself a stroke."

I seized the moment.

"Clear her out of the hallway," I said. "Calm her down. We'll be right behind you."

Under normal circumstances, I don't think Meat Foot would have left us alone in his mother's bedroom, if even for a moment. Are there "normal circumstances" that call for one to leave a hated troll nemesis and handsome black stranger alone in one's mother's bedroom? The hallway was narrow. To squeeze past would require a close proximity, and no good could come from that. The wailing continued. Anxiety bled into Meat Foot's indignation. He made for the doorway, nodded to Terrance, and Terrance let him pass. Terrance joined me in the room.

"C'mon, Mom," I heard Meat Foot say. "Let's go to the family room."

"They're in my bedroom!"

"They're leaving. Let's give 'em a little room."

"I don't make room for that ugly little shit."

"They'll be out of here in a second."

"Who is that nigger? I want his name."

"You can't talk like that."

"They're in *my* house!"

Their voices receded. Her blathering grew unintelligible. The moment had arrived.

"What are you doing here?" I whispered.

"I was in the den," he whispered. "Back at your place. We heard shouting in the street, and saw you from the window, getting chased around the Caddy."

"Like Little Black Sambo," I said.

"I think I've heard enough racist shit," he said.

"Quite. Sorry about that."

"Your mother and grandfather are worried sick."

There was a fire in his eyes that I'd never seen before. His hands were shaking. He was high on adrenaline. I pointed at the book.

"It's right there, Terrance."

Had it been our den and not Little Miss Sunshine's bedroom, I could have grabbed a folding chair from the closet, climbed, and grabbed the book myself.

"That's it, huh?"

I was disappointed by his unenthusiastic response.

"It is! No mistaking it! Come over here and grab it!"

Terrance sighed. He looked up at the book, then down to me, and then toward the door.

The door. The way out. The way out of everything. The gateway to his new life.

"You're probably going to hate me forever, Buddy. But no."

I shot him a gaze of the coldest steel.

"What do you mean, *no*?"

"Where would we hide it?"

"Under my shirt! Under *your* shirt! Wherever! That book is coming with us."

"People are waving guns, Buddy! There's no good way. We need to get out of here before someone gets hurt."

"I offered to loan you thirty thousand dollars. I offered to help you, and I still would, even though your mother is gone."

"It was a wonderful gesture. I'll always be grateful."

"I don't care about 'always.' Show your gratitude *now*!"

"You're my unit of care, Buddy. Consider this my final task as your family nurse. I've got one goal—to get you out of this house alive. So let's do it."

Nuts to him! I looked around for a possible step stool. There was the Pennsylvania Dutch blanket chest, five feet long, and dragging it across the room would have made plenty of noise, but to hell with it. Terrance saw my intention and stepped in the way.

"We've got nowhere to hide it," he said. "If he sees you with it, it's *Guns & Ammo* all over again. He's not letting you leave with it, and if they see that you want it—that it was the reason you charged in here—they'll *know.* As of now, they know nothing. Look at it. It's just sitting on a shelf, gathering dust. Leave it. Someday, you might get another shot at it. Not today."

He was right. I hated him for being so. I gave the relic a final look.

We passed through the "family room." Little Miss

Sunshine and Meat Foot made way for us. His arm was around her, and there was regret on his face. The anger had passed. The whole thing had all gone too far. His lips were tight, his eyes averted. Little Miss Sunshine possessed the opposite bearing. Her eyes burned holes in us. We were halfway through the room—halfway to the staircase, to the way home—when she spoke.

"Your mother was a whore, your father was a retard, and your grandfather was a drunk. I know all about you, Buddy Hayes."

I stopped in my tracks.

"You're a walking corpse," I said. "I can smell the rot on you. Die, creature, and be done with it!"

Her visage twisted, like that of a sinister puppet.

"You're disgusting people," she said. "Everyone says so. Anyone who knows you talks about how *disgusting* you are. You're the laughingstock of the neighborhood."

"What *neighborhood,* hag? Have you looked around? They're all gone, all dead. And you're next."

"I think that's enough," Terrance said.

"Who are you?" Little Miss Sunshine demanded. "I want your *name,* nigger."

Terrance gave a cold laugh. "You're getting a thrill out of that, huh? You think you're the first old lady to call me nigger? I was a nurse. I heard it all the time."

"Please, Mom," Meat Foot said calmly.

"Your father quit the stuff," she said to her son. "He stopped. For you and me, he stopped. And then he'd go over to that basement of theirs, and he'd come back stinking of it!"

"He got hit by a truck, Mom."

"He fell *in front* of a truck, because he was too drunk to see straight, and he was coming from *their* house, *their* basement, and they're the ones that did it to him. Oh, that filthy, *ugly* little carpenter! Always blitzed out of his mind. I told him—'You want to be the town drunk, that's your business, but my husband is in the program, and he's been to rehab *two times,* so don't go pulling him down into the gutter with you!' Guess what? He didn't care. They didn't care! They don't care about anyone but themselves!"

It wasn't just any truck. It was an ice cream truck. Mr. Ding-A-Ling. Spring comes, I hear the distant, synthesized strains of *It's a Small World After All,* and I think of death. The song wasn't playing at the time of the accident. The driver had finished his route and was racing back to the Ding-A-Ling warehouse. Dusk had fallen. The Husband came out from between two parked cars, to the edge of the road, and tripped in a pothole. He stumbled. First Street is a narrow one-way.

Fun fact: Mr. Ding-A-Ling was also drunk at the time.

Meat Foot held his mother close. He looked at us with tired eyes.

"Get the fuck out of here, would ya?"

So concluded our charming exchange. Terrance and I descended the stairs, went out the front door, stepped down into the street, and Terrance went to his car, and I went home, and no further words were exchanged between us. Terrance turned the ignition in his rusted Honda Prelude. He buckled his seat belt. I know this because he had to have done the former and always did the latter, but I didn't see it, I was gone, up the front stairs, into our majestic family home, back to the place where I belonged.

Did he watch me go? Give one last look as he drove away? I'll never know. We were headed in different directions.

- 18 -
CIRCULAR STRUCTURES

I'm anxious to hear Puppa's opinion. He's an experienced reader. He'll be able to separate the Buddy in these pages from the one he calls grandson. I'll perform a reading. An abridged, G-rated version, of course. I'll stick to the thrilling bits, or the humorous ones, and leave the lubricious stuff to Puppa's imagination.

As for Mummy? I forbid her from consuming my opus in any form! She would paint a picture of the events in her mind, and there I'd be, dancing and drinking, fighting and fornicating, making a general fool of myself. It's untoward. A mother should not fantasize about her son in this manner.

A Friday. I'd go with my country-gentleman-meets-Irish-brawler number. Navy blazer. Khakis. Tweed cap. The hair beneath the cap: pomaded and coiffed. The body beneath the blazer: smartly dressed and amply perfumed. I am never lackluster when it comes to dress. That morning, I sought to dazzle.

It's a happy accident of nature. The first perennials to bloom are the most beautiful flowers of all. I went to our garden and prepared a tulip bouquet. *In the spring, a young man's fancy lightly turns to thoughts of love.* My fancy had turned. I bound the flowers with a pink ribbon and made my way to the library. I felt dashing. There's something about an elegantly dressed young man, promenading along, carrying a bouquet. The sight provokes; it delights; even if the young man is as ugly as me.

I entered the library. The Alluring Librarian was at the author catalog, adding new cards to the M section. It was wasted work. The card catalog would soon be history. Everything was going digital.

She wore a tasteful light blue blouse, paired with a knee-length skirt in tan. On her feet: my blue suede penny loafers. It was a new outfit. The colors were unlike her. The vibrancy of my contribution seemed to be working its way up.

I was tired of frightening her. I went quietly to the front desk and gently rang the bell. She turned from her work.

"Buddy!" exclaimed The Alluring Librarian, at a volume well above library-appropriate. She floated toward me. I doffed my cap. I almost thought she'd throw her arms around me, but she stopped short of that and instead reached out and gave my bicep a little squeeze.

"Are you okay?" she asked.

"I'm fine. No one got shot. That's the important thing."

Her beautiful eyes went wide.

"No one *got shot?* What are you talking about?"

Could it be? Had Terrance really kept it all to himself?

"Oh. You haven't heard. There was an attempted robbery on our street. The plot was thwarted. Reports say that a firearm was involved. The neighborhood watch newsletter is all abuzz."

"Oh. That's scary. But I wasn't asking about that. Are you okay since Terrance left?"

"Things are back to normal," I said. "Normal has a lot going for it. How are you?"

"I'm sad," she said.

"But you're still seeing each other," I said.

"Kind of. I don't know. It's hard. 'Better a neighbor near than kin far away.'"

"*Luke?*"

"I think *Proverbs.*"

"I think you're right."

I wanted to touch her. On the arm, maybe, as she had done to me. A quick squeeze of the hand, perhaps. I didn't. To touch her would have been too much.

"Those flowers are beautiful," she said.

"They sure are."

"Are they for me?"

Her tone was uncertain, but not uninviting. If I had offered the flowers, she would have taken them. My motives might confuse her, and the intrinsic assumptions might make her uncomfortable, but she would have accepted them, and taken them home. They were beautiful tulips, in the most commanding tertiaries that eyes can comprehend. Reds. Yellows. Purples. They'd brighten up anyplace. Maybe—just maybe—when she was alone, in her dreary South Ilium apartment, and the only color there cast by the flowers I had given her, maybe she would stop, take a moment, give her crooked little smile, and say "Huh."

"No," I said. "These are for Dolly. I want to surprise her. She loved Terrance. I figure she could use some cheering up."

"That's sweet."

"It's also why I'm here. I don't know where she lives,

and, like a fool, I failed to score her digits. You dropped her off with Terrance that night. Would you mind filling me in?"

Terrance would have pushed back on my request. Terrance was no longer here. The Alluring Librarian drew a map for me with words. I knew the street. Dolly's residence was only a short walk from ours.

"Do you have a moment to assist me in the media section?" I asked.

"The media section!?" exclaimed the librarian. "I thought you said you'd never set foot in there."

"Indeed. Library media sections are just another feature of western civilization's long decline. They attract riff-raff and promote illiteracy. If you're just dying to see *Kung Fu Kidz,* you can get it at your local Blockbuster."

"We try to make the library useful for everyone."

"Well, at last the media section may prove useful to me. I'd like to pick up a couple of DVDs for Dolly. I'm thinking *9 to 5* and *Steel Magnolias.*"

"We have both."

"And they're free to borrow. It's a great thing about library materials, don't you think? They never belong to you. They give you a reason to come back."

It wasn't a plan. This was more "keeping the pieces in play." The odds were stacked. At any point, the whole thing could come crashing down, and all my labors would be thrown to waste.

Her beauty would fade. No. That's not right. Her beauty would change. The edge would dull. It would become less like a weapon, and more like a handsome piece of décor. She'd grow weary, as everyone does. She'd want for comfort, as everyone comes to do. Finding someone you can talk to. It's a kind of falling in love.

"I work late," Hephaestus whispered to Aphrodite. The Alluring Librarian had had her roll with Ares, but he was gone, and I was still here, pounding away at my anvil. There'd be other Gods. Lesser ones. If I could outlast Terrance Johnson, who's to say I couldn't outlast the lot?

Dolly. I'd present my flowers. I'd ask her out. Dating is courtship and a gentleman courts with marriage in mind.

After that, I'd take a bus to North Ilium. There was a Craigslist posting I meant to explore. **Studio Loft – Perfect for Artist - Clean building – Utilities included**. I had an appointment with the superintendent. Happy coincidence: It was only blocks away from The Cantina Wagon. I'd stop in after the showing, enjoy a spicy lunch, and catch up with the guys. After that, it was back home, and back to work.

It wasn't a plan. It was what it always had been: a set of wants. Business, inspiration, gothic fornication. Art drooling into commerce. Hard logic bleeding into the carnal. The wholesome and the taboo. I dared, reader. I dared.

- - -

The checkerboard was arranged on a stool, close to his harness. Puppa pointed out his intentions, and I executed them on his behalf. It wasn't looking good for me. In a few moves, he'd have a king, and he'd squeeze me out shortly after. It was inevitable.

His socket was empty. It had been an oozy morning.

Mummy had grilled me for details. I told her some but couldn't tell her all. Hearing about the pistol would have given her a conniption. I left out Little Miss Sunshine's mention of my "retard" father. I had no idea what that meant, nor any desire to know. I left out *Tarzan*. The tale was cast as a Keystone Kop affair, with lots of running up and down stairs, a series of close calls, general slapstick hysterics. I pumped up the farce and let the darker realities lie.

Mummy forbade me from ever interacting with them again.

"There's something I need to tell you, Puppa. Last Wednesday. When I ran into Little Miss Sunshine's house."

It wasn't easy to budge his eye from a game in progress. At that moment, his eyeball leaped.

"I saw it, Puppa. I saw it! *Tarzan of the Apes!"*

"Argh gizzit?!" Translation: *Where is it?*

"In her bedroom. Where their bay window is. It's just sitting on a high shelf, stuffed in with a bunch of her dead husband's gumdrops. She has no idea what it is!"

An odd tingling invaded my lobes. My *brain* lobes, I'm saying. Synapses crackled. From Puppa's eye, a laser, boring into me. His empty socket transformed into a bottomless pit—into a black hole, bent on swallowing the universe. My soul beat with the savage cadence of drums. A data transfer commenced. Telepathy! I heard him! As clear as ever, in a voice I'd known since childhood but hadn't heard in years, and that I never thought I'd hear again.

"She has the book," Puppa said inside my brain. *"Our* book. Our relic. And we're going to get it back."

Time passed. Each day, like the one before. Drops of summer rain struck the window, and the city without cowered under a gunmetal sky. The city of Ilium. Upstate New York. Ours is a three-story brownstone. We live on a quiet, decaying street.

The telephone rang. It was Mummy, the ID warned, calling from downstairs.

"Hayes Interactive. This had better be important."

"You have a letter. It's in your mailbox."

"I receive correspondence every day, Mummy. No need to call—"

But the line was dead. She'd hung up.

I descended to the second story and checked. It was a typical white envelope. The return address: someplace in "Kew Gardens, New York." The sender: Terrance Johnson.

I returned to my desk. The moment called for a snuff. I took a pinch of the baccy and snorted it up my right nostril. It hit my sinuses like the head of a struck match. I took another pinch and sent it up the left. The nicotine was on me in an instant, followed by a sneezing fit. It cleared the mind. I opened Terrance's epistle and read.

Buddy,

That was some scene, eh? I was eager to get out of there, and I'm sure you can understand that, but I'm sorry that we didn't share a proper good-bye.

I'm in a new show. It's a drama. A "what if the Nazis won?" kind of thing, but interpreted through movement and song. You will absolutely hate it. Please find the enclosed ticket. Front row center, Saturday, July 31st. You won't have to miss any work. Just take the Amtrak. I'll be waiting for you at the station.

I'm still staying with my friend, but it's no problem. He wants you to come. I told him the whole thing. I told him about you and your family, and Dolly, and Viktor and Oleg, and all the wild things that would happen at the music night, and I told him about Little Miss Sunshine and Meat Foot, and Tarzan, and everything that went down in that house. I told him you're a writer. He asked if you've ever acted. I told him that you perform every day. He'd like to meet you.

You'll say no. But why? Come down. Come down Saturday, or Friday if you can, or take Friday off, come Thursday night, or stay a week. Call it pleasure. Call it business, because maybe that's what it will turn out to be. Call it whatever you have to call it to make it right in your mind.

Your Friend,
Terrance Johnson

I went to the den. I didn't take the letter with me. Terrance had mentioned *Tarzan,* and while he didn't explicitly reveal the discovery, its presence was sure to lift Mummy's eyebrow. I did take the ticket. *Long Knives,* the show was called. Yikes.

"You should go!" Mummy gushed.

"Go?"

"It sounds wonderful!"

"It sounds dreadful."

"Wouldn't you like to go and see Terrance? See New York, with a real New Yorker as your tour guide? What an experience!"

"Terrance is not a real New Yorker. He's a temporary transplant."

"And what about this writing business? And possibly . . . acting? Buddy! It's the opportunity of a lifetime!"

I rolled my eyes.

"The kind of opportunity that only a mime can bring. It's all silliness. This two-bit Marcel Marceau is probably just looking to squeeze me for ideas. He'll drop me the moment my lemon runs dry."

"Terrance wouldn't associate with that kind of shark."

"How little you understand the entertainment business. Besides, I'm an aspiring *novelist,* not a playwright—although I must admit that the stage has always held a certain appeal to me."

"If this man runs a theater, he must be in cahoots with all kinds of artistic people. Maybe some in publishing."

"I'll be the toast of Kew Gardens, Queens."

Mummy's harelip scar went to a sparkling rosé.

"Terrance is interested in *our* story?" she asked.

"Terrance is interested in Terrance's story, and I'm sure his friend is too. We'd be a subplot, at best."

"We'll be famous!"

"Fiction can be unkind, Mummy. Be careful what you wish for."

I turned to Puppa.

"Boo shoo ohhh." Translation: *You should go.*

"It wouldn't be right. You'd like to see it too. You both would. The only fair thing would be for us all to go, for us all to see it, and for us all to pinch our noses *together*; to mock the postmodern absurdity of it, from concept to execution; to joke and laugh about it all the way home. Going by myself—it would feel like a betrayal."

Mummy stood. Puppa dangled. They were shoulder to shoulder now, looking down on me. In terms of deference—deference to my position, to my authority—there was none. I was a boy, and forever would be in their eyes.

"Go, Buddy. We'll be fine."

"I can't."

"We'll enjoy it. Father-daughter time. We'll be like roommates!"

"It wouldn't be fair."

"Go, Buddy. Pay attention to everything. Take note of every detail. And then come home and tell us all about it."

I was dressed in the latest fashion. Jacket: brown herringbone, narrow lapel. I'd had it taken in so that it was now a size too small, in spirit with the nincompoop style of the day. Shirt: red and white gingham, western cut, with the top three buttons left manfully undone. Dark jeans and pair of classic Chuck T's completed the statement. On my head: Puppa's bowler. A step too far? One accessory too many? Perhaps. But it was my best way of taking him with me.

A pair of conductors made their way along the aisle, back to back, taking tickets and punching them as they went. A conduct*or* tended the row opposite; a conduct*ress* tended mine. Anticipation brimmed. I was a young millionaire, clad in finery, off for a weekend's pleasure. *Noblesse oblige.* Unrequited flirtation was called for.

It's hard to transpose familiarity between contexts. In this case, hard to transpose nudity, or beguiling white lingerie, or impossibly high stilettos, with the staid uniform worn by Amtrak's finest. The conductress was lissome. Awkward. She wore an ugly, captain-style hat. She recognized me before I recognized her. Her recognition demanded its return. I thought: *Jeez, I had better recognize this woman!* When I did, I gasped.

The Mute. Her eyes spun like off-kilter gyroscopes. Her respiration quickened, ever so slightly, and her cheeks went flush. The "sex flush." Or maybe she was disgusted. With me. With herself. With the inner animal who brings nothing but regret.

Her eyeballs ceased their riot. They came to rest on mine.

"Ticket?"

It was the first word she ever spoke to me. Her voice was normal. Utterly normal. So normal that there is no other way to describe it. I smiled up at her, wiggled my eyebrows, and waved my ticket back and forth in a teasing way. Her expression asked: *Are you serious?* I just kept wiggling my eyebrows.

"This is my first time on the Empire Service." My tone had the quality of pillow talk. "If you can suggest anything that would make my trip more . . . *pleasurable* . . . I'd appreciate the advice."

She snatched the ticket from my hand, mutilated it with her hole punch, and placed it in a slot on the top of my seat.

"Sit on the other side," she said. "By the Hudson. It's a beautiful view."

The Hudson. I've got a view of it from my chamber window. The river runs parallel to First Street and is no more than a quarter mile away. I'd follow its course: past Kingston, past Poughkeepsie, and southward, past those soulless places that New Yorkers call "Upstate" but Upstaters call "no, thank you," and down, to the blighted megalopolis at the river's mouth. Such dangers. Such adventures. And if anything happened—if all else failed—the Hudson could serve as a breadcrumb trail to lead me home.

The train was pointed south. A great hydraulic hiss. The iron wheels cut loose, and we were rolling. I was ready to try something new.

EPILOGUE

The Hayes gardens. Our flowerbeds. We'd never compete in the Tour again, but our backyard oasis was an undefeated champion, and no one could take that away from us. Appearances had to be maintained. My spade worked the soil. A sensation struck me. I felt drawn downward, toward the Earth, by forces stronger than gravity. I dug. I planted my boot on the shoulder of the shovel, sank the blade to the hilt, and drew heavy clumps of earth. I tossed each load behind me, without consideration for where it landed. The day was brisk but fair. Overhead, a dazzling blue sky.

The hole was knee-deep. Something *ting*'ed off the spade. I stooped down, sank my hand into dirt, and drew it up. A diamond. An enormous one! As large as the Hope, I'd wager, but without the blue cast. The diamond I'd found was the picture of flawless transparency. Oh, how it sparkled!

Is this Mummy's? Did she drop it while gardening? Is it Puppa's? Did he secretly bury it here, in the hope we'd discover it after his death?

I pocketed the diamond and kept digging. Waist-deep, and I hit more treasure. An emerald this time, and as big as a walnut! I pushed the soil from the gem with my filthy hands. The green within it was the greenest green imaginable.

The two gems made me a rich man. I was playing with house money, and I should have climbed from the hole, thrown my spade to the ground, and vowed to never dig again. But the extra-gravitational pull was just too strong. I kept digging. The treasures kept coming. Chest-deep, and I hit a sapphire. Shoulder-deep, and I unearthed a scattering of ancient gold coins. My pockets were bulging. My head was the only part of me that stuck out above the ground. It was an odd perspective. The world without seemed made for giants. If someone had happened by, they might have mistaken me for some kind of grotesque garden ornament.

Stop. Climb out. Cash in. But the force would not relent.

Soil ejected behind me by the spadesful. I was fully absorbed by the Earth. I kept digging. I descended deeper. Five feet below. Ten. Every so often, I'd look back the way I'd come. On my first backward glance, the hole was the size of a beach ball; on my second, it was basketball size; so on and so forth, on to soccer-ball size, on to tennis-ball size, until, at last, the world I had left was nothing but a pinprick of light.

My path felt true. Straight down, and to the center of the Earth. At some point, I'd hit a pocket of magma and be burned to a crisp. The light was long gone. I was burrowing, without bearing, through the infinite darkness.

I thought of something Puppa used to say. "The human brain can only contain thirty years of memory. Ten years of childhood. Ten years of adolescence. Ten years of early adulthood. After that, it's all as one day, and that day is spent solely in reflection."

My digging shifted to a horizontal course. I didn't feel it happening. Up was down. Left was right. One feels nothing in the void.

My digging shifted to a vertical course. Back toward the surface. No telling when this happened. A nothingness of feeling all feels the same.

A final stroke of the spade. It broke upward, into the open air. When I emerged, I did so into another world.

ACKNOWLEDGMENTS

The author would like to thank the following individuals:

Masha. The love of my life.

Virginia, William, Peter. Loving parents.

Luke, Lindsey, Patty, Kaitlyn. Siblings, and comrades in arms.

Owen Sherwood. Lifelong pal, and an artist of rare vision.
www.owensherwood.com

Liam Harrison. Old chum, and gifted animator.
www.mesmeric.tv

Rob Hammer. Cousin, and a master of his craft.
www.robhammerphotography.com

Theresa Yetto, Marie Yetto, Charles Hammer, and Mark Hammer. Not a day goes by.

Deane Bogardus, Amelia Fusco Costello, Steve Fletcher, Martin Monahan, and Bob Moore. My teachers.

Andriy, Angela, Andy, Anya, Brian, Bryan, Cavan, Challen, Christine, Dan, Dan, Dave, Evan, EY, Greg, Gus, Jon, JY, Kiera, Kerri, Konstantin, Maire Kate, MaryNicole, Megan, Micah, Morgan, Natasha, Nick, Scott, Scott, Shura, Tara, Tina, Todd, Tom, Tommy, Vita, Yura, and Yuriy. An embarrassment of riches.

Mark Gottlieb. Agent. Thanks for believing.

The wonderful team at Turner.

Don't think I forgot about you, Dennis. My best friend of thirty-five years. Roll it, Den.